MR
ROSENBLUM'S
LIST

— *or* —

*Friendly Guidance for
the Aspiring Englishman*

MR ROSENBLUM'S LIST

or

Friendly Guidance for the Aspiring Englishman

SCEPTRE

First published in Great Britain in 2010 by Sceptre
An imprint of Hodder & Stoughton
An Hachette UK company

1

Copyright © Natasha Solomons 2010

From 'The Links' by Robert Hunter, published by Wiley & Sons.
Reprinted by permission of John Wiley & Sons, Inc.

Constance Spry's 'Coronation Chicken' recipe reprinted
by permission of Grub Street Publishing Ltd.

ISBN 9781444709841

Typeset in Monotype Sabon by Hewer Text UK Ltd, Edinburgh

Printed and bound by Griffin Press

Hodder & Stoughton policy is to use papers that are natural,
renewable and recyclable products and made from wood grown in
sustainable forests. The logging and manufacturing processes are expected
to conform to the environmental regulations of the country of origin.

Hodder & Stoughton Ltd
338 Euston Road
London NW1 3BH

www.hodder.co.uk

On his ninetieth birthday, I promised my grandfather that I would dedicate my first novel to him. So, this is for Mr P.E. Shields O.B.E., 1910–2000.

And for David, with love.

CHAPTER ONE

It will be cloudy and dull this evening and tonight with periods of rain; the rain being moderate or heavy in many districts. Fog will be extensive on high ground with fog patches along the south coast. Tomorrow, more general and heavy rain will spread from the south-west with temperatures of approximately fifty-seven degrees. That concludes the weather summary; a further news bulletin may be heard at a quarter to . . .

JACK ROSENBLUM SWITCHED off the wireless and nestled back into his leather armchair. A beatific smile spread across his face and he closed his eyes. 'So there is to be more rain,' he remarked to the empty room, stretching out his short legs and giving a yawn. He was unconcerned by the dismal prognosis; it was the act of listening to the bulletin that he savoured. Each evening during the weather forecast he could imagine he was an Englishman. When the forecast was stopped through the war he grieved on behalf of the British, aware what loss this absence would inflict, and when it started again he listened in religiously, happily considering all the Englishmen and women hearing 'light drizzle on high ground' at the same instant as he. Through the daily weather reports he felt himself to be part of a nation; the prediction may be sleet in Scotland and sunshine in the West Midlands but the ritual of the weather forecast united them all. The national preoccupation had been rightfully restored and in his soul Jack rejoiced.

He stared out of the window, watching the rain trickle down the pane. Beyond, the tatty grass of the garden ran up to a dilapidated fence, and on the other side was the heath. No one had mended the fence. It had been falling down since 1940 but there was no new wood with which to mend it. He could have found some on the black market with a little *Schwarzgeld*, but the simple truth was that he, like everyone else in London, had ceased to notice the shabbiness of his surroundings. Over the last ten years the city had slowly decayed, cracks appearing in even the smartest façade, but the people of London, like the spouse of a fading beauty, had grown far too familiar with the city to notice her decline. It was left for those who had returned from exile to observe with dismay the drab degeneration of the once great capital. London was blackened and smoke stained, with great gaping holes strewn with rubble.

Jack was not like the other refugees who, in the most part, were quite happy to build their own tiny towns within the great city. He agreed with his neighbours that the role of the Jew was not to be noticed. If no one noticed you, then you became like a park bench, useful if one thought about it, but you did not stand out. Assimilation was the secret. *Assimilation.* Jack had said the word so often to himself, that he heard it as a hiss and a shibboleth. He was tired of being different; he did not want to be doomed like the Wandering Jew to walk endlessly from place to place, belonging nowhere. Besides, he liked the English and their peculiarities. He liked their stoicism under pressure; on the wall in his factory he kept a copy of a war poster emblazoned with the Crown of King George and underneath the words 'Keep Calm and Carry On'. Their city was crumbling all around them; the peopled dressed in utility clothing, there were only wizened vegetables, dry brown bread and miserable slivers of bacon from Argentina in the shops, yet the men shaved and dressed for dinner and their wives served them the grey food on their best patterned china. All the British were alike – even as the Empire collapsed and the pound tumbled, they maintained that they were at the centre of the world and anyone coming to England must be here to learn from them. The idea that the traveller from India or America might have some wisdom to impart was ludicrous. The British stood tall in their trilby or bowler hats and discussed the weather.

Jack had lived amongst them for fifteen years. He felt like one of those newfangled anthropologists employed by Mass Observation, but while they were busy surveying the population, listening in on the conversations of coal miners in pubs and on buses, housewives and earls in Lyons Corner Houses, Jack was only interested in one sub-species: the English Middle Class. He wanted to be a gentleman not a gent. He wanted to be Mr J.M. Rosenblum.

Jack aspired to be an Englishman from the very first moment he and his wife Sadie disembarked at Harwich in August 1937. Dazed from the journey and clutching a suitcase in each hand, they had picked their way along the gangplank, trying not to slip in their first English drizzle. Sadie's brand-new shoes made her unsteady, but she was determined to arrive in her host nation smartly dressed and not like a *schnorrer*. Her dark-blond hair was plaited into neat coils around her ears and Jack noticed that she'd carefully masked the heavy circles beneath her eyes with powder. She wore a neat woollen two-piece, the skirt a trifle loose round her middle. Elizabeth, barely a year old and unaware of the significance of the moment, slept on her mother's shoulder, tiny fingers curled in Sadie's plaits. All the refugees, with their piles of luggage, clutches of small sobbing children and pale-faced Yiddish speaking grandparents, were herded into haphazard queues.

3

Seeing others with parents, cousins and brothers-in-law, Jack experienced a gut-punch of guilt. Acid rose in his throat and he gave a small burp. It tasted of onions. He cursed in German under his breath. Sadie had made chopped liver and onion sandwiches for the train ride into France. He hated raw onions; they always repeated on him. That whole journey, he knew he ought to be mulling over the momentous nature of their trip but he watched with an odd detachment as Germany vanished in a blur – God knew if they'd ever see it again. '*Heimat*' – the idea of home and belonging – was gone. And yet as the train rushed through Holland and France, all Jack could think about was the taste of onions. Sure enough, he arrived in England in his best suit, shoes polished to a gleam, hair neatly trimmed and his breath reeking.

The refugees had waited beside the dock in the falling rain, none daring to complain (they'd learned the hard way to fear the whims of bureaucrats). A man walked along the lines, pausing to talk and pass out pamphlets. Jack watched his progress with fascination. He had the straight back of an Englishman and the self-assurance of a headmaster amongst a gaggle of unruly first-form boys – even the immigration policeman nodded deferentially on asking him a question. Jack admired rather than envied elegance in other men. Jack himself was slight with soft blue irises (hidden behind a pair of wire-rimmed spectacles) and sandy hair receding rapidly into baldness. He rued his small feet, which turned inwards ever so slightly. When standing still, he always had to remember to turn his feet out, to avoid looking pigeon-toed.

Reaching Jack, the man handed him a dusky blue pamphlet entitled *While you are in England: Helpful Information and Friendly Guidance for every Refugee*. He gave another, identical, to Sadie.

'Welcome to England. I'm from the "German Jewish Aid Committee". Please study this with great care.'

Jack was so taken aback that this man with his twirling moustache was both an Englishman and a Jew that he stuttered – quite unable to talk. The man gave a tired sigh and switched effortlessly into German.

'*Willkommen in England. Ich bin—*'

Jack shook himself out of his stupor. 'Sank you, most kindly. I will learn it hard.'

The man beamed his approval. 'Yes, jolly good.' He pointed to the pages in Jack's hands. 'Rule number two. Always. Speak. English. Even halting English is better than German.'

Jack nodded dumbly, carefully storing this piece of advice.

'And this? He will truly tell me everything that I must be knowing?'

The man smiled tightly, impatient to be moving down the lines. 'Yes. It tells you everything you need to know about the English.'

Jack clasped the flimsy pamphlet in trembling hands. He glanced along the rows of refugees sitting on travel trunks, nibbling apples or glancing at newspapers in half a dozen languages. Did they not realise that they had just been handed a recipe for happiness? This leaflet would tell them – Jews, *Yids* and *Flüchtlinge* – how to be genuine Englishmen. The booklet fell open upon the list and Jack read avidly, his lips mouthing the words, 'Rule one: Spend your time immediately in learning the English language . . .'

Jack spent his first few months in London living according to the rules set out in *Helpful Information*. He took English lessons; he never spoke German on the upper decks of buses and joined no political organisations, refusing to sign a petition for the repositioning of a tram stop, in case later it could be misinterpreted as subversive. He never criticised government legislation and would not allow Sadie to do so either, even when they had to register with the local police as 'enemy aliens'. He obeyed the list with more fervour than the most ardent *Bar Mitzvah* boy did the laws of *Kashrut,* and it was whilst adhering to it, that he had an unexpected piece of good luck.

Sadie had sent him out to buy a rug or a length of carpet to make their flat above Solly's Stockings on Commercial Road a bit more homely and Jack strolled along Brick Lane, idly sucking the salt crystals off a pretzel. He was aware that he ought to be eating an iced bun, but as he recited item number nine, 'An Englishman always "buys British" wherever he can', he consoled himself that in this *shetetl* buns were hard to come by. It was a brisk morning and the steam from the beigel shops hovered in the atmosphere like bread-scented smog. Boys peddled newspapers, trolley-bus conductors yelled for passengers going to 'Finchley-Straße' and stallholders hustled for business, from tables sprawled along the uneven pavement. The air was thick with Yiddish, and Jack could almost imagine himself back in Schöneberg. With a shake of his head to drive away this stray homesick thought, he scoured the stands for carpets. He spied clocks and watches (ticking or with their innards spewing out), barrels of herring, *heimische* cucumbers, lettuces, a broken hat stand and then, at last, a length of mint green carpet. He tossed his half-eaten pretzel into the gutter for the pigeons and pointed to the roll.

'Him. The green carpet. Is he British?'

The stallholder frowned in puzzlement, his usual sales patter forgotten.

Impatient, Jack flipped over the roll to inspect the underside and to his delight saw a Wilton stamp and the Royal Warrant of His Majesty the King.

'Super! I take it all, please-thank-you.'

'Right you are. I got more if you want it, guv? A bloomin' trailer load.'

Jack thought for a minute. On the one hand, he had only ten

6

pounds to his name. On the other, he could see the potential in selling on the rest of the carpet, if he could get a good price. He glanced back at the Royal Warrant – surely this was a sign?

'Yes, all right. I take everything. I pay two pounds and I must be lending this trailer.'

Sadie was appalled when Jack returned home with twenty rolls of carpet in shades from mint to mustard and magenta. For a week Elizabeth crawled through carpet tunnels, and they all perched on carpet benches in the evening to listen to the wireless – but that trailer load of carpet marked the beginning of Rosenblum's Carpets. At first Jack acted as a middleman, selling on remaindered stock at a premium to other refugees looking to add homely touches to squalid apartments, but soon he realised that there was enough demand for him to open a small factory right there in the East End.

Sadie observed her husband easing into their new life with a mixture of wonder and concern. She knew that the neighbours whispered about him behind his back, calling him a *deliberate assimilator*. As though he was guilty of some silent betrayal.

For her part, Sadie felt off balance in this new place. She disliked leaving the safety of the East End, and rarely strayed beyond the boundary of the Finchley Road. Jack informed her that it was not done to shake hands with strangers on omnibuses or in tramcars (for which she was grateful, having been disconcerted by the hostile stares she received on formally greeting every passenger in the courteous Germanic way). Now reassured that she understood the customs, she agreed to take the bus into the West End with him. There was only one seat downstairs, beside a rotund woman whose doughy face was crowned by an enormous hat decorated with butterflies on wires. Insisting that Sadie took the seat, Jack climbed the stairs to the top deck in search of another. The conductor bustled round dispensing tickets. Sadie stiffened.

Jack always bought the tickets – his English was *wunderbar* and more to the point, he had all the money.

'Where to, madam?' said the conductor, reaching her seat and jangling his box.

Sadie gave a timid smile and pointed at the ceiling. 'The Lord above, he will pay.'

The conductor spluttered in wordless outrage, and Sadie felt the pudgy woman beside her swivel and stare, the butterflies on her hat wobbling as she sniggered.

When at home Jack explained her mistake, Sadie couldn't help feeling that the English language was deliberately designed to confound outsiders. She refused to speak another word to him in that *verdammt* tongue for the rest of the afternoon, and since he would not chat in German, they sulked side by side in silence, until Jack went out. He insisted that they spoke only English (something in that cursed pamphlet for sure) but speaking with her husband in her disjointed newcomer's tongue transformed him into a stranger. He looked the same, but the easy intimacies were lost.

'He'd already changed his name. He was Jakob when she fell in love with him, and Jakob when she married him, but when a clerk wrote down 'Jak' on his British visa, he took it as a sign.'

Sadie perched on the uncomfortable settee sipping a cup of black coffee. There was a murmur as Elizabeth woke from her nap, and then a little cry, 'Mama. Mama!'

Sadie put down her cup, spilling a few drops on the mauve rug in her hurry to fetch her daughter, and gave a little tut of discontent that Jack had taught her baby to call her 'Mama' instead of 'Mutti'. Tonight, when he returned from the factory and could mind Elizabeth, she would go to Freida Herzfeld for some *Kaffee und Kuchen,* kitchen gossip and illicit German chatter. Then she might go to the synagogue – the only place in this city where she felt at home. There the words were the

8

same: Hebrew in the grand *schul* on *Oranienburger Straße* and Hebrew in the handsome brick building behind Stepney Green. When she closed her eyes and listened to the deep song of the cantor, she imagined herself back in Berlin with her mother beside her in the women's gallery fussing as to whether Emil was behaving himself in the room below. Sadie could almost make out the off-key intonations of Papa as he mumbled his way through the service.

Rosenblum's Carpets quickly outgrew its cramped workshop and expanded into premises off Hessel Street Market, until it was the largest carpet factory in London's East End, supplying some of the best middling hotels in the city. Half the men in the Rosenblums' street were gone, and goodness knew where – Canada? The Isle of Man? Even Australia, if the rumours were true.

The police came for you at dawn. It was a haphazard system, and sometimes if you were out they never came back. Sadie fretted that Jack would be taken, and to humour her, he agreed to this unconscionably early walk to the factory. He never actually believed they would take him, after all, he was an almost-Englishman applying through proper channels to become a genuine citizen (and he could finish *The Times* crossword in under two hours, which Jack was sure must be some sort of record). But when he arrived at the factory that September morning, he realised he'd forgotten his breakfast. Sadie always packed him a paper bag with matzos and a slither of rubbery cheese from his weekly ration, as well as a thermos of foul smelling coffee. His stomach growled.

'*Mistfink*,' cursed Jack, resorting to German in his exasperation.

He pictured the brown bag on the kitchen table and decided to go back for it. He trotted the half-mile back home.

The police were waiting for him on the doorstep. Jack didn't even try to turn around. They'd found him and it wouldn't be British to run like some coward–criminal.

The stench from urinals always brought it back – one whiff of ammonia and mothballs and he was back in 1940 in a makeshift cell in a London police station with five other refugees all facing internment, and all complaining loudly about cold benches and haemorrhoids. Jack had not joined in the discussion; he'd sat with his head in his hands and wondered how it was that he, the most promising Englishman of all his acquaintance, could still be labelled a 'class B enemy alien' (possible security risk) and arrested. With his knowledge of marmalade and Royal Family history going back to Ethelred the Unready, it scarcely seemed possible that he could be anything other than a 'class C' (loyalty to the British cause not in question).

Jack couldn't understand how this had happened. He'd obeyed the rules to the letter and they'd still taken him – clearly the points in *Helpful Information* weren't enough to make a chap blend in. He fished out the pamphlet and began to make his very first addendum:

Regard the following as duties to which you are in honour bound:

1. SPEND YOUR TIME IMMEDIATELY IN LEARNING THE ENGLISH LANGUAGE AND ITS CORRECT PRONUNCIATION. *Have done so but it is not so easy. Even English lessons do not assist. Cursed German accent IMPOSSIBLE to lose.*

2. REFRAIN FROM SPEAKING GERMAN IN THE STREETS AND IN PUBLIC CONVEYANCES AND IN PUBLIC PLACES SUCH AS RESTAURANTS. TALK HALTING ENGLISH RATHER THAN FLUENT GERMAN – AND *do not talk in a loud voice. (Unless talking to foreigners when it is the done thing to shout).* DO NOT READ GERMAN NEWSPAPERS IN PUBLIC.

Do not read them AT ALL or you will be considered a 'class A threat' and a spy.

3. DO NOT CRITICISE ANY GOVERNMENT REGULATION, NOR THE WAY THINGS ARE DONE OVER HERE. *Very hard to manage at times <u>like this</u>.* THE FREEDOM AND LIBERTY OF ENGLAND ARE NOW GIVEN TO YOU. NEVER FORGET THIS POINT.

Jack snorted. Loyal as he was, he couldn't help but notice that his was a funny sort of freedom. With a sigh, he realised that this very thought was perilously close to criticism, and turned to the next point.

4. DO NOT JOIN ANY POLITICAL ORGANISATIONS.

It was points five and six that Jack pondered the most. While useful for the newly arrived refugee, Jack now realised that they were in serious need of clarification.

5. DO NOT MAKE YOURSELF CONSPICUOUS BY SPEAKING LOUDLY, OR BY YOUR MANNER OR DRESS. *Don't gesture with your hands when talking. Keep them stuck to your sides or the English will think you strange and over-emotional.* THE ENGLISHMAN GREATLY DISLIKES OSTENTATION OR UNCONVENTIONALITY OF DRESS. *Remember, 'bland is best'.* THE ENGLISHMAN ATTACHES VERY GREAT IMPORTANCE TO MODESTY, UNDERSTATEMENT IN SPEECH RATHER THAN OVERSTATEMENT. HE VALUES GOOD MANNERS. (YOU WILL FIND THAT HE SAYS 'THANK YOU' FOR THE SMALLEST SERVICE – EVEN FOR A PENNY BUS TICKET FOR WHICH HE HAS PAID.) *Always apologise, even when something is plainly not your fault – if a man walks into you on the street, apologise profusely.*

6. TRY TO OBSERVE AND FOLLOW THE MANNERS AND CUSTOMS AND HABITS OF THIS COUNTRY, IN SOCIAL AND BUSINESS RELATIONS. *Yes – but what ARE the manners and customs? This point requires some significant expansion.*

7. DO NOT EXPECT TO BE RECEIVED IMMEDIATELY INTO ENGLISH HOMES, BECAUSE THE ENGLISHMAN TAKES SOME TIME BEFORE HE OPENS HIS HOME WIDE TO STRANGERS.

8. DO NOT SPREAD THE POISON OF 'IT'S BOUND TO COME IN YOUR COUNTRY.' THE BRITISH GREATLY OBJECT TO THE PLANTING OF THIS CRAVEN THOUGHT.

A policeman banging on the bars of the cell interrupted Jack's scribbling. He looked up with a start to see his wife and small daughter standing outside, and flushed with humiliation. He didn't want them to see him caged and stinking. The first week he'd been here, they had met in the visitor's room, but now thanks to Mr Churchill's exhortation to 'collar the lot' every room in the police station was full with refugees waiting for transfer to internment camps.

Sadie reached through the bars and stroked his unshaven cheek.

'*Meine Liebe . . .*'

'In English, darling,' murmured Jack with an anxious glance at the guard.

'The little one misses her papa.'

Elizabeth peeked out from behind her mother, pulling faces at one of the old men sitting at the back of the cell, who was plaiting his long beard into spikes to make her laugh. Jack planted a kiss on the back of Sadie's hand and did his best to seem cheerful.

'It's not so bad. I'll sausage through. Moishe here has been teaching me backgammon tricks. Did you speak to Edgar?'

'*Ja*. I visit him at his office, just like you say. And Lottie, she tell me he visits police every day and he goes to see magistrate and he shout. Then he drink whisky.'

Jack tried to smile, knowing his friend was doing all he could. If anyone could help him, it was Edgar Herzfeld. Edgar was a gentle, sedentary fellow, until something roused him.

'And Freida, she tells me give you this,' Sadie leant forward and kissed him tenderly on the mouth. 'You see? More exciting when kisses are not from your wife,' she said, doing her best to seem light-hearted.

As she left, Sadie slipped a small package wrapped in a handkerchief through the bars. Jack sniffed at it. Apple strudel. Sadie and Mutti, her mother, always baked strudels on Fridays in Berlin. Today must be Friday. He took a bite and his teeth tingled on the sultanas. Sadie's younger brother Emil hated sultanas. He always picked them out and lined them up in neat rows along his plate – it drove Sadie crazy. 'Think of all the currants you've wasted!' she used to say, 'if you lined up all the currants you've not eaten, they'd stretch all the way to the *Zoologischer Garten*.' Jack closed his eyes, and saw a row of sultanas end on end – every one that Emil had ever refused to eat – and wondered how long that line would be at the end of the boy's life. That moment, Jack felt a crushing sadness against his ribs. He swallowed, trying not to cry, but a tear escaped and trickled down onto his strudel, making it taste salty. He worried about Emil and Mutti and the others left behind, but right then, he only had space for his own unhappiness. He was cold, the cell smelled of piss and he was homesick.

At dawn one morning the prison was emptied and he was herded into a second-class compartment of an extra-long passenger train at Waterloo Station. Sandwiched between a pair of elderly Viennese gentlemen, Jack knew he should be concerned about where they were taking him. Instead, after three weeks sealed into a damp, high-windowed cell, he felt a tingle of excitement in his belly.

The train rattled through the city, an endless warren of brick streets and grey skies. Plumes of smoke still smouldered from last night's *Heinkel* raid. He saw people crawling over the wreckage of crumpled houses and closed his eyes in disgust. The lurching rhythm of the train lulled him to sleep. His head bumping against the glass, he dreamt of strange things, open skies filled with larks, emerald fireflies in the night and chequered flags on the side of a hill.

Then one of the Viennese gentlemen was shaking him awake, offering him a piece of stale bread that he did not want. Jack turned back to the window and realised he had woken in another England. This one was green. Before they left Berlin, he had imagined that this was what Britain was like. He smiled – so England was meadows and sheep, thatched roofs and silver rivers after all.

The train pulled into a station and Jack was shoved onto the platform by the throng. The air smelled of salt and he could hear the sea. The afternoon sun was so bright to his prison-accustomed eyes that it made him blink, and it took him a moment to realise that someone was calling his name.

'Jack! Jack Rosenblum!'

Jack peered into the crowd and saw a figure frantically waving a wad of papers.

'Edgar?'

A slight man with wild grey hair hurried towards him, pushing aside the unwilling bodies and enfolded Jack in a crushing embrace.

'I've done it! You're safe, Jack. I can take you home to Sadie.'

Jack swallowed and stared at Edgar, as his legs began to tremble, like a lush before her morning gin.

'I went to a judge and I tell him, "This man, this Rosenblum of Rosenblum Carpets, is a true ally against the Nazis."' Edgar spread his arms for emphasis, bumping the men streaming by on either side. Refusing to let his recital be interrupted he continued. 'I tell the judge in his funny long-haired wig, "On the day war is declared this man turns his profitable factory over to the British war effort. Do not question Jack Rosenblum's loyalty!"'

Jack nodded dumbly, unable to speak.

'The judge agreed. You are now "class C" alien and can go home.'

Jack's tongue stuck to the roof of his mouth. 'This place? Where am I?'

Edgar gave a shrug. 'Dorsetshire.'

'Pretty,' said Jack, as a tiny bird with dappled feathers landed on the handle of his leather bag, and stared at him with round black eyes. It flapped its wings and took off in a gust of song.

CHAPTER TWO

FROM THE MOMENT he arrived home, Jack devoted his spare time to meticulously expanding the bullet points in the *Helpful Information* pamphlet, until there was no room left and he had to insert supplementary pages at the back. There was nothing he liked more than to make another little note, an observation upon English customs such as 'the British housewife makes a purchase of haddock on Friday mornings' and record this titbit of invaluable knowledge. Jack prided himself, that should another booklet be commissioned, the German Jewish Aid Committee could turn to no greater expert than himself.

The factory continued to grow, the vast looms churning out parachutes and kitbags and coarse canvas tents, so that the Rosenblums were able to move into a small terraced house in Hampstead, with a brass door knocker and a cobbled patio backing onto the heath. As the days seeped into weeks and then into months, Sadie grew tired of her husband's list. Every evening there he was, hunched in his chair before the gas fire, the wireless blaring, scribbling, scribbling in his little book. The only time he faltered, and his pencil drooped was when Mr Winston Churchill or Mr John Betjeman came over the airwaves. She couldn't understand this obsession to be English while she could feel that other life drifting further away, like steam from a kettle through an open window. There had been no news from Mutti, Emil or Papa for months. Jack went out every Friday for a copy of the *Jewish Chronicle*, and together they pored over the news. It was full of sinister rumours.

While Elizabeth napped, Sadie would curl up on one of the pre-war Rosenblum rugs and read Mutti's recipe books, trying to glut her appetite on visions of *Sachertorte* or puff pastry *Windbeutel*.

Then, one Sunday morning in March 1943 it began to rain. Sadie knew Jack was upstairs somewhere with his *verdammt* list. The sky turned a deep shade of grey and the city was bathed in a false twilight. Water poured from the gutter and rain shattered the shimmering surface of the pond beyond the boundary. After an hour the water gently lapped the fence posts at the bottom of the garden leading to the heath. Staring out of the window, Sadie imagined she was Mrs Noah bobbing along in her house-shaped ark. She went and stood at the sink, gazing out at the pond sleepily. There was a deep-throated quacking from above, and then a cloud of ducks descended from the sky and landed on the pond. She smiled to see them; she liked the irritable sound they made when they quacked – they were like housewives bickering over bread. Then, she noticed something odd: a grey-haired woman was feeding them in the rain.

The kitchen was filling with a peculiar smell, sweet and singed; it was poppy-seed cake, slightly overdone so that the seeds on the top were beginning to burn. Sadie never made poppy-seed cake and had not eaten it since they had come to England; nor could she recall even having seen poppy-seeds for sale. It was Mutti's favourite cake, better than Baumtorte, vanilla crescent or even toasted marzipan squares. She would eat slice after slice, getting the tiny seeds stuck in between her teeth so that she looked like a gap-toothed witch from the pages of the Brothers Grimm.

Sadie opened the door to the terrace and went out into the rain. She walked across the wet ground in her flimsy carpet slippers. The air was brimming with the aroma, as though the rain carried the fragrance of toasting seeds and sweet dough.

As puddles formed in the soil, they too gave off the scent of a bakery amongst the terracotta flowerpots. Sadie walked to the fence and pushed aside two broken panels. Holding in her tummy, she slipped through the gap and stood on the bank of the pond. There, on the other side, stood her mother. She was wearing her long black skirt, a white apron and a neat blue scarf over her hair, while she fed scraps of burnt cake to the quacking ducks. Sadie stepped straight into the stagnant water. It was shallow and lapped the edge of her dressing gown, turning the bright fuchsia into dirty brown. The robe fanned out behind her like a train, her curlers forming a crown upon her head.

Closing her eyes, Sadie took a breath, drawing the sweet scent inside her. She mustn't open them. She must not. Must not. If she did, Mutti would be gone and there would never be poppy-seed cake again.

Sadie walked home the long way, oblivious to the curious glances of passers-by. She knew there would be no more letters from Berlin. Yet she felt nothing, only silence.

'What is wrong with you? Are you a crazy?'

Jack stood on the pavement, thin lipped. He stared at her for a second, then thrust a horsehair blanket over her shoulders and hurried her into the house, tense with disapproval.

'I saw you. You were in the pond.'

Sadie said nothing.

'What if someone else saw you?'

Sadie ignored him and marched into the kitchen, the dangling hem of her dressing gown smearing mud along the polished hall tiles. She could feel Jack trailing after her, stuttering in confusion. She didn't care. She grabbed Mutti's recipe book and wrenched it open, snatching at the pages. With a cry she tore out a leaf and crumpled it into a ball, crushing it so that the ink began to run from the sweat on her hands.

18

'*Scheiße! Scheiße!* It's all for nothing. I am lost.'

She hurled the book at the stove where it crashed into the cooker hood and slid onto the floor. Jack grabbed hold of his wife, hugging her to his chest, smoothing the hair from her eyes.

'Hush. Hush, what has happened little one?'

Sadie could not speak, and from the back bedroom Elizabeth began to wail, woken by the noise.

'Poppy-seeds,' she choked, breath coming in rasps, 'there were poppy-seeds. And there will be no more letters.'

Jack stared at her and for the first time since his brief internment he was frightened. He reached out and stroked her hand.

'This will not do, *mein Spatz*. People will decide you are eccentric. You cannot walk into ponds in carpet slippers on a Sunday morning. It is not safe.'

Sadie felt like she might puke with anger. 'This. This is what concerns you? *Arschkriecher!*'

Jack took a breath and licked his dry lips, 'Odd habits are all very well for the English but we must be invisible.'

Sadie tucked a strand of dark hair behind her ear, and gazed at her husband unblinking.

'Very well. I shall be invisible.'

As she turned and walked away from him, Jack knew in his belly that something had broken. He almost heard it snap, but he could do nothing but watch her go, the damp fabric of her dressing gown clinging to her bare legs.

The end of the war was both a challenge and an opportunity. It meant that, no longer limited to wretched utility garments, Jack could now acquire the proper attire of the Englishman and, after careful deliberation, he decided that this meant nothing less than a bespoke suit from Savile Row. In his neat hand he recorded this as item one hundred and six on his list. Jack went to Henry Poole for the first time in October 1946. It cost him a small fortune just to acquire the requisite number of clothing coupons, let alone the cost of the clothes, but had been worth every halfpenny: that suit was the livery of the English gentleman. The store smelled deliciously of cedar wood, and the tailor called him 'Sir', measured his small frame without a sneer, and the suit was delivered twelve weeks later, wrapped in crepe paper inside a pearlescent box with the Henry Poole crest emblazoned in gold. His pattern was to be kept in the company vaults alongside those of Churchill, Gladstone and Prince Albert. When he put on the suit, he felt taller than his five feet three inches, his bald head appeared to shine less and his nose felt, well, less pronounced. It was how the Emperor had wished his new suit to be.

As car production increased once more, Jack was able to complete item number one hundred and seven: An Englishman drives a Jaguar. The summer of 1951, after the factory had shipped a particularly large order of sage velvet plush carpets to New York, Jack took delivery of the Jaguar XK120. He had been on the waiting list for two years, and when the moment arrived he was overwhelmed. The night before he had stayed awake and imagined himself driving along Piccadilly in his Henry Poole suit, at the wheel of his racing green Jag, beside his wife with her purple rinse and perfect nails.

However, item one hundred and eight (An Englishman's wife has a purple rinse, nice nails and plays tennis and bridge) was problematic. Sadie was devilish at bridge but did not play tennis and refused even to consider the rinse, complaining that it was an unnatural hue to have upon one's head. Considering she was quite content to have dazzling violet carpets on her floors, he felt it illogical for her to protest, but knowing his wife's temperament decided not to press the point. He would have to be English enough for the both of them.

Apart from the deficiencies in his wife, Jack had fulfilled nearly all the items on his list. He had the suit, the car and the house in a leafy part of the city. He procured his hat from Lock of St James and tried his best to adjust the brim to precisely the correct degree. He ate lunch three times a week in the best of the squalid restaurants in town where he was waited upon with grovelling respect. (He mistakenly put this down to the power of his suit, when it was in fact due to his extravagant tipping. The waiters accepted his outlandish, foreign generosity and silently despised him for it.)

He took his wife to Covent Garden and to Wigmore Hall and made donations to the right charities as well as the wrong ones; giving equally to the fund to restore St Paul's roof as well as to the fledgling Israeli state.

There remained one more item on Jack's list. He knew it to be the quintessential characteristic of the true English gentleman and without it he was nothing. Item one hundred and fifty: An Englishman must be a member of a golf club.

For Jack membership of a golf course was the rebuilding of Jerusalem, Atlantis and the perfect salt-beef sandwich all at once – but it was proving troublesome. He flicked a catch concealed in the carved Griffin of his Victorian desk and a drawer popped out a few inches. He pulled it the rest of the way to reveal several tidy compartments filled with visiting cards and neatly filed bills. A fourth spilled over with paper. This was where he kept his correspondence with the golf clubs of England. The communication consisted of a copy of each application and a polite, but firm, response from the club secretary declining his admittance. Jack was persistent to the point of stubbornness; he had arrived in London with nothing but his suitcases and twenty pounds in his pocket. Within ten years he had one of the biggest carpet factories in London, so a single rejection from a snide official of a golf club was not going to dissuade a man like Jack Morris Rosenblum.

To his dismay, the single rejection rapidly turned into five, then ten, until every course in a twenty-mile radius had turned him down. The secret drawer was getting full and the papers were beginning to jam his desk. It was time he took advice. He spoke to Saul Tankel, the jeweller, who was considered to be a source not only of diamonds but information.

'It's no good, no good at all. They'll never let you in. Not with that *schnoz*.'

Saul laughed, pushed back his thick, jeweller's spectacles onto his forehead so that they resembled a pair of antennae, and waved with enthusiastic dismay; he looked like an alarmed grasshopper.

'There is us and them. And *they* will never, ever let you in. Anyway, what will you do? They play on Saturdays.'

The problem of playing on Saturdays had already occurred to Jack, and did not unduly concern him. He hadn't yet the courage to tell his wife, but he considered golf as an excellent alternative to a tedious morning spent at synagogue. Saul seemed to sense his thoughts.

'You know what would happen if you did get in?' He asked, jabbing a surprisingly large finger two inches from Jack's controversial nose. 'You will play on a Saturday, when everyone else is in *schul* praying to Him,' Saul gestured to the heavens, or rather a light bulb hanging inches above their heads, but Jack took the point. 'And you will play the best game of your life. And finally you will get the hoop-in-one.'

'A hole,' Jack corrected.

'What?'

'A hole-in-one. Golf has holes not hoops.'

'Ah. So, then you will get the hole-in-one. And you will be able to tell no one. Because you played on Saturday, against His wishes on the day of rest!'

Saul jabbed at the light bulb so fiercely that it swung back and forth, clocking him on the head.

'You see? You see?' Saul exclaimed excitedly, taking this as a sign of God's wrath.

Jack was not convinced, but the information was useful. The next letter he signed under the pseudonym Professor Percy Jones. The professor received a much more favourable response from a previously frosty club secretary.

1 February, 1952

Dear Professor Jones,
    Thank you for you kind enquiry concerning membership of the Lawns Golf Club. We are indeed open to new members. I sincerely look forward to making your acquaintance.
Regards,
Edward Fitz-Elkington, Esq.

Jack turned the letter over and over until it grew quite worn along the folds. He decided to write back to the club secretary under his own name, mentioning that his good friend Professor Percy Jones had been told membership was not full, but the reply was inevitable.

Dear Mr Rosenbloom,
    I am sorry to inform you that there has been a misunderstanding. Membership is now full. I would be pleased to place you on the waiting list, but I must warn you that the current wait is approximately twenty-seven years.
Yours sincerely,
    Edward Fitz-Elkington, Esq.

It was hopeless. He could not produce the evidence of the professor's letter without admitting that he had impersonated him, which he imagined the secretary would not take kindly. He did business with everyone: Anglicans, Catholics, socialists and even the odd agnostic, but they never became friends. He had known some of these men for fifteen years and for fifteen years they had enquired after the health and happiness of his wife, but they had never once suggested meeting her. He had never been invited to dinner at a colleague's house. That was what restaurants were for, he thought grimly. They were for meeting with those whom you could not have to your house: actresses, Americans and those like him.

Jack wrote one final letter to the Sanderson Cliffs Club, offering free carpets for all the buildings and enclosing a colour chart with the season's latest range. Considering the scarcity of good carpets, in fact the scarcity of everything, Jack knew it to be a generous proposal – and he even had a precious letter of recommendation. He was more hopeful than he had felt for months because Mr Austen, a woollen merchant from Yorkshire, had actually offered to nominate him for membership. Jack was elated; this was fate. The Sanderson Cliffs was the perfect club; their course was legendary, the best in North London. Even during the war they retained twenty greenkeepers to nurture that perfect grass and, according to legend, they used tweezers, nail scissors and water imported from the Nile, so smooth were the greens. If he closed his eyes and looked into the future he could see his name in gold lettering on the polished boards: *Mr J.M. Rosenblum, Captain.*

So optimistic was Jack that he finally bought a set of clubs. He had never actually played a single round of golf; he had never even been on a golf course, nor had he held a club, let alone taken a swing. He put on his Henry Poole suit and went to Harrods. He rode the elevator to the sports floor in a state of hushed reverence, and the shop assistant led him to the selection of golf clubs. The room was oak panelled with dim overhead lights, and in the gloom the steel of the clubs seemed to glow. Jack felt the sweat start to tickle his forehead. The assistant passed him a club.

'Try this six iron. Beautifully balanced, sir. Specially designed to make striking the ball that bit easier.'

Jack held it in his hands and he felt his throat catch. He hadn't wanted anything this much since he was a small boy and had saved up for a bright red steam engine that really worked. The assistant passed him another.

'This nine iron has fine grooves. Used by Bobby Jones himself. Top of the range with polished lightweight steel shafts. The newest technology. Very *aerodynamic*.'

That was it. Jack had to have them.

'Excellent choice, sir,' cooed the assistant as he began to wrap them and Jack counted out the crisp pound notes. 'Now, will sir require a new bag to put them in?'

Jack selected one in a rich tan with a crimson stripe stitched along the side. He thought they were the most beautiful objects he had ever seen.

The clubs rested in the corner of his office, still in their wrappings, propped up against a chair. Jack would sit behind his desk and gaze at them. Then, when he could bear it no longer, he would cross the room and reverentially pull out the nine iron or the sand wedge and grip it in his hands. After a few minutes – he never risked a swing, as he didn't want a single graze on that metal – he would meticulously rewrap the club and tenderly place it back in the bag.

On Friday, Mr Austen paid a call. He had been trying very hard to get Jack into the Sanderson Cliffs; he'd written a generous letter of introduction and had pointed out the usefulness of Jack's offer of carpets. Waiting for an answer had been most unpleasant; while Mr Austen was perfectly fond of the odd round, he couldn't fathom Jack's fixation. That was because Mr Austen was born an Englishman like his father and grandfather. There were Austens in Hampshire and Warwickshire going back at least twenty generations – there was even a rumour that they were distantly related to that greatest of English novelists. Edward Austen knew never to leave home without his hat, but to remove it immediately on entering a church. He knew when to use a fish fork should the occasion arise and he was aware that cake forks were bourgeois. He could tell by the cut of a man's suit or the angle of his hat, as easily as by the tone of his voice or the wax of his moustache, where he ranked in the social order compared to himself. Such men as Mr Edward Austen never worried about membership to golf courses. They presumed their superiority above every other nation, as confidently as they knew that the 7.03 to Victoria stopped at Vauxhall.

Jack waited for Mr Austen in his small office, off the main factory floor. The clatter from the mechanical looms made the furniture vibrate and Jack's temples throb, but he liked to be in the thick of things. One wall was entirely covered with samples from the new season's range of innovative tufted carpet, in a rainbow of colours. Rosenblum's Carpets might not have the cachet of a Wilton or an Axminster but Jack was secretly sure that his product was quite superior. Hearing a loud knock on the door, he rose to greet Mr Austen and shook his hand with enthusiasm.

Mr Austen liked the outlandish little man and his perpetual cheerfulness. He always found his accent surprising; those Germanic vowels and softly hissing consonants had not faded one jot over the years that he had known him. He felt sorry for him, it must be awful to sound like the enemy and have everyone take you for a Kraut.

'Ah, nice clubs. May I?'

'Of course.'

Jack watched, concealing his concern for his treasure, as Mr Austen pulled out a short iron and stood – legs slightly apart, shoulders tilted – and raised the club. He brought it down in a controlled arc, a proper golfer's swing.

'They're a good heft. I like them.'

Jack beamed. *Heft*. That was an excellent word. He must remember it.

'Where did you get them?'

'Harrods.'

Mr Austen laughed unthinkingly. 'Really? You didn't? My good fellow, no one actually *buys* clubs at Harrods.'

Jack flushed, embarrassed to be found out once again. He stared at his clubs in their white tissue paper. Their shine no longer looked radiant, but taunted him. Perhaps everyone would be able to tell that he had bought his clubs from Harrods, and then they too would laugh at him.

Mr Austen slid the iron back into the bag and reached into his pocket. There was no point putting it off any longer. He pulled out a sheet of stiff notepaper embossed with the Sanderson Cliffs emblem.

'I've heard back. Not good news, old man. It's a no-go. Terribly sorry.'

Jack sat down, dumbstruck. It couldn't be true. Mr Austen had recommended him, and he was one of *them*.

'You needed more nominations; my paltry one wasn't quite enough.'

'But you said others had been admitted. That membership was still open.'

Mr Austen fiddled awkwardly with the label on the golf bag. He wished old Rosenblum would hide his disappointment better – it made this damned uncomfortable – always so emotional these continental Jews.

'Mm, yes. Think that was part of the problem. Apparently the quota's full.'

'Quota?'

'Yes.'

Quota. Jack turned the word over slowly. He hadn't heard that for a while, and with it he knew the game was lost. They would never, ever admit him to any golf course inside or outside London. Despondency seeped into him, like cold water into a leaky rubber boot.

'You told them about the carpets?'

'Yes,' said Mr Austen. He was longing to leave. He'd done his bit, really he had. The suggestion of free carpets had gone down particularly badly. 'Think they can buy their way in anywhere, don't they?' The club president had complained. 'They make all this money on the black market, depriving us of things we need then sell them back to us. Worse than the blasted spivs in my opinion.' He did not mention this to Jack.

'I'm terribly sorry. You'll have better luck with the next one. Try Blackheath.'

Jack bowed his head; he did not tell him that Blackheath, the oldest of the English courses, was the very first he had approached. The office door swung open and Fielding, the factory manager entered, staggering under a swaying tower of files.

'Sorry to disturb you, sir. Shall I come back later?'

'No. It's quite all right, I'm just leaving,' said Mr Austen, relieved to have an excuse.

Fielding dumped the pile of paperwork on the desk. 'I need you to make a decision on these new machines, Mr Rosenblum.'

'Leave them here. I'll look at them later,' said Jack, shooing away the young man.

There was no room left in his mind for business; it was full with this latest disappointment. He was disconsolate and needed to wallow in a few minutes of misery. His usual ration was ten minutes; after that he would force himself to start thinking of solutions and a plan. As this was a particularly heinous disaster he allocated himself an extra five minutes of despondency. The clock read ten forty as he lowered his head into his hands and let out a sigh.

At ten fifty-five Jack decided to get ready for the Sabbath, which involved pouring a large whisky and reading the paper. He settled into his armchair and flicked through *The Times* to the sports pages but something in the property section caught his eye: a large cottage with tangled roses growing up the walls and a thatched roof. He had only ever seen a thatch once before, on a train journey to the sea. Next to the picture of the house was another one of a view; it was grainy and slightly blurred, taken from the top of a hill looking down over a patchwork of fields that lay under a cloudless sky. The photograph was black and white but Jack could tell that it was the bluest sky he had ever seen. There were flowers at the front of the frame peeping out amongst the hedgerows and dots of sheep in the distance. He peered closely at the small print. 'House offered for sale along with sixty acres of land. Splendid aspect. Apply Dorset office.' Sixty acres. And in Dorset. He could hear the birds singing as he looked at that photograph and he hadn't heard birds like that for a long time.

There was a distant chime as the bells of Bow Church struck the half hour and hurriedly Jack got up, put on his hat and left the office. The golf course was the last item on his list, and pursuing the list had not led him wrong yet. He needed a plan.

The carpet factory was situated in the East End in a large red-bricked Victorian warehouse with posters for '*Rabenstein Ltd. Kosher sausage manufacturer for first-class continental garlic sausage*' and '*Hats, Frocks and Fancies by Esther de Paris*' pasted all over the walls. Jack sniffed: change was coming – he could smell it as a hint of turmeric and cumin mingled with the yeasty scent of baking *challah*. There were holes where buildings used to be; a single missing house in a terrace like a knocked out tooth in the mouth of a boxer, and vast craters filled with rubble. Such was the scale of the repairs that the clean up had barely started, and nature had crept back into the East End; there were patches of grass and wild flowers, green, white and yellow, springing up amongst the waste. A small clump of forget-me-nots poked up between broken pavement slabs and lilted in the wind next to a lamp post. These were memories of the meadows that once covered the ground and that still lurked deep beneath the concrete crust.

He was considering this, alongside his other more serious concerns, when he walked right into an idea. He turned left down Montague Street and saw the sign. It read in Yiddish: 'MILCH, FRISH FUN DI KU'. He remembered hearing that years ago those living in the East End couldn't get milk from the countryside and so had their own herd in the middle of the city. The last cow had departed long since but the sign remained, hanging haphazardly on the disused gates, to serve the purpose of providing divine, or bovine, inspiration for Jack.

'That's it! Milk fresh from the cow!'

The sound of birdsong echoed in his ears and for a moment he almost muttered a prayer under his breath. If you couldn't get milk from someone else's cow, you had to get your own. No golf course would admit him and so he must build his own.

CHAPTER THREE

'AND TELL ME, *mein Broitgeber,* since you know everything – why couldn't we go to Israel?' Sadie muttered at her husband as the green Jaguar wound its way along the narrow country lanes. She was younger than Jack, still in her forties, but had long since resigned herself to a premature old age. She had neat grey-blond hair and on the rare occasions when she laughed the rolls of fat around her middle wobbled ever so slightly. Now they shook with agitation. 'You want to be like everyone else. So let us go to Israel, where everyone is like us!'

Jack said nothing, concentrating hard on not steering into the jutting hedges and gave a little sigh. He liked being called '*Broitgeber*', or 'my Lord and master', but wished her tone was a touch more sincere. 'Israel is a place for the young and I am old. It's too much to build a whole new country. A golf course is enough for me.'

He had bought the cottage without telling Sadie, which in hindsight may have been a miscalculation. He knew he would have to tell her sooner or later, but wanted it to be a *fait accompli.* Sadie would have railed against it, and he knew with quiet self-assurance that this was the right thing to do. He had also taken the rather dubious decision of not telling her that their house in London was up for sale, which resulted in the first viewings being cloak-and-dagger affairs. The estate agent bundled visitors round the house while Jack watched from a window for Sadie to return with spurious items, which he'd sent her out to find, like flea powder and anchovies. So when a week later, while reading the *Jewish Chronicle*, Sadie discovered that her house was 'under offer' she was more than a little surprised. So surprised, in fact, that it had taken several brandies to calm her down.

'And why could you not build this thing in London? Why this godforsaken place?'

'London's full. And fresh air is good for nerves.'

'What do I care for fresh air?' Sadie's words came out in a sigh as she sank miserably into her seat. 'You sell my house from under me, you take me to *alle schwartze yorne* and then you have the nerve to mention my nerves! *Du Blödmann.*'

Her litany of tribulations descended into disgruntled mutterings.

'It will be better. You will be better away from it all,' replied Jack, his grip on the steering wheel tightening.

'No. I need to be *there.*'

The Rosenblums' lives were divided into two – a neat line severed each half. There was the old life in Germany that was *before*. Then, there was the new life in England, which was *after*. Sadie thought of her existence purely in these terms of *before* and *after* but this left no room for *right now*. Her life was a blur of other times. The car reached a straight stretch of road and Jack hit the accelerator. The engine snarled and they surged forward, forcing Sadie to clutch the scarf covering her hair. She frowned and burrowed into her seat. Most of the luggage was in the removal van but she had insisted on her box being placed carefully in the boot of the car. That box was all that was left of *before*. It contained half a dozen photographs: there was one of Sadie, aged eleven, and her brother Emil, aged three, both dressed up in sailor suits as well as pictures of each of Sadie's parents smiling at the camera. The rest were family portraits belonging to Jack. Sadie wished that all the photographs were hers – he didn't deserve them. He couldn't even remember who the people were in his pictures – the bearded men in tall black hats or the round, smiling women – she would have taken better care of remembering the people who belonged to her. His behaviour was downright careless. She felt the back of her neck itch in irritation.

In the box, Sadie also had a tattered Hebrew prayer book that once belonged to her grandpa, Mutti's recipe book and a neatly folded white linen towel. Their families had been in Germany for five hundred years and that box was the sum total of their combined histories. Jack's great-grandfather had been a famous cantor in the synagogue, his honey voice echoing the ancient prayers each *Shabbas*. No one remembered that but Sadie – she thought of it sometimes when she listened to Jack tunefully crooning Caruso in the bath. There was no memento of the tortoises she kept as a girl, or the click of their claws as she and Emil raced them along the quarry tiles in the hall. Only she remembered how Emil used to cheat at chess, and the bishop-shaped dent in the wooden wainscot – caused when he hurled it at her when she objected. Under a loose floorboard in the maid's room, they used to hoard their treasures as children: a shiny *Pfennig*, a piece of green glass, a lump of elephant dung stolen from the zoo, carefully dried and wrapped in a napkin. Sadie wondered if they were still there. Did Emil look at them again before they took him?

Unless she looked at the photograph, Sadie could no longer quite recall her brother's face – it was like he was staring back at her through a bowl of water. She couldn't remember whether his eyes were blue or grey. The only thing worse than remembering, she decided, was starting to forget.

Sadie liked the Jewish calendar because it was all about memory. She had a list of her own: remember to keep the Sabbath, remember to keep the dietary laws as they remind you that you are a Jew; at *Yom Kippur* atone for your sins and, most importantly, do not forget the dead. During life there is the birthday and afterwards *Yahrzeit*, the day of death, and

33

she knew as she celebrated her birthday each year that there was this other anniversary waiting, like an invisible bookend. She liked the ritual of the Jewish year – it was a tightly strung washing line for her to hang her remembrances along.

Jack was humming under his breath beside her, and she pulled her scarf closer over her ears in an attempt to block out the sound. She could ask him to be quiet but then she would know he was still singing in his head, which was just as cross-making. The narrow lanes frothed with cow parsley that brushed the side of the convertible. Sadie glowered and muttered, 'We're lost and I hate the countryside. *Du Dumpfbeutel*. No one will come and see us, not even Elizabeth.'

Jack winced at the mention of Elizabeth. She was soon to start her studies at Cambridge University and the thought that she would not visit them in their self-imposed exile was terrible. 'She will come,' he insisted, 'we will sip champagne and eat strawberries on the lawn and then I'll drive her to Cambridge.'

Elizabeth had gone to Scotland with a girlfriend for the summer but had promised to come and see them before term started. It was now three weeks, ten days and seven hours since she had gone and Jack experienced a pain in his gut whenever he thought about her absence.

'My girl will come. Of course she will.' Sadie said nothing, satisfied that she had needled him successfully but Jack, momentarily distressed, did not notice. 'This will be her home until she gets married and has a family of her own.'

He could not admit out loud the obvious fact that his beloved daughter had left and was now busy with her own life, preferring instead to pretend that she was merely on holiday and would return home to him soon.

'You're joking yourself. She's gone,' said his wife with a sigh.

Jack took his hands off the steering wheel and covered his ears. 'Hush!' A moment later he tried a conciliatory tone, 'Sadie, doll, try to be happy.'

She frowned – after all these years, he still did not understand. 'I don't want to be happy.'

They reached a ramshackle set of crossroads and a blank signpost.

'You see, silly old man, this place doesn't even have a name.'

Jack winced with the effort of trying to remain patient.

'Of course it does. The signs were simply painted out during the war and no one's replaced them. Everyone in the village knows where they are. Probably aren't enough strangers passing to warrant the effort of replacing them.'

Blue smoke from a nearby bonfire hovered, making strange patterns as the sunlight tried to penetrate. Jack felt Sadie shiver beside him and he tried to make casual conversation. 'I read that the corpses of highwaymen were buried under crossroads.'

She was not reassured. They passed the village hall where a small group of men were hammering wooden tent pegs into the sun-baked ground. Several of the younger men had removed their shirts as they worked, the muscles beneath their skin coiling like rope. They all stared narrowly as the Jaguar passed. Jack was perturbed – it was part of his grand scheme of assimilation that they would simply seep unnoticed into village life, like rain into damp earth, and he did not like their scrutiny.

He steered the car round to the left, turned by a steep hill and then noticed a broken gate leading along a roughly hewn dirt track. 'This is it!' he cried, recognising this to be a great moment in their lives – in years to come when he stood at the front of the driveway and ushered in the chauffeured cars to his golf club for the Wessex Cup or the qualifying match for the British Open, he would remember the moment when he saw the place for the first time.

He steered the car up a potholed driveway lined with beech trees, which shaded them coolly as the Jaguar bounced along from one hole to the next. 'Need to get this fixed,' he said resolutely – a course such as his would need a proper road.

The trees grew thicker and the light through the leaves played weird patterns over the car bonnet and upon their skin. Jack noticed two black eyes watching them through the gloom, then a shape disappeared into the thicket. He remembered a green painting of a wood in the book of fairy tales he'd had as a child.

And then they were back in the daylight. He pulled the car up beside the front door of the house. It looked rather different from the picture that was sitting snugly in Jack's breast pocket. The thatch was still there, but even with scant knowledge of thatches, he felt that they shouldn't have bald patches. A blackbird darted out of a large hole and another picked at a loose bit of straw. The lime-washed exterior was grimy in the sunlight; the roses grew feral and obscured the boarded-up windows. The walls were made of wattle and the house gave the impression that it wished for nothing more than to slump back into the earth. Jack furrowed his brow, climbed out of the car and ripped away the rotten wood nailed to the window frames. There was a tinkle of broken glass as a pane fell out. 'Need to fix that,' he muttered, less resolutely than before.

Sadie hadn't moved; she sat fixed in her seat and stared at the house curiously, breathing in deeply – there was a familiar scent, something she knew well but had not smelled for a long time. Jack plucked a rose from the wild tangle round the door and presented it to her. She ignored him, so he stuck it in her headscarf.

'Ouch!'

The stem of the rose was covered in sharp green thorns, and she pushed him away. Unperturbed, he opened the car door for her and offered his arm, which she rejected, brushing past him to stalk across the drive to the front door.

'The house looks sad now but with a lick of paint it will be perfect,' he called producing a bunch of old-fashioned cast iron keys, each the size of a giant's finger. 'Ready?'

He slipped one into the big keyhole on the studded door and as he turned it there was a satisfying click. He heaved open the door and entered the dark hallway, Sadie close behind him. She gave a little scream. '*Scheiße!* Something touched me!'

Jack wedged the door so that a shaft of light illuminated wisps of a torn cobweb. 'See, it's nothing, doll. Nothing but us.'

Glancing up, Sadie saw the low ceiling was criss-crossed with hulking beams, stained black with soot and age. On the walls the lime plaster was beginning to flake and where the sun fell it shone upon spots of mould and creeping damp. She ducked under a low archway leading into a rudimentary kitchen – it certainly wasn't Sadie's idea of a kitchen. There was a filthy stove, a heap of wood to drive it, a worn oaken table with a few broken, upended chairs, and as she looked about her, she saw there was no sink. In fact, not only was there no sink, there was no tap. She tried not to dwell on the significance of this unsavoury fact nor think of her porcelain bidet abandoned to its fate in Hampstead.

Jack had followed her and, having given up trying to peer through the dirt-caked windows, was heaving against the stable-style door that lead to the back garden.

'Just a minute. Nearly got him. Oh . . .'

His voice trailed away, as he saw the land stretched out before him. Wordless, he seized Sadie's hand and oblivious to her protests, led her outside. The fields lay under a shimmering heat haze and the bees hummed in every bush. The lawn sloped gently into fields full of waving grass tinged with buttercups, and high above their heads a kestrel hovered, its wings not appearing to beat.

Here was his golf course. Jack narrowed his eyes and, whether it was the effect of the sunlight or sheer excitement, he could hear a wireless commentary. – 'Well, *this is the first British Open to be held at the new course at Pursebury Ash. It is a fine day for it. Looking to the seventh you can see Sam Snead taking a practice shot. Ah, yes, here comes Bobby Jones with the owner of the course, that well-known English Gentleman, Mr Jack Rosenblum. Ah yes, it's going to be a great competition.'*

Jack saw the little flags waving amongst the tightly mowed grass and the yellow of the bunkers. He beamed, closing his eyes for a moment, as he listened to the cheering of the crowd.

Realising that Jack was lost in a daydream, Sadie turned to go inside. A voice from inside the hedge made her start.

'Mornin'.'

An old man was squatting in the shadows behind her, camouflaged by leaves and sprouting cow parsley. His face was the colour of wood stain, and he looked as if he was growing out of the hazel boughs. Sadie took a step back.

'*Ja*, hello, may I help you Mr . . .'

'Curtis. Jist Curtis. You can help if yer likes. I is huntin' for pignuts, Mrs Rose-in-Bloom.'

Sadie stared at him. 'You know my name?'

'Aye.'

He offered no more explanation, and Sadie continued to gaze at him, her mouth slightly open.

'Them last ones flew away,' he added conspiratorially.

He plucked two leaves off the hedge and made flapping motions.

'I am sorry? I beg your pardon?'

'Them last ones what lived in your house. They flew away.'

Sadie did not understand. 'They took an aeroplane?'

'Nope. Beds a-made of pijin feathers. 'S bad luck to sleep arn pijin feathers. They's wings grow back in the night and then they flies away. With you in bed or not.'

'Oh.'

'Yoos heard of them legends about gins, right?'

'Djinns?'

'Aye. Well they ent gins or Djinns but pi-jins. They is very dangerous things, pi-jins.'

'Pigeons?'

The man tapped his nose.

'What about goose feathers? I have an eiderdown of goose, will they fly away too?'

The man screwed up his face in concentration. 'Nope. Don't think so. Jist pi-jins. But I will make a sure.'

He stood, clambered out of the hedge, gave Sadie a little tip of his hat and wandered away down the hill. Aching with tiredness, all Sadie wanted was to lie down and sleep and determined to find a bed. Attempting to ignore the fustiness of the house, she climbed the wooden stairs and tried the nearest room. A cast-iron bed covered with a moth-eaten quilt rested in the middle of the room. She leant against the rough plastered wall and wondered aloud, 'How did I get here?'

A robin landed on a branch and cocked its head, as though the question were addressed to it. Sadie knelt to open the low window but the catch was stiff and splinters of rotting wood broke away as she forced it ajar. The air was full of dust that swirled in the spotlights of sun, and above the glass a fat cobweb wobbled in the breeze. She stared out at the shining fields, listening to the ribald song of the robin and found herself thinking of her grandparents, who had come from the *shetetls*. They had lived as peasants in villages in the east and sowed corn and potatoes, reared sheep and goats. A wind blew into the bedroom carrying tiny seed cases and the same odd scent; it was not the sickly ammonia scent of mice, nor the honeysuckle, but something familiar from her childhood. She walked to the window and slammed it shut. There was a tinkle of glass as another ancient pane shattered and fell to the ground in a cascade of sharp rain. She sighed, drew the curtain and lay on the bed, scrutinising the thick oak beams in the sloped ceiling above her head. The curtain was faded chintz and it fluttered in the breeze like a giant butterfly. On the floor lay a pile of faded books and she reached out to grab a volume from the top. The spine had come away, the cover was damp stained and it smelled vaguely of mould, but she opened it anyway and idly read the contents page. It was a collection of folklore: 'The Dorset Oozeer', 'Apple Bobbin' at Midnight', 'The Drowners', and she skimmed through the titles, searching for any reference to pigeons. There was none. The rest of the books were novels by Thomas Hardy and once must have been a smartly bound nineteenth-century set, but now they were scarred by brown water marks. She shoved all the books in the corner of the room so that their dank stench could not reach the bed, lay back down and closed her eyes.

She woke with a jolt to find that it was dark and, for a moment, she was back in Bethnal Green underground station in the midst of an air raid. She reached out automatically for Elizabeth – the child always slept curled against her hip, oblivious to the booms overhead – but Sadie's fingers brushed the wiry hair on Jack's leg, and she remembered where she was. She kept her mouth tight shut, worried that if she opened it the darkness would pour inside and choke her, sat on the edge of the bed and listened to the gentle rasp of Jack's breathing. There was another sound: a soft thudding and flapping. She tried to shake Jack awake but he would not stir. The scrabbling grew louder and screeching cries came from the wall. She dug her nails into her palms – she was a middle-aged woman and would not be tyrannised by night-time noises.

She slid out of bed and followed the sound to a door built into the wattle wall in one corner of the bedroom. As she fumbled with a bolt, the door burst open and a cascade of creatures flew at her, their panicked fluttering filling the air as she screamed out, terrified that they would get tangled in her hair. Looming grey shadows poured out from the cupboard and flapped across the ceiling; she could not tell if they were outsized bats or birds. There was only the thud, thud as they flew into the walls or collided with the window glass. She ran to the window, flung it as wide as she could and then escaped from the bedroom, slamming the door behind her.

She raced downstairs in the darkness until she reached the hall, where the flagstones felt icy cold on her bare feet. She didn't like to think of Jack asleep in the room with all those creatures – supposing they flew away with him? Then she would be left alone. She laughed at her silliness but her voice echoed in the empty house and, as she padded into the sitting room, she gave a slight shudder. Their furniture had been delivered but was still covered in white sheets, and she wished that she had a torch or even a candle. She could make out the shape of their sofa, an old high-backed Knole. Jack had bought it after reading that the Knole sofa was the oldest of all English designs and boasted a proud aristocratic lineage. Ladies had to be careful whom they sat next to on a Knole sofa as, with a flick of the wrist and a pull on the cord, the sides and back came tumbling down to form a makeshift bed – it was a dangerous and licentious sofa. Right now, it proved very useful and Sadie gladly removed the sheet, tugged on the cords and lay down. She wrapped herself up in the dustsheet, screwed her eyes tight shut and waited for sleep.

CHAPTER FOUR

JACK WOKE THE next morning feeling disorientated. He was lying in a neat, low bed in an unfamiliar room, with his hair sticking up around his ears like meadow grass. Light grey-blue feathers lay scattered across the floor and a dead bird rested next to the window. Throwing off the covers he jumped out of bed, landed on bare wooden boards and bounded across to the window – unhelpfully positioned at the height of his knees – and bent down to look out. Rolling down to the foot of the hill were the fields for his golf course; the grass was thick with dew and clumps of cloud floated lazily across the sky like tufts of duckling down. Early morning sunshine streamed in through the filthy window, and he gave a contented huff as he saw the pond glitter in the distance. There was no sign of Sadie – this was a good house; it was big enough for them to lose one another in.

Jack yawned, stretched and went downstairs to the small back parlour that he decided would be his study. It was dingy, the walls smoke-stained and the thick layers of dust made him cough. A pile of dead leaves had blown in from outside and a half-burned fire mouldered in the broken grate. Underneath a bookcase lurked a sprung mousetrap, with a tiny shrivelled form pinned to the base. He looked away quickly – really must get a cat, much more pleasant than a trap. He disliked the paraphernalia of death, even bestial ones and, while he knew deep down that hunting or shooting was as English as golf, he couldn't stomach death being part of the game. Even if it was an un-British sign of weakness, he never added any kind of blood sports to his list. He had hated the rabbits in the butchers' shops during the war – strung up in their blood-smeared fur, eyes filmy, humming with flies – and he couldn't bear Sadie to buy them, not even when the only alternative was a tin of 'potted meat in natural juices'. It was not only dead animals that repulsed him, a wriggling fish with a line in its lip, suffocating in air, distressed him too. He liked that the English language separated animal and food: cow and beef, sheep and mutton. It was more civilised than German: *das Rindfleisch,* bull-flesh. It was too literal. Perhaps that was why he hated rabbit – rabbit was rabbit whether it was hopping in a meadow or skinned and ready for the pot.

A box of papers rested on the floor. He removed the lid, rifled through the pages and in a moment found what he was looking for.

A Guide to the Old Course at St Andrews, Scotland,

By Mr Tom Morris.

1884

Printed for T.R. Johnson in St Paul's Churchyard.

It was a yellowed and dog-eared pamphlet, which he had discovered in a second-hand bookstore off Piccadilly sandwiched between a guide to the Lake District and a volume on lesser-spotted quails. He had read it at least fifty times and was almost word perfect. He stroked the battered pages with affection. It was like the commandments given to Moses on the Mount – the blueprint for his destiny. With the wisdom of Tom Morris he would build the greatest golf course since the end of the war: an Old Course in the West Country. He didn't have the sea, that was the only slight hitch and it probably couldn't *officially* be a links course with only a duck pond, but other than the lack of ocean, the differences in topography, soil, wind direction and grass, it would be a perfect copy of St Andrews.

Jack's cheeks flushed with excitement – his entire life had been building to this great event. They had barred him from the London clubs, but this would be the best course in the south of England and he would select the members. He envisioned himself sitting in state at the kitchen table, reading a vast pile of correspondence from lords of the realm and club secretaries beseeching him for admittance, in letters dripping with adjectives.

He went out into the garden, the wet grass making dark patches on his leather slippers, and listened to a cuckoo calling from a distant copse. He unfolded the central pages of the pamphlet to display a map of the Old Course, which he held up to the prospect before him. He wondered how long it would take until it was all finished – five months, maybe six? It was all about positioning the holes and he had Tom Morris to help with that. The holes themselves couldn't take too long to dig – it was the greens that would be more tricky. They needed regular watering and he would have to find out where the springs on his land lay.

'The springs on my land.'

The words caught in his throat like a piece of bread. He stared at the ground before him, awed that this patch of green and this slice of steep hill belonged to him and Sadie – it scarcely seemed possible that he could be allowed to have so much. He would be the perfect country gentleman and take good care of these fields. What he needed first was a tweed cap and a walking stick with a bone handle – that was the wardrobe of a country gentleman with sixty acres, and Jack knew the importance of being properly attired (rule number five: always adhere to English conventions of dress). He returned to the house shouting, 'Sadie, I'm off to buy a hat.'

Sadie was already up; she had managed to fall into a fitful

sleep but had risen at dawn to begin the immense task of cleaning the house. There was only one tap, a spluttering stream in the back kitchen that had been just sufficient to wash the floors – there was, of course, no hot water and the large tin bath in the kitchen also provided a dismal hint that there was no bathroom. Yet the bare, grimy house with its lack of electric light and strange nocturnal sounds reminded Sadie of her childhood. As a girl there had been long holidays in Bavaria with her family, in an ancient house on the edge of a wood. It was a memory that, like a favourite novel, had been hidden by shelves brimming with more recent matter, only to emerge that morning when she was woken by the cooing of wood pigeons in the chimney. The childhood holiday cabin was full of privations: a well in the garden, candles for light and no maids. Back then it had seemed like an adventure. She was older now, had a twinge in her knee, her back ached at night and she liked ease but somehow this house reminded her of *before*. Filled as it was with misplaced memories of a distant, underwater childhood, she thought she could lose herself here. Perhaps, she would fall through the cracks in the kitchen wall and re-emerge in Bavaria forty years before.

She did not share these feelings with Jack – he would not understand, nor would he wish to. She resolved to accompany him, and since she knew he did not want her to come, this gave her a kernel of pleasure. From the landing she called down to him, '*Broitgeber* you must wash before we leave.'

Jack frowned – he had taken a notion to buy a hat, and once fixed upon something there was no time for distractions. He followed the voice of his wife upstairs. She had disposed of the dead bird and was tidying the bedroom, making up the bed with starched white sheets so that it looked almost inviting. A trail of silver feathers led to the cupboard in a corner of the room; the door was ajar and the inside was coated in a layer of yellowing excrement.

'Jack, you must get a man in to fix the ceiling. It's an aviary up there. And the birds fly down into the cupboard.'

Jack kicked a feather with his toe, disinterestedly. 'I'm going. You stay here and worry about the birds.'

Sadie studied her husband. He was still wearing the clothes from yesterday; he had grass stuck to his back, a feather on his cheek and a growth of stubble across his chin. She gave him a sly look. 'You wish to make the correct impression, hmm? They'll think we're slovenly foreigners unless you wash.'

Jack knew that she was right – it was rule thirty-seven on the list (Englishmen of all classes take great pride in excellent personal hygiene). He couldn't possibly risk the condemnation.

She watched his face contort at the prospect and pointed to a small wooden washstand in the corner. Set into it was a chipped jug and a round porcelain bowl painted with blue nymphs. Underneath lurked a sinister pink and white flowered pot. Jack it pulled out.

'Is this for pissing?'

He dangled it upside-down.

'There is a toilet outside. Do not use that unless you intend to empty it yourself.'

Jack considered this, then looked out the open window – there was not a house or person in sight. He knelt down and unbuttoned his fly. An arc of urine sprayed onto the tangled flowerbeds below.

'That,' said Sadie, 'is neither English nor hygienic.'

He pretended not to hear.

'There is a small room down the hall that will be perfect for Elizabeth.'

Jack fastened his fly and jumped up, alert with interest, 'Will she be able to see my course from her window?'

'Come and look.'

He followed Sadie along the corridor, his elbow brushing the peeling wallpaper, the bare floorboards creaking underfoot,

46

into a room beneath the eaves. A thatched dormer window had a splendid view across the valley below but he surveyed the room critically – it needed to be just right for his Elizabeth.

Sunday afternoons, that was his only regret on leaving London. He used to take Elizabeth to the Lyon's Corner House on the high street. Every week the ritual was the same: he held the café door open for his daughter, listening happily to the tinkle of the bell. The waitress glanced up as they came in, 'Your regular table, sir?'

Jack saw in his mind he and Elizabeth being led to their booth by the window with an excellent view of the street. The waitress passed him the menu but he did not open it, instead handing it straight to his daughter. On those Sunday afternoons Jack was silent. He knew that his accent betrayed him, after fifteen years in London he still spoke with the measured tones of a foreigner, so he let Elizabeth talk in her flawless English voice, and answered her in little whispers that could not be overheard. For that hour, they would sit in the window booth, sipping warm, sweetened orange juice and nibbling stale jam roll, and Jack was happy. He would listen with a tear in his eye as Elizabeth chattered about books and of how she dreamt of travelling to America, all the while marvelling that he, a man born in a shabby Berlin suburb, had produced such a creature. The waiters and waitresses, the diners at nearby tables, only heard the voice of the pretty girl and so, Jack believed, he appeared to all of them a genuine Englishman.

Now, standing in the neat bedroom, he tried to work out how many more weeks it was before he could expect Elizabeth's visit. He gave a tiny sigh – part of him wished that the world had not changed, and that fathers could still keep their daughters with them and forbid holidays in Scotland.

Later that morning, as the Rosenblums drove down the lane towards the village hall, it occurred to Jack that he was slightly unprepared for their expedition to the country. In addition to preparations for the golf course, he might need to install indoor plumbing for his house – this was a nuisance, since he had intended to leave the house entirely to Sadie and devote all his energy to the more important matter of the course. Yet, this inconvenience was not a thought that worried him unduly – he merely acknowledged it and then let it float away. He wished he were alone; while in London he succeeded in passing most days without spending more than fifteen minutes in the company of his wife, today he seemed unable to be rid of her. He knew a good husband would be more sympathetic to her unhappiness, but to his mind a person should want to live, if only out of curiosity. He realised she missed Emil – so did he. There was an Emil-shaped hole in the universe. And Elizabeth would have liked an uncle. With a start Jack realised his daughter was the same age Emil had been when he died. Quickly, he thought of other things.

As he slowed to take the corner by the village hall, a burly man in a stiff wool suit stepped into the road and waved at them, forcing Jack to brake sharply. The man stood in front of the car, looking them up and down with steady interest but saying nothing. He seemed to be waiting for something, and then, clearly losing patience he snapped, 'Well, Mr Rose-in-Bloom, are yer comin?'

Jack experienced the same confusion as his wife had the day before. It must be the done thing here to know everyone's name – clearly a local custom. So, not knowing the man before him, Jack felt rather awkward and searched for the suitable English phrase 'I don't believe I've had the pleasure, Mr . . .'

'Jack Basset. But I is jist called Basset. None of yer misters.'

'Glad to make your acquaintance, erm, Basset.'

Jack offered his hand, which Basset shook slowly before scratching at a tiny shaving nick in his muscular neck. He made no move to get out of the way of the car. Peering round him, Jack noticed a motley crowd gathering in the shade of the hall; the women dressed in floral frocks and wide-brimmed hats and the men sweating uncomfortably in hot, special occasion suits.

Basset waited for a moment and then cleared his throat. 'Well? Are yer?'

'Of course.'

Jack had no idea to what Basset referred but did not want to cause further upset so enquired with the utmost politeness, 'May I ask where the car park is?'

'Car park? He wants to know where the car park is?'

Basset started to cough with laughter, a button popped off his shirt and a fleshy triangle of hairy stomach poked through. Embarrassed, he straightened and pointed to a field across the road.

'That there is the car park. Put him in corner. I'll get gate.'

Jack steered his beloved Jaguar through a flock of nonchalant sheep and parked under a tree, eyeing the animals suspiciously. The Rosenblums allowed Basset to lead them onto the village green, where a battered white marquee was erected in the centre of the grass. Peering inside, Jack glimpsed plump girls selling fat hunks of red meat. Mounds of dark hearts, piles of kidneys and blue-tinged ox tongues lay on steel trays. Beside them rested baskets filled with misshapen vegetables and trays of grey fungus. He saw a table covered in the limp bodies of pheasant, duck and hare; they were skinned and raw, and the pretty girl presiding over them had a tiny smear of blood on her smooth cheek. Leaning up against a bench was a pile of rifles, and he wondered where they had come from – the trade in de-commissioned arms was strictly illegal. A heap of ammunition lay baking in the sun. 'This is England,' thought Jack, 'you can sell anything here, and some poor bugger will buy it.'

Basset ushered them inside the tent, where it reeked of

cider and warm bodies. While the women argued over filched rabbits and game, the men drank and, judging by the stench, they had been here a while.

'This is Mr and Mrs Rose-in-Bloom,' announced Basset guiding them into the midst of the crowd.

Jack stood quite still and let them all stare, while Sadie took a small step closer to him. A ragged woman viewed them suspiciously, eating the biggest peach he had ever seen; it took him a moment to realise what the round yellow-fleshed fruit was – it had been so many years since he had seen one.

'Rose-in-Bloom's a funny name,' said the woman, 'sounds English but yoos foreign, ent you?' There were little pieces of peach flesh smeared round her mouth and caught in her brown teeth.

'We are British now. We love England. We feel very English,' Jack declared.

The woman wasn't to be deterred. 'Yoos British *now*. What was you before, then?'

Jack hated this part, the declaration of his otherness.

'We were born in Berlin. We came to England before the war.'

'Berlin – that's in Germany.'

He nodded. 'Yes, it is.'

The ragged woman was not impressed. 'So, you is a Kraut,' she corrected herself, 'you *was* Kraut. You sounds Kraut.'

'No. I am a British Citizen.'

'Why 'ave you come to Pursebury?'

'To build a golf course.'

This was unexpected.

'A what?'

'A golf course.'

Jack was standing in the centre of a growing crowd, where he was proving to be the most popular attraction at the fair – this did not please him, as he was trying his best to be inconspicuous. He never understood how, when he always obeyed the list to the letter, dressing in the uniform of the English gentleman, he was instantly identified as a rank outsider.

'I shall build the greatest golf course in the South-West.'

The faces in the crowd stared at him dubiously.

'Everyone in the village shall have membership,' he announced proudly with a magnanimous wave.

No one seemed especially excited at this prospect and continued to stare.

'This ent golfing country. It's skittling country,' said Basset. 'Ever played skittles?' he asked with a note of challenge.

'No, I haven't.' Jack was intrigued – an English game he hadn't heard about. He was filled with instant enthusiasm.

Seeing this, Basset smirked. 'I'll learn you,' he said and led him away with a glint in his eye.

Choosing not to witness Jack's latest escapade, Sadie wandered from the tent into the village hall. It was an unusual building; the pitched roof and walls were all made of sage-coloured corrugated iron while inside it was wood-panelled and decked with multicoloured flags. Framed photographs of the Royal family adorned every wall; the pictures of King George all draped in black crepe. A small army of women stood at the back of the hall guarding the tea table. Sadie was used to London where good food was scarce; it wasn't like anyone went hungry – there was enough to eat – it was just plain. Food had lost its colour; there were drab potatoes, grey meat and tinned vegetables. Spices were a rare luxury and it took all of her skill to make her cooking taste of anything much at all. In contrast, the table in the church hall was a monument to excess and could have been the tableau of 'gluttony' in a painting of the Deadly Sins, heaving as it did with sandwiches of rare beef – blood turning the bread red – and baskets of brown speckled eggs, bowls of cream and trays of bright strawberries. She recalled the delicate pastries of the chefs in Berlin – the light folded palmiers and vanilla sugar biscuits – those were fragile pieces of artistry but this English feast was something different. She couldn't remember food being such lurid colours – the dripping beef and scarlet strawberries looked obscene next to the faded floral patterns on the women's dresses. She became conscious of someone staring at her, and turned to see a thin woman, hair swept into a severe schoolmistress bun, standing very close.

'I'm Mrs Lavender Basset. Secretary of the Parish Council fourteen years runnin' and chairwoman of the Coronation Committee. Will you be wantin' some tea?'

Sadie swallowed, shyness making her perspire, and her blouse cling underneath her arms.

'Thank you. That is very kind. I'm Mrs Sadie—'

Lavender cut her off with a snort, 'Oh. I knows who you are Mrs Rose-in-Bloom.'

She led Sadie to the front of the hall and filled a plate for her with a fat slice of Victoria sponge oozing with cream, made pinkish by the jam. Sadie didn't want to eat. The food was too much, and she worried that once she started she'd cram the sponge into her mouth, unable to stop. She always felt self-conscious eating in front of strangers, but Lavender was scrutinising her through owlish spectacles. Glancing around the hall Sadie realised that all the women were waiting, teacups poised on saucers, watching. Feeling a little sick, she took a bite and forced a smile.

In the field beside the hall, Jack was not faring well at skittles. He shook his head in total bemusement. Curtis, a tiny old man, gave him a friendly tap on the shoulder.

'Nope. Like this, Mister-Rose-in-Bloom.'

Curtis clasped the rock-hard ball, took a run up and then, falling to his knees, slid along the wooden alley on his belly.

The ball rolled from his hand and collided with the skittles, knocking them flying in a perfect strike.

'Now, that there is the Dorset flop. Nothing like the piddling Somerset wump. Much more effective. 'S why we beats them nillywallies every time at t' Western Skittlin' championship.'

'Yer turn to try,' growled Basset and thrust the ball once more into Jack's damp palm.

'Trick is to let go of the ball at last minute. Got to do it sharpish like. Skittles knocked over with yer noggin doesn't count, mind,' added Curtis tapping his head.

The others grunted in agreement at this sound advice. Jack rubbed the ball against his trouser leg and prepared to bowl again. The rules were beyond him; he knew only that the general aim was to knock down as many as possible and that somehow, whenever it was his turn, the skittles remained resolutely upright on their wooden platform, whilst, when Curtis, Basset or one of the others bowled, the skittles clattered to the ground. Steeling his nerves, he took a deep breath, stepped back a few paces and began his run-up along the grass. Reaching the wood of the skittle shoot, he screwed his eyes shut and threw himself onto his belly, knocking all the wind out his lungs. He slid two yards along the ramp and stopped. Jack opened his eyes, and realised that everyone apart from Curtis was laughing.

'Yer forgot to let go of the ball.' the old man said sadly. 'An ersey mistake.'

'Loser 'as to drink,' said Basset thrusting at Jack a brimming mug of a sweet, apple-scented alcoholic drink.

As the afternoon wore on, Jack became dimly aware of jeers, of Basset and the other men discarding their jackets, of shirts being unbuttoned and raucous shouts of, 'Drink, Mr Rose-in-Bloom, drink!'

His head was really swimming now and the combination of home-brewed cider with hot June sunshine was making his vision cloud. He closed his eyes for a moment and heard a voice mutter, ''Ee's a goner. Skittled. 'Ee'll be seeing Dorset woolly-pigs soon.'

There were more snickers and hissing mirth. Then another voice. 'Dorset woolly-pigs. Them is idiots wot believe that.'

There was a derisive cry from Curtis, 'Don't mock. Yer doesn't josh about the Dorset woolly-pig. A noble beast of strength and savagery. If yer'd saw one yerself, yer wouldn't say things.'

Jack tried to open his eyes and failed.

Curtis rumbled on in his deep burr, 'I saw it. More 'an thirty yer ago. But I saw it.'

Jack struggled and with supreme effort opened his eyes. The sight that greeted them made him think that he was indeed skittled. A tree was standing in front of him: a huge knot of branches covered with leaves and woven with drooping flowers swaying on a pair of stout legs. There seemed to be a man inside, but he was almost entirely hidden by the vast framework of twigs, and perched at an odd angle on top of his head was a misshapen crown of leaves studded with daisies. Unsure if he was in the midst of a dream, Jack closed his eyes again.

'Git moving, you drunken bastard,' yelled a voice.

Concerned that he was being addressed, Jack opened one eye to see the tree-man lumber forward. He swayed and staggered across the field where he paused, and then slipped into a ditch. There were shouts, and a rush of children surged towards him, yanked him out and then, clutching the branches, pulled him onwards. A minute later the strange procession disappeared up the hill, the crowd resumed their business, and Jack drifted back into his stupor.

When he woke up, he realised his legs wouldn't work. He looked at them, told them to move but they stayed on the ground, splayed out in front of him, immobile. The field was quieter now, the crowd had thinned, and his wife sat on the ground by his feet. She did not look pleased.

'Scold later,' he murmured.

She studied him for a moment and then heaved him upright but it was no use and, his legs as weak as a newborn lamb's, he slid back down.

'Just get me to the car. I can drive us back up the hill.'

Sadie said nothing and, pursing her lips in profound annoyance, half dragged, half carried her husband to the front of the hall where only the stragglers remained. Together they staggered past Curtis snoring beneath a wooden bench, their feet crunching on snatches of twig and fallen blossoms that had been discarded by the tree-man as he lumbered up the lane. In the distance there were cries and shouts and Jack could smell bonfire smoke. Vicious gnats whined in his ears and tried to bite him as he slipped into crevices and potholes. It was still warm, making his damp shirt mould to his back and, as they reached the shade of the trees, he paused for a moment to rest.

'You go on. I'm going to wait here for a minute,' he panted and, with a self-sacrificing little wave, slumped to the ground. A moment later, he watched indignant, as Sadie stalked off up the winding lane without a backward look.

'Fine. You just leave me.'

He wiped his damp forehead with the back of his hand and stared at several cows chewing the cud by the side of the road. There was an unpleasant heavy sensation in his belly and a pulsating pain was building in his temples. Outside the hall lounged a few young men, smoking and idly rolling up the battered tents. A gunshot rang out and Jack winced in pain as the sound pierced his aching skull. Birds rose in a flurry out of the trees and an empty tin bounced along the ground. He frowned – someone had purchased the guns; he did not like men playing with such things – even air rifles and toy pistols disturbed him. A crew of youths reloaded the rifles and stared curiously at Jack as he ambled unsteadily past. He swaggered a little and wished, not for the first time, that he were five inches taller and wearing his Henry Poole suit – the next time he was in London he would purchase another. With relief, he saw that Sadie was waiting for him across the lane.

'This where we parked the car?'

He pointed to an iron gate and she nodded. Jack heaved at the gate; it was heavy and squealed like a trapped rat. The car's dark paintwork shone in the afternoon sun and Jack shambled to it, fumbling in his pocket for the key, but sitting in the driver's seat, eyes shut and chewing happily, was a large woolly sheep. The words burst out of him before he was aware of it. 'GET OUT! HELP! FIRE! THIEF!'

The sheep looked at him in surprise, scrambled to its feet and leapt out, clipping the top of the door with its hoof. Swaying slightly, Jack rubbed the door with a corner of his shirt.

'It's scratched. *Mein Gott. Scheiße! Kaputt!* It's scratched.'

He only lapsed into German at moments of extreme stress, as he prided himself on what he considered to be his great emotional self-control. The boys across the road paused to watch the peculiar little man shout at his car.

Sadie caught a glimpse of them and gave a wave. 'Stop being ridiculous. Your beloved car is fine. You're making a scene.'

Jack stopped running his hands frantically through his hair, opened the car door and sat down but, just as he was about to swing his legs inside, he realised that a long black face was gazing up at him. He prodded the second sheep.

'You. Out.'

Reluctantly, it got to its feet and climbed out the car.

'They is not used to such luxury,' said a voice.

Jack looked round to see a stocky youth with a lopsided grin standing by the car, toying with an empty cartridge casing.

56

'Yes, well, no harm done.' Quickly he recovered his good temper. 'Jack Rosenblum.'

He shook the young man's hand.

'Max Coffin,' said the boy.

Jack thought for a moment through the apple haze in his head.

'What do you do, Max?'

'Work at farm.'

'How would you like to earn some extra cash?'

Max flexed his arms awkwardly. 'Always want extra cash.'

Jack liked this bit and felt his mind sharpen, and the sense of bleary sickness subside. He owned the biggest carpet factory in North London and there wasn't a house in the whole of Hampstead Garden Suburb that wasn't fitted with a Rosenblum peach, peppermint or lavender plush pile carpet. He was good at striking a bargain – pay what you have to and then add a little bit extra so that the men really want to work that bit extra for you.

'What do they pay you at the farm?'

'Three pound a week.'

Jack paused for effect; this was part of the process – the boy needed to feel that this was a real negotiation and he was being taken seriously.

'I am creating the greatest golf course in the entire South of England and I'm going to offer you the opportunity to share in that triumph.'

The lad stared at him blankly.

'Come and work for me,' Jack explained with an expansive smile. 'I'll pay you and your friends,' he gestured to the young men folding away tables outside the village hall, 'Three pound ten a week.'

Max's eyes widened for a second and then he scrutinised his fingernails, trying to appear indifferent. Tactfully, Jack pretended not to notice his surprise. 'Go and discuss it with the lads.'

Jack watched Max saunter back to the village hall. The lads huddled in animated discussion.

'Are you sure this is a good idea?' Sadie asked, concerned.

'Of course.'

Max returned, hands in his pockets, clearly relishing his sudden elevation to negotiator and spokesman.

'Five of us wants to help.'

'Wonderful,' said Jack, 'The course will be the jewel of England.'

'But we wants three pounds twelve.' Edgy and uncertain, he glanced back at the group of boys.

Jack whistled and Max looked stricken, as though he knew he shouldn't have pushed it. Jack thought for a moment, watching as the boys reloaded a rifle and lined up another row of bully-beef tins.

'I tell you what. If you promise to throw those guns in the river, it's a deal.'

'A'right,' said Max.

Jack shook the young man's hand and studied him for a moment before he returned to the others.

'What did you do that for?' Sadie's voice brimmed with irritation. 'Always interfering.'

'And you're always complaining. All is well, my darling. It has started. They will help us build our golf course.'

'*Your* golf course.'

'I am sure they can help on the house once the course is underway. These boys today are remarkable. Turn their hand to anything.'

They climbed into the car and he started the engine. Sadie surreptitiously knocked a shiny, round sheep turd off her seat. Hearing the car fire up, Max leapt into action and swung open the gate.

'Goodbye. I shall see you on Monday!' Jack said with a wave.

He drove the car at walking pace. The sky was a bold, unbroken blue and the buttercups in the hedgerows glowed yellow. The dandelion clocks sent seed parachutes flying on the breeze and into the car where they tickled his cheek. They passed a row of ancient dwellings with sagging roofs and untidy gardens filled with blue forget-me-nots and tall lupins in purple or yellow. Bumblebees filed in and out of nodding foxgloves. Jack briefly closed his eyes – this evening sunshine felt different from the close heat of London. In the city he felt the grime cling to his skin while this felt clean, as though the sunshine was warming him inside like a generous bowl of curried mutton stew.

CHAPTER FIVE

SADIE SPENT THE next day scrubbing the house. The same light blue feathers littered every room and white bird excrement had sprayed the flagstone floors and spoilt the walls. She wondered about the people who lived here before. The house had been deserted for years, save for the birds and mice that she could hear scratching at beams in the attic. She did not know from whom they had bought the place but she liked not knowing. It made the house belong more to her; the only history that mattered now was theirs. 'I don't have space for other people's memories,' she murmured as she crouched in her petticoat and washed away the dirt and the recent past, the years of neglect.

Jack sat in the sunshine listening to the birds. The sound came from every tree and bush, filling the air with a constant high-pitched chatter. He thumbed through a battered copy of the '1951 Golf Year Book' scouring the advertisements for tools and brands of fertiliser. There were captions proclaiming the virtues of 'DORMAN SIMPLEX JUNIOR PNEUMATIC SPRAYER' and telling him to 'OBTAIN THE FINEST TURF OF ALL FROM SUTTON'S GRASS SEEDS – THEY ENSURE SUCCESS!' He wondered whether he ought to buy some for his greens – he didn't want the grass to grow either too long or too coarse, it had to be just right.

Lost in this pleasant reverie, he started when the gate clattered loudly and half a dozen men stomped along the driveway. He recognised them from skittles but now they were unsmiling and had changed into stout leather boots.

They were all big men, broad shouldered and bull-like. He glimpsed a flash of steel studs on the bottom of the boots as they marched across the gravel. Trying not to be alarmed, Jack strolled through the garden to greet them, just as Basset began to hammer furiously on the ancient front door.

'Why did you do it?' Basset shouted, jabbing a finger accusingly at Jack who stood there whitely on the porch, dropping his golfing annual in shock.

'I beg your pardon?'

'That's right. You should beg my bloody pardon. The lads won't work now. Not less I give 'em another fifteen bob a week which I ent got. So what am I going to do? Watch my harvest rot in them shittin' fields?'

Basset paused for breath. He flushed with anger and struggled to articulate the words through his rage.

'This man 'as thieved my boys. For 'is feckin' golfin' course.'

Flecks of spittle caught in the corners of his mouth.

Jack shuddered; he was not used to this kind of unbridled rage. There was something feral about Basset's fury and he made no attempt to disguise his contempt for the neat Mr Rosenblum and his pristine shirt. Jack surveyed the orgy of enraged faces and heard their muttered curses.

Sadie watched from the kitchen, lurking out of sight – this was Jack's mess. She wanted to disappear, to dissolve into nothingness or to fly away and leave behind only a pile of feathers. She gave a tiny laugh; perhaps that was what happened to the last residents of the house.

For a brief moment, even Jack wanted to go back to London, and thought with a pang of his friend Edgar and their evenings together playing backgammon. In fifty years of friendship, Edgar had never once shouted at him and, God knew, he sometimes deserved it. At that moment, Jack decided this golf course was for Edgar and for everyone who had been banned from the other courses. Basset would not stop him from obtaining the last item on his list; he must be resolute. He stared at the man swollen with anger before him, and concentrated on the little wiry hairs sprouting from his nose and ears, the green eyes and the thinning blond hair. Basset exuded self-assurance; he was the leader of this tiny piece of England. From his muddy boots to his red-veined nose Jack Basset was an Englishman. And Jack Rosenblum wanted to be part of his village – he was going nowhere.

Jack swore to Basset that he wouldn't lure away the farm boys with promises of riches until after the harvest was in. The farmer grunted a grudging assent, and led his friends away. Retreating into his study, Jack poured himself a medicinal whisky, and breathed a heavy sigh. It was June and, according to the leather-bound copy of the *Encyclopædia Britannica*, the boys would be busy until late September. Jack was sorely disappointed; the coronation of the new Queen was set for the following June and he was resolved on having the finishing touches completed well before then. He would invite a selection of gentlemen – Mr Austen as well as Edgar Herzfeld – to partake in a small tournament dedicated to Her Majesty. He could already see the gleaming silver cup laid out on a long table covered with a white cloth and piled high with bottles of champagne, trays of sandwiches, pickles and poached salmon. If the men only began in October, they would barely have started the course before winter arrived, and he knew from reading Tom Morris that new grass had to be planted in mild weather, for when the ground froze they could do nothing at all. At present, the fields were full of meadow flowers and long grass and it would need a great deal of mowing to transform them into greens like those at St Andrews.

Jack made a decision and, needing someone to announce it to, walked into the kitchen where Sadie was carefully flouring her hands. Throwing open the door with a bang, he cleared his throat.

'I am going to build the course by myself.'

Sadie looked at him in wonder, eyebrows knitting together in doubt but Jack met her pessimism with drama and held his arms aloft.

'With these two hands I shall dig my way to victory!'

Sadie shook her head in contempt and brushed her fingers through her hair leaving two white streaks of flour like badger stripes.

'My mother warned me that craziness ran in your family. I should have listened but no, I was young and foolish and easily impressed by your red bicycle and your thick hair.'

She gave a rueful cry and turned her back on her husband. He waited, disappointed by her unsatisfactory response and then retreated in silence.

Over the next month, his study metamorphosed into a labyrinth of plans, maps, drawings and letters. He joined Stourcastle library and ordered every title on golf that he could find. They lay stacked in tottering piles across the floor, partly submerged by detailed drawings of various Scottish, English and American courses. He was captivated by Bobby Jones's account of the transformation at Augusta. There were botanical sketches of the flowers he had used and detailed layouts of the planting and water features. Jack wondered if he could divert a river too – perhaps dam the Stour and make it flow over Bulbarrow and across his course; it looked so beautiful in the pictures and, according to Bobby Jones, it was not difficult.

Jack decided that the course at Augusta was man's perfection of nature. Jones was an omnipotent magician; at his command woods vanished, hills subsided and valleys rose. Even those who preferred the ancient links had to concede that Bobby Jones had transformed Augusta into an Arcadian paradise. A canvas of verdant green provided the background, like the painted backdrop of an Old Master, and into this was woven a thread of glittering streams filling large pools, which reflected the wide-open blue of the sky. Then there was the miraculous marriage of water and scented azaleas and dogwoods – reds, pinks and gold – sparkling in the mirror ponds so that Jack could smell the fragrance rising off the photographs. There was a vista from every rise – a glimpse of a trickling stream surrounded by blooming camellias, or the curve of a yellow bunker echoed in the angle of a lake. Such perfection was designed to give the spectator a sense of profound satisfaction; Capability Brown would have been proud to inspire such a pupil. Nothing was out of place; every blade of grass was considered, the shade and texture of the greens and the gradient of each hillock the result of meticulous planning and planting. This was living art; man creating beauty in flowers, water, earth and sky. No sculpture or drawing could be considered more daring. The gardens of Babylon or Bobli were no greater than these.

Yet Jack was also transfixed by Robert Hunter, author of the celebrated tome *The Links Courses of England and Scotland*, who declared, 'it should be remembered that the greatest and fairest things are done by nature and lesser by art'. Hunter was a Romantic and valued the sublime on the golf course. Bunkers were only true hazards when formed from sand blown in by the turbulent North Sea. The rough should be toughened blue seagrass and the greatest vista was that of the crashing waves against the horizon. Beauty is small scale – a mere construction of prettiness by mankind, who cannot manufacture the sublime magnificence of nature. Bobby Jones may smooth a hillock or alter the course of a stream, but he cannot fill an ocean or grow a granite-tipped mountain. Hunter knew of no course that could rival the ancient links. Yet, Jack reasoned, Hunter had not actually *built* a golf course and Bobby Jones had.

Torn by the conundrum of whose approach to choose, Jack took off his glasses, nestled into his high-backed armchair and lit a cigarette. He was not a regular smoker, perhaps smoking three cigarettes a week, but they helped him think. He struck a match and let it burn between his fingers, watching the bright orange flame flicker before shaking it out. He inhaled deeply and coughed. The smoke curled upwards and lingered alongside the beams embedded in the low ceiling. He stretched out his short legs and closed his eyes in consideration. While he liked the photographs of the course at Augusta, he remained concerned that diverting the Stour single-handedly might conceivably be ambitious for a novice. Similarly, the purchase of thousands of exotic flowers may be beyond his means. Nonetheless, he was adamant that his course would be one of the best and, like all great visionaries, he was not going to be dissuaded by trivial inconveniences.

Mr Robert Hunter's command to utilise the natural obstacles provided by the terrain was compelling. Jack's land was full, overflowing in fact, with natural obstacles: there were the water meadows at the base of the valley filled with sprouting bog plants, and the slope of the hill was really very steep, an incline of approximately twenty per cent which, Jack understood, already made his course one of the more challenging. The edges of the course were tightly wooded and hedges divided the land into thin strips.

Considering this, Jack tried to blow a smoke ring and choked. His eyes began to water and tears streamed down his cheeks. He reached for the nearest liquid, which happened to be the whisky decanter, and took a large gulp. This made the coughing worse and he spluttered whisky from his nose. It took a minute for the fit to subside and exhausted he settled back in his chair. He contemplated why he was so drawn to the game of golf – what had compelled him to pack up his life, gather his petulant wife and move to this place? Yes, he

65

wanted to be an Englishman but there had to be something more, a reason for his obsession with the game. Perhaps he liked golf because it had rules – within those little laws lay a logical order. If you played the game and obeyed the rules, then win or lose you were safe. The game contained and held you safely within its structures. For the hours of your round, you could live in this perfected world of flowers and silver pools, and exist according to the boundaries of the game. Golf was a great list of rules, all by itself. He sucked on his cigarette, exhaled a small funnel of smoke and reached a decision. He must combine the two great models: he would create a links course according to the wisdom of Robert Hunter but using the techniques of Bobby Jones. He would create a St Andrews in the Blackmore Vale – even if he had to demolish the entire western face of Bulbarrow Hill.

There remained one niggling doubt, like a small stone in his shoe, and so Jack decided he must do what any logical man would – write to Bobby Jones for advice. He went over to his desk, pulled out a piece of crisp white writing paper and reached for his pen.

Dear Mr Jones,

I have recently purchased sixty acres of land in the county of Dorsetshire, which I have undertaken to turn into a golf course. I am a great admirer of your triumph at Augusta, and hope that you would condescend to bestow upon me a little of your advice. I intend to have my course completed before the following summer. I enclose a map of the land. My only slight inhibiting factor is that currently I must undertake all work myself. I do not wish this to impede any suggestions you may decide to bestow. Please, be assured sir, that I am five foot three and a half inches of sheer tenacity.

With regards,
Your humble servant,
Jack M. Rosenblum

Jack sealed up the letter and placed it carefully in his pocket. First thing tomorrow, he would take it to the post office to be weighed. He did some rough calculations in his head. Presuming that the letter went into the first airmail post tomorrow, it would still not reach Mr Jones's publisher until a minimum of four weeks later and a delay of anything up to twelve weeks was certainly very possible. He then assessed that it would sit in a secretary's in-tray for another week and would not be forwarded to Mr Jones, undoubtedly a very busy man, for at least another fortnight. All in all, he would consider himself fortunate if he heard back at all before Christmas. He simply could not wait that long. Whilst he would incorporate Mr Jones's advice the instant he received it, construction must begin right away.

He stood up and brushed himself down. There was no more time to waste – he'd already lost a whole month in preparation. He must start this very instant. He went straight to the ramshackle barn at the side of the house that had been converted into a tool shed. Unable to procure any labour from the village, the previous week he had requested two caretakers from the London factory to come to the country. He agreed to pay an exorbitant bonus and Fielding, the factory manager, was very unhappy, but it had been worth it – in seven days they had plumbed a bathroom and fixed up his tool shed. He surveyed the gleaming racks of tools; he had no idea what most of them were, but they looked wonderful. They had cost a pretty penny, using up a tidy chunk of the Rosenblums' savings account, but he was sure they were all vital to the construction of a golf course. There were five different types of hoe as well as rakes, trowels, mowers and a fearsome array of heavy rollers and, on a hook just beyond his reach, rested a steel spade with a red-painted handle. He moved an old seed crate into position to use as a step and, standing on tiptoe, unfastened the spade, but it was heavier than he thought and clattered to the ground. Retrieving it with a curse and getting a lightweight hoe for good measure, he headed for the door. He had no notion what a hoe was actually for, but felt more professional with a tool in each hand.

He hurried out to the field and stood in the biggest of the meadows with his local Ordnance Survey map, surveying his land.

'Bugger it. I ought be wearing my new cap.'

He plunged his hands into his pockets, wishing he'd thought to write to Mr Bobby Jones earlier. Then he'd have a proper plan and real advice.

'Never mind. Can't be helped.'

He closed his eyes and tried to visualise Tom Morris's plan of St Andrews. He had stared at it long enough that he could see it in his mind and, as he opened his eyes and gazed at the landscape once more, he saw it with St Andrews superimposed on top. To the north, where the sea should be, was the one part of the original that Jack recognised he could not recreate. There was a rise to the south at St Andrews but on his land there was a dew pond. He did not know how to drain a pond and he wondered briefly if there was a plug to pull like in a bath – a straw bung, perhaps, that once removed enabled the water to flow back into the centre of the earth. There was also a strange hollowed-out path cut into the side of the hill, just where he wanted it level for the first green. On the Ordnance Survey map it was labelled 'the coffin path'. He supposed this was the route the dead were taken to the little church – the lane was too steep and so coffins had to be carried along the gentler path across the fields – and now the centuries of use with heavy, lead-lined boxes had sliced a deep gouge into the soft earth underfoot. Interesting, but no use for golf – he needed a perfectly even surface. It'd have to go. Well, then, he decided, that was a good place to begin. On balance, he considered it would be easier to fill in the path than empty the pond. He would pack it with earth and level the ground. Buoyed with enthusiasm he thrust his spade into the soil. Instantly there was a crack as metal hit rock. He bent down to inspect the damage and saw that the spade had struck a piece of flint. He hesitated for a moment, removed it carefully with his hands and tossed it aside. From his pocket he retrieved a crisp pocket-handkerchief and meticulously wiped his muddy hands.

'There now, that's what it's all about. Getting one's hands mucky.'

He thrust the spade into the earth once more and again, there was a clink as it collided with stone. He bent, plucked out the object, cleaned his fingers on the dirt-smeared pocket handkerchief and stood upright, slightly painfully this time. An hour later, there was a low pile of stones and a hole but the sunken path was no less hollow.

'How on God's earth am I supposed to fill these blasted holes without digging more holes for earth to fill them?' It was a real conundrum.

He was damp with perspiration and his fingers were blistered. He sat down with a tiny sigh on a tufted molehill, the size of a well-fed snoozing sheep, and put his head in his hands, inadvertently smearing mud across his cheeks. Old grassed molehills covered nearly an acre, rising out of the ground like giant mossy pimples.

'That's it!' He jumped up in excitement. 'I will dig up the molehills and use them to fill the holes! That'll kill two birds with one stone.'

It was genius in its simplicity. None of his tools were right for slicing off molehills, what he really needed was a giant cheese wire. He made some estimates – there were enough molehills to plug the voids and, if there were enough left over, he would use them to fill in the dew pond. 'It's going to be a triumph – I can sense it.'

Later that evening, Jack returned to his study and consulted his maps. Every bit of him ached with tiredness; his eyes were bloodshot, irritated by the tiny flecks of soil that had endlessly been thrown into his face as he worked. Clasping a stiff whisky in one hand, he traced over the land with a shaking finger. After ten hours of labour he had succeeded in moving three molehills. 'Not to worry,' he told himself, brightly, 'tomorrow I shall be quicker. First, I had to mould my tools, and now they are made, I shall get on like a donkey, stubborn and efficient.'

The cheese-wire plan had worked. He'd found a piece of wire and managed to work it through the base of the mound. The molehills, however, proved to be extremely heavy, forcing him to construct an elaborate pulley system in order to lift them. This took several hours and many buckets of water from the pond to use as counterweights. The system was very unsteady and, if he got his measurements off, the buckets would waver and empty their loads all over his trousers. The molehills were loaded onto the pulley and then deposited in the holes, where they sat, round and grassy like cupcakes in odd-shaped cases. He was sure he had read somewhere that molehills grew in the wet, so he poured water over them in the hope that they would melt into the right space. In a few months, with a bit of luck and a little rain, they would expand to fit perfectly and his land would be smooth and level.

In blue ink, Jack circled the area on the map. When it was even, he would flatten it with the heavy rollers and cut the grass. Then, and only then, could he trim his first green and make the very first hole. He reached into his desk drawer; the rejection letters had all been disposed of, and in their place rested a small book of fabric samples. These had been sent from the factory as Fielding had wanted him to consider diversifying into curtains, but Jack needed the cash funds for the golf course – construction was going to be expensive. He kept the samples anyway to select a colour for the flags. He held the fabrics on his lap and stroked a vibrant blue and cream stripe, then a crimson check.

CHAPTER SIX

MOVING THE MOLEHILLS was a gargantuan task and he made slow progress, inching around the field like a shadow on a giant sundial. He had been at work for a month now and there were bare brown circles where the molehills had been removed. The land was riddled with these round marks amid the lush grass. His pulley system was wheeled out of the barn at first light and, in the sun-soaked silence of the afternoon, the mechanism bobbed up and down as he rearranged the great piles of earth. Word spread throughout the Blackmore Vale about the Jew's quest to construct a golf course on Bulbarrow. At first he was dismissed, but then, when his molehill contraption was glimpsed, it was decided that here was a sight worth seeing. Jack never took a day off to rest, his task was too important, and so on Sunday afternoons people came from villages all around to gaze at the unusual spectacle. They gathered with picnics on the brow of the hill, and stared happily at the peculiar little man with his giant cheese wire invention. They clapped as the pulleys lifted the tufts right off the ground and groaned when the system faltered and deposited its buckets of water over him. Binoculars were passed between family and friends to afford a better view. No one offered to help. It seemed to them that here was a man devoted to a unique and solitary calling. They considered him to be somewhere between a prophet and a lunatic. Some wondered if, like Noah or Moses, he was compelled by the voice of God. Others were convinced he was a madman, but as long as he was not dangerous, they were happy to eat egg sandwiches and ginger cake and watch the small man move piles of earth as the sunlight shone off his polished head.

Away from the crowds on top of the hill, Sadie watched her husband quizzically. She hardly recognised the darkly sunburnt figure with tiny muscles showing through the thin skin on his arms. At dusk he crossed the fields and opened the kitchen door with a bang, collapsing onto a high-backed chair.

She studied him before speaking. 'So, you only come inside for meals now?'

He shot her a beseeching look. 'Too tired to argue.'

Sadie hid a tight smile. It was more fun if he didn't enjoy it. 'You're an old man, you work all day and for what?'

Jack only nodded.

'We live in the same house, at the edges of each other's lives. Nearly twenty years of marriage and it has come to this,' said Sadie slapping the table with her palm for emphasis.

Still he said nothing. This irked Sadie; she was plaguing him and he was not fighting back. As long as he didn't walk away – she couldn't bear that. She fetched a loaf of bread and some cold beef from the larder, slapped it onto a plate and handed it to him. He ate hungrily. He would have to stay and listen whilst he ate.

'Thank you,' he said and smiled.

This was too much for his wife.

'*Mein Gott!* Always so cheerful! It's not natural. Why can't you be even a little bit miserable? Then, maybe, we'd have something to talk about after all these years.'

'Why do you have to chew over everything like a piece of gristle? The past is in the past. For pity's sake, let it stay there.'

There was a note of anger in his voice that pleased Sadie. At last, she had got to him. 'You are sunshine at a funeral.'

Jack gave a sharp laugh. 'And what is wrong with that?'

'Everyone wants good weather for a wedding, but at a funeral the sky should have the decency to be overcast. It is simple respect.'

Jack finished his bread, sent his wife a wary glance and stalked out of the kitchen. She gave a sigh of exasperation and contemplated following him into his study to torment him further, but deciding against it, she sat down, wondering if he took the trouble to remember anything at all.

Despite the usual quarrels with her husband, Sadie felt more peaceful than she had for many years and certainly since Elizabeth had left. In the mornings she was woken by the scent of roses seeping in through the open windows. The sounds of the wood pigeons in the roof no longer alarmed her. She had a pair of white doves sent down from Harrods and installed them in an old dovecot she discovered in the garden; they started to breed and the air was full with the cheeping of baby birds. Leaning against the house stood an ancient nodding lilac tree, its branches spindly and heavy with sprays of sweet-smelling blossoms. Butterflies and humming bees moved amongst the tangled flowerbeds and snails left their silver trails across the damp earth. The sky was bigger here than in the city and she lost herself for hours as she watched the branches on the ash trees, the leaves shifting in the summer wind like glass inside a kaleidoscope. Sometimes she did not get dressed, she would come downstairs in her curlers and nightdress and lie on the dew damp ground and stare at the clouds drifting across the changing sky. In the thick July heat she spent whole mornings resting on the unkempt lawn and if she felt drowsy she slept; there was no one to chide her for eccentricity. Sometimes as she lay watching the scudding clouds, she imagined Emil beside her in the long grass. It was he tickling her wrist with that strand of green. She was careful to look straight ahead at the soaring larks, so as not to spoil the game.

There was still that familiar scent in the garden, a flower that smelled of her childhood. Finally, she traced it to a rose – an unremarkable yellowing bloom with dark leaves marked with blight. Its fragrance was of endless summer holidays a long time ago. It made her melancholy and yet it reminded her of a time *before*, when she was happy. She did little to the flowerbeds except trim a space around this rose.

The garden was thickly overgrown. There was a tumble of plants: roots, stems and leaves all entwined. She cut back a few of the unruly shrubs and trimmed the plum tree's lower branches to open up the view from the kitchen window but the rest of the garden remained covered with a layer of brambles. She had not had a garden before; in London they had a terrace and a balcony with wrought-iron railings, and each summer she planted begonias and pansies in earthenware pots, but an actual garden was different. The grass had gone to seed and rabbits loped in the long flowers, their ears poking up above the daisies. There was an orchard at the bottom, where the grass sloped off and the hill began to run steeply downward. At the side of the house the garden reverted to scrub; the hedgerows crept forward and brambles and bright yellow gorse bushes made it impassable. The stinging nettles were five feet tall, yet butterflies landed on them effortlessly, somehow never getting stung. Sadie neither planted nor weeded; Hitler had declared the Jews weeds and plucked them out wherever he found them. She knew that a plant was only a weed if unwanted by the gardener, so she refused to move a single one, and they sprouted up wherever they wanted, between flagstones on the terrace or in a riotous mass in the unruly beds. The garden had been here for too many years for the Rosenblums to make any sudden changes.

On rainy days Sadie turned her attention to the inside of the house. The front door had been waxed and the great iron knocker glistened. Every room was limewashed, the flagstone floors cleaned with lemon soap and the curtains rinsed and rehung. The crooked sign had been reforged and 'Chantry Orchard' hung proudly on the gate. The thatch had been patched; it would be redone next spring and under the eaves a twittering family of house martins were learning to fly. Early one evening, Sadie stood in her kitchen, a solitary gnat buzzing around her, while she continually swatted it away. The ancient kitchen table had been restored so the knots shone and it smelled softly of paraffin. A black enamel range with four hot plates nestled in the inglenook and threw steady heat out into the room. She was shelling peas for dinner; she liked popping them from their pods into the pot but rogues kept escaping and rolling across the floor.

The door to the garden flew open and an unkempt Jack burst in, his few remaining strands of hair wild and coated in grass. Belatedly, he had decided to assist Sadie in a few details of refurbishing the house. Until the clubhouse could be built, they would need to offer members refreshments in the house after a round, so it needed to be properly attired. There was no use in having the best golf course in the South-West, only to be let down by poor facilities. He helped himself to a large glass of milk, then took a tape measure out of his pocket.

'I just need the measurements and then you can choose the colour.' He knelt down and calculated the dimensions of the kitchen floor. 'Sixteen feet by eleven and a half,' he said, writing it down on a pad.

Sadie put down the dishcloth and studied the floor. The flagstones were a brown Marnhull stone, each one a different shape, worn and notched with the pattering of three hundred years of footsteps. The surfaces were polished smooth in the centres and covered with deep grooves at their edges. They were like the rings of a tree, displaying on their faces the history of the house and its families.

Jack handed her a folder filled with samples of carpet in

every hue. They had names like 'Apricot and Peach Salad' and 'Morning Daffodil.'

'I like that one,' he said, pointing to a page with a red pile called 'Crimson Battle'.

Sadie held up the swatch. 'Too dark.'

Jack leant back on a kitchen chair. 'Well, choose a lighter one then.' He was growing impatient. He wanted to get back outside – there were a few more hours of light and he could move at least one more molehill.

Sadie looked down at the flagstones.

'I know we're carpet people and we've bought this house with carpet money. But I don't want carpets.'

'Are you crazy?'

'I'm very serious. These stones and their markings – they're like wrinkles in an old face. I've got an old face and I don't want someone to come and carpet over me.'

Jack chuckled; he liked it when she said surprising things. 'My darling, you sound a little cuckoo-bird.'

'Cuckoo?'

'Yes, cuckoo-bird. Means *meshugge*. I heard it yesterday.' He explained vaguely, having overheard someone describing his vision as cuckoo. 'We don't need to have carpets if you don't want them. How about a tiger skin for the hearth?'

She ignored him pointedly. 'I am going to take a bath.'

Until the new bathroom was fitted, Sadie had used the old system of strip washes over the sink and the pleasure of a hot, soap-filled bath had not yet lost its novelty. She climbed the stairs to her new bathroom with the same excitement Jack experienced each morning as he went to dig his golf course.

The bathroom had an elegant claw-footed cast-iron bath, framed prints of tea roses on the walls and a polished wood floor, but the best part of the room was the low mullioned window with a view across the Stour Valley. Sadie ran the bath, the water thundering against the metal sides like an express

77

train, and poured perfumed salts into the steam. Slowly, she unfastened her blouse and unclipped her skirt. Out of habit, she folded them and placed them in a neat pile on a rocking chair. She stood there, naked, and stared at her face in the mirror – it was the face of a woman in middle age. There were lines around the eyes and mottled marks on her cheeks and neck. She wondered when it was that she got old.

The face didn't feel like it was hers. It belonged to someone else; it wasn't the face that her family had known. They wouldn't recognise her now. She had never seen her mother as an elderly woman; soon she would be older than her mother had been when she died. She held out her own hands; they were beginning to display the thinness of an older woman's hands and were slightly swollen around her wedding ring – she'd never be able to take it off now.

Sadie climbed into the hot water and shut her eyes. The glass in the windowpane misted up; she wiped it with her palm and looked out across the fields. She had been about to order curtains for the bathroom but Jack poked fun at her. 'Who's going to spy on you? Badgers and birds?' Now she was glad the window was bare – the landscape already looked different from when they had first arrived. It had lost its bright June sheen; the verdant fields faded to a hot brown after the grass was cut for hay and the wheat stubble turned gold. She was aware of the weekly changes in the countryside in a way she had never noticed in the city. In London there were only four seasons, and she had handbags for each. Here, summer was a thousand shades; the elderflower bushes found in every hedgerow and copse smelled sweetly in the middle of June and now, a month later, they were all brown and withered. Yet, the honeysuckle and the jasmine were in full bloom and their scent lingered in the summer air. The foxgloves had drooped and been replaced by the flowering bindweed, which climbed up the stems of the dead plants.

The sun was low in the sky and the parched fields glowed pink in the evening light. At the edge of the garden, just beyond the orchard, she saw a deer nibbling the leaves of a hawthorn tree. It glanced up as if it sensed her staring through the window. Neither moved; the deer listening and Sadie lying naked in the warm water, watching.

As she got out of the bath and towelled herself off, she studied the large cracks in the wall, running all the way from the heavy oak beam in the ceiling right down to the floor. They had called in a builder when she first noticed them but he found their concern entertaining and explained, 'They is like livin' things these old houses. The stones move. It don't matter. Supposed to. Those newfangled houses, they is no good. These old 'uns like to move. Stretch a bit. There's one in Okeford that moves out so much I swear he walks down the street.'

Sadie had never thought of a house as a living thing before – it was a thing, which one filled with other things, like furniture and books. Yet the walls here were painted with limewash so that the stone could breathe and at night the house did feel almost alive, with its creaking and the sounds of the stream, trickling, trickling. She closed her eyes and imagined she could hear the stones of the house sigh.

She went back down to the kitchen to find that Jack had gone. There was an almighty crash and a rumbling clatter from close by. Clad in her bath towel, her feet still bare, she followed the noise to the sitting room.

Jack was standing on the hearth with a crowbar as black rubble and grime poured out of the chimney and onto the floor. It was as though he had opened a sluice gate. As Sadie watched in dismay, he changed colour; his hair went from white to black and his face turned grey, except for the shining whites of his eyes. A minute later the tide slowed. He took a piece of wood and poked around, causing more soot to tumble out and small clouds of smog to form in the living room.

79

Sadie stared in horror. 'I've just had a bath.'

Jack did not turn around. 'Hope you kept the water. Think perhaps I might need a wash.'

He stuck his hand back inside and reached into the back of the chimney. 'There's a shelf here. And. There's something on it.'

He pulled out a charred object and laid it on the mat. Sadie peered at it from a safe distance and felt a little sick. It was a skeleton of some sort. Jack gave it a poke. 'What is it?' He dumped another item next to the skeleton.

While Jack had been reading endless books on golf, Sadie had read the volume on ancient folklore.

'It's a cat. People put mummified cats up the chimneys. Thought it kept out evil,' she said.

Looking closely at the bones, Jack could make out the shreds of bandages.

'And there should be a Bible. The cat keeps away witches. The Bible is for Him.' Sadie gestured to the ceiling.

Jack was intrigued and he picked up the other object, which was indeed a book. He murmured a *Brocha* to humour his wife and opened it with reverence. The print was small and divided up into tiny chapters – it looked like a *goyische* bible. He read a line to Sadie.

'"Asylum: a place of refuge; a place of protection. Atheist: one who disbelieves in the existence of God."' He paused, rubbing his nose and leaving another black smear on his spectacles. 'The Christian Bible is more different from the Torah than I had thought.'

Sadie took it from him, flipping to the front page and read, '"*Johnson's Dictionary of the English Language*. To which are added an Alphabetical Account of the Heathen Deities. Published 1775." Yes, hmm. Funny sort of bible.'

Jack gave a short laugh. 'I'll bet you the hole in my beigel, that whoever put it up there thought it was a bible.'

Sadie smiled. 'The words are the same, just in a different order. I am sure He can rearrange them.'

Jack chuckled and Sadie turned, laughing with him. She looked pretty, he decided, with her wet hair curling around her face and in this light her eyes were quite green. In these brief interludes Jack could almost remember the woman his wife had once been. He recalled the first days of their courtship when, half in love, they were still shy with one another. In a fit of boldness he'd confessed that he liked Christmas carols and secretly always wanted to go to the service on Christmas Eve in the *Berliner Dom,* and listen to the singing – Christians had all the best tunes. Sadie laughed and goosed him, challenging, 'Well? Why don't we?' They'd snuck in and sat in the very back pew, their thighs brushing, as the congregation bellowed the refrains of 'O Tannenbaum'. Somewhere between the third and fourth verse, Jack realised that a small, gloved hand was sliding into his. He clasped it, his heart beating like butterfly wings. Afterwards, exhilarated by their daring, Jack kissed Sadie for the first time. They stood beneath the Christmas tree in the *Gendarmenmarkt,* cheeks flushed with excitement and cold, and Jack leant towards her, wondering if he ought to remove his spectacles.

Jack chewed thoughtfully on his lip. In half an hour he would return to the field and she would sink back into her silent gloom but, for an instant, they were in the same place – like travellers from opposite ends of the world happening upon the same village, and he did not want the feeling to pass, not just yet. 'Let's put up the *mezuzah*,' he said.

Ordinarily, Jack despised the trappings of religion. They only served to show up one's differences. He was willing, however, to humour his wife in order to maintain this fragile equilibrium. Besides, he reasoned, a *mezuzah* was only a small brown box by the front door – another Jew would recognise it while an Englishman wouldn't notice it at all.

Sadie looked at him, surprised and pleased. Clutching her towel, she went into the kitchen and fetched a carved wooden box, a few inches long and with a space at the top for a nail. She held it up and shook it so that the parchment inside rattled.

'What are the words on the paper in the *mezuzah*? Do you even know?' Jack enquired, hoping that he was not jeopardising the peace.

'No. But they're supposed to ward off evil and bring good fortune to the household.'

'With a cat, a dictionary and a mystery prayer I believe we are very well prepared for all eventualities.'

He placed a handkerchief on his head as a makeshift *yarmulke* and Sadie handed him a prayer book. It was evening now and the house martins zoomed under the eaves to their twittering young. Jack's voice mingled with the birds as he sang a Hebrew prayer. His song was ancient; it sang of Israel and a desert land of milk and honey. The village of Pursebury Ash had never heard such a song before but the woodlarks continued their own choruses and the wind played gently in the long grass. Jack hammered the *mezuzah* to the doorframe in a single movement, his arm rising like Abraham's, ready with the knife.

CHAPTER SEVEN

JACK WORKED AS the long ears of corn turned golden and the days became slowly shorter. He laboured in the fields by the light of the high summer moon, the badgers watching him silently as he heaved piles of earth. As July slid into August, he finished moving the molehills. He retired his pulley system to the barn, fetched his mowing contraptions and for the first time in years the grass was cut. He left it long around the edges so that the rough remained strewn with frog orchids, goosegrass and bright pink ragged-robin. He read about the different kinds of grasses for the greens, the advantages of seed versus turf and ordered long hoses to keep everything watered. The dew pond would not be drained; it was filled by a spring whispered to have magical properties. The cold water seeped out from the depths of the earth, emerging from between the stones at the bottom. He could not tell how deep the pool really was, as the surface was covered with giant buttercup lilies. Sometimes, he glimpsed the silver shadows of fish and wisps of pondweed swaying in invisible currents but he did not like water, never having learned to swim. He poked a tall branch into the dark water, where it sank and was swallowed, never touching the bottom. It was good that he did not know the true depth of the pond: it was said to be so deep that it flowed for miles beneath the earth. One afternoon, he watched a duck bobbing on the surface – it dived under water and he waited for it to come up quacking, a fish in its beak. He waited and waited but the duck never reappeared. A few minutes later, a small boy throwing sticks in the pond many miles away at Ashbourne, was surprised to see a duck surface, certain he had not seen it dive.

By the beginning of September, the first hole was nearly finished. In the moonlight, Jack carried a large watering can from the pond to his green and poured it over the young grass. He had planted the finest seed he could find, ordered specially from Switzerland. He knelt down, tenderly stroking the soft stems, now three inches high and ready for their first cut. He went to the barn and fetched the mower, a hand-pushed roller with hundreds of tiny blades and, with the utmost care, slid it across the precious surface. Every few yards he had to stop, remove the basket and empty the cuttings. At midnight, he had finished mowing and the green was smooth, like a shot of silk in the darkness. It remained sparse but cutting would help it grow and put down good roots. He filled another watering can, mixed in a spoonful of fertiliser and sprinkled the grass once more.

He was so tired that his muscles trembled. 'Must carry on . . . must carry on,' he chanted over and over, clenching his fists in determination. Elizabeth would be here in a week or two, and he was resolved on having the hole finished.

He felt a flicker of excitement in his belly – finally, he was ready to cut the first hole. He had purchased a special tool for this: a long metal tube with a serrated top that lay in readiness by the pond, the new metal glinting coldly in the light of the moon. He ran his finger along the sharp edge, cutting himself foolishly, and a drop of blood fell to the ground. He licked his finger and carefully removed his torch and the map of Bulbarrow from his jacket. Trying to avoid smearing it with blood, he spread the map along the ground, weighted it with rocks and with a pencil marked with an **X** the spot where the hole was to go. It corresponded to the first hole on Tom Morris's plan of St Andrews; Jack had laboured mightily to get the land to match, and the stream trickling down from the dew pond haphazardly mirrored the Swilcan Burn running in front of the first hole on the Old Course. He wished that Tom Morris's greens were a little smaller – after two hours of mowing and trimming with scissors he was exhausted.

There were other drawbacks; the Bulbarrow stream ran at a different angle to the Swilcan Burn and instead of skirting the green it simply cut it in two. Try as he might, he simply could not get the green level and although he removed the molehills, the incline remained sharp – a ball placed at the top rolled straight down into the pond at the bottom. Similarly, the fairway remained bumpy as, despite all his watering and a hefty dose of summer rain, the molehills did not grow. They remained, grassy lumps, wedged into the furrows and dips of the land. These minor impediments aside, he was thrilled by his miraculous progress.

Clutching his map in one hand and a brass compass in the other, he walked carefully across the new grass to mark the position of the hole. He gazed learnedly at the compass and searched for the North Star. He wasn't absolutely sure how to use a compass but the cowboys in the pictures always looked at the stars, unless it was daylight when, well, he didn't know what they did then.

Suddenly, he swayed on his feet, his eyes closed and he fell fast asleep. A little snore rumbled forth from his throat and he snapped awake in surprise. 'Here. The hole will go here.' He plunged a stout stick into a random spot declaring, 'I shall decide by instinct.'

Instantly the stick hit a rock, so he shifted it a little to the left where it sank into the wet earth with ease. 'Clearly, *this* is the right spot.'

He slid the hole cutter into the ground and hammered it in with a piece of wood. Heaving and puffing, he hauled it out to leave behind a neat, round hole, a foot deep and perfect.

'Now for the cup.'

He fished an old soup tin out of his pocket, parcelled in newspaper and preserved especially for this purpose. He unwrapped it and rinsed it out in the stream, the last flecks of beef consommé trickling away. Gingerly, avoiding the jagged edges of the tin, he slid it into the hole. Finally, it was ready – this was the part he had been waiting months for. As he picked up the black-painted pole with its neat blue and white chequered flag and slotted it into the hole, he felt a twinge of regret that Sadie was not here to watch his first triumph. There was a time when they were friends. He would have liked this moment better if his Sadie and Elizabeth were here.

The bright squares on the flag glowed whitely in the darkness and fluttered in a tiny breeze. Jack stood back and admired his handiwork. Eventually, after all his effort, the first hole was finished. He had felt a similar sense of achievement when his factory produced its first roll of carpet, but this he had done with his own hands. No man would help him and so he had laboured like Samson night and day (and golf courses were much more useful than temples). 'One hole made – only seventeen to go.'

He felt slightly dizzy at this thought and craved sleep. In the morning, he would drink ginger beer for breakfast to celebrate and then he would play his very first hole. He'd had a case sent down from Fortnum's, and he wondered how he could persuade Sadie to join him. To have his wife toast his success with a ginger beer, and then walk round the course with him (shaded by a white parasol and marvelling at his every shot) would be very pleasant. In London he could sometimes buy her goodwill with a box of glazed honey cakes from one of the bakeries in Golders Green or a print scarf from Liberty's, but while he sensed that she was different here, he had no notion of how to curry favour.

He hoped Sadie would be impressed by the brilliance of his swing. After all this time and painful hard work, he still had not played any golf – he was determined to wait until the first hole was ready and to try his swing on a proper course. He'd tee off tomorrow morning. He glanced at his watch and hesitated; tomorrow was already here – it was two o'clock in the morning. Should he take out his clubs and try a shot in the dark? No, he decided. He'd waited this long. He would play a hole properly, like a gentleman – after breakfast.

He staggered back up the ridge to the house, so tired that he felt as if both legs had turned to lumps of clay. He paused on the edge of the garden and gazed down to the opening hole, where the flag waved as though in acknowledgement. Reaching the house, he climbed the stairs and, only removing his mud-caked shoes, slumped into bed next to his sleeping wife. He tucked himself in beside her and stroked her rigid back. 'I know you are not pleased now, but you will be,' he whispered. 'This is for both of us. Wait until the course is full with people and then you'll feel better. You'll see.'

He kissed the nape of her neck, something he would never dare to do when she was awake. As he went to sleep, he saw himself teeing off and hitting a ball high up into the far reaches of the sky, where it became a shooting star and disappeared into the black night.

Jack woke late to the sound of bells; it was nearly twelve o'clock. The room was empty and he could hear Sadie in the kitchen. He waited until it was silent, signalling she was in the garden, and then traipsed into the bathroom to wash. He helped himself to one of the new fluffy towels sent from London and, hesitating before using Sadie's Parisian soap, he strolled naked onto the landing.

'Can I use your good soap?'

There was no response, which he took for ascent and liberally doused himself in lily of the valley. He cleaned himself carefully, washing the last crusts of dirt from his ears and hair and took a brush to his fingernails. He had been somewhat careless of his appearance the last few weeks but this morning, for his hole of golf, he needed to be pristine. He whipped up a lather and shaved meticulously, then took the scissors and comb from the bathroom cabinet and trimmed the hair protruding from his nostrils. He dabbed cologne behind his ears and on the top of his head, and scrupulously scrubbed his teeth with peppermint powder.

Clean and sweetly scented, he padded along the landing to the bedroom. Hanging in the wardrobe, wrapped in tissue paper, was his new suit. It was a green and yellow golfing tweed with plus fours, a matching cap and canary coloured socks. He pulled it on, humming cheerfully to himself, and scrutinised his reflection in the long mirror. He looked just right, a proper golfer. Once it was a little more lived in it would be perfect. He laced up his brown leather studs and clattered down to the kitchen leaving small holes in the wooden tread of every stair. The case of ginger beer was set out in readiness and Sadie had left some bread and fruit on the table. He cracked open a bottle and took a gulp; it was fiery and made him hiccup.

'Well, is today the day?' demanded Sadie coming into the kitchen.

Unable to speak, Jack nodded.

'Do you know what to do?'

Jack scrambled to his feet in excitement at her interest, wiping sticky ginger beer from his mouth with the back of his hand.

'I've been reading all about the perfect golf swing. First there is the grip, the *Vardon* grip.'

He grabbed a saucepan from the countertop and clasped it in both hands to demonstrate.

'It's all about power. You need to place your hands in a neutral position so as to deliver the force flush to the back of the ball and send it whooshing down the fairway!'

He swung the saucepan through the air and knocked a chair flying. Sadie frowned unimpressed, but Jack's torrent of enthusiasm now unleashed, could not be stopped.

'Do you remember – we saw a reel of Bobby Jones at the Masters?'

Sadie wrinkled her forehead. 'Yes, I think so. It was at the front of a Veronica Lake picture.'

Jack barely recalled the film – some tedious weepy that Sadie had wanted to see – but the newsreel footage of Bobby Jones was something else. He had gone five times just to watch that swing: the elegant poise, feet shoulder width apart, elbows tightly in, head still, left arm straight, wrists cocked and then the sheer force; hips pivoting, as the club sweeps down in a perfect symphony of coordination with muscles, joints and mind all working together.

'Bobby Jones's swing – that's as close as a man can get to magic.' He shook his head, awed by the thought of his hero. 'I mean, I realise that mine won't be like that, not at first. I'll need to practise.'

Sadie considered him curiously but he did not notice, already lost in reverie.

'I have a course of my own, well, a hole, to learn upon. Maybe in a year or two, I can enter the British Open as a gentleman amateur, like Bobby Jones.'

Sadie stared at him, and wondered if she should knock sense into him or pity him.

Jack, unable to read the thoughts of his wife, was once again overwhelmed with the unfamiliar sensation of desiring her company. At that moment, there was nothing he wanted more than Sadie to share in his triumph. He felt almost shy, a bashful suitor once again.

'Will you walk round with me? Watch my first shot, *mein Spatz*?'

She did not turn round, merely dismissed him with a tiny shake of her head.

Jack retreated to the barn to collect his clubs. He would have liked her to accompany him but, he reasoned, perhaps it was for the best, just in case he wasn't a natural – he didn't want her to be disappointed in him. His clubs were propped in a corner, carefully wrapped in two old blankets to protect them from cold and draughts. With the tenderness of a new father, he peeled off the layers and hoisted them gently over his shoulder. All the exercise had made him stronger; he had lost the hint of fat around his middle and had small muscles on his arms and legs, but still the bag of clubs felt heavy. Smiling broadly in the morning sunshine, he walked down to the field. Everything was leading up to this moment; the orange lilies in the flowerbeds had burst into bloom that morning especially for him. Tiny white butterflies floated before him like a guard of honour. How many Englishmen could say that they had played their first hole on their very own golf course?

He paused on the rise leading down to the first tee, closing his eyes in the warm sunshine, and felt tingles of happiness. In a few days Elizabeth would come to visit and he would stand on this spot and show her the golf course. He was proud of his daughter, and he wanted her to be proud of something he had achieved. The dirty factory with its noisy machinery was a place she avoided, but this was different. She would look at the hole he had dug and the land he had heaved, and she would realise that her father was a man with vision. Finally, with his golf course, he really would be somebody; the kind of man a daughter could admire. He would drive her to Cambridge and they would talk about the magnificence of his achievement.

With a grunt he picked up his clubs and, as a shaft of sunlight illuminated the tee, he jiggled from foot to foot in cheerful anticipation. The next moment he stopped dead. 'No. No. It can't be true.'

He blinked and rubbed his eyes, certain that he was not seeing right but, as he looked, he realised with a tightening of his stomach that it was true. His beautiful new grass had been torn up in great chunks; deep gouges ripped up the fragile green and the turf was yanked back. Massive holes were furrowed across the rough and the fairway, some several feet across. The molehills had been wrenched up and scattered, and a vast pile of twenty or more lay mouldering in a heap on the middle of the green. For a whole minute he stood paralysed with horror, staring at the waste of all his toils, as the dismal Romans once surveyed the wreckage of their sacked city. Then, dropping his clubs he ran up to the ruins, tripped and fell. He heard something crack underneath him and for a horrible moment was sure it was a bone in his leg but feeling no pain he eased himself up. On the ground lay his flagpole snapped in two, its chequered flag torn and spattered with mud. A shout of rage snarled from him like the war cry of some wild beast.

'Bastards! Jew haters!'

His brand new trousers and dapper jacket were smeared in filth and stained with grass. He was heartbroken. How could they do this to him? What had he done to so offend them? In that moment, his vision of standing on the ridge with Elizabeth faded away; he was destined to remain a nobody.

Despair rolled over him in dark waves. It would take months to repair the damage, if it were even possible. The course would never be finished before the coronation. And what next? He could repair the spoilt hole, nurture the greens, smooth the land, water the grasses, only to have them destroy it all again? But who? In his mind there was no doubt: Jack Basset. He fixed all his fury and hatred upon him. So English, so self-assured, he would surely take pleasure in the misery of a foreign Yid. He would find him and show him the misery he had inflicted. The only question was where to find the . . . the . . . Here Jack faltered, trying to think of a word strong enough to convey his wrath. English failed him, '*Jack Basset ist ein Schweinehund! Pig-dog bastard!*'

He wondered what day it was – he had lost all track of time during the past weeks. Sadie had ceased to scold him for working on *Shabbas*, which after they had left the city had been his only method of counting time. At first, every Saturday morning as he rose early to fetch his spade and start digging, Sadie would plead with him not to work. Then, the supplicating tone gave way to reproach and finally to silence. Now, there was no marker to inform him which day was which and consequently the weeks seeped seamlessly into one another.

He stood motionless and listened: the air was still. He climbed upon the mound of molehills in the centre of his green; all was quiet save for the chattering of the skylarks and the wind in the leaves. He peered into the distance – there was no one in sight. From the hill above came the peal of bells. Sunday? It must be Sunday and that meant Basset would be in the pub. They all went there after church – Jack had seen them on previous Sundays walking down the lane in their best clothes, talking and laughing.

His cheeks flushing with anger, he made his way across the fields towards The Crown. It was only as he crossed the stream that fury gave way to worry. All he wanted was to be one of them and, failing that, to be ignored. He did not want trouble – that was dangerous. If only he'd got to play a hole and try out his swing, then perhaps he could have forgiven them. All that work and not a single shot – it was too much to stomach.

He gave a sigh, rage subsiding into unhappiness. Above him the humped back of Bulbarrow Ridge lay like a sleeping giant beneath the sky. In the distance was the ringed hill fort of Hambledon; the Iron Age earth walls made deep cuts into the side of the hill, its outline jagged and roughly hewn like a badly thrown pot. The woodlands were a series of dark green shadows on the hillsides and he stared at them, wondering what forgotten beasts lay hidden in their depths.

When he reached The Crown it was teeming with people. He recognised several of the faces by the bar. A man with whiskers and wearing a patched blue suit with too short trousers gave him a wave and raised his glass. Jack felt himself redden as all the heads turned to stare, before returning to their conversations and their pints. He watched the wall of men slouching on bar stools or leaning against the counter, their backs to a vast inglenook fireplace decorated with brass bits, stirrups and a massive yoke.

He wondered what he should do next; he had the feeling that they were expecting him and he did not have a plan. Now he was here, the urge to shout at Jack Basset and threaten worldly violence upon his household did not seem the best way forward. He found Basset in the gloom of the pub. He was a large, tall man and, despite the protruding belly, there was the hint of power in those shoulders. For a second Jack found himself wondering whether Basset would have a fine golfer's swing.

Jack had good bar presence; he was neither tall nor aggressive but with a forced smile he was the next to be served and put a crown down on the bar. 'I'd like to buy all these gentlemen a drink.'

The elderly barman grunted – he wasn't used to this. 'Please yerself.'

'They won't want a drink?'

There was a shout of objection from Basset. 'What you sayin', Stan Burns? When 'ave we ever turned down free booze?'

There were snorts of laughter and poor Stan began topping up pint glasses along the bar. Basset clapped his arm around

Jack and pulled him into a corner where a group of men were huddled. 'Move y're arse, Curtis,' growled the farmer to the tiny, unsteady man of indeterminable old age, swaying dangerously on his bar stool.

'No, please. I prefer to stand,' objected Jack.

The men were the same bunch who had trounced him at skittles. He half wondered whether he ought to buy a skittle set and make an alley in his barn, so that he could practise and then thrash them all.

Basset slapped Jack on the back, making him stagger forward. 'A toassst. A toast to our new friend Meester Jack Rose-in-bloom.'

The men raised their mugs and drank to the bottom. Jack tilted his and took a small sip, all the while watching the others.

'We seen what happened to your land and offers our condo-lin-ses,' Basset slurred through his pint of bitter.

Jack felt the hair on his neck prickle and tried to edge away from him. 'So you admit it then? You ruined it all? All this spite from such a big man. I thought only women and girls did such things.' Angry again, he spluttered carelessly.

'Now, now, easy. Some might git offence at that,' warned Basset.

'We ent guilty. Twasn't us,' confided the man in the patched suit.

Jack snorted derisively.

'It was the—' started the man.

'Hush, Ed.' Basset took a step closer and placed a thick arm around Jack, who with a wince wondered how he could extricate himself.

'I think it is time to tell our new friend our secret,' Basset said in a stage whisper.

The men gathered closer as though they didn't want to be overheard and Curtis gave a loud hiccup and slid off his bar stool. Standing, he barely reached Jack's shoulder. Jabbing a finger at Basset he hissed, 'Don't ee start that. Leave the man alone. What's ee done to yoos?'

He was instantly hushed by the others and Basset leant in so close that Jack could smell the beer on his breath and see the yellowish whites of his eyes. 'I is about to tell you that which 'as never been shared with no stranger. The . . .' he paused for dramatic effect, 'Legend. Of. The. Dorset. Woolly. Pig.'

Jack took another sip of beer and suppressed a shudder. He detested beer, especially bitter – much preferred whisky – but it was important to blend in. He should have stayed at home, had a good rest and started to rebuild in the morning. Eventually they would grow tired of destroying his course. A man on his left, in a pair of dirty overalls, added sagely, 'Aye. Tis a big honour. Yer hearin' this legend. It's only Dorset folk what have seen it.'

'Yes, tis Alf. This tis a first,' said Basset.

Jack thought he had better go along with the game. 'What is a Dorset woolly-pig?'

Basset gave an elusive smile. 'The Dorset woolly-pig is a beast only found in the heart of the Blackmore Vale. Only true-hearted Dorset men 'ave ever seen 'im and then only rarely. 'Ee is a majestic beast of unusual savagery. Could eat a small child if he wanted. 'Ee 'as the snout of a pig, tusks of a great wild boar an' the fleece of a ram an' can only be killed with an arrow of pure gold.'

Jack played along. 'And have any of you gentlemen seen one?'

Curtis had dozed off but he awoke with a start, when Basset nudged him with a sharp elbow. The old man stared at Jack without blinking, slowly taking in the spoilt suit, mud-streaked hair, and tired blue eyes. He cleared his throat and spoke in a rumbling voice. 'I sawed him. You folk don't believe me but I sawed him an' I shan't talk about it anymore. Yoos are all a bunch of turds. An' stinkin' dung heaps.'

Basset gave the old man a vicious nudge, making him scowl and then relent. He set his cider tankard down on the bar with a thud, and when he sensed his audience was ready, spread his arms with an expansive flourish.

'Twas three score year ago. And twas 'bout two weeks after mid-sommer an' a real scorcher o' a day. I were mindin' sheep on top of Bulbarrow. It was so 'ot that I thought I'd 'ave a little nip o' special cider like, before goin' home for my supper. I must have fallen asleep, cos of the sunshine, mind, and when I awoked – well, there 'ee was. The great beast were starin' at me. 'Is eyes blazed like a burnin' wheat field and 'is woolly coat glowed as if it were a snowy January. Never seen anything like it.'

Jack's eyes narrowed. 'What kind of tail did he have?'

Curtis swallowed hard and stroked his stubble – it was many years since someone had listened this intently to his story. He was fed up with the others and their teasing, but this new chap had proper respect. Rose-in-Bloom seemed like a bright young fellow.

''Ee had the curled tail of a pig. And great curved tusks. Like those but on his chops.' Curtis pointed to the head of a ram with magnificent curly horns that was mounted above the bar.

'Weren't you afraid?'

Curtis furrowed his brow and took a sip of cider to help him think.

'No,' he said slowly. 'No. I don't remember that I was. 'Ee was like nothing else. I jist looked at 'im and 'ee looked at me. And then 'ee were gone.'

As he said 'gone' he blew on his fingertips and opened his hands to reveal his empty, if slightly grimy, palms.

Jack turned to the rest of the men. 'Has anyone else seen him?'

They looked at each other.

'Old Tom Coffin did.'

'And Matthew Clinker.'

'Aye, but they's dead now. Long since – may God rist their souls.'

There was a general muttering amongst the fellows – a prayer or curse, Jack couldn't fathom.

'I is only one left,' said Curtis. 'An' trouble is – you 'ave to really believe in 'im an' be pure of heart. That's why these noggerheads ent seen 'im.'

The others didn't seem to take offence at the insult but just chuckled and refilled Curtis's pint.

'We is truly sorry for the mess in yer field. It's a nasty shame. But only a woolly-pig can make that much trouble. An' a big 'un at that,' said Basset.

'Aye. Was the woolly-pig what done it. No doubt at all.'

Jack glanced round the sombre faces. So, they were going to blame their barbarous savagery on a fairy tale. Well, he would go along with their ludicrous game. He surveyed the ram's head on the wall and, for a moment, he felt that the glassy orange eyes were staring back at him.

CHAPTER EIGHT

WHEN HE ARRIVED home Sadie was waiting for him on the doorstep. Her face was pale and her expression almost compassionate. Jack was touched, and reached out and brushed her cheek with his fingertips. 'Thank you.'

Sadie flinched and stomped inside the house, 'Not your stupid course. I would have dug that up myself if I'd only thought of it. It's Elizabeth. She's not coming home.'

Jack went cold. He felt the last remnants of optimism trickle out of him like the dregs of tea from a kettle.

'She telephoned to say that Alicia Smythe's father will take them both to Cambridge. She said it would be easier – save you the bother of collecting her, and the long journey.'

'It would have been no trouble.'

'I told her that. She was very insistent.'

Jack crumpled – the anticipation of Elizabeth's visit and then driving her to university had carried him through all the hours of hard labour. The trip was to have been a great adventure for them both, but Mr Smythe had stolen it from him. Jack thought of Arnold Smythe: banker, six feet and three quarters of an inch tall, handsome, blond moustache and a hearty handshake. He would get to take both girls to tea in Cambridge and walk with them through those ancient college quadrangles. Jack could just picture him (moustachioed and smiling) with two lovely English daughters – all of them at ease and where they belonged, and with a pang, he wondered whether Elizabeth had planned this all along. Was she so embarrassed of her father and his foreign voice and looks?

Yes, he could understand her preferring Mr Arnold Smythe as a stand-in father.

Jack was tormented by the idea that Elizabeth was mortified to be seen with him. He had thought that he was different to the others. He was the one chap in their circle who knew to buy marmalade from Fortnum's, and who realised that Lux was the only brand of soap flakes that would pass muster (and was not to be confused with a kind of smoked salmon beigel). Yet, it seemed that his own daughter knew him to be a fraud and a foreigner. He must return to his list, and rehearse the subtleties of Englishness. This had to be done properly, and so he found a spot in the garden well concealed by an overgrown willow, carried out his list, the wireless, the papers and a bottle of whisky, set down a canvas chair and took up his studies once again.

It was over a month since he last glanced at a newspaper (item forty-nine: an Englishman studies *The Times* with careful attention) and the city and financial crisis seemed oddly distant. As he turned to headlines about the 'Chronic Housing Shortage', 'National Debt Crisis' and 'Expense of the Health Service', he realised that he was no longer a man who cared about such things. He folded the paper into a neat stack, deciding they would be useful in lighting the fires when the weather turned cold.

There was a soft thud as a plum hit him on the head and then rolled into the long grass. He picked it up and rubbed it on his not-quite-clean trouser leg. The skin was dark purple and shining and, when he bit into the yellow flesh, tasted faintly of honey. He yawned, switched on the wireless and took a large slug of whisky. Number seventy-one – an Englishman listens to the BBC – felt quite natural to him. He'd been desolate when his set was briefly confiscated during the war (they would have taken his bicycle, camera and car too if he'd had them). The local bobby who came round to collect it was apologetic, but he was under orders to remove wirelesses from all 'class B' enemy aliens. He gave Jack a ticket, and promised to return it the minute he was reclassified as a 'class C'. On seeing the dejected look on Jack's face, the bobby had assured him that he wouldn't let any of the chaps down the station listen to it. Six months later, the wireless was indeed returned unscathed by the same policeman, along with a bag of almond biscuits baked by his wife. The incident remained in Jack's mind, a symbol of the vagaries of government legislation (not that he'd ever criticise), and the kindness of the ordinary Englishman.

The clipped tones of the announcer introduced John Betjeman and Jack nestled into his deckchair, closing his eyes in anticipation. He remembered his programmes during the war – Betjeman, like the great Churchill himself, had reminded the public of what they were fighting to safeguard: a resolutely English way of life. Jack heard the voice of the poet as a rabbi hears the Song of Solomon. Each broadcast was a lament for an England he saw slipping away. Sitting in his garden, he joined with Betjeman in his ardour for feather-grey slate roofs, flowering currant bushes and the ancient place names of Fiddleford, Piddlehinton and Fifehead Magdalene. He felt himself to be one of the broadcaster's select society of ardent anglophiles, devoted to the preservation of everything great about this little island. He too loved the water meadows brushed by hedges of wild rose and adored the idea of bluebells in April. Quietly, he promised himself trips to St Ives, Brownsea Island and the Isle of Man, and swore allegiance to Betjeman's quest to block the march of the pre-fabricated bungalows across England's green and pleasant land.

Betjeman's fascination with churches he could not share. However ancient, ivy clad or pretty the ramshackle tombstones in the churchyard, churches remained a symbol of Jack's un-Englishness. If only what they stood for had some name other than 'The Church of England'. They were stone watchtowers to remind him if he ever got too comfortable or ever began to feel even a little bit English, that he did not belong. He listened to today's talk on churches obediently but, unlike those on every other subject, he did not weep with sympathy. He fidgeted, trying to pay attention until finally, in an admission of abject failure, he switched off the wireless.

He folded up his chair, trapping his finger in the hinge and his temper snapped in a torrent of German obscenities, '*Himmeldonnerwetter*', before he recovered enough to curse in English, 'Shit and skulduggery.'

He stormed into the house and lurked sullenly in his study, irked by his own shortcomings and worrying about Elizabeth. He wanted her to be pleased by her English father and here he was abandoning his studies. He must try harder. He pondered the other topics Betjeman had touched upon: seaside towns, the architecture of Bath, Victorian novelists. Now, that was a good one; he could cultivate his admiration of the novelists – Mr Betjeman was very clear that this was a vital aspect of Englishness. Jack had never read the British Canon – he had been taught Shakespeare in school, but it was Goethe and the Brothers Grimm that he loved. When the Rosenblums were waiting anxiously in Berlin for their British visas, Jack had prepared for the trip by reading Byron's poems and a Polish translation of P.G. Woodhouse. He understood only a little Polish and read the adventures of Mr Bertie Wooster with the help of a German–Polish dictionary. It all got rather lost in translation, and the novel appeared to him a very peculiar sort of book and had dissuaded him from sampling further the pleasures of English literature. Now, having listened to Betjeman, he realised that this was a grievous error – being an English Gentleman was a state of mind and, while it was too late for him to attend Eton or Cambridge, he must cultivate his mind with the reading of a gentleman nonetheless.

After all, was not Elizabeth reading English Literature at Cambridge? Jack flushed with joy at the delightful prospect of discussing voluminous tomes with his daughter and impressing her with shrewd insights. He drew up a reading list according to the principles of Mr Betjeman, who was very specific about the importance of the Victorian novelists above all others. He listed them: Thackeray, Dickens, Mrs Gaskell, Thomas Hardy. Yes, he would begin with Hardy because he was the author of Wessex. The house conveniently contained, in seventeen dusty volumes, the complete works of Hardy. Jack had stacked these neatly in his study because he admired the faded bindings and gilt-edged pages. To atone for his inability to appreciate chapels and churches, he would read some Hardy.

He scanned the titles: *Tess of the D'Urbervilles, The Mayor of Casterbridge, Far From the Madding Crowd.* Then, one caught his eye: *Jude the Obscure.* 'I didn't know Hardy wrote about a Jew! *And* an obscure Jew.'

In an instant Jack went from feeling excluded by his Jewishness, to glorious exultation. The Great Victorian Novelist of Dorset had written about an obscure Jew like him. 'This is me!' He clamoured excitedly to the empty room as he wielded the book. He had been quite prepared to cultivate his enthusiasm for Hardy but he could see that this would not be necessary.

He attempted to read *Jude* over breakfast the next morning but he was finding it very tricky to concentrate. On balance, P.G. Woodhouse was easier to read, even in Polish. He gave an unhappy sigh and pushed the book aside, miserably adding 'Victorian novelists' to 'English churches' on the list of things he could not properly appreciate, despite having being recommended by Betjeman. He considered that at this rate, when Elizabeth finally returned, she would notice no difference in her father at all, and began to butter his toast with such aggression that it disintegrated into a mush of crumbs.

Jack rubbed his aching temples; he loved England and wanted to listen to the slow trains rattling through the green countryside via Millford Vale and Blandford Forum. He liked the British Railways: platforms selling soggy sandwiches and paperback novels, cramped compartments filled with suited holiday folk all gazing out of smeared windows at rushing fields. These trains were pleasant things that made you smile to think of them, like a hot cup of tea. They were not like those other trains – the ones of Mittel Europe that stole men's souls.

But there was that other side of England, the people like Basset, who did not want him and who tore up his land pretending it was the work of a giant pig. It was not the first time, or even the second or third that such a thing had happened to Jack, though it was the first to be blamed on a mythical beast. His factory in the East End had been vandalised on countless occasions. It occurred continually in the run-up to the war, as people did not like that a Jew (and a German) was making money in their city. The walls were daubed with paint, bricks tossed through the windows and every Monday morning Jack helped clean up the damage. It got better during the war; vandalism then was an unpatriotic act, especially on a parachute factory. In the vast, anonymous city such petty hatred did not upset him. The dislike was placid, impersonal and he accepted that his position as a new arrival made him the perfect scapegoat. Here, amongst the dappled clouds and cooing wood pigeons, the hatred punctured his idyll and disturbed him.

He sat in the kitchen miserably chewing his toast and slurping a cup of black tea. Sadie bustled around, scrubbing pots and muttering under her breath, until finally she abandoned an encrusted casserole dish, letting it clatter into the sink and, fixing Jack with a hard stare, demanded, 'When are you going to start work again on that wretched course?'

'It's broken. *Kaput*. Finished.'

'So, you must fix it.'

While Jack's obsession irked her, Sadie discovered that this miserable man, who refused to shave and dripped from study to deckchair like a cat caught in a rain shower was even more bothersome. *Gott in himmel!* She needed him to be fizzing with optimism. '*Dann wurstel dich durch!*'

'Sausage through? How can I?' Jack gazed steadily at his wife and brushed crumbs off the book beside him. 'I don't want to rebuild because I cannot bear them to destroy it again.'

There was a dull bump as the post hit the doormat, and he went into the hall to collect it. He recognised the handwriting of Fielding on a white envelope and opened it with a sinking feeling. The letter from the factory manager contained the usual requests for new machinery. The looms were near obsolete, (everyone wanted tufted and pile carpets nowadays) but Jack was reluctant to invest in case he required more money for his course. Fielding was pressing him for a decision, but Jack had no room in his mind for such things and guiltily slipped the letter to the bottom of the pile.

Then he noticed something most unusual. Amongst the usual bills there was a cream envelope made from expensive watermarked paper. He took it into his study – such a pretty piece had to be opened with the silver letter knife. He fumbled in the drawer and pulled out the shining blade, carefully slicing open the envelope to remove a smart cream 'At Home' card.

Piddle Hall

Dear Mr and Mrs Rosenblum,

My wife and I are hosting a little gathering for drinks on Friday. We would be delighted if you and Mrs Rosenblum

could join us. We look forward to welcoming you to our
delightful piece of country. Be so kind as to come at seven.

Regards,
Sir William Waegbert

Jack's hand shook with excitement. This was a letter from a real English knight, not a mere gentleman but an actual member of the aristocracy. He marvelled over the invitation; did it mean that he was finally about to be accepted as an Englishman? He wished again that Elizabeth was here – then he could have shown her the card and she would realise he was a proper gentleman. Still trembling, he read and reread the invitation, admiring Sir William Waegbert's close hand and genteel loops. He must strive to make his own handwriting more gentlemanlike. Clearly, his was far too easy to read – one must work to decipher the words of a real gentleman like Sir William Waegbert. Jack tried the name aloud, 'Sir William Waeg-bert.' It sounded most auspicious. Much smarter than 'Arnold Smythe', and a fragment of Jack's jealousy of that man broke off and vanished.

There was one slight difficulty with the otherwise delightful invitation – Sadie was also invited. While Jack knew that it was usual to include a man's wife, Sadie was not like most wives. He hoped that she would behave – he could not bear for her to make a scene – and wished for the thousandth time that she would rinse her hair blue, paint her nails and be like other women. Jack realised it would take all of his persuasive powers to get Sadie to agree to accompany him; the party was on Friday night and she never went out on *Shabbas*. She would not even pick flowers, for the law states that nothing shall be broken into two halves on the Sabbath. Jack ventured into her territory to plead his case and found her kneeling amongst the flowerbeds cutting the dead heads off cala lilies.

Without a word, he squatted down beside her and handed her the invitation. Putting down her shears, she read it in silence and passed it back to him, leaving a bright yellow smear of pollen across the pristine surface. He winced but uttered no reproach. 'Well, will you come?'

'It is on *Shabbas*,' she said by way of answer.

'Ah, well, no, not quite.' He had been thinking about this on his way into the garden. 'It states an arrival time of seven o'clock and dusk is not until eight thirty. And, therefore,' he gave a little cough, 'by my calculations *Shabbas* will not be in until nine thirty.' He actually had no idea when dusk was, but he spoke with such assurance that Sadie did not question him. She picked up her scissors and continued to snip away at the flowers, placing the fallen heads into a bucket. She moved a stone and instantly the soil was teeming with ants. Jack shuddered, repulsed by the wriggling black bodies and tiny pinkish eggs.

Seeing his revulsion, she gave a snort, 'Everything is home for something.'

'Please,' said Jack, 'please.'

Sadie did not seem to hear him. She gave a little chuckle of glee and pointed to a small blue bloom, 'A cornflower.'

There was the sound of knocking on wood, like a tiny, powerful fist against a massive door. Above them a brilliant woodpecker, white and red, hammered with his beak against the bark of a tree. Sadie listened acutely to the sound, alert with interest.

'I like his outfit,' said Jack, pointing to the bird's brilliant plumage. 'He's a dapper little fellow. And an excellent percussionist. I'm sure with the right contacts, he could perform at the Wigmore Hall.'

Sadie's face brightened until she was almost smiling. She rocked back onto her heels and glanced up at her husband.

'Very well, I'll come,' she said and carried on snipping.

CHAPTER NINE

JACK WAITED FOR Friday like a small child for sweets to come off ration. When it finally arrived, he dressed himself meticulously in his Henry Poole suit and carefully selected a lilac silk tie. He combed his few strands of hair and shaved with a new blade. He even speculated whether he ought to grow a moustache for the occasion, but, on balance, did not feel confident enough with regard to the etiquette on facial hair. There were bound to be nuances of meaning in the angle or the shape of the curl and then there was the troubling question of whether or not to wax. It was safer to shave. He would study the gentleman of the aristocracy and then perhaps reconsider.

Sadie was waiting for him by the car. He was relieved to see that she was very respectably dressed in a pale olive frock – the colour matching the soft green of her eyes – with a white cardigan and matching shoes. She clutched a bouquet of garden flowers. 'We mustn't go empty handed. We're not *schnorrers*.'

Jack smiled, pleased by her good thinking. This was their very first evening out since their arrival in the countryside. He had been far too busy with his golf course to drive out with his wife and she was indifferent to excursions, preferring to stay quietly in her garden watching the birds. The evening was warm and Jack had peeled the top off the car. He gripped the steering wheel tightly to hide the slight trembling of his hands. If only he had finished *Jude* then he would have something suitable to talk about. Privately, he was already certain that he preferred Byron to Hardy, mainly because he was shorter in height as well as length, and Jack always felt a firm sense of solidarity with other small men.

The verges had been mown and the evening was heavy with the smell of freshly cut grass; dotted amongst the dark green of the hedgerows were speckles of scarlet wild strawberries and the whitish flowers of the brambles. The edges of the road teemed with bounding rabbits and every now and again they passed one stretched out on the tarmac, its fur bloodied. Jack stared straight ahead and suppressed a shudder.

He had memorised the map and was confident of the route but, in case of misadventure, he had allowed an extra half hour for the fifteen-minute journey. They arrived in fourteen minutes, shortly before half past six. The invitation strictly stated seven o'clock, so he pulled the car to the side of the road and they waited. He had the card with him; it was soiled now but he kept it anyway, safely tucked in his jacket pocket, half expecting to be questioned and turned away by the staff unless he could produce it. In front of them were the gates to the house. They were elaborate wrought iron and supported by two towering gateposts made of blond sandstone, each one topped with a screeching, weather-beaten eagle. A wall, seven feet high, ran from the gates all around the estate, so they could not see what lay beyond. A narrow driveway led away and immediately wound tightly to the right, heightening Jack's sense of expectation. They sat in silence until six fifty-five staring at the austere eagles, which gazed back at them, beaks tilted imperiously.

At six fifty-five Jack started the engine and they drove slowly along the gravel drive. It was lined on both sides with towering bushes of rhododendron and ancient magnolia trees. The land sloped down to a lake where a small flock of sheep grazed on the banks in the company of a brilliant white horse. On either side of the lake parkland was dotted with spreading oaks and Jack noticed a herd of deer grazing in the distance. In a minute they reached the house, a handsome stone manor, the front façade covered with ivy and tumbling wisteria, the evening sun glinting off the windows. They drew up to the main steps, whereupon an elderly man in a grey suit slowly descended. Jack leant out of the car, trying to shake his hand, 'Delighted to make your acquaintance, Sir William Waegbert.'

The man gave an almost imperceptible bow, 'Thank you for the compliment, Mr Rosenblum, but I am not the illustrious Sir William. My name is Symonds. The butler.'

Jack flushed with embarrassment – his first blunder and he'd not even parked the car.

'Would you be good enough to leave the automobile by the stables, sir?' said Symonds, pointing to a low building around the corner.

Jack steered the Jaguar to the smart stables at the back of the house. They had recently been reroofed with black slate tiles and the wooden walls were newly painted duck-egg blue. Two horses wearing nosebags gazed nonchalantly at the newcomers. A groom polished riding tack to a gleam, while a nut-brown mare fidgeted and tried to back into a wall as a girl in breeches attempted to pick muck from her hooves with a blunt knife. Jack parked alongside a line of other vehicles in the far corner of the yard. The automobiles were in stark contrast to the shining, well-cared for horses. There was an Austin, its bodywork battered by what appeared to be hoof-prints, the wheel arches eaten away by rust. Next to it was a Rolls-Royce, but it was a model dating to before the Great War – its exhaust was missing and there were holes in the leather upholstery where tufts of horsehair stuffing poked through.

They walked back through the yard, Sadie stumbling on the cobbles in her heels. Having taken to walking barefoot over the grass, it felt strange to her to be wearing shoes at all. Symonds was waiting for them at the front of the house.

He must have been in his seventies but Jack noticed with admiration his excellent upright bearing.

'May I show you into the rose garden? Sir William and Lady Waegbert will join you shortly, Mr Rosenblum, Mrs Rosenblum.'

They followed the servant into the formal garden at the front of the manor. Jack still found the English manner of speaking most peculiar. They so rarely made absolute statements or asked you to do something but instead continually spoke in rhetorical questions – 'would you?' 'may I?' – when what they truly meant was park here, wait there. They liked to give you the illusion of choice, when really there was none.

'Will you be quite comfortable here, sir? And may I bring you a drink, sir?'

'Yes. Thank you. A whisky.'

'With soda or ice?'

Jack paused, wondering which was the correct answer. Which would give him away as a phoney and a foreigner? 'A dash of soda, please,' he said, trying to sound casual.

Symonds gave a tiny bow and Jack relaxed – he had chosen wisely. He must remember that. No more neat whisky: whisky and soda.

'And for the lady?'

Now it was Sadie's turn to look stricken, she shifted uncomfortably from foot to foot, heels sinking awkwardly into the grass. Nice, middle-class Jewish ladies didn't drink. Occasionally she might have a glass of champagne if they went to the opera but only in the Stalls bar, never from the Crush bar. She had once tried a sip of gin and tonic and had rather liked it but Mrs Ezekiel had seen her, and she had told everyone at *schul* on Saturday that Mrs Sadie Rosenblum liked a gin. Gin, Sadie decided, was a danger to one's reputation. Jack, however, knew better; only yesterday on the wireless Mr Betjeman had described how gin and tonic with a slice of lemon was one of the great joys of an English summer's evening. Betjeman explained that it evoked the old days of Empire and the nostalgic pleasures of a misremembered past, and noted wryly that even English ladies enjoyed a little 'G and T' amongst friends.

'A gin and tonic, with a slice of lemon if you've got it,' said Jack firmly.

Sadie opened her mouth to speak and then shut it again meekly, smoothing an imaginary crease in her dress. She was still clutching the flowers.

'May I take these, madam?' asked Symonds.

Sadie hesitated. 'They're for Lady Waegbert.'

'The man doesn't think they're for him,' said Jack irritably.

She allowed him to take them from her, watching as he vanished into the house. They were left standing on a lawn, neatly clipped and rolled into smart stripes. Pyramids of Yew were planted in straight lines across the grass and loomed above them. She wondered whether it was usual to be left hanging about in the garden, waiting for one's host.

In fact it was not. Lady Waegbert liked to greet her guests personally – however unwelcome. She could not see why her husband had invited such ludicrous people to her house – just because people were odd it was no guarantee of their being entertaining. And now, they had arrived so outrageously early that no one was ready to receive them.

'Surely *everybody* knows that seven o'clock means seven thirty,' she complained bitterly to her husband.

'Darling, they are foreign, *Germans*. They are always punctual.'

'They are not punctual. They are early,' she said, as if it were one of the worst crimes in society. 'And to arrive before your hostess has even had time to put on her lipstick.'

The Rosenblums, in the shadow of the Yew Pyramids, were oblivious to their violation of the social niceties. Nor did Jack realise that they had been invited solely for entertainment value. The other ten guests had all been asked to stay for dinner, and Jack was intended to provide the pre-dinner cabaret. Sir William was not a cruel man but he enjoyed the bizarre or ridiculous, and he had heard the strange tales about the Jew of Bulbarrow, who was trying to build a golf course in forty days and forty nights with only a shovel. This was too good an opportunity to forgo, so risking the wrath of his wife he dispatched a rash invitation.

Sir William, growing tired of his lady's complaints, went out into the garden to meet his guests. He rubbed his hands in delight as he saw them standing together. They were better than he had hoped – she was merely old-fashioned-looking, a plump woman in a faded frock and silly white shoes – but he was very promising. To Sir William's eye, Jack's treasured Henry Poole suit was garish and the lilac tie lurid. The fact he wore a suit at all for what was merely drinks was also highly entertaining. A gentleman wears a jacket and tie for drinks and a suit only for dinner. Sir William, however, was the model of perfect breeding and, as he shook their hands with real warmth and profuse apologies at his own lateness, Jack and Sadie suspected nothing.

The remainder of the guests arrived punctually late at seven thirty. They appeared on the lawn with Lady Waegbert just as Jack was attempting to steer the conversation to the first four pages of *Jude the Obscure*. He had also stashed a collection of Hardy's poems in his breast pocket in case any one was in need of an urgent quotation.

'*Jude*, eh. No never read it. Tried *Tess* once. Heard she was quite a gal, a real corker,' confided Sir William with a wink.

Jack made a silent promise to read *Tess* next. The combination of whisky, sunshine and nerves was making him feel a trifle faint. The men drew around Sir William eager to meet the promised Jew, like a crowd gathering for a circus act. He introduced Jack to several smart-looking gentlemen, including Mr Henry Hoare, a man of about sixty in a patched flannel jacket and heavy horn-rimmed spectacles.

'So, do tell us about this golf course, then. The only reason we've come to this ghastly pile at all is to hear about it,' said Mr Hoare.

Jack looked worried – he recognised this to be an instance of English wit but did not like it and hoped Sir William had not taken offence. The baronet, however, remained unperturbed and smiled encouragingly.

'Well, the course will be the greatest in the whole South-West. It is the most important labour of my life,' Jack declared.

He looked at the expectant faces and took another sip of whisky. It was nearly a week since he stopped construction but he found his enthusiasm for the project returning in great waves as the alcohol warmed his throat.

'I am following the example of Mr Bobby Jones – in my view the greatest player and designer of courses in the whole of golfing history.'

'Jones is a gentleman, too. A true amateur, none of your *sporting professionals*,' added a man in a dull green tweed.

Sir William gestured to Symonds, who scuttled over to take a whispered order, reappearing, as if by magic, moments later with another glass of whisky and soda for Jack. As he sipped, Jack felt warm and pleasant, and became expansive. He wanted these men, these leaders of society, to understand, no, to fully appreciate the wonder that was Bobby Jones. He spread his arms like a rabbi deep in explanation of the mysteries of the Torah.

'There is no one quite like Mr Jones. He truly is a remarkable man. His is a gift straight from Himself,' said Jack, in a voice quivering with emotion and raised his eyes to the cloudless sky. 'Augusta is paradise on earth. There are flowers in red and yellow and gold and blue and silver lakes with multicoloured fish. The sand in the hazards is so fine it feels like ground silk. Parrots roost in the trees and help to find any lost balls. Nightingales sing and the air is scented with honey from specially kept bees. When the light is just so, the grass looks blue, and you believe you are playing a round in the sky.'

'Jones, you say?' Sir William asked, caught off guard by Jack's description.

'Yes, Mr Bobby Jones, Sir William Waegbert.'

'Oh, please, please, just plain old Sir William.'

Jack grinned, gratified at the perceived honour of calling a knight by his abbreviated title. He was relaxing with Sir William's kindness and the growing effects of the liquor.

'And you say that your course will be the greatest?' demanded the man in mossy tweed.

'Yes. For the very first time in the illustrious annals of the sport, I am combining the two great models. Not only am I using the inspiration of Mr Jones's brilliance at Augusta, but also the triumph of Old Tom Morris and the revered wisdom of Mr Robert Hunter. I shall create a links course on the side of Bulbarrow. It will be a perfect copy of St Andrews.'

'Links are by the sea are they not?'

Jack sighed and plunged his hands into his pockets. 'Yes. I may have to dam the Stour. We shall see.'

Sir William beamed. His eccentric guest was proving most amusing and he rewarded him with a benevolent smile.

His confidence growing, Jack risked an observation. He phrased it as a question, in the English way. 'Waegbert is a German name, is it not?'

'Good God no! It does sound Germanic – I'll give you that. Bit like Wagner or what-not. No. It's Anglo-Saxon. There have been Waegberts at Piddle Hall since nine seventy-three. William is Norman. There have been Williams in the family since William the Conqueror. Apparently my ancestors thought it was a good idea to flatter the blighter by naming Waegberts in his honour.'

Jack nodded, overwhelmed by this sense of history. He fully expected that Noah had two Waegberts on his ark.

Sir William was usually quite happy to talk about the grand ancestry of the Waegberts at some length, but he wanted to hear more about the golf course. 'When will it be finished?'

Jack frowned – he did not want to admit to the catastrophe, as that would show weakness. And that was not British. Rule sixty-four: an Englishman keeps his head in a crisis *no matter what*.

'In time for her Royal Highness Queen Elizabeth's coronation. I shall hold a competition to celebrate the momentous occasion.'

'Excellent. Excellent. Can anyone play?' enquired Mr Hoare, rubbing his palms.

Jack considered this – he had not resolved the finer details of his plan yet. 'No. I believe I shall restrict play to members only.'

'Jolly good. Well, we shall have to become members then, Sir William, eh?' Mr Hoare gave his friend a nudge.

'If we are accepted, Henry. We do not know the conditions of membership,' said Sir William seriously, with an appeal to Jack.

It was one of the proudest moments of Jack's life. A knight, a real live knight (with stables, horses, a Rolls-Royce and a family going back to nine seventy-three) was asking him, Jack Rosenblum, if he could have membership to his golf club. His cheeks turned pink, he felt the blood pounding in his ears and tears prick his eyes. He wished Elizabeth could hear this. Some men at this point may have demurred, wanting to slight a man who was part of a class that had universally rejected his own applications to a hundred golf clubs, but Jack was not such a man. Friendship was too precious a commodity to refuse in this sad world. A tear trickling down his cheek, he clasped first Sir William's hand and then Mr Hoare's.

'Of course. Of course. I would be delighted,' he said, his voice cracking with emotion. 'You will be my very first members. I shall have your names put up on the board in the clubhouse in gold letters.'

The two men were taken aback by the emotional outburst of the slight man. Sir William did not know whether to laugh or take offence at the notion of the Waegbert name being sullied on a board in a common clubhouse.

Across the lawn, as she remarked upon the weather, Lady Waegbert tried to get a better look at Jack's shoes which, as she rightly suspected, were made of suede. This was really too much for Lady Waegbert, who viewed suede as a symptom of moral degeneracy. That her husband had willingly encouraged these people into her house was quite unbearable. Sadie's skirt length, cut at the knee instead of mid-calf in the New Look, merely revealed her to be a woman without style; at least she had let her hair go grey, instead of indulging in one of those dreadful blue rinses that the middle classes all seemed so wild about. It was nearly eight thirty and time for dinner. These people should have gone by now. The middle-classes or Jews – they were all the same to her – never knew when to leave. It was most unpleasant. If they did not go soon, she would be forced to ask them to stay, and that would be frightful.

'Do stay and dine. My wife would be simply delighted,' said Sir William.

Jack glanced over to Lady Waegbert – it pained him to refuse such an elegant and thoughtful woman but he had promised Sadie that they would return home before the start of the Sabbath. He knew Sadie was terrified that she would be made to eat pig and, while he was not sure how anyone could be *made* to eat anything, he had promised. So it was with genuine regret that he politely declined Sir William's invitation.

They made their farewells and left the party on the lawn.

Jack felt easier than he had all summer; he was tired of being the Jew and the Yid – it was lonely and dangerous. He had tried again and again to impress the need for assimilation upon Sadie. 'We need to become part of them. If *they* come back – whom do you think they will give up first? Us! Us! You and me! Only if we become like them, can we hide amongst them. We must not be poppies in the wheat field.'

He felt almost happy as he and Sadie walked back across the lawn towards the house. This, he thought, is the beginning. Dusk was drawing in and gnats hovered above them.

'I need the lavatory,' announced Sadie.

'Can't you wait?' Jack was irritated; he did not like to ask if his wife could use the toilet.

'No.'

He frowned. 'You ask. I'll wait here.'

Sadie scowled, and he knew that the tentative truce of the evening was over. He watched as slowly she went up the front steps and disappeared into the murk of the house. The light was fading; a family of house martins flew to their nest in the eaves and he could just make out the North Star appearing in the evening sky.

Ten minutes later she had not reappeared and, growing restless, he ventured into the manor. It was still, except for the wafts of laughter coming from the terrace where Sir William and his guests were now being served supper. Jack stood in a large, oak-panelled hallway hung with a dozen or more portraits; austere men and women glared at him from their frames, their hands resting on the heads of supercilious-looking dogs. Hanging beside them was a mounted certificate with the red mayoral seal of Dorset; he squinted to read the ornate calligraphy.

Sir William Waegbert of Piddle Hall,
Mayor of Dorsetshire, 1945 AD

Jack was impressed – so his new friend had been mayor as well and hadn't even mentioned it – he admired this British modesty. A minute later he began to fidget; where on earth was his wife? A door was ajar and he pushed it open to reveal a large, panelled room with a vaulted ceiling stained black with smoke and age. The flagstone floor was covered with an ancient rug that once must have been handsome but was now foot-worn and thin. Dangling from one wall was a tapestry of a hunting scene; silken men rode on horseback, their thread hair flying out behind them, accompanied by a pack of woven hounds all chasing an animal into a forest. In the background there stood a purple castle and a lake brimming with writhing sea monsters.

On the opposite wall was a massive stone fireplace, the mantelpiece hewn from a single slab of rock and supported by two elaborately carved sidepieces teeming with magical creatures. There was a unicorn, a ho-ho bird, a pair of griffins whose clawed feet made the bottom of the pillars, and a wyvern – a winged reptile whose red eyes were shining jewels set into the stone. Beneath the mantelpiece was engraved a forest of twisting branches, some in leaf, others in bud, while yet more had burst into sandstone flowers. Peeking from between two branches Jack noticed another beast. It had the head of a pig and carved tusks that entwined the magnificent horns sprouting from its skull. On its back grew a woolly fleece which, even chiselled in stone, appeared to him soft and white.

'It's a Dorset woolly-pig' said a voice behind him.

Jack turned to see the elderly servant standing in the doorway. It must have been a trick of the light, but the old man's eyes were a startling shade of green.

'He is a myth of this county,' explained Symonds. 'The older people in these parts still believe in him.'

'Do you?'

Symonds only smiled. 'There he is again.' He pointed to the tapestry and Jack realised that the poor creature pursued by the hunters was none other than the woolly-pig. In the medieval work the brute was as large as the horses the men rode and its eyes were woven with crimson fury.

'Why would you harm such a magnificent beast?'

The servant gave a sad smile. 'They were said to be plentiful during ancient times and could grant the pure-hearted their true wish. But then the knights hunted them for sport and the woolly-pigs grew angry and refused to grant any more wishes, pure of heart or not. They hid in the depths of the oldest forests and gored any who tried to find them. As the trees were hacked down and the woodlands became smaller and smaller, they died of sorrow. A few are said still to wander the forests bleating of their sadness.'

Jack thought of his wife, filled with nothing but sorrow, wandering the earth remembering the dead and happier times.

CHAPTER TEN

LATER THAT NIGHT, Jack surveyed the wreckage of the opening hole and wished it really were the woolly-pig who was to blame. Post-war Europe was a drab place, tired and devoid of wonder, and a mysterious creature surviving from antiquity to create a little havoc in the modern world was an appealing thought. A wild pig destroys hedges and golf courses out of rage that they are in his way – Jack couldn't imagine that a pig gave a fig whether the land belonged to a Yid, a Kraut or the Queen of England. For the first time in months, he thought of Berlin. He saw the city with a towering barbed wire fence splitting it in two and imagined a woolly-pig crashing through the night, tearing up the wire as if it was a bramble hedge. Yes, the world would be much improved with a dash of magic.

He sighed and loosened the knot in his tie. The night was black and starless, and he felt that he was walking with his eyes closed, as he stumbled over the broken ground and jutting earth. Above there was a whooping cry and a flash of white. 'Must be an owl. Out hunting,' he muttered quietly, to reassure himself. The clouds cleared for a moment around the moon, and there was a beat of wings, and then he felt cool air rush against his arm. The glow caught the barn owl's plumage, bright as bone in the dark. Then the sky clouded over again and the bird was gone.

With a vast yawn that made his jaw crack, Jack slumped upon the heap of molehills. His eyes were slowly adjusting to the darkness, and he watched the tiny undulations on the surface of the pond; it was never still and never the same. The water was covered with tiny white flowers that appeared like miniature stars on the black plane. A frog sat on a lily pad, took one look at him and dived into the cool water. He had never seen a spring before – he had only read about them to Elizabeth in fairy stories when she was a little girl. There was something remarkable about the way the water trickled out of the ground that seemed as mystical as any seam of gold or imagined mine filled with precious gems. Gnats swirled, landing on his cheeks as he tried to swot them away with his hat. He bent down and washed his hands in the cold, fresh water. Then, he made a cup with his palms and took a long drink – the water tasted pure and was as clear as Sadie's wedding diamond. He took off his shoes and dangled his swollen feet in the water, feeling the current tickle his toes.

On the banks of the stream, he noticed several prints in the mud. He studied them carefully. Several looked like rabbit – he knew those well from the tracks in Sadie's kitchen garden – and he recognised a bigger set that he guessed were deer. Then he saw something else. Embedded in the earth were two neat trotter prints. They were ten times the size of an average pig and could only belong to a giant boar.

The adrenalin surged in Jack's veins and then, half a second later, it vanished. Of course there are prints, he reasoned. They wanted to blame the mess on a woolly-pig so they would place the evidence; they must consider him a simpleton to think he would believe such childish stories. There were no boot prints that he could make out in the darkness but he supposed Basset and the rest must have waded up the stream to disguise their tracks. 'I wish I could catch the sneaky bastards,' he muttered, and that gave him an idea. Traps. They were pretending that it was the woolly-pig, and he was pretending to believe them. So, he must go a stage further and lay traps all over his land, purportedly to catch the beast. He would place them everywhere as he rebuilt the course and then, if they tried to destroy it again, the traps would imprison the real culprits! He imagined Jack Basset and his friends caught in a massive bear pit, all of them pleading for mercy. He would be generous and decline to report them to the police and then, in return, he might earn a little respect. Under the whispering leaves, he flopped onto his back and lay spreadeagled on the cool ground, listening to the earthworms churning beneath the soil and pondered Basset's fate.

The following afternoon it rained; it hadn't for a fortnight but now it poured and Bulbarrow Hill disappeared into a filmy mist while bullets of rain battered Sadie's rose bush. A gossamer strand of spider web was suspended between two buds like a silken trapeze and raindrops hung there, glistening like jewels on a necklace. Driven indoors for the first time in a month, Jack sat in his office and studied the topography of Bulbarrow. He laid maps carefully across the floor and wondered what kind of traps would be best – the notion of bear pits was very tempting; they could be disguised with branches and grass and, if he dug them deep enough, they would hold a man. They would need to be ten or twelve foot deep with straight, slippery sides but unfortunately, after weeks of endless shovelling, he was reluctant to mine any more holes.

Jack lit one of his rare cigarettes and sat back in his battered armchair for a good think. Catching the perpetrator would be satisfying, but was not absolutely necessary; the most important thing was to protect the course. Time was ticking away and to have any hope of a match on Coronation Day, he needed to make progress and he simply did not have the time to dig mantraps. What was required was a deterrent. Basset and the others needed to *believe* he had traps: vicious, sinister contraptions capable of snapping a man's leg in two – that surely must put them off. Then, he could quietly restore his poor butchered fairway in peace.

At nine o'clock Jack decided to go to the pub. He had not seen Sadie all day, only heard her singing to herself, and slipped out so as not to disturb her. The rain stopped; the evening turned warm and close, and he walked alone through the fields. One was never alone in the city; one could be lonely or ignored but there was always the buzzing of other people – even in the house one could hear them outside in their cars or jabbering in the street. Here there were only the swallows. Flying so high in the sky, they were like scribbles of birds in a child's drawing as they chased the insects, surfing waves of high pressure after the rain. He flicked away a biting fly and saw his arms had turned a deep shade of brown and the little hairs were all bleached white. Under his hat even his bald pate was tanned. He felt that he had ripened, just like the blackberries that were slowly turning from red to deep purple on the bramble bushes.

The doors of The Crown were thrown open and people spilled into the garden. Jack Basset perched on a wooden bar stool like a great heron on a pebble, the rickety seat creaking ominously under his hefty frame. He drank his pint with ardent concentration and, on seeing the other Jack, greeted him like an old friend.

'Evenin' Mister Rose-in-Bloom. Found any woolly-pigs yet?'

Jack shook his head. 'Not yet. But I will.'

The men looked up in surprise. Jack was pleased. Good, he thought to himself, let them all believe I am a crazy Jew-Bastard. He cleared his throat and met Basset's cornflower blue eyes. 'I am going to capture the woolly-pig.'

There were suppressed muffles of laughter and a small gaggle of men gathered around Jack.

'How?'

'Traps, Mr Basset.'

'Wot sort, mind?'

'I have a few designs . . . what would you recommend?'

Basset liked to be consulted. He took a drink. 'He's too big for a badger trap. 'Ee'd break it with his tusks. What d'you use for bait?'

'A pit and leaves. Tis only way. Mush Rooms are best for bait. Nothin' but Mush Rooms.' Curtis piped up, elbowing his way to the front of the group. He seemed about to speak again, then changed his mind and sulked in silence.

Jack reached into a pocket and pulled out his hand-drawn map of Bulbarrow, marked with a series of red crosses that looked a little like grave markers. 'These denote the position of the traps,' he explained, waving the map in front of them quickly and then hiding it from view – he didn't want them to get too close a look, just in case it encouraged them to go searching for a trap that wasn't really there. 'I believe I shall stick with my own designs. They are more dastardly.'

He slid a hand into his jacket and produced another sheet, decorated with a diagram of the supposed contraption to catch the beast. A large cage was concealed in the earth and just beneath the ground were a set of vicious serrated jaws, ready to snap if the wire was touched. He pointed proudly, 'It's a hair trigger. A mere snuffle from the creature and *wham*!' He clapped his hands shut and surveyed the curious faces, wondering if he had pushed it too far. 'I don't mean it any harm. I only want to catch one. Put Pursebury on the map.'

Basset snatched Jack's plans of Bulbarrow. 'Tis already on the map, Mr Rose-in-Bloom.'

Jack knew they were laughing at him – all of them except Curtis, who was staring at him with an odd expression. The old man was the smallest grown person he had ever seen; he was the size of a child but wizened and thin. He'd tipped a pint of cider down his trousers, which now clung to his stick-like legs making him look, if possible, even more frail. He was standing right up close to Jack, so close that he could smell the sweet scent of apples and sweat.

Curtis had entered into that part of old age where it becomes impossible to fathom the precise number of years. Even Curtis wasn't sure. The baptismal records for the last century had been removed to the county office and he had no other way of checking; he guessed that he was somewhere between eighty-five and one hundred and thirteen. His face was creased with more lines than usual because he was worried.

'Yer really want to see the beast?' He spoke quietly, almost in a whisper.

'Yes,' answered Jack. The word came out before he was aware that he had spoken and, at that very moment, it was true – he did want to see a woolly-pig. It would mean that the men in the village had not ruined his hopes and had not lied, and that the world was not such a grey place, devoid of the ancient and unknown.

Curtis shook his head, 'Traps. Huh. Won't find 'im like that. Won't even catch a glimpse of his tail. Yer believe in 'im. That summat but that's not t' whole apple cake.'

The other farmers ignored Curtis. He gave them a little sly smile, while they continued to stare at Jack.

'Mister Rose-in-Bloom?'

Jack turned to the gnarled face that was as crinkled as the bark of an ancient oak tree.

'Come.' Curtis beckoned with a stubby finger and pointed to the door of the pub and beyond into the darkling light.

In a minute they were on the road outside the pub. The old man raced along on his short legs so that soon Jack was panting to keep up. Long shadows barred the road and branches were all thin hands waving in the stillness. Jack wasn't sure if it would be rude to puncture the atmosphere; perhaps silence was necessary to hunting the woolly-pig. He chanced a whisper.

'Where are we going?'

'Your house. Pick up t'car,' Curtis said loudly. 'I'm a bit deaf. Don't talk quiet.'

Jack looked around and realised they were in fact at the end of his own driveway; somehow he hadn't noticed in the dark.

'Why do we need the car?'

'We is goin' to Hambledon. It's three miles and I ent walkin'.'

They reached the Jaguar, which stood gleaming, reflections of clouds moving across the bonnet. Curtis ran a hand lovingly along the shining paintwork. 'Ent she a beauty.'

Jack tiptoed inside to get the keys, wondering if the expedition was actually a ruse so that Curtis could go for a drive in the car. Not that he minded – he would have quite happily taken him, although probably not at half-past eleven at night for a trip up an ancient hill fort. He tried to be quiet to avoid waking Sadie, and opened the front door as smoothly as he could. Silence. Holding his breath, he took the car key and pulled the door shut.

He started the engine and peeled back the hood so that the car was open to the night sky. Curtis climbed onto the rear and perched upon the curved boot, his feet resting on the front seat.

'Are you sure that you're quite comfortable?' asked Jack.

'Yup. I likes to feel the wind in my ears.'

They drove along the roads without seeing another soul. The headlights caught the bright stripes of a badger running at full pelt along the verge, and soon the windscreen was spattered with moths. At the foot of Hambledon Jack paused when Curtis gestured for him to park.

'Stop 'ere.' Curtis nimbly hopped out. 'We is goin' up there.'

He pointed to a narrow, tree-lined track that fell away into the darkness and led the way at his usual rapid pace. Jack kept tripping over tree roots as he struggled to keep up. Trees grew on either side of the pathway, their canopies spreading and meeting in the middle like the fingertips of two hands touching. The green-tinged tunnel was sunk ten feet below the trees.

'Why is the track in a ditch?'

The old farmer gave a snort.

'Ent no ditch. This path is two thousand years old. These is the wearin's and tearin's of all those feet an' carts an' soldiers an' head-hunters.'

'Head-hunters?' Jack wasn't sure that he had heard correctly and trotted a few yards to catch up.

'Aye. Head-hunters. They dug up round here afor t' Great War an' found skulls with 'oles in. They 'ad been worn by the weather an' had 'oles in 'em for where they'd bin put on spikes, like.'

Jack cast round in the gloom, half expecting to see an Iron Age savage ready with a skewer for his head. They emerged from the tree tunnel and reached a gate, which Curtis vaulted. He then began to climb the sharp incline as Jack scrambled after him. Jack must have been at least thirty, maybe as many as fifty years younger than Curtis but there was no question as to who was the more agile. The hill was sheer, the slope even steeper than that of Bulbarrow, and into the side were cut deep, circular grooves many yards deep. Jack gasped for breath and he had a stitch. Although it was late, the night was warm and the air he gulped felt humid. He concentrated on where he was putting his feet, carefully trying to avoid the patches of thistles and round brown cowpats in the dark. He felt like he had been climbing for an hour, though it couldn't have been much more than twenty minutes. Then, eyes still fixed on his feet, he bumped right into Curtis.

'Righty stop 'ere. We is at top.'

Jack flopped down beside him and closed his eyes. 'You climb so fast. You're not even out of breath,' he gasped, his own coming in rasps. He heard the squeal of a bottle being unscrewed and then a flask was thrust into his hand.

'Drink,' commanded Curtis.

Jack took a deep glug; it was like drinking apples set on fire. It made him cough and want more at the same time. Curtis snatched away the bottle.

'That's enuff. Yoos ent used to it yet,' he explained, not unkindly.

'What is it?' Jack's eyes were watering.

'Erm. Jist a special cider brew. Apples and thingy,' he answered cryptically.

Jack lay on his back and felt the stuff warming him all the way down to his toes. He closed his eyes and was suddenly very sleepy.

'Are you ready Mister Rose-in-Bloom?'

'Ready for what? Are we waiting for a woolly-pig?'

'Nope. Not tonight. Tisn't t' right time. And yoos isn't ready.'

Usually Jack would have objected to this: he was perfectly ready and this was exactly the right time, only he hadn't brought his camera. And it was dark. But, whether it was the heat, his drowsiness or the effect of the special brew cider, he was happy just to lie here and listen.

'Open yer eyes.'

Summoning all his energy, Jack opened them. The moon was high and bright and the stars were so clear that he felt he could reach out and touch them. He wasn't used to skies like these; in London on a cloudless night he could make out the Plough, but there was always light from street lamps and the steady glow from houses and offices. On Hambledon Hill the only light was the stars and, as they shone, they filled up the whole night sky. Jack knew that he was gazing across time to stare at light that had travelled billions of years to reach Dorset. He stared at one hovering star that emitted a pale green glow. It danced in the air, floating above his head before disappearing. Then, he saw that there were scores of them –

not in the sky but near to the ground – tiny, pale green lights that flickered and floated as they swayed upon long grass stems. He reached out to touch one and it twinkled just out of reach before drifting away.

'W-what are they?' he stammered.

'Worms. Glow-worms. Jitterbugs. What we are seein' is a jitterbug orgy.'

'A what?'

'An orgy. Them is the female ones that glow to attract a mate. Tis jitterbug mating season.'

Curtis handed him the flask and he took another swig. The green lights began to blur and sway like a miniature firework display. Every blade of grass seemed to hold a glinting emerald light.

'In years gone by, hignorant people thought these is fairies,' Curtis scoffed.

Jack could see why. There were no wings on the glow-worms, but he could hear a soft batting, like the whirring of a clock. A single light hovered as though treading air, and then darted in a jabbing pattern above his head. Curtis pointed with a stubby finger. 'Only males 'as wings an' they doesn't usually glow. They is right lazy bastards.'

Jack stared at another pale light nestled in the prickly palm of a thistle. As he watched, the light dimmed. He blinked and it was dark.

'Ah,' said Curtis, 'once she's mated, she puts out 'er light. She lays her eggs, she fades and then she dies.'

Through his alcohol haze, Jack wondered whether the male jitterbug was performing a dance of grief for his dying mate.

Jack and Curtis lay in a large ditch, that formed part of a series of Iron Age trenches designed to defend the fort against other marauding head-hunters. Each dugout had grass walls nearly fifteen feet high and Jack marvelled at their construction.

'How did the head-hunters dig these ditches?'

Curtis took a swig of cider. 'Antler horns and wooden pick axes.'

The place felt ancient; they were lying in a fort nearly two thousand years old. Jack could hear the whispers of the earth and knew that here was deep time. The woolly-pig was part of that world, a remnant from another, older age.

Curtis heaved himself onto his elbows; his battered hat perched at an odd angle and a clump of burrs were stuck to his shirt.

''Ave you 'eard the legend of Arthur and the Round Table an' all that stuff?'

'Yes. Don't they think it was at Cadbury Castle now and not Glastonbury? I read it in *The Times*.'

Curtis spat on the ground in disgust. 'Those Somerset folks. They nickered our 'istory. Tisn't Glastonbury nor Cadbury Castle neither. Tis Stourcastle. Dorset. That's where the Saxon King were – old Wessex. Bloody, thievin' Somerset folks. Jist cause they hasn't got enuff stories of their own they goes stealin' ours.'

Jack rubbed his eyes and tried to focus. The green lights were a blur and the sky was sinking towards earth – it was a star-sprinkled blanket a few inches from his face.

'King Arthur was in Stourcastle?'

Curtis nodded. 'Aye. But 'ee wasn't called Arthur, mind. 'Ee were Albert.'

Jack closed his eyes and dreamt of King Albert. He was a mighty woolly-pig with tusks of gold, and when he opened his mouth a stream of green lights poured out and filled the sky with stars.

CHAPTER ELEVEN

JACK WOKE THE next morning in his own bed with no memory of getting home. He sat up and immediately lay back down, rubbed his eyes and blinked several times. He felt as if he had been asleep for a hundred years and was now rousing from a magnificent and enchanted slumber. His very soul was rejuvenated, and he had a furious craving for a soft-boiled egg. Putting on his worn leather slippers he wandered downstairs and went outside to check the car. It was parked neatly in the driveway, paintwork unscathed. Then he noticed the driver's seat: it was pulled all the way forward as though a child had been driving.

Despite the drinking and the late night, he was filled with more exuberance than he had experienced for over a week. He had the first two members of his Great Golf Course and his stomach tingled when he considered this remarkable turn of events. As he changed out of his pyjamas and into his work clothes, he decided that now it seemed appropriate he hadn't yet played a hole. It was right and proper that the first hole should be played on the morning of the Coronation. That was to be the greatest British Event since the end of the war and would mark the beginning of a new era: the Illustrious Elizabethan Age.

He collected his molehill contraption from the barn and wheeled it along the rugged track down to the field. For the first time in nearly a fortnight he was not disheartened by the monumental task before him and was instead flooded with energy. Humming 'Land of Hope and Glory', he loaded up the first bucket of water and tugged on the pulley. He hoped the threat of traps would be enough to ward off any would-be saboteurs but, just in case, he had bought several from a gamekeeper on Bulbarrow. They lay bundled in a sack by the pond, since he could not quite bring himself to set them. The bucket of water wavered and the first molehill was hoisted up; he swung the contraption and dumped the heap of earth into a ditch. One down. He turned to the next molehill, but someone was sitting on it. Curtis was perched on the edge, head in his hands. He picked up a blade of grass and started to peel away the outer layer, while Jack watched him in silence. He didn't know what Curtis did – he didn't have a farm, though sometimes he minded other people's sheep, but Jack didn't even know where he lived. Triumphant, Curtis held up a thin sliver of white, the inside of the leaf he had been peeling.

'This 'ere is a wick – dip him in pig fat and yer got yerself a candle. Now,' he said turning to Jack, ''ow has the woolly-pig hunt bin farin'?'

Jack winced; he did not like lying to the old man but could not confess that when confronted with daylight and a clean head, he did not believe in the woolly-pig. Saying nothing, he pointed towards the sack by the dew pond. Curtis picked it up and tipped out the traps so that they lay in the long grass, a heap of glistening metal jaws. He gave a shudder. Jack had to agree – they did look rather evil now he studied them, and one serrated edge was encrusted with dried blood and tufts of fur.

'I was told they were humane,' he said, sounding unconvinced.

'Aye, very humane,' said Curtis. He lifted his trouser leg and showed an angry red scar all the way round his ankle, where the skin was mashed up like flesh-coloured marble.

'*Zum Kuckuck!* That was from a trap?'

Curtis preened in Jack's dismay. 'It is. Got done by a trap on Bulbarrow. Jist mindin' my own business. Found a pheasant – weren't poachin', it jist flew into a sack I 'appened to be 'oldin' like and then *crack*.' He smacked his hands together to show the movement of the trap shutting on his leg. 'I were lucky them trap didn't take my leg off.'

Jack was appalled. 'I don't want to kill them. It. The woolly-pig. I don't even want to hurt it. I want to trap it.'

'Well then, don't use them things. Evil buggers,' said Curtis bitterly.

Jack paused. Much as he did not wish to maim another man, he also did not want his course destroyed. He thought for a moment. 'I want to *see* a woolly-pig, but I don't really need to catch one.'

To his surprise the old man jumped up and began to shake his hand.

'Spectacular! Tis good news. No noggerhead can never catch one of them nanyhow. Yer might be from forin lands but yer gets the beast and 'is thinkin'.'

Jack held onto Curtis's arm, 'I won't use any traps. But I am a very private man and I don't want any of *them* on my land. Perhaps, you could tell Jack Basset that I am using these things to catch the woolly-pig. Then he will leave me alone.'

'Yer wants me to tell folk that yoos is an evil and nasty bastard not to be buggered with?'

This was not quite how Jack would have put it. 'Yes.'

Curtis frowned and tapped his nose confidentially. He helped himself to one of the shovels and, with a neat thwack, sliced off part of a molehill, lifted it and dumped it into a ditch. Jack watched, amazed at the tiny old man's strength.

'Righty ho?'

Jack agreed and turned back to his machine. The ground was hard and cracked – yesterday's rain had been absorbed like milk into blotting paper and the earth was as dry as before. They could only dig a few inches at a time, scratching away layers of dried dirt. Curtis dug twice as fast, but it was still very slow. The wind was strong and whipped the mud flecks into their faces, so that soon Jack began to tire. He felt a hand on his shoulder.

'Here 'ave a nip,' said Curtis, drawing the flask from beneath his jacket.

Too tired to argue, Jack took a small sip. Instantly, he felt fiery strength burn along his veins. He seized the bucket and poured the contents over a patch of cleared green. Then, he filled up another and another, until, in half an hour, he had tipped fifty loads of water over the brown grass.

'With a little sun, it will be back to green in no time. May I show you the rest of the course?'

They walked slowly to the top of Bulbarrow. Before the war, the area had been wild scrub and yellow heath but it had been converted to grazing during the 'Dig for Britain Campaign', yet in the last couple of years the edges were reverting to gorse as the thicket took over once more. The land wasn't rich enough for crops; only sheep and sturdy Dorset cattle could graze on the spiky grass and thistles that grew there. The fields lay in a neat patchwork, the hedges at the corners like green embroidery holding them together. It was a peopled scene; the land bore the marks of a thousand years of cultivation. The last corn had been harvested, the stubble burnt and the land ploughed, ready to be replanted. From a distance, the brown furrowed fields looked like they had been combed. Groups of whitewashed cottages huddled together in villages, while beyond Hambledon a column of smoke spiralled upward from the orange flames of a bonfire.

Jack and Curtis climbed up Backhollow, a great crater cut into the hillside during the Middle Ages. Now it looked like a giant, semi-circular amphitheatre with grass seats in the hill; however, they weren't seats but grass shelves built to create more land for farming at a time when the population was beginning to starve. It had never been used. Instead, the

Black Death had come along killing half the peasants and Backhollow became the haunt of deer and ghosts.

Curtis paused for a moment halfway up the slope and pointed happily at a big, cream ball. 'Look, a giant puffball.' He gave the ball a kick and it exploded into dust that flew up into the air. ''Ee's a mushroom. Lovely on toast.'

Jack looked around and saw half a dozen of the things in the hollow. The largest were nearly a foot in diameter and looked like huge footballs growing up from the earth. He gave one a gentle nudge – it was soft and spongy; he prodded it a bit harder and it disappeared with a puff as billions of tiny dust particles blew into his face. He coughed and brushed them away as Curtis cackled with laughter.

'Them is spores,' he said, as Jack picked them out of his hair. 'An' if ivry spore in a giant puffball grew up to be another puffball, all tigether they 'ud be twice as big as earth 'imself.'

'That would be an awful lot of mushroom.'

Curtis picked up a small one, the size of a tennis ball, and handed it to him. This one didn't explode, but was firm and rubbery and smelled of earthy fungus.

Curtis snatched it back. 'Aye, well, we doesn't want to waste 'em.'

Jack noticed that Curtis appeared to have a duffle bag under his battered jacket. From the top of the bag sprouted a few feathers, which looked suspiciously like pheasant. Observing Jack's look, hurriedly he dropped the mushroom into the bag.

'It's a feather duster. I do my dustin' on a Tuesday. Always use a pheasant duster, gives a lovely sheen.'

Jack said nothing – after all, it was none of his business. He picked up another small puffball and handed it to Curtis, which the old man cheerfully popped into his bag.

'Nice mushroom supper.'

Every morning for the next month Jack found the older man waiting for him. Working side by side, they heaved the last of the molehills off the spoilt green and into the ditches, smoothed the hillocks as best they could and carefully watered the withering grass. Whenever he thought Jack wasn't looking, Curtis poured a precious drop from his hip flask into the water buckets for the green, confident that the grass needed nothing more than a nip of special brew – it was much more powerful than any of the fancy fertilisers his friend insisted on buying from London stores.

Curtis had the strength of a much younger man and together their progress was swift. Jack enjoyed the companionship; although, he tried to avoid the topic of the woolly-pig, worried that the only reason the old man had bestowed his friendship was in the mistaken belief that Jack shared his faith in the creature. The elderly farmer grumbled continually as he laboured. 'Why did you choose this effing field, yer ninnywally. Everywin knows that stones grows 'ere. Chuck one away and two grews to take his place. Buggerin' hell.'

Jack mounted a large calendar on the wall in his study. Every evening at dusk, he went into the room and crossed off another day from the calendar, shadowed by a sombre Curtis.

'Don't worry, Mister Rose-in-Bloom, we'll git him done.'

Jack shook his head – the cider fumes fading and the panic rising – and took the bottle of whisky from the cupboard. He poured himself a stiff drink and squirted a tiny drop of soda into the amber liquid. 'Whisky?' he asked Curtis who shook his head, preferring the flask in his pocket. Jack settled into his chair, Curtis choosing a low stool by the grate, stretching out his short legs and warming his bare toes in front of the flames. Jack switched on the wireless – it was time for Betjeman. The two men closed their eyes and listened. The voice described in nostalgic tones the joy of old buildings, thatched roofs, limewashed cottages, and how the strength of England lay in her wild woodlands and mud-caked walls.

'Aye. Aye,' murmured Curtis in agreement.

Jack was too exhausted to find his way up to bed and so, for the third time in a week, fell asleep in his chair in the study. He was vaguely aware that he'd not seen his wife for several days. He heard her in the garden and noticed that the larder remained stocked with bread and cheese for him to pillage for meals, but he was too busy with his golf course to worry himself with her. When the course was finally finished, and she could look out of her kitchen window on to the first tee to see players hitting balls in the sunshine, she would feel much better. He felt a little uncomfortable about the neglect of his wife but – as with all things that were unpleasant to him – he tried to think about something else. Whisky. He would have another whisky and then a little sleep.

A few hours later, Sadie threw the bedcovers off, too hot to sleep and realised she was alone yet again. The night air was sticky and the scent of the night flowers was sickly sweet. She reached for the bedside clock: midnight. With a yawn she climbed out of bed, put on her dressing gown and tiptoed downstairs, unwilling to disturb the darkness. She retrieved her box from the kitchen dresser and sat down at the table. The moon was so strong that she didn't need any other light in order to see the picture of her brother. Emil smiled up at her from the curled, brown print. His was a face that would never grow old.

Next she picked out a white linen towel, stiff with starch and with an embroidered rose in the right-hand corner. It was neatly ironed into folds and wrapped in tissue paper. Mutti had given it to her when she left for England, insistent that a lady always needed a clean towel. Sadie must be able to wash, be clean and nicely groomed; it showed one's respect for the adoptive country. English people were always clean and tidy and she needed to be the same (it was one of the few items on Jack's list that she agreed with). Sadie never could bring herself to use the towel and it remained pristine in the neat folds of her mother's ironing, still smelling of lavender soap and starch.

Sadie sighed and wondered whether she ought go back to bed but knew she wouldn't be able to sleep. Murmurs were coming from Jack in the study – he was so tired from digging, from trying to become one of them. She went to the window and gazed out across the night-time garden; it was growing bare now – the late summer flowers were dying and the ground cover crept back to expose the cold brown soil. Soon it would be winter and she would tuck up the plants in armfuls of straw and wait for spring. The flora would return, undamaged by death and a sojourn underneath the earth. She inhaled deeply, and breathed in the cinnamon perfume of her favourite rose.

Playing in the woods surrounding the Bavarian cabin, Sadie and Emil had discovered a baby vole underneath a dog rose. The vole was tiny, smaller than her pinkie, and almost hairless. She scooped it up in her pinafore, and laid it in a cardboard box, which they lined with handfuls of dry grass. They fed it with boiled cow's milk through a pipette borrowed from Emil's chemistry set. Sadie picked a flower from the dog rose, to place in its bed so the vole wouldn't be homesick, and Emil laid the box beside the stove. It died anyway. They held a little ceremony, Emil wearing Papa's *tallis* and *Yarmulke* and reciting from Grandpa Landau's prayer book, while Sadie read the dormouse passage from *Alice in Wonderland* (they didn't know any stories about voles and hoped the vole-ghost would understand). Finally they wrapped the tiny corpse in a napkin and buried it beneath the dog rose.

In her Dorset garden, Sadie thought of Emil and Mutti and Papa and school holidays, while she breathed the scent of the flowers and let the weeds flourish. She removed the last item

138

from the box: Mutti's cookery book. She had not touched it since the day she glimpsed Mutti in the pond. Opening the worn pages, she noticed cooking spatters from long ago and imagined Mutti bustling in her Berlin kitchen, pans bubbling. Once, Sadie tried writing down her memories, attempting to preserve them in a nice book to pass on to her daughter but it did not work. The meaning kept disappearing in the spaces between the words, and her story as written was never quite how she remembered it. Now Sadie wondered whether it would be better for her to cook her way home to them. Perhaps she would find them in the smell of slowly simmering *cholent* or cinnamon *rugula*.

Sadie's mother was a great cook and had ordered her life entirely round meals, keeping time via the contents of her larder. Mutti knew it was tomorrow when the big loaf of bread she baked yesterday was going hard. It was summer when Sadie brought her the first plate of rose petals ready to be iced in order to bejewel her lemon rose cake and autumn was gooseberry fool, or a big round summer pudding, oozing with blackberries, strawberries and the last of the blackcurrants. For Mutti there were no hours of the day, only meals: breakfast, lunch, tea and supper. Things were either before breakfast, after lunch or between tea and supper. A time like three o'clock meant nothing – it was instead that space shortly before apple strudel and freshly boiled peppermint tea. Then there were the recipes themselves that fitted into neat categories: the conventional ones like 'dishes so that you can tell it is summer', 'meals for times that are cold and wintry', but there were others like 'biscuits for when one is sad', or 'buns for heartbreak'.

Sadie stroked the battered volume. The spine was coming away and the cloth cover loose, and she glanced through the index, neatly inscribed in her mother's curling hand and smudged with mixtures from a hundred mealtimes, until she found the one she wanted: 'Baumtorte' – part of a category called 'cakes to help you remember'. Unlike Jack, Sadie preferred German to English because she liked the literal meanings of the words; they were put together like tidy building blocks and felt good in her mouth as she said them. 'Baumtorte' was a good word, meaning tree (Baum) cake (Torte), since it is made of layers like the rings of a tree. Sadie, like her mother and grandmother before her, had baked a Baumtorte whenever she needed to remember. She'd baked a cake after Jack kissed her for the first time that December night, another when he proposed (in a noisy train carriage on the way back from Frankfurt, so that she couldn't hear him and he had to repeat himself), another when they were stripped of German citizenship and one more after Elizabeth was born. She made the last one with Mutti on the day they received their exit visas. They'd asked for six (Jack, Sadie, Elizabeth, Mutti, Papa and Emil) but there were only three. They hadn't cried – they'd baked a Baumtorte.

Sadie read out the recipe, 'Whip together a batter made of eggs, the right amount of sugar, sufficient flour and the perfect quantity of vanilla'.

The quantities were never more precise than that – she had to know the correct amount in her heart before she began. 'Oil a tin and heat up the grill, spread a thin layer over the bottom of the pan and grill until it is done.'

More and more layers would be ladled on and then grilled until the side of the cake looked like the rings of a tree. Sadie first baked the cake as a young girl. It had been thin as there were not so many memories to record in the layers. She glanced at the clock on the kitchen wall – nearly one o'clock – time to bake another Baumtorte. She would bake a layer for everyone she needed to remember.

She went into her larder and counted out three-dozen eggs from a large metal basket dangling on an iron nail. She had started to keep chickens as their shit was good for her beloved plants; they were as good layers as they were shitters and, having no friends to give the eggs to, she stored them in the cool of her larder.

'A vanilla pod.'

She had just one and it had travelled with her all the way from London. She bought it in the days before the war and kept it all those years and, upon giving it a sniff, happily discovered that it had not lost its scent. A mountain of butter given to her by Curtis rested under a tea cloth; she did not ask whose cows it had come from. There was a sack of flour from the mill and a large enamel flask filled with milk, which would be useful if she needed to loosen the batter – all she wanted now was a basin big enough to mix the ingredients. None of the kitchen pots was sufficiently large and then she remembered the tin bath that was in the house when they first arrived; she would give that a good wash.

Still clad in her pink floral dressing gown, she began to whip up the batter. She did not weigh any of the ingredients, trusting her instincts. She mixed them in the echoing bath; at first she used a wooden spoon but finding it too small, she carefully washed her feet with soap, dried them on a clean towel, hitched up her dressing gown and climbed into the bath to stir the batter with her feet. She found the widest cake tins in the cupboard and put layer after layer of the oozing mixture under the grill, and when each tin was completely full, carefully removed the cake inside and smothered it in a layer of sharp lemon icing. Each cake was placed on top of another and then another until, when dawn came, there was a cake towering many feet high with a thousand layers of rings; every layer holding a memory.

Sadie fell asleep on the kitchen floor, still holding her spatula. When Jack rose half an hour later, he did not see her lying hidden in the shadow of the kitchen range; helping himself to a glass of milk, he disappeared into the field to carry on digging. While Sadie slept, the smell from her baking drifted out into the lane where several women from the village were walking. Jack was not the only person in the village counting down the days until the coronation; the women had formed a Coronation Committee and were busy pinning posters to trees along the lane, when the scent of baking overwhelmed them. It had a strange smell, not merely dough or sugar but the fragrance of unbearable sadness.

'We should ask Mrs Rose-in-bloom to join us,' murmured Lavender. She had not thought of the plump women with the German accent since the day of the fair, but knew somehow that the baking was hers. 'We always need good bakers.'

The women followed the smell along the driveway leading to Chantry Orchard, like several middle-aged Gretels searching for the gingerbread house in the wood. The kitchen door was open, and they saw Sadie stretched out on the floor, still fast asleep. On the table above her stood the Baumtorte. It was as tall as Curtis, and the women stared, uncertain.

'Should we wake her?' asked Myrtle Hinton, a portly woman with greying hair, tied back with a scrap of yellow ribbon.

'Well, we can't be leaving her sleeping 'ere. Poor soul will catch cold,' tutted Lavender. She wondered what could make a middle-aged woman bake through the night and sleep on a stone floor. Mrs Hinton napped on the barn floor when her sow was a piggin' – but that was different.

Mrs Hinton gently shook Sadie awake, 'Mrs Rose-in-bloom?'

Sadie opened her eyes, alarmed to find her kitchen full of women.

'We are the Coronation Committee. Would you join us for a meetin' in the village hall?' asked Lavender primly.

Bleary eyed, Sadie nodded. 'I must dress.'

'No, dear. It's only us. Put on a housecoat.'

Sadie shrugged and buttoned up her dressing gown. She glanced at the Baumtorte – it was a thing of magnificence; she had used the juice of three precious lemons for the icing. If it were a tree, it would be hundreds of years old – a cake like this should be shared.

'Help me carry the Baumtorte,' she said.

As though part of a stately parade, the women filed to the village hall. Several others were already waiting for them, busily setting out chairs and handing round sheets of paper, but they all paused to watch the procession of the Baumtorte. They placed it on a table at the front of the hall while they discussed the day's business. Lavender chaired the meeting with unquestioned authority. Sadie tried to feign polite interest – it was all very pleasant but she wondered what these things had to do with her. Lavender cleared her throat and opened an envelope.

'Now, I've been requestin' suggestions from all residents. I have only had a few suggestions, and only one that I am able to read in polite company. It is from Mr Jack Rose-in-Bloom. He wishes to propose a game of golf to be played at 'is new course in honour of Her Majesty.'

Sadie looked up in astonishment; Jack had not confided his plans to her. Lavender appealed to her but Sadie shook her head, embarrassed.

'I know nothing at all. My husband tells me nothing.'

Lavender smiled – Mr Basset never told her anything either. It seemed men were all the same – English or foreign. 'Well, if there are no objections, perhaps Mrs Rose-in-Bloom would be good enough to tell Mr Rose-in-Bloom that the Coronation Committee approves the match.'

It was time for tea and Sadie went to her Baumtorte, which rested on a makeshift table, bowing under its weight. She cut slices for each of them with a huge knife – the thinnest that she could manage. The women ate, and it was the most remarkable cake that they had ever tasted. It was sweet and perfectly moist with a hint of lemon but, as her mouth filled with deliciousness, each woman was overwhelmed with sadness. Each tasted Sadie's memories, her loss and unhappiness and whilst they ate, Sadie was, for once, not alone in her sorrow.

CHAPTER TWELVE

J ACK WAS TOO preoccupied with his golf course to notice the unusual behaviour of his wife. Parading towering cakes through the village on a Wednesday afternoon while wearing rose-patterned slippers was not blending in, but Jack was driven by his obsession and was therefore spared the bother of being embarrassed.

Jack and Curtis restored the opening hole on the golf course; it was more battered than before and the grass still needed time to recover, but the damage had been repaired. Jack checked the post each day for a letter from Bobby Jones, eager to hear from his hero. There was none, just an ever-growing pile of anxious letters from Fielding at the factory.

Dear Mr Rosenblum,

I have nothing good to report. I'm very concerned about the looms. The machines are getting old and finicky (much like my missus, if I'm allowed my little joke). Soon one is going to break down beyond repair. The emergency funds are almost empty – please wire more cash.

When are you coming back?

Yours truly,
George Fielding

Jack did not reply. He was reluctant to wire money to the factory – he needed every farthing for the course. Surely the looms would be fine for another season or two? They could sausage through. He felt a pang of guilt at his neglect of business, but he had room for nothing in his mind except the golf course, and the possibility of a letter from Bobby Jones.

He knew it was too soon to expect a reply from America but still he hoped. That afternoon he confided his disappointment to Curtis.

'He might be a busy man, but I am in serious want of advice.'

Curtis paused for a long moment leaning on his spade and looked up at the sky. A dragonfly hummed as it skimmed the pond. He liked being asked for advice; when it was requested one was duty bound to give an opinion, whether or not one knew anything on the subject. He swallowed, rubbed his nose and folded his arms behind his back.

'Tis my 'pinon that tis time to write him another letter. Tis always the danger that Mister Jones were not in receipt of yer first epistle. Besides 'ee might like gitting letters.'

Jack stopped digging and gazed at his friend – this was something he had not considered. He always told his employees that persistence and determination were the most important rules in business and yet here he was, hesitating, when he ought to be tenacious.

'You're quite right, my friend. Very right, indeed. I'll write to Mr Jones tonight and then, I think, I'll write each week to tell him of our progress.'

Curtis smiled, revealing a set of surprisingly strong white teeth. 'Tis an excellent idea. Only good will come of it.'

That evening the friends tripped into Jack's study to cross off the day's work and settle down to write to Bobby Jones. There was no sign of Sadie, but she had left out an apple strudel, which Curtis munched as he helped Jack compose the letter.

Dear Mr Jones,

*I am not sure if you received my last letter, so I
thought I had better write you another one, just in case.
I am building a golf course in Dorsetshire with the
assistance of my good friend Mr*

Here Jack paused, realising he only knew Curtis's first name.
'Mr Curtis? Is that correct?'

'Aye, well, Curtis Butterworth,' the old man replied,
through a mouthful of apple and pastry.

*Mr Curtis Butterworth. We have completed the first
hole, using Old Tom Morris's map of St Andrews
as a model. We do not have the sea to make this a
true links course but we do have the advantage of an
excellent dew pond. I had hoped to have the benefit
of your advice before proceeding much further, but
my course must be finished in time for Her Majesty
Queen Elizabeth's Coronation on 2 June next year, so I
am trusting that you have not taken offence that I was
compelled*

He stopped again, 'compelled or forced?'

'Forced,' said Curtis, ''s more forceful.'

'Yes. Good.'

*I was forced to commence without the benefit of your
inspirational wisdom. Here is a drawing of our first
hole. It is a little hilly, but I hope that will merely add to
the challenge. We are proceeding at a pace*

'Tell 'im 'bout the trouble with the woolly-pig,' interrupted
Curtis excitedly.

'Are you sure? I want to seem professional.'

''Tis an unusual difficulty, but twould be a lie not ta even mention it,' said Curtis directing a hard stare at his friend.

Jack sighed. He could not risk the old man discovering he did not believe in the woolly-pig – let Bobby Jones think him a little crazy, it could not be helped.

> *and despite tremendous difficulties with a vicious woolly-pig that wreaked havoc and destruction, we are now doing well. Please write back very soon with your recommendations, even though you are a very busy man.*
>
> *With regards,*
> *Your humble servant,*
> *Jack M. Rosenblum*

Jack folded up the letter and put it into its envelope, already addressed and waiting. He poured a whisky and settled back into his chair. The two men sat for a moment sharing a contented silence. 'If only we had more men to help. We are three times as fast with the two of us,' remarked Jack.

'Aye. Tis a right shame.'

The next day Jack went down to the field at daybreak. The air was cool and the first of the blackberries were covered in thick dew. A noisy wood pigeon called to him from the orchard as he staggered under the weight of his tools. He glanced about for Curtis but unable to see him, decided to start alone. As he reached for his spade, he heard a voice.

'Mister Rose-in-Bloom, come, come!'

Curtis stood on top of a rise pointing towards the road. Jack scrambled up beside him and squinted into the distance. Coming up the lane through the early morning mist was a giant combine harvester. It was bright red, with glinting teeth like a colossal mechanical dragon. Jack had never seen such an immense piece of machinery in the British countryside, and amongst the hedged lanes and hedgerows it appeared to be a creature of the apocalypse.

'That's 'im. 'Eard 'ee was comin',' said Curtis sagely, ''Ee's from America.'

Jack frowned. 'It won't fit through the gate. Too narrow.'

'Nope. They will rip out all them 'edges. All of 'em, so 'ee can plough the whole side of Bulbarrow.'

Jack shuddered; it sounded barbaric.

'You isn't thinking. Use yer noggin,' said Curtis, tapping his head with a grubby forefinger. ''Alf the tennants in Pursebury will be put out to grass.'

Jack sighed. It was a sad world when men could be put out of work by a machine. Yet, such was civilisation and progress. 'Where will they be?'

'Pub.'

Curtis insisted on taking the short route cutting through the maize field. The towering plants dwarfed both men and instantly Jack became disorientated. He could only glimpse the blue sky above his head and the tall green plants growing densely on every side. Curtis called, 'This way, Rose-in-Bloom!' and Jack fought through the towering foliage frantically trying to follow the sound of his voice. He thought of Livingstone lost in the African jungle, suffering from green blindness, and started to panic. It would be terrible to be missing for ever in a maize field not half a mile from one's armchair. He took a deep breath and prepared to scream, but a moment later emerged in the lane in front of The Crown.

It was early in the morning, yet the pub was already full. There was a hum of agitation as men in work clothes gathered at the bar talking in hushed voices. No one looked up when Jack came in, but then he no longer looked different from the others, dressed as he was in mud-spattered trousers and stained sun hat. Curtis coughed and clapped his hands.

Everyone ignored him. So, he clambered upon a bench by the bar and threw his hat on the ground.

'Mister Rose-in-Bloom wishes ter offer any of yer put out by the arrival of the beast from Hamerica gainful employment.'

The men turned to look at Jack with tired faces.

''He'll 'ave to join the queue.'

Jack noticed two men seated by the bar. They were about thirty years old and clad in grey flannel suits. A pair of cheap trilby hats rested on the counter, and the men were not drinking. He grimaced; he had learned not to trust chaps who refused a tipple in pubs. One of the men, a fellow with sandy blond hair and a wisp of a moustache, turned and gave him a thin smile.

'Good morning. I represent Wilson's Housing Corporation. If you are in need of a job, I'll take you on at five pound a week for general building.'

Jack frowned. 'What are you building?'

'Bungalows. We have permission for forty in the water meadows at the edge of the village. Want them up sharpish. Hence the most generous wages.'

Jack's frown deepened into a scowl. He did not like this young man, nor did he like bungalows being built on ancient water meadows. He knew people needed somewhere to live, but he could not understand why they did not put plumbing in the old cottages or rebuild the ones that had tumbled down at the bottom of the lane.

'Five pounds?'

'Yes. But you'll have to prove you can work a full day. No offence, but you're not in the first flush of youth. And since you're not English, we'll put you on probation for a few weeks. Just to make sure you don't slack.'

His companion sneered. 'Lazy foreign bastards. All the same. Just remember. We. Won. The. Bleeding. War.'

Jack reddened with rage; he had not been this angry since

they mutilated his golf course. His eyes glittering with fury he glanced round the room. Curtis moved in closer to stand beside him, lips drawn back into a silent snarl.

'Well,' said Jack, trying to control the furious tremor in his voice, 'this young man will pay you five pounds. I'll pay you five pounds and ten shillings.'

The farmers in the bar looked at Jack in surprise. Hunched miserably in the corner, Jack Basset stiffened; he did not speak but stared at the other Jack. The blond man in the suit was taken aback by the unexpected competition. Wordlessly, his companion wrote a note and slid it across the bar. The fair-haired man glanced at it.

'We'll pay five pounds twelve and sixpence.'

Jack swallowed. He did not know how on earth he was going to pay them this much but he had to win.

'Five pounds and fifteen shillings,' he whispered.

The thin man stood up. His companion was desperate to up their offer but he put a hand on his arm to restrain him; they had no authorisation to go higher. He snatched his hat from the bar, and addressed the room.

'Fine. But remember you'll have to work for a shitty little Kraut. When he goes broke and you come crawling back to us, we'll only pay you four pound a week and not a farthing more.'

They left, crashing the heavy wooden door behind them and Jack sat down in shock, scarcely aware that Basset was buying him a drink. He trembled as he considered the consequences of what he had just done – he would need to take out a loan to cover the cost of the wages. And use the carpet factory as collateral – he couldn't possibly wire money to Fielding now. He grasped the glass in front of him and, barely conscious of what he was doing, drained the contents. He cursed himself for getting overwrought, 'I'm a *Dumpfbeutel*. Oh yes. Emotion is always bad in these situations – it never ends well.'

'What?' Basset motioned for Stan behind the bar to pour Jack another drink.

Jack drank and as the liquid warmed his gullet he gained in confidence. He took Basset's hand and shook it warmly.

'It is a good day. You're very right,' forgetting that Basset had not actually spoken. 'With all you splendid fellows, I'll actually finish the golf course. For sure I will. For sure. '

He toyed with his empty glass. 'I built up the carpet business from nothing, everyone said I was a *meshuggenah hund* but I proved them all wrong.'

Twenty men had been put out of work by the great machine. Jack learned from Curtis that Basset and the others were only tenant farmers, permitted to work the land in return for hefty rents. Curtis drew his friend a map of Bulbarrow in the dirt to show how the valley of little dairies was changing.

'Them big farms, now they 'as got themselves beasts from Hamerica, they wants all the land back. All the little farms is bein' gobbled up by the big 'uns.'

Curtis kicked away a piece of flowering nettle that was standing in for a field boundary.

'Yer see? Them giant machines can plough whole o' the buggerin' hill in a single day.'

Jack agreed sadly and absent-mindedly began to nibble on a strand of wild mint, which he'd been keeping in his pocket in case he felt snackish.

'It's a new era, Curtis. Britain and her hedgerows must make way for progress. I don't like it. I don't like it all.'

Jack wrote a careful list of the men he was hiring and added them to the payroll of the London factory. It was cripplingly expensive and Fielding was irate, penning Jack a furious letter, which he scanned guiltily and shoved in the back of his desk. The bank agreed to a loan, but he had made none of the investments he ought to have over the last few months and the quarterly profit was down. He was concerned, more for those who relied on him for their wages than for himself, but he signed the loan papers nonetheless, sent them back to the bank and tried not to think of them again.

The rate of progress on the course rapidly increased. These countrymen had worked on the land all their lives, and understood the quirks of soil and scrub. Basset informed Jack that the marsh at the bottom of the course could not be drained – the soil was clay and there was nowhere for the water to run. For the first time Jack had an expert onsite; Jack Basset's brother, Mike, had actually played a round of golf whilst on holiday in Margate. Jack and Curtis listened to him attentively. He advised them on the placing of the hazards and that a stream cutting the green in two was highly unusual. He also persuaded Jack that nine holes would be ample – 'Players who wants eighteen 'oles can jist go round again, like.' Jack agreed to this solution with relief.

Yet, something had shifted within Jack and he no longer dreamt of demolishing the side of Bulbarrow Hill in order to mirror the Old Course. The slow beauty of the country had crept upon him, and he wanted his course to be defined by the rise and fall of the landscape. Mike was adamant that the greens ought to have a less acute angle. A flat surface was impossible – Jack's land consisted entirely of the south face of Bulbarrow Hill. Jack listened to the men, and learned to listen to the landscape, until it seemed to whisper the direction they should go, and the positions of the holes. He did not want to dig too deep and disturb the ridges of the hill; it was best to go around them, let the edges of the mounds and ditches define the rough. He felt time as he dug and raked with his men: the soil was millennia old and held countless lives and deaths – things born or budded, died and rotted.

At midday the men disappeared home for a hot dinner and returned at two o'clock, ready to work again. Whilst they laboured in the afternoon, Jack drew Robert Hunter from his pocket, sat down on a Mackintosh square and read to them from *The Links*.

> 'The true links were moulded by divine hands. Links-land, the fine grasses, the wind-made bunkers that defy imitation, the exquisite contours that refuse to be sculpted by hand – all these were given lavishly by a divine dispensation to the British. With wind and wave, with marram-grass and river's tide, the Great Creator moulded the links of Britain.'

He was soon overwhelmed by his enthusiasm. 'You see, you see? This is why Britain is Great. God gave you the best golfing land in the whole of the world. It's providence.'

He reached into his pocket and wiped his eyes with his once white monogrammed handkerchief.

'Before Robert Hunter very little had been written on the art of golf course construction. It is a very *elusive* subject. I would like to share with you, my friends, the rules I have devised from his methods:

'Number one: Select well-drained, slightly rolling land.

'Two. Avoid clay soil.

'Three. Do not go into hilly country at any cost.

'Four. Shun also that country broken by streams and ponds. They are most objectionable.'

At the end of this little speech Jack coughed. 'I am aware that perhaps, according to some, the land here on Bulbarrow does not quite conform to Mr Hunter's recommendations, but sometimes the most beautiful things are created in the most unusual places. Think of a pearl found in the belly of a fish.'

'Aye. An' I once found a nest o' blue robins' eggs in middle of a dung heap,' added Curtis, jumping up in a single bound in his enthusiasm. 'Lil' spicketty eggs in a steamin' pile o' chicken shit. Lovely they wis.'

Jack grinned. 'You thieved the words from my mouth, my friend.'

The men listened to Jack, intrigued by his passion and energy. Here was a man who disobeyed the rules he himself devised; his golf course was in the worst possible site and had every known drawback. Yet, he believed in it nonetheless and had absolute faith in their ability to produce a modern-day miracle.

At the end of three weeks two holes were complete. The days became shorter, like a tree-trunk steadily shaved and sanded by a meticulous carpenter, and at dusk the men slipped home to supper by their fires leaving Jack and Curtis alone. The two friends sat on a bank at the top of the hill and surveyed the landscape – the seasons were on the cusp. It was early October, two weeks earlier and the girls were still in summer dresses walking down the lane, and in two weeks' time the leaves on the flowering plum tree would curl and fall to the ground in purple shades. The air was cold and Jack gave a shiver. He was worried; every Friday he paid the men but he did not pay Curtis, and they had been working on the course together for so long that he did not know how to broach the topic.

'My friend, I do not wish to insult you. But I would like to compensate you for your hard labours.'

Curtis wrinkled his face in displeasure. 'Friends durst pay.'

'Friends also do not take advantage of one another. That is not friendship.'

The old man continued to scowl but Jack knew he was right, and refused to be swayed.

'Let me give you a gift then. Choose something of mine, anything at all.'

Curtis shrugged; he was not hungry or cold and therefore was quite content. Putting an end to the discussion, he got to his feet and started to walk down the hill. Jack followed, always a few paces behind. They passed the two neat flags wavering in the evening air and reached the marshes at the bottom of the valley. All of a sudden, there was a flash of light, and a ball of fire hovered above the bog. A grey goose gave a low shriek in surprise and flew up into the sky in a flurry of wings.

'A will-o-the-wisp!' Curtis gasped in excitement.

The ball of light drifted in the air, weaving between the tall reeds. The water looked as though it had caught fire, and the flaming reflection trembled on the surface. Jack watched in awe as the wisp singed the tall reeds and he remembered Moses and the burning bush. Then, it flickered, and was gone.

The two men retreated to Jack's study, where he set about his weekly letter to Bobby Jones. It was an unusual predicament for Jack, to write letters without knowing if they would ever be read or answered but it was also strangely liberating, and he found that he confided all his fears to the legendary golfer.

Dear Mr Jones,

    It has been a long week. I confess that I am worried we will never finish in time. Winter will come and turn the fairways to mud and we will be able to dig no more in the fierce frosts. I am also running out of money. This is a secret. Even my wife does not know how little we have left. I must finish by spring.

    This evening I saw a will-o-the-wisp. I knew it to be nothing but a ball of phosphorescent light but I wanted it to be magical, or mystical. Wouldn't you like to live in such a world, Mr Jones? A world of magic instead of concrete and bungalows?

Regards,
Your humble servant,
Jack M. Rosenblum

Curtis sat quietly while his friend wrote. He waited until Jack sealed up the letter, and had placed it carefully inside his jacket pocket.

'I can have anything?'

'Yes, of course.'

'I'd like 'im,' said Curtis pointing to Jack's gold watch lying discarded on the bookcase, the strap dangling over the spine of *The Woodlanders*. Jack had taken it off the first week he arrived in the West Country and had not used it since. It was half hidden under a mounting stash of bills and papers but still glinted in the twilight. He pulled out the old timepiece and pressed it into his friend's hands.

'Please. I would be honoured. It is yours.'

Reverently, Curtis slipped it into his pocket. ''S excellent. Won't be late no more. Time keepin's very important.'

CHAPTER THIRTEEN

SADIE WAS BUSY cooking her way through the recipes in her mother's book, and the house became filled with scents of her childhood. Sometimes, she took her baking down to the village hall for the women to eat. Each time she ventured into the wood-panelled room Lavender Basset tried to persuade her to stay, 'Come an' have a nice cup o' tea wi' us, Mrs Rose-in-Bloom. Her Majesty's Coronation Committee could do with an outstanding baker like yerself.'

Sadie set down her tray of almond macaroons or cherry and coconut pyramids on the trestle table and shook her head, avoiding the eyes of the smiling women.

'Very kind, Mrs Basset. Much obliged, I'm sure. But I can't stay.'

Sadie wouldn't be tempted into eating a morsel but hurried away, as soon as she could be sure she wouldn't cause offence. Walking back to the house, listening to the laughing of the larks as they took flight, she thought of her London friends – Freida and the others at the synagogue. It was strange, but she did not really miss them. Once a week she telephoned Freida from the red call box outside The Crown, but the conversations were always rather unsatisfactory. Freida prattled with gossip about Bernie Solomons' bad leg (rumoured to be housemaid's knee, his wife worked all day in the fishmonger's and Bernie was suspected of keeping house), the difficulty in getting kosher eggs or enough branches for the *Sukkah*. When she'd finished, Freida paused expectantly for Sadie to chatter, before prompting her with, 'your turn friend, what's new?'

Sadie sighed. There was nothing new. There were only the rhythms of sun, rain and falling leaves. She could hear the murmur of cheerful conversation drifting up the lane from the village hall. For a moment, she wished she could have said yes, she would like a cup of tea and have sat and sipped and listened. But she always said no, and couldn't possibly join them now. She picked up her pace, and hurried home.

The Coronation Committee only met on a Wednesday, so the rest of the time she left cakes, biscuits and loaves of honey-coloured bread out on the table in the kitchen and forgot about them. After a taste, enough to fill her mouth and remind her of the texture of lavender and rosewater cream-filled buns, they lay abandoned on the wooden table.

Jack and Curtis, passing through the kitchen on their way to the study, presumed that the offerings laid out were for them and ate hungrily. Jack took them as signs from his wife, small gestures of conciliation. He did not realise that this new burst of cooking was another act of remembrance and took the vanilla crescents, the sand cakes and *Pfefferkuchen* as tokens of a well-concealed affection. He suspected that in some wordless way she understood he was in a spot of bother – being nearly out of money – and that these sweetmeats were a silent symbol of companionship. They barely met, passing as shadows, but he felt for the first time since that day a softening in his wife. He bit into a slice of Stollen, rich with a thick seam of marzipan, and was returned to the tiny flat by the *Zoologischer Garten* in Berlin. As he ate, he heard the howling of wolves from the zoo at dusk, and remembered the smooth roundness of his new wife. There was a time, long ago, when he loved her every day. When the course was finished, he would sit in her garden and ask her the names of the flowers.

As a consequence of the cakes, Jack started to sleep in the bedroom once more. Also, it was getting colder at night and

159

he liked the warm body of his wife; sleeping in his chair he woke in the small hours, shivering in the dark. This morning he tried not to disturb her as he slipped out of bed in the creeping dawn. He opened the curtains a crack so that he could see to dress, and a cool light poured into the bedroom.

Sadie was only feigning sleep, she rarely slept for more than a few hours: her nights were haunted by people who had lost their names, and who rifled through her dreams trying to find them. From the bed she could see across the valley and the water lapping the edge of the garden. Just then, she noticed that the ducks were leaving the pond – there were clouds of them circling high in the sky.

'Jack. The ducks are leaving.'

They were the first words she had spoken to him in several days and, realising this, he put on his spectacles and stared out the window at the dark shapes moving smoothly into the distance. The air filled with the sound of quacking, striking a melancholy note in the morning stillness. Jack shuddered; he hesitated and then, uncertainly, placed his arm around Sadie. In a minute the ducks were gone and the pond lay empty, its surface rippled only by the fish gliding underneath the surface. They were bereft.

'Come, I'll make tea,' said Jack, feeling that this would mark the sorrow of the occasion.

After breakfast, Jack decided to light the fire in his study, and with meticulous care cleared away the piles of maps and books lying near to the grate – it would be a disaster if Robert Hunter or Old Tom Morris went up in flames. There was rustling behind him as Sadie rumpled the papers on his desk. He gave a tiny sigh – a man's study was his own. She scrutinised the calendar on the wall above him.

'What day is it?'

Jack peered at the date. Why was she asking him? The woman had eyes of her own. 'Twenty-second of September.'

'*Nein, du Mistkerl*. In the Hebrew calendar.'

Jack shrugged. 'How would I know?'

He was now late – Curtis and the men would be waiting for him in the field and he did not like them to start without him, but Sadie was not to be dissuaded. She went over to the bookcase, pulled out a tattered Hebrew almanac and flicked through the pages.

'I've forgotten. How could I forget?' Sadie raised her eyes to the heavens and muttered an apologetic prayer.

Jack continued to look at her blankly.

'It's Rosh Hashanah, Jewish New Year, the Day of Judgement, the Day of Remembrance . . .' she snapped.

'Yes? And what does it have to do with me?'

Two pink spots appeared on Sadie's cheeks and her eyes flashed with anger. 'Go. Go to your fields and your new friends, then. I'll say *Kaddish* for the dead. I am sure they'll understand.'

Jack stood up sharply, took one last look at the curling tongues of flame in the grate, and retreated into the kitchen. Lying on the table were the fruits of Sadie's sleepless night: a platted loaf of *challah*, studded with currants, sprinkled with cinnamon and warm from the oven, with a jar of honey resting beside it. He studied the bread on the cooling wire, and considered his wife. One. She scolded him. Two. She was stubborn and indifferent to happiness. Three. She baked for him during the night, making all the treats and sweets he recalled from those brief months in Berlin – they were happy then, ignorant of what was to come. Elizabeth was conceived there, in that tiny flat with its glimpse of the stone elephants outside the park, and Sadie had laughed and been kind to him. Jack picked up the *challah*, tore off a piece, dipped it in the honey and popped it into his mouth. He chewed pensively, took another bite and then another. In ten minutes the entire loaf was gone. Wiping the crumbs from his mouth, he returned to the study.

'I'll sit with you,' he informed her with a puff of resignation.

Sadie's lips flickered into an almost smile. She liked the ritual of Rosh Hashanah and liked to think of all the other Jews, busy with their own recollections; it was a rite of shared sorrow, *The Day of Remembrance*. Most days, she thought about *before* alone, in silence, but this was a whole day dedicated to remembering. She thought back to the final Rosh Hashanah in Berlin, the last with her family. Back then, she had not known that soon she would be saying *Kaddish* for them. She was young in those days, a mere girl – she had been late to synagogue, arriving in a flushed hurry of joy, and apologised to the disapproving women as she squeezed her way through the tightly packed chairs to Mutti, who scolded her for her tardiness on *today of all days*. Sadie claimed it was because she couldn't find her coat but this was a lie. She was late really because her new husband had persuaded her back to bed to make love. He kissed the backs of her knees and the inside of her wrists, and had tugged her laughing onto the small wooden bed. She did not know that day, but Elizabeth began to grow in her belly. Perhaps that was why she became so unhappy, because she conceived on the Day of Remembrance. The dead that she was too busy to remember grew alongside the child in her womb and, long after she gave birth to her daughter, wormed their way into her conscious, insisting that she say *Kaddish* for them every day. Once, she had confided this thought to Jack and he became angry.

'Life, that is the most precious thing! Life. It takes the place of death. Wedding has precedent over a funeral. I choose joy over this pointless sorrow.'

The *shofar* blowing was Sadie's favourite part of New Year: the eerie note of the hollow ram's horn calling through the centuries. It sang of the symmetry of time and was one constant in an ever-changing world. She listened to the *shofar* with her family and later, in England, she would close her eyes and pretend she was a girl again. She knew the *shofar* was the same for her grandparents, her great-grandparents and for King Solomon in the Temple.

'Let us go and cast away our sins into the river.'

Jack perked up; he had abandoned any thoughts of working with the others on the third hole today. While he was dubious about the prospect of ditching his sins into a body of water, it meant going outside and quietly checking on the course. Curtis and Mike would be in charge; they were smoothing the tee and shaping the bunkers but some determined rabbits were continually disrupting progress.

Together, they walked down towards the dew pond at the bottom of the large field. The small duck pool by the house was rejected, as Sadie was insistent that the water must contain fish.

'A fish's need for water symbolises the Jew's need for God and, as a fish's eyes never close so His watchful eyes never cease.'

'Well, there are bloody great fishes in the dew pond and the stream. Curtis saw a pike,' added Jack, not awed by his wife's reverent tones.

It was a damp morning, the clouds hovered low in the sky, and the air smelled moist and earthy. Jackdaws circled, cawing overhead in the trees and leaves lay in mushy piles that squelched as they trod. Jack peered up towards the third hole where he could see several men digging and Basset leading two great carthorses down the steep slope. They lumbered unsteadily, their huge hooves trying to grip the slippery ground, until they reached the flat area of mud that was to be the green for the third hole. Jack paused and watched with interest as two men hitched the horses to a pair of stone rollers.

He was reassured that they were managing spectacularly

without him, despite wishing that he could climb up to admire the progress. Basset had promised he would bring the horses to level the ground before they put down turf. The horses were old, but Basset kept them in a rare gesture of sentiment, even though he claimed they were merely a back-up in case a tractor broke down. They were bred from a mare belonging to Basset's grandfather, and Jack supposed the old farmer liked to think of the line carrying on. The horses were enjoying their brief respite from retirement, and steadily pulled the massive roller across the muddy ground.

A few more weeks at this pace and Jack would have another hole done. There was a chance, if the winter was not a cold one, that he would have all nine holes completed by spring. He uttered a little prayer to heaven.

'Listen, please don't be offended that I don't really believe in you. But, just in case, I would be most obliged if you could make this winter a mild one. I'd very much like to finish my course. Otherwise, there is a very good chance that I'm finished – *fertig*. And, if you really are there, I am sure you don't want that. There is enough unhappiness.'

He was not sure whether this was the right tone for a prayer – it had been quite a while since he last addressed God. He thought as a concession that perhaps he ought to cast off a few sins. If the slate was clean, God might be more inclined to favour his request.

The grass was vivid green under the blackening sky; rain began to drizzle and a fine mist slowly rolled into the valley below, obscuring Jack's view. He helped Sadie climb over the stream to reach the dew pond.

'Are you sure there are fish?'

'Quite certain.'

'Then empty your pockets.'

'That's all?'

'Yes. And feel contrite.'

Obediently, Jack emptied his pockets. There were several crumbs, a piece of string, a receipt for straw and a bag of humbugs. He tried his best to be contrite, but it was hard because he always tried not to dwell on regrets, although he did regret the paper bag of humbugs that was slowly sinking to the bottom of the pond. He watched Sadie, her eyes closed and her lips moving in prayer as she turned her pockets inside out and flapped them over the water.

'Hey, there's nothing in them. They're already empty,' he objected.

She opened her eyes and stared at him.

'Of course I emptied them first. I don't want to actually throw anything away. You cast away your sins *metaphorically*.'

'Oh.'

Now Jack really did regret the loss of his humbugs – they were still on ration.

'Say *Kaddish* with me, Jack.'

He sighed, but he supposed, as the English say – in for a penny in for a pound. Round his neck he wore his battered sun hat on a string – it would have to do for a *Yarmulke*. He placed it on his head and started to sing, his voice mingling with the cries of the birds and the falling rain. Yet, there was a strange sort of harmony to the sound. The wind shook the branches of the willow tree above their heads making tiny drops of water spatter their faces.

'*Yis'ga'dal v'yis'kadash sh'may ra'bbo, b'olmo dee'vro chir'usay v'yamlich malchu'say.*'

The dead are held in our memories; we carry them with us through life; one generation to the next, so that our people live on in the minds of our daughters and our sons.

Jack sang the names of those they had lost while Sadie pictured their faces and, for a few brief moments, saw them dancing on the water before her.

Then there was another sound: the rich long note of a horn.

It rose up through the mist and echoed against the hillside. Sadie clutched Jack's arm.

'A miracle! Thank God! It's a miracle!'

Tears ran down her cheeks. God had sensed her loneliness and here, in the wilderness, he had found them and sent her the sound of the *shofar*. They were alone no more; the note of the ram's horn united them. It rang out across the centuries and cut through the fog to find them. She rubbed Jack's knuckle with trembling fingers, whispering Papa's old words, 'The sound of the ram's horn is sharp. It is like no other sound. It pierces the armour of the heart.'

For a moment the mist cleared and there was a flash of scarlet and rushing limbs. Jack moved to the edge of the pond and stared towards the horizon. There was the sound of barking and pounding hooves, and then a pack of hounds raced into the meadow below, closely pursued by red-coated riders on thundering horses. The horn cried out again and the hunt disappeared back into the haze. In the distance the note rang out for a final cry, and then silence.

Sadie was sobbing now. Jack passed her a rather grubby handkerchief and noisily she blew her nose. 'It's a miracle, Jack isn't it?'

He reached for her hand, 'Yes, darling, a miracle.'

CHAPTER FOURTEEN

AUTUMN SLID INTO winter. The leaves fell to the ground, blew into piles, turned crisp in the frost and rotted away. The branches were jagged against the pale winter sky, and at night Jack and Sadie listened as the windowpanes rattled and the winds rose up and hissed through the empty attics above their bedroom. Jack dug out extra blankets from one of the boxes and they huddled under it at night, hostilities suspended as they clutched one another for warmth. Each evening Sadie filled the earthenware water bottles in an attempt to ward off chilblains. She kept a chamber pot underneath the bed; it was too cold to traipse down the landing to the bathroom, and in the morning the urine in the bowl was ice covered.

Progress on the golf course was halted by the thick frost. The ground froze one night and did not thaw the next day or the day after that. There was nothing to do, except wait. Jack paced his fairways, admiring the five chequered flags, each one frozen mid-flutter. He now realised his course was rather testing (though he was sure it would be much admired by expert players). From each tee the respective hole was invisible, hidden behind the slope of the valley or masked by scrub. The greens were uneven and steep. The rough was a mixture of wild grass, dogwood and gorse and a ball entering it would be lost for ever (in Jack's view adding to the challenge). Despite these drawbacks, it had a magnificent position. The view across the countryside was vast and open, and Jack felt his smallness against the great expanse of earth and sky.

November eased into December, bringing the thickest frost of the year, and Elizabeth. Jack was filled with joy at the prospect of seeing his daughter. He missed her noise. Young people filled the house with bustle and life; one could feel the world turning and moving onwards.

Elizabeth was the only girl in her class to go up to Cambridge and Jack was a little in awe of his daughter's achievement. He'd left school at sixteen eager to join the busy world and was unsure as to the proper English method of educating girls. (The information in *Helpful Information* was entirely unhelpful on this point, merely stating that Jews should not expect their sons to be doctors, lawyers or dentists since those occupations must be reserved for the offspring of English professionals). Once a year (or so it seemed) Mr Austen presented to Jack a neatly folded copy of *The Times* announcing the marriage of Miss Marianne Austen or Miss Jessica Austen to a Mr So and So Esq. This appeared to be the pinnacle of an English girl's achievement, until the following year when the same paper was waved under Jack's nose so he could admire the 'safe arrival of Henry Edmund So and So, seven pounds and six ounces'.

Sadie was the one who vocalised concern and consternation – 'Don't you want to find a nice boy? Your father will give you all the carpets you could ever want.' But Jack wanted something more than carpets for his daughter, and if it was Cambridge she wanted, then Cambridge it must be.

Elizabeth knew she was her parents' connection to the alien, English world and was not above exploiting their ignorance. Most girls went home for the weekends and when at college they were strictly supervised, but she was expert at circumventing rules and avoiding home visits. Even so, she was deeply curious about her parents' strange journey into rural England. They had never really done anything interesting before, her father made lists and sold carpets, while her mother gossiped and wept when she thought no one was listening.

Sadie cleaned the house and made up the little bedroom under the eaves for her daughter, filling it with all her old childish things. There was the school desk, scratched with ten years of homework, and volumes of Dickens and Shakespeare. In a packing crate she discovered a stash of bedtime stories that she used to read to Elizabeth. Jack didn't want his daughter speaking German – it was the first and second rules on his list. But, Sadie wanted Elizabeth to hear a little of her language and so read *auf Deutsch*, the pranks of Till Eugenspiel and the macabre adventures of Stuwelpeter. She wasn't sure the little girl understood every word, but Sadie wanted her to know that *Deutsch* was also a language of stories and magic. She wouldn't let those *Schweinepriester* take all her words from her. The child promised her mother that she wouldn't tell Papa about the German storybooks. Sadie cherished their secret. As a girl Elizabeth shared everything with Jack – they were forever laughing at some joke or disappearing off to cafés without inviting her – but those forbidden bedtime books belonged solely to Sadie and Elizabeth. During those minutes, she could be *Mutti* at last.

Leaving his wife fussing, Jack left early to collect his daughter from the station. There was a deep frost, the leaves coated with white and the grass hidden beneath an arctic layer. The ponds froze and birds pecked miserably at the solid surfaces. The Jaguar was parked inside the barn, covered in a horse blanket and it took him a good ten minutes to fire it up. He packed hot water bottles, which he wrapped in blankets, along with a flask of tea mixed with brandy for the journey. The roads were icy and he wondered about the wisdom of driving a sports car; he would have to put chains on the tyres if it snowed.

Elizabeth was waiting on the platform, stamping her feet to keep warm, her hands buried in a pair of red woollen mittens. She had two ancient suitcases, filled with a term's worth of books, washing and memorabilia. For a moment Jack didn't recognise the young woman standing very straight in the smart caramel-coloured coat; every last trace of the schoolgirl had vanished. He was the same: small, balding, bespectacled and smiling. Elizabeth ran to him and planted a kiss on both cheeks. He received her affections awkwardly and bashed her nose with his, not expecting the second kiss. Suddenly embarrassed before this elegant, adult creature he tried to prise her cases from her grasp. A moment later a porter appeared and firmly piled the luggage onto a trolley.

'Let me look at you, Daddy.'

She stood, hands on hips and gazed at her father, who shifted from foot to foot under her scrutiny.

'You're thinner. And browner. Your hat's on funny.'

She reached out and fiddled with Jack's trilby for a moment, took a step back and shrugged.

'It never sits right,' she sighed.

Jack felt himself flush like a schoolboy and walked briskly after the porter to hide his mortification. All his hats were purchased from Lock of St James, the best hatter in London, and yet they never sat right. He wished she wouldn't always draw attention to it; he was trying as hard as he could and hated it when he shamed her. They caught up with the porter, who loaded the bags into the trunk as Jack slipped him sixpence. Elizabeth rolled her eyes in mock exasperation.

'Oh Daddy, when will you learn not to tip so much?' she said when the porter was out of earshot.

Jack winced; she'd told him that before – people sneer at you, if you tip too much.

'But it's nice to be generous. It's Christmas.'

She waggled a finger at him playfully. 'Only Americans tip that much. The English are mean.'

'Thank you for coming, love, it means so much to your mother.'

She smiled at him, the quick, bright smile that made dimples form in either cheek and she looked happy. Jack relaxed. 'It's all right,' he thought. 'It's all right. I'm a *klutz* but love has brought her back to me.'

Her face was rosy pink from the cold; the heating had broken down at Salisbury and the last miles inside the train were freezing so that even the car seemed warm in comparison. Eagerly she wiped away the condensation from the window and watched the English landscape unfold – the trailing rivers iced over and the frost hanging in the rushes on the riverbanks. She had never left London as a child, except for a school trip to Minehead, and now barely heard her father chattering as she stared in amazement at this new world. Smoke puffed from every chimney and the cottage doors were festooned with wreaths of holly. It was not yet four o'clock but daylight was already fading and candles began to flicker in the windows. The fields glimmered in the dusk and Elizabeth wanted to stroke them; the gathering frost looked as soft as goose down.

Sadie was waiting anxiously at home; she'd been checking the window for signs of them at least an hour too soon. Then, in a crackling of gravel, they were there. Elizabeth flung open the heavy front door and embraced her mother, burying her face in the familiar soft cheek and neck. Sadie always smelled softly of Chanel No. 5, and there it was, but mixed in with it was the heady scent of damp earth and woodsmoke.

'*Mein lieber Schatz! Mein Kind,*' exclaimed Sadie, her face buried in her daughter's hair. She covered her face with exuberant kisses, and ushered her into the kitchen. Sadie felt a tug of joy at the prospect of feeding her little one, and sat at the table to watch her eat, hiding her smile behind her hand as Elizabeth demolished half a dozen vanilla crescents. And yet, they had been apart for so long that there was a distance between them; they were two strangers who needed to become acquainted. She felt that Elizabeth was different – a young woman now, beginning her own life and exuding confidence. In contrast Sadie felt middle-aged and tired. Her clothes were faded, her hair grey and in the mirror she could see creases round her eyes and thin lines on her top lip. She remembered when she was young like Elizabeth with thick hair and smooth skin. Elizabeth looked English: she had dark Jewish hair but bright green eyes and the creamy pink complexion of the classic English rose, and now she spoke with the quiet self-assurance of a graduate of one of The Universities. No one would guess that she was conceived in a tiny apartment in a Jewish suburb of Berlin. She listened to Elizabeth chatter about new friends, the tutors she liked and the ones she didn't, new words peppering her conversation. Sadie didn't understand but did not like to expose her ignorance to this smart new daughter who drank tea with milk.

Jack marched into the kitchen, a scarf wrapped around his face, his eyebrows covered in frost. Elizabeth smiled – he looked like a peasant from a storybook *shetetl* in his layers and woollen cap, rather than the dapper London businessman.

'Come see my course.'

Swaddled in her coat and woollen scarves, Elizabeth followed Jack outside. The winter's moon hung low in the sky. The frost was so thick that it shone white, bathing the countryside in a ghostly light. It was a good night for stories, so Jack told his daughter all about the legend of the woolly-pig. She listened in silence as their feet crunched through ice on the iron ground. They paused at the ridge by Backhollow, the moon illuminating the weird grass ledges; at the bottom of the slope a hoar frost hung in the ash trees. It coated the spindly trunks and dangled from the branches like silver streamers, each twig coated in tiny crystals. In this strange other world of glittering white Jack could almost believe in the tale of the woolly-pig.

'Perhaps there really is such a creature. It might be a wild boar. After all they still have them in France,' conceded Elizabeth.

Jack was delighted; he loved it when she believed his stories. He reached deep into his jacket for a flask and passed it to her.

'Here, drink this – it'll keep you warm. Don't tell your mother.'

His coat was purchased from Curtis. It was lined with rabbit fur and had a handy inside pocket for keeping all manner of hidden things, from a poached pheasant to a hip flask or scrap of fabric for polishing a flagpole.

Elizabeth took the flask and unscrewed the cap with difficulty through her mittens, tilted it and had a sip. Apples burnt the back of her throat. She coughed and handed it back to her father.

'God, Daddy, what is that?'

Jack shrugged, 'Just cider from our orchard. It's not very good. You must taste the stuff that my friend Curtis makes.'

He took another swig and gave a loud hiccup. He hadn't yet made a batch that didn't give him hiccups – it was most upsetting.

'Come, you must see the first hole. I dug it all myself.'

Sadie sat alone in the kitchen. They had been gone for two hours and she was starting to worry. There was a chicken roasting slowly in the oven as a special treat and soon it would go dry. It was pitch dark outside, the lamps kept going out and there was the uncanny howl of a fox in the distance. She felt like crying. It was always the same – they would go off and

173

forget all about her. Every Sunday in London, Jack had taken Elizabeth to the Lyons Corner House in the high street. Not once had they thought to ask her.

Nearly an hour later, Jack and Elizabeth flung open the kitchen door and erupted into the room in a flurry of noise, treading wet boot prints across Sadie's clean floor. She frowned but said nothing; she didn't want to be a scold on her daughter's first day home.

'Well, sit down. It's all ready.'

Sadie lit the candles on the kitchen table and the room basked in the flickering glow. She had wanted everything to be perfect tonight but she was simmering with resentment like the chicken bones in the pressure cooker. Elizabeth reached for the mashed potatoes and took a huge spoonful as Sadie watched, running a hand absent-mindedly over her own spreading middle. There was a thickening roll that never used to be there, which felt like it wasn't really part of her. She remembered when she used to be able to eat like Elizabeth. She flung the vegetable dish on the table. For a moment rage bubbled inside her. It wasn't fair – Elizabeth had everything: youth, the possibility of happiness, and Jack. Sadie watched as Jack gazed at his daughter, his eyes wet with love. Once, long ago, he'd looked at her like that. She slammed down the gravy jug.

'The chicken's dry. Everything's spoilt.'

Later that night Jack waited until his women had gone to bed, enjoying the few moments of stillness and watching the embers dying in the grate. He would like a fireplace like Sir William's, decorated with mythical beasts, ho-ho birds and woolly-pigs. A little magic was a good thing.

He hadn't seen Curtis in several days. It was as though when the cold came he disappeared into hibernation, like the badgers and ferrets. Jack yawned – it was getting late. He stretched luxuriously and ambled into the kitchen to fetch a glass of milk before bed. He sloshed it into a mug, and as he wondered whether or not to warm it, he noticed Elizabeth's exam results lying on the table and picked them up, smiling in anticipation – he presumed she had done well or she would not have left them out for him to peruse. Then he noticed the name on the envelope. This was not *his* Elizabeth – this was another girl. Elizabeth Margaret Rose.

Jack placed the letter back on the table. This was what he wanted: an English daughter with an English name. Now she had the names of a queen, a princess and the most English of all flowers.

She was not even the first to change her name – he reasoned. At nine days old she was named Ilse for her great-grandmother by the rabbi at the synagogue in Berlin. In spite of his wife's railings Jack insisted that Ilse had her name altered to the English version, Elizabeth, when they reached the shore at Harwich. Sadie had been furious, names were important; the history of the Jews is carried forth through names: *Jack son of Saul and Sadie daughter of Ruth*. Jack had broken the chain. He objected; he had merely translated her name into English, in essence it remained the same. He did not want his small daughter, so tiny and brimming with promise, to be crippled by a German-sounding name.

Sitting in his warm kitchen fifteen years later, Jack reasoned, he had no right to be unhappy that Elizabeth had changed her own name once again. He was sad nonetheless: she no longer had *his* name. She was his daughter still, but not in name. Most fathers had to wait until their daughters were married to receive this blow, but for Jack it had come early and he felt it bitterly.

He tiptoed upstairs to Elizabeth's bedroom and pushed open the door. She was not sleeping, but curled up in her mother's rocking chair, chewing her plaits and reading a magazine. Christmas carols played softly on the wireless. She did not hear him, and he watched the small figure, struck by the childishness of her pose. She was a girl-woman, and he felt his heart within him ache.

'Well done. A good result, Elizabeth Rose.'

He said her new name, testing it, trying it out in his mouth like a new taste. It sounded very fine. She looked at him sharply as though trying to read his thoughts.

'It's easier for other people to say, Daddy,' she said, her green eyes appealing to him to agree, not to contradict her.

'Sure, sure,' he said nodding.

He understood: she was tired of always being *the Jew*. She did not look like a Jew – only the name betrayed her and without it she was free. He remembered when she was at school. All the other girls had tall fathers who smoked cigars, understood cricket and kept a box at Covent Garden to listen to Wagner. He sighed inwardly; it was his own fault that she didn't let him take her up to Cambridge. For a second he imagined the way she saw him: he pictured himself in a garish suit talking too loudly with the other elegant parents on neat college lawns. No wonder she forbade him from accompanying her.

He sat down beside her and pretended to interest himself in her magazine. He had done this, he started her on this course to Englishness, and it was what he had wanted. It had driven him to write his list and made him come here, to the countryside veiled in ice to build his golf course, but for the first time in all his years in Britain, he felt a sense of loss.

'I remember when we came here. We were in the East End, jumbled with all the other Jews. I thought it would be safer to have an English name so I considered calling myself Jack Rose-bloom for a while.'

'Jack Rose-bloom,' Elizabeth said the name slowly.

'The thing sounds ridiculous in English.' He took her warm hand and brushed it against his lips. 'You're quite right, my darling. Mr Rose does sound better. Mr Rose sounds like Mr Anyone. In fact,' he added with a rueful smile, 'I think it sounds rather English.'

He flicked a stray cobweb from an oak beam.

'I should add it to my list. Item one hundred and fifty-one: an Englishman must have an English name.'

His heart filling with tears, Jack vanished into his study; it was time to write to Bobby Jones. He had not written a letter for several weeks, there had been no progress in the frost, but he missed the act of writing; it helped one get one's thoughts in order. He opened the drawer and pulled out a piece of paper.

Dear Mr Jones,

The weather here has been terrible. I don't suppose you in sunny Augusta know the bitter chill of a midwinter freeze. My bones creak, and I feel like Captain Scott, only with more tinned soup. My daughter has come home. I don't know if you have children, Mr Jones, but they grow away from you so fast. We name the things we love. God created the world and then he named it. The world and its names appeared at the very same instant, 'Let there be light, and there was light' and so forth. God named us, in love, according to my wife who believes such things. A man names his child, and that moment she becomes more than a tiny crying creature, but a person. It is sad when a father is no longer allowed to give his child her name. What else have we to give?

Your friend and humble servant,

Jack Rose

And with that, after hundreds of generations of Rosenblums, the name was severed, more cleanly than with a knife or axe. Jack Rose took half the name, made it English and anonymous, and another little piece of history disappeared.

CHAPTER FIFTEEN

JACK TRIED HIS best not to think about the matter of the name but found that it troubled him. It haunted him even more than his money troubles or the cold weather halting progress on the golf course and he was relieved when distraction arrived a few days later in the form of Freida and Edgar Herzfeld. They were visiting second cousins in Bournemouth and decided to make a short detour to call on their good friends the Rosenblums.

Edgar was partial to a game of golf. His fascination was not synonymous with a wish to be considered an Englishman, he merely liked the click of the ball and eagerly joined a Jewish Golf Club. He appreciated what he took to be Jack's passion for golf, but could not understand why the man needed to build a course of his own. The Finchley Club was anti-Semitic, most certainly, the others had quotas, but why not join a Jewish club? Why go where you were not wanted? Edgar liked the Jewish Club, where they served excellent schnitzel, everyone was familiar and nothing needed to be explained.

Jack was very fond of Edgar and was eager to extend membership to him as soon as the course officially opened. Jack would need to practise a good bit before they played together as he needed to be quite certain that he was a better golfer than Edgar, but in the meantime it was very pleasant to show his old friend his triumph. He walked him up to the fifth hole, where from the tee the entire Blackmore Vale could be glimpsed. It was damp and dark, the sky seeming to hover only a few feet above the muddy fields. Edgar was impressed.

His friend had disappeared into the wilderness like Moses, and had performed a great feat.

'I like it. I like it very much. How many members do you have?'

Jack pondered this. 'Well, there is Sir William Waegbert and Mr Henry Hoare and yourself. So three.'

Edgar thought the position was charming, or would be in spring, but he was concerned at the steepness. He wanted to help Jack; he suspected that he was not an experienced golfer and could perhaps benefit from a little advice.

'I'd dearly like to play a few holes. I think it'd be useful. Test them out.'

Jack considered this. Trying the course sounded like it might be a good plan. If there were any changes, they could be made when work resumed. He did not want Edgar to know that, as yet, he had not played a round himself.

'Yes. I should like a second opinion. But, I will walk round with you. I'd rather listen to your thoughts than be worrying about my own game.'

Edgar was surprised, but he shrugged. 'Well, if you really prefer. I'll fetch my clubs.'

Jack wanted to be the first to play, but he considered that since Edgar was only trying out a few holes and not the completed course, it did not really count at all. The sky turned black and then white as the snow fell to the earth in a silent avalanche of flakes.

'Oh! This is too bad,' exclaimed Edgar sadly returning with his clubs, 'I'll just have to come back in the spring.'

Jack was perturbed. Now that Edgar had suggested the course ought to be played, he was not willing to wait. A touch of snow would not deter the man who had single-handedly built a golf course.

'It's not bad,' said Jack, putting out his hand and looking optimistically at the sky.

'Are you sure? I don't want to damage your greens,' said Edgar looking doubtfully at the looming clouds.

'It'll be fine but we should go right now.'

He hoisted Edgar's bag of clubs over his shoulder and led him back down towards the first hole. Flakes were fluttering to the ground in kaleidoscopic patterns, and landing softly on their woollen hats and scarves. Jack blinked to brush flecks of snow from his eyelashes. They traipsed to the first hole, Jack lugging the clubs through the battering wind. Edgar was losing his enthusiasm. He was very cold and a little hungry, and this no longer seemed like a good idea. They could barely see more than a few feet and the valley disappeared behind a solid bank of fog.

'Which club do you want?' enquired Jack politely through muffled layers.

'What does it matter? How the hell do I hit the ball?'

Jack paused to consider; he was determined that Edgar should try the course. They said they were going to play a few holes and so, weather be damned, they were going to play. With the utmost care, he placed the bag on the ground and began to build up a little pile of snow. He stopped when it was a few inches high and popped the ball on the snow-tee.

'Here.'

Edgar selected his driver and got ready to take a swing. Jack admired his stance, he wasn't Bobby Jones but he looked respectable enough as he lifted the club high above his shoulder, turning his hips, and then swung down to the ball. There was a click, and they watched the ball fly off into the mist.

'Good shot,' said Jack in awe.

'How can you tell? We have no idea where it went.'

'Well, we'd better look then.'

Jack hoisted the bag back onto his shoulder and took off along the ridge. Edgar followed him, using the driver as a walking stick to stop him from slipping. The ground was now completely covered in gleaming snow and only the flags flickering through the haze indicated that this was a golf course at all.

Bent against the wind, Jack battered through the falling flakes, pursuing the direction he thought the ball to have taken. The temperature was dropping, and his fingers were getting stiff and numb. He glanced around for Edgar, but could not see him.

'Damn.'

It was most inconvenient to lose him so close to home. He sighed; he wanted to search for the ball not the man. There was a sneeze behind him.

'Ah, good, there you are. This way, Edgar.'

Jack put out his hand and half dragged his friend down the hill towards the pond. The snow was falling quickly now, and gathered in drifts by their feet.

'Come on, Jack, let's go inside. It's too cold. We'll never find it. Looking for a white ball on white snow. It's madness.'

Jack studied his friend. He was the image of dejection; most of his face was now obscured by layers of clothing, only his nose poked out and it was shining red with cold, his eyes were watering and he was shaking. Then, he saw something on the surface of the pond, a round object with a small cap of gathering snow.

'Look! It's your ball. See how far you hit it!'

Sitting proudly on the top of the frozen water was Edgar's ball; he had sent it a good three hundred yards. Edgar stumbled to the edge of the pond for a closer look. Tiny cracks like a thousand microscopic tributaries appeared in the surface of the ice, but it had not broken. He marvelled at his own power.

'I've never hit a ball so far in my life. *Wunderbar*. What a course!'

Edgar laughed with glee, pumped Jack's arm and slapped

him on the back. The two men marched back to the house leaving two neat sets of footprints. As they approached the back door, they could see a figure waving to them.

'Who's that?' said Edgar,

Jack was not sure. There was a tall man wearing a deerstalker, certainly not Curtis. 'Sir William Waegbert?'

The aristocrat stamped and waved his arms partly in greeting and partly to keep warm. The tips of his moustache had a light dusting of white.

'Yes. Yes. Happy Whatever it is that you do and all that. Your wife said you'd gone orf to play a round of golf.'

Jack shook his head sadly. 'Not a whole round. Course isn't finished.'

He opened the door to the kitchen and ushered his companions inside. The snow melted off their boots and formed little puddles on the flagstones. Unconcerned, Jack trotted to the larder to fetch his bottle of whisky. They sat around the table as he sloshed some of the liquid into three glasses.

'Soda, Sir William?'

'Good God, no. Far too bloody cold.'

Jack grunted his agreement and took a deep swig.

'So, how is the course? I've come to investigate.'

'Wonderful,' announced Edgar, his cheeks flushed from freezing air and the excitement caused by his great shot in the blizzard. He was a gentle man, calm and cautious; his game of golf in the driving snow was the greatest act of daring he had undertaken in the last ten years and he felt like Shackleton in the Antarctic in his audacity.

'Best course. It will be fantastic. Super-incredible.'

Jack smiled, filled with happiness. Here he was, sitting with his old friend, glorying in his achievement, and his new friend, a knight of the realm. Sir William slid the bottle across the table and topped up all three glasses to the rim. He raised his glass to the others, and took a gulp. Edgar followed and toasted Jack.

'To you, old friend.'

Edgar was filled with a comfortable burning from his throat to his belly; he felt warm and magnanimous. Despite his own personal victory, sending the ball a good hundred yards further than ever before in his fifty-seven years, he was still aware of the painful shortcomings of the course. The tees were blind, the greens steep and the hazards poorly placed. He was not a man usually prone to exaggeration or wanton praise, but he was unused to the powerful effects of whisky and as he drank he became loquacious in his enthusiasm.

'You mark my words,' he said, jabbing a finger in the vague direction of Sir William, 'it is going to be the triumph of the South-West. Everything this man does turns to gold. His carpet factory is the best in London. No one believed he could do it, and then – miracle. You want a good carpet at an excellent price. Only Rosenblum's will do.'

Here Jack fidgeted uncomfortably on his hard wooden chair.

'Rose's. It's just Rose's.'

Edgar raised an eyebrow.

'Oh?'

'Yes. I've changed the name. Not yet, but I will. It's Elizabeth's idea. Jack Rose. Less of a mouthful. Don't know why I didn't think of it before.'

Edgar continued to contemplate his friend in astonishment but Sir William gave a slow nod.

'Yes. Probably for the best. No point having a Kraut name if you can help it.'

Edgar swallowed, momentarily lost for words. With another sip of whisky he recovered and returned with enthusiasm to his original topic.

'This place will be his next big success, mark my words!

You did a smart thing, getting membership now my friend. Very smart indeed,' he added with a flourish.

Jack watched as Sir William stretched his legs comfortably under the table. It was very pleasant in the warm kitchen. Sadie had been baking at her usual pace and the cupboards were brimming with seasonal sweetmeats. He fetched a plate of honey cakes from the larder. Then he sliced Stollen into fat chunks and placed it on the table, taking it as a great compliment when Sir William helped himself to a large piece. Glowing contentedly with single malt in his belly, he happily prattled away to Sir William. He'd accepted that nine holes was sufficient, but now buoyed by the whisky and Edgar's effusions, he was feeling particularly optimistic.

'I will have nine holes by spring, and then another nine by the end of the year. I want this to be a course for champions. The British Open will be played in the Vale of Blackmore.'

Thinking this was a toast, Edgar raised his glass and drained it. 'The British Open! To the Blackmore Vale!'

Sir William leant forward confidentially.

'And Bobby Jones. I believe you mentioned he was the chap whose designs you were following?'

Jack fidgeted awkwardly in his chair. He had been checking the post every day for a reply from his hero but none was forthcoming. He had even driven to the big post office in Dorchester to make certain that there had been no mistake. There was no mistake. There was just no letter.

'Yes. He is the greatest of them all. A true champion in our dreary age, but he is a busy man, a very busy man,' he added sadly.

Edgar slumped in his chair and began to snore softly. Jack smiled at him fondly, his eyes brimming with affection.

'He's a good man is Edgar Herzfeld. You'll never find a better.'

The booze unloosened something within Jack and he turned warmly to Sir William.

'And you. It is very good of you to take such an interest in my humble little course – a real, thorough interest. You are a good friend too, sir.'

Sir William did not reply. He stayed until the bottle of whisky was empty, then climbed back into his decaying Rolls-Royce and drove away into the snow.

That night there was no question of the Herzfelds leaving. Freida and Sadie retreated into the kitchen so they could chatter *auf Deutsch* uninterrupted by Jack's reproachful stares. They sat warming themselves by the hulking range, waiting for the tea kettle to boil. The making of tea was a useful distraction; the women could fuss as they fiddled with the packet of loose leaves, spilling some on the floor, which then needed to be swept up. Once the strainer was found (Jack had filched it to use for a new concoction of fertiliser), the pot must be left to brew for the right amount of time. But when the tea was poured and the biscuits set out on a rose-patterned plate, there was nothing left to do but talk to one another.

Freida wrapped her hands around her cup and turned to her friend. '*So*, do you have the television yet?'

Sadie shook her head. '*Nein*. No signal. Bulbarrow Hill. He is in the way.'

Freida raised a plucked eyebrow, 'Ach, what a pity! Watching the television on a cold night is one of life's little pleasures.'

Sadie shrugged and stirred another teaspoon of sugar into her cup. She had no interest in such novelty items.

'How will you watch the coronation?' said Freida.

Sadie knew this was one of the items being furiously debated by Lavender and the Pursebury Coronation Committee, but she never stayed long enough at the village hall meetings to discover if a solution had been found.

'Is that a new sweater?' asked Freida, pointing to Sadie's

mauve knitted cardigan, knowing perfectly well that it was not, but reaching for something to say.

'*Nein.*'

Sadie refilled the teacups.

As it grew dark Edgar and Jack sat smoking cigars and sipping port by the fire in the sitting room. A backgammon board was set up in front of them on a low table and they played in silence. Elizabeth perched on a squat milking stool beside her father's armchair. She peered forward watching the game critically.

'Don't move there, Daddy, or he'll win. Put it there.'

Jack obeyed, Edgar laughed, 'This is called cheating.'

Jack took a puff of his cigar and watched the smoke curl upwards. It floated to the roof beams and hovered there in a small cloud. Later, Sadie would complain about the smell.

'Let me have some of your cigar,' said Elizabeth, taking it from her father's hand.

'Don't breathe, suck,' commanded Edgar. 'Like this.'

He demonstrated and blew a column of blue smoke into the fireplace where it spiralled away up the chimney. She tried but it made her cough and she gave it back to her father in disgust. 'I'm tired. I'm going to bed. Goodnight Daddy, 'night Uncle Edgar.'

She leant over and kissed the shiny top of her father's head.

'You're a good girl.'

Jack settled back in his chair and watched as she tidied away the backgammon set. This evening her hair was damp and drying in feathery curls around her face. She reminded him of Sadie all those years ago, before the sadness took her. He closed his eyes against the heat of the fire and pictured the girlish Sadie. She was so young and with such soft edges; she had the kind of bosom a man wanted to lay his head on at night. She was a delicious plumpness; like the perfect roast chicken. When they locked him up in that cell for being an 'enemy alien', he dreamt of her every night. He missed Elizabeth for sure, but it was Sadie's face he saw in the darkness. With a start Jack opened his eyes. He listened to the wind outside and through a crack in the curtains watched it blow the snow into great white piles in the garden.

Elizabeth was going to make some young man happy, thought Jack, but he would never appreciate her, not until it was too late. It was the sad lot of the middle-aged man to value youth and happiness long after it had vanished. He helped himself from a supper tray, and turned to Edgar with a melancholy smile.

'When did we get old?'

'I am not sure', said Edgar matter-of-factly. 'Here, have a herring.'

CHAPTER SIXTEEN

B Y CHRISTMAS EVE the house was buried in two feet of snow. Jack cleared a path through to the orchard but the field beyond was smooth and perfectly unmarked like a sheet of white paper before a word has been written. Sound was muffled through the snow; the cries of the birds were muted and strange. The bright white dazzled him every time he went outside but it was oddly peaceful; time seemed to have slowed with the snow. Everything took longer; walking down the lane for a pint of milk was an expedition. The telephone cables came down with the first flurry and the bright red telephone box was buried uselessly under a vast drift. The boundaries beyond Bulbarrow signalled another far off and unreachable realm. Pursebury Ash was a miniature, ice-filled island.

Sadie looked out of the kitchen window. A robin was balancing along a sugar-coated branch with a bright berry in its beak, trying not to drop its precious cargo. The wind blew and flakes fluttered from the bough of a birch tree in spirals to the ground. Icicles dangled like doll-sized mountain ranges from the eaves and in the distance the whiteness bled into the horizon and disappeared round the curve of the earth. She could hear Elizabeth and Jack in the sitting room arguing over backgammon.

Alone in the quiet kitchen, she opened the sturdy farmhouse dresser, took out her box, removed the lid and laid out her family on the battered table. Her brother's face smiled up at her and she felt a twist in her stomach. Next, she took the picture of her father and placed it on the table, first dusting away the toast crumbs. It was tattered at the edges, beginning to yellow and curl, but it wasn't a good photograph in any case; he looked stern and cross. It was taken when he was a young man and Sadie still a baby. He had a neatly trimmed black beard in the snap but he had shaved it off when she was small and she didn't remember it. Yet this was the only picture she had of him and, as her memory began to wear and fade, the face in the photograph seemed to loom where once her father's had been.

She placed the picture of Mutti beside her father. It was taken shortly before Sadie left for England and showed a fretting, middle-aged woman doing her best to look cheery for the camera. She wasn't worrying about things to come – this was no premonition – she was concerned whether she had picked up enough chicken schmaltz for supper. The mismatched photographs presented an odd couple: her father glowering in his twenties and her mother twenty years later, huddled in middle age, so that husband and wife looked more like mother and son. Sadie reached into the box for another picture: a studio print of Jack, Elizabeth and herself taken several years ago for the holidays. She arranged all the photographs in a circle, her family together.

'Sadie Rose. Sadie Rose,' she said, to the pictures, introducing herself. This new name was strange; it had an unpleasant taste like strong mustard and burnt her tongue. It was one more thing to take her away from them, to separate her from *before*. Her family had known her as Sadie Landau and later, when she married Jack, as Sadie Rosenblum. This Sadie Rose was someone new, and they would never be able to find her. When Emil was small, they used to play hide and seek in the apartment building, hiding in the hallway shadows or the creaking elevator car. She would crouch in the space underneath the stairs, listening as he called, '*Sadie, Sadie Landau, I'm going to find you.*' Now she could see him walking through the fields calling for her, but she wouldn't hear. He had the wrong name.

Several days ago, she'd found Jack completing forms for new passports for the entire family, under this unfamiliar name. Of course she had remonstrated, scratching at him and trying to grab the papers and rip them into little pieces.

'Give me back my name! You can't take it from me.'

'Stop being hysterical. It is sensible. It's all part of the naturalisation process.'

'I don't want it.'

'Well, I want to have the same name as my daughter. Families share a name.'

'Why do we even need new passports? Are you taking me on holiday?'

Sadie's face contorted into a mocking smile, knowing exactly why Jack always applied for passports. He wanted to feel that this place was home and not exile, but there was always a flicker of doubt and, like Houdini or the Scarlet Pimpernel, he liked to have an escape plan. Just in case. Despite everything, she knew that he was an outsider like her.

That afternoon, the Roses walked together by the banks of the river Stour. It had frozen over and a wintry carnival erupted in what had been water meadows and were now ice fields. Boys in greatcoats and girls in mufflers skated over the still surface. Jack shuddered, he did not like deep water, solid or not. When he looked at it, he could feel the wetness pulling him downwards, his breath escaping in bubbles above his head and hands grabbing at the fronds of weed as he sank deeper into blackness. He shook his head and clapped his hands to drive away such gloomy reflections. Elizabeth, ignorant of this aversion, took his hand and dragged him resisting out onto the river. He wobbled, his feet sliding away from him.

'*Scheiße!* Let me go. I don't like this at all.'

Elizabeth laughed and pulled him along. 'Look, we're like Moses, see, see!'

Sadie smiled and shook her head, 'No, no he parted the sea *then* walked.'

Jack succeeded in crawling back to the bank where, breathless, he rested against the trunk of an alder tree. 'You see, even Moses would not walk on water. It's not natural.'

Tiny silver fishes were suspended in the ice, and he peered at them, wondering if they would unfreeze and swim away in the thaw. The air was punctured by the happy shouts of children upon toboggans and makeshift sledges made of coal sacks, which left dirty smears on the white ground. Half-wild dogs careered madly, chasing sticks and barking at the sky. The poplars were so laden with snow that they leant forward heavily like stooped old men. The willows on the banks dangled down into the river, their branches frozen in a silent waterfall.

Jack and Sadie perched on a tree stump on the shore, watching Elizabeth skate. Jack could hear the earth shiver and hum and felt that he had fallen to the other side of the world; this was an arctic, unearthly place – not the muddy, wriggling place he knew but some strange netherworld. Elizabeth was hidden for a moment in the crowd of skaters and Sadie scrambled to her feet, anxious at losing sight of her. Jack smiled, he understood his wife's concern, even though they were parted from Elizabeth for months at a time. A moment later she reappeared, her red hat a crimson streak against the blur of white. She skated to a halt by her parents and grabbed on to a branch to steady herself.

'I'm hungry.'

'Well, let's get you something to eat.'

He offered her his arm and heaved her onto the glittering bank. The three of them strolled along to where stalls had been erected between the trees at the edge of the skaters.

There were chestnuts and cobnuts burning gently in the coals, twists of home-made liquor to warm the throat, and the smell of sausages and sizzling fat. Elizabeth, catching sight of her mother's tight smile, wavered for a second. Then, she pointed to a sausage. 'One of those.'

Jack gestured to the man, who speared a sausage, popped it onto a piece of bread and handed it to Elizabeth, who ate hungrily, a little smear of grease trickling down her chin. Jack ignored Sadie, indifferent to her disapproval. Elizabeth was not a Rosenblum, she was a Rose and could eat pig if she wanted. What did it matter? The smell burnt the inside of Jack's nostrils, it was so delicious, salty and smoky. He had never eaten pig before, it was a taboo he obeyed, instinctively and without resistance. Fish he ate and whenever the opportunity arose he mixed milk and meat. Pig was the one deep-rooted aversion he did not think to overcome. It was as unnatural as drinking seawater. Yet here in the darkling light, the hissing of sausages mingled with the wind in the stripped branches.

' . . . And another.'

The man passed it to him, and Jack hesitated only for a moment before biting into the bread and blackened pork.

The sun dipped behind the bank of bare trees, and dusk crept forth. The children were taken home to their beds, and the river took on a different shade. The ice gleamed blackly in the darkness and the skaters moved faster and faster, fuelled by cold and alcohol. They took swigs from bottles and shrieked into the night. Jack did not like it.

'Where *ist mein kind*?' Sadie's voice trembled.

Jack patted her arm. 'She'll be fine, dolly. She's a big girl.'

A second later Elizabeth glided into view, her cheeks bright with exercise, and waved happily at her parents. Jack went to the edge of the river and beckoned to her.

The Roses picked their way back along the meandering

river. As they turned the corner the cries of the last skaters drifted away into the night air. Jack thrust his hands deep into his pockets, grateful for the soft fur lining.

'*Snow is a white, white word*,' sang Elizabeth into the darkness.

She took hold of her mother's hand and tried to make her run and skip. Sadie stumbled to keep up, unaccustomed to moving so fast and young. Elizabeth skidded to a halt. 'Look,' she whispered, still clasping her mother's mitten.

A clamour of rooks rested upon the shadow of a dead tree, its branches outspread like pairs of lifeless arms and grasping fingers. There were hundreds of them, sitting on every limb of the tree. The birds were black, black against the snow.

'They is nasty creatures,' said a voice.

Curtis appeared in their midst. Expertly, he skimmed a large stone, which bounced across the ice and hit the tree carcass with a hollow crack. The rooks beat their dark wings and rose into the sky, circling with angry caws.

''arbingers of death,' he added cheerfully.

Elizabeth laughed.

'And them mare's tails sproutin' in the frost. Terrible omen, for sure,' he said pointing to where a green brush like plant poked through the snow.

Elizabeth snorted. 'Do you know any tales that aren't nasty?'

Curtis was crestfallen. He thought for a moment.

'Well, I does know that comfrey flowers is an excellent cure. Can't remember what for 'xactly. But tis excellent. Also, you mustn't wash on New Year's Day, or yer'll wash yer family away. That's a good 'un.'

He reached into his pocket and passed a flask to Jack, who tried to drink surreptitiously while joggling from foot to foot in an attempt to stay warm.

'It's a night as dark as a badger's backside,' said Curtis,

replacing the flask. 'Yer shouldn't linger here. The Drowners will get 'ee.'

Elizabeth laughed into her mitten. 'The Drowners?'

Curtis swiped the flask from Jack and fixed Elizabeth with a hard stare. 'They puts out precious things upon river bank. Yer know, things that yer have treasured and lost. Then, when yer creep down to the edge of the water to grab it, they snatches yer and pulls yers under.'

Jack shuddered; he felt the cold water closing above his head once more as he sank to the bottom of the river.

'You shouldn't say such things in front of my girl,' Sadie scolded the old man.

'She don't believe me anyhow. Modern wi-min.'

Elizabeth suppressed another giggle. She liked the books coming from America – Kerouac, Faulkner and Arthur Miller – that was the future. She was going to save up for an airplane ticket and go to America after graduation – Europe and the Old World were worn out and threadbare. Curtis and his folk tales belonged to another century.

They reached the gate at the foot of the hill leading to the golf course. Curtis leant against it and, steadily ignoring Elizabeth, waggled a finger at Jack and Sadie.

'Lost people in this village to the Drowners. I 'ad a cousin who 'ad a lovely gold watch, present from his granpa. Went out drinkin' one night and lost it. Was very upset, got a big hidin' from his pa when 'ee got home. Then. A year later. Maybee five. I doesn't remember. Anyhow tisn't important. Walking home 'ee sees 'is gold watch on river bank. It'd bin snowing like, and it were twinklin', and he bends down to git it, and then . . .'

His voiced trailed off and he gave a little wave into the darkness.

'And then what?'

'Well, 'ee was niver seen again, was he,' said Curtis crossly, slamming the gate.

'If you never saw him again, how do you know about the watch and the Drowners?' said Elizabeth.

'Hush,' said Jack.

Curtis scowled, offended by the impertinence of the girl; he did not want to be dismissed like an old fool. Sadie took Elizabeth's arm and gently pulled her towards the house. Jack and Curtis watched as the two women trudged across the garden and then a few moments later, the lights flickered on in the kitchen. The two men paused companionably in the night air.

Jack stared at the criss-crossing tracks littering the white field; there were marks from the sledges of the village children and deer prints, but next to them, lying deeply embedded in the snow, was a large round trotter print. Was it possible? He pointed to it. 'A woolly-pig print,' he said, with an air of conviction to mollify his friend. '*Yom Tov* woolly-pig.'

His voice rang out into the night. For a moment he waited, and then he was sure he heard a deep-throated grunt echoing a reply across the snow.

The weather did not improve for the last days of the year. New Year came and the ice stayed, snow drifting against the ancient walls of the cottage. The flags on the golf course were dotted across a white ocean, and as he dug narrow walkways across the endless snow, Jack found the tiny, frozen bodies of birds. One morning he discovered the fat little robin that had hopped along the gate in autumn, tugging at worms and watching him, head cocked. He saw a splash of red feathers and, stooping to look, found the robin, stiff and half buried in the frost. It was as light as his handkerchief in the palm of his hand and he felt, as he covered the flame-coloured bird, that he was burying the last piece of colour in a white world.

It was fortunate that Sadie, schooled by rationing, was in the habit of hoarding food or they would have gone hungry.

Luckily, her pantry was piled high with tins, buckets of flour and crocks of eggs, which Jack traded for pitchers of milk. The hens huddled in the barn, their coop covered with blankets and Sadie took them water twice each day since inside the barn water froze in a few hours. The novelty of the cold changed into tedium.

The hot water pipes froze and Sadie boiled kettles on the kitchen stove. Jack refused to wash – 'I need my dirt to keep me warm' – but on New Year's Day, Sadie decided that it was time to bathe. She had never seen in a New Year dirty. With a scowl, she placed her hands on her hips and cleared her throat.

'*Broitgeber*, I believe it is a rule on your list. An Englishman is always clean, is he not?'

Lying in bed later that night, he decided the water had gently broiled his innards, since he was less cold than usual. He went to sleep with ease and dreamt he was at Augusta, lying contentedly in the sunshine, listening to the trickling of temperate streams, the piping song of nightingales and the pock of golf balls.

When he awoke, it took him a moment to realise he was still in the midst of the dismal British winter and not in the great Georgian pleasure garden. He was only disappointed for a moment and slid smiling out of bed and into his slippers. He adjusted his fleece-lined dressing gown and bounded onto the landing. There was a powerful draught whistling along the staircase and he concluded that a window must have blown open in the night. Rubbing his hands for warmth he scurried down the wooden stairs to close it, before Sadie or Elizabeth caught cold. He could hear the wind howling in the kitchen and hurled himself at the door to open it. Mayhem greeted him: the ceiling had come down in the night. Plaster and debris were strewn everywhere and melted snow pooled on the flagstone floor. There was a large hole above his head and he could see the thatch sagging ominously. A twig landed on his head, and he noticed the remains of a bird's nest on the stove.

'*Mistfink*. Shit-heaps and buggering hell.'

The family surveyed the wreckage as snow fell gently into the kitchen turning the dust and rubble into a thick, rancid mess. The north wind hissed through the hole sending flurries of snowflakes and filth across the stone floor. Jack was almost out of sorts. He needed every penny for his golf course and did not have money for niceties like roof mending. Gazing up at the sky through the large opening in the kitchen ceiling he wondered if the repairs could wait until spring. Perhaps he could offer the thatcher membership of the course in lieu of payment.

Sadie and Elizabeth shovelled armfuls of ceiling plaster, scraps of wood and liquefied black dust into large, wet piles, which Jack scooped into sacks. After an hour, the flagstones had turned to mud and they began to skid along the floor. Sadie slipped by the kitchen dresser, grabbing hold of the base to steady herself. She noticed the low doors were ajar, and frowned, biting her lip in anxiety – precious things were in there and she didn't want them ruined. She knelt down in the dirt and shoved the wood with her fist. The cupboard door bounced open and water poured out. Snow from the roof had melted and run into the dresser, flooding every cabinet. The crockery was covered in slimy filth but she didn't care about that, or the vases or the linen tablecloths. She only cared about her wooden box. She eased it out and left the kitchen without a word.

She crept into the hall, feeling bile rise in her stomach.

'Please let them be all right. *Bitte. Bitte*,' she murmured.

Her hands trembling, she lifted the carved lid. The photographs floated in water, the faces blurred and featureless, all drowned in the deluge. Sadie picked out the picture of her mother, rubbed it gently against her sleeve and held it up in the daylight. The face was gone – she had wiped it off. There was only a piece of soggy, grey paper on the floral swirl of her housecoat. She reached for the other pictures and tenderly laid them on the ground. Every one was ruined. The paper disintegrated into mush as her shaking fingers touched them.

She picked up the sopping linen towel, Mutti's last gift, and held it to her face and breathed in, but the scent of her mother's starch and perfume was gone. Sadie had preserved that small towel immaculately in its tissue paper for nearly twenty years – its starched folds and the marks from Mutti's iron – and now there was nothing left.

She sat down on the stone floor and was sick; she retched and vomited again and again until the muscles in her stomach ached. Then she lay down; the stone cool against her cheek. A small pebble trodden inside from the driveway was trapped under her face and she could feel it slicing into her skin but she didn't move. Without the photographs, in a year, or in five years, she would forget their faces. They had no graves, no names engraved in stone; they needed her to remember them. She closed her eyes. Perhaps if she slept and then woke she would still be in bed and this wouldn't have happened. She opened her eyes. She was still here. The box was still spoilt.

Suddenly, eyes feverishly bright, she sat up. Through the closed door she could hear the happy chatter of her husband and daughter. She had an idea; she knew where to look for her photographs.

She fastened her robe tightly around her waist and, clasping her box, slipped out of the back door. The snow was knee-deep, and she had to stoop against the battering wind. It lifted the flaps of her flannel dressing gown and blew it open, making her pink nightdress flutter like a great moth. Her slippers were instantly sodden but she did not notice. It was mid-morning but the sky was pumice grey, filled with murky half-light hinting ominously of blizzards to come. She crossed the garden and opened the gate out into the blank expanse of the field, an odd figure, trudging across the whiteout in her floral housecoat, her grey hair limp in the damp air. The still rooks on the dead tree at the edge of the river eyed her as she passed.

Breathless, she paused and craned upwards to look at the sky, and remembered winters like this at the old house in Bavaria. They were snowed in one December and stayed in the house in the forest, marooned from the outside world. She'd helped Mutti make goulash and vegetable broth, and tied a scarf round her hair and pretended that they were peasants. She wished then that they could stay in the rickety house for ever, and she would never have to return to school or the city. In her mind, the Bavarian house was part Chantry Orchard – the sound of the wind through the eaves at night was the same – and also like a picture from the storybooks she read to Elizabeth. Sadie wished she could recall how the house actually looked, the colour of the shutters and how the chimney appeared poking above the treetops. Sometimes, in her dreams, they were all still there in the cabin in the wood. Mutti hunched over the stove, Papa sleeping in his chair and Emil building models out of balsa wood in front of the fire. She was late, and they were waiting for her.

She manoeuvred past a fallen branch blocking the path along the riverbank and sat down to rest on a stump, not bothering to brush the seat clear of snow. She was exhausted without being tired and wanted to slip down into the downy whiteness and close her eyes. Elizabeth and Jack did not need her; they would get on better without her. Jack had his golf course, and he would prefer not to see her again or to have her spoil his smiling content.

Her fingers were turning blue at the tips, and she could

feel them tingling uncomfortably but she liked the pain – she was supposed to suffer. The others had stayed and died, therefore she deserved to be unhappy. Jack did not understand this, however much she tried to show him, and so she placed burrs in his socks to give him blisters to mar the unbroken cheerfulness of his day. When she bothered to cook his supper she made all the food he disliked eating: kidney pie, rabbit and marzipan tarts. It was good for him, she reasoned, he needed to be a little sad. Making Jack a tiny bit unhappy, and nurturing her own hurt, were acts of love in Sadie's eyes.

She stared indifferently at the river and waited. The trees creaked under the heaving mass of snow, and the ice on the river groaned and sighed. She had always been a spectator, living on the edge of catastrophe, set apart from those who had lived and died in its midst. She felt like a series of women, like a paper-doll chain of Sadies, each connected by her fingertips to the next, but every one separate. There was the girl Sadie, then the Sadie before the war and the Sadie who escaped. Then the Sadie in London, and now this strange plump, middle-aged woman, who felt indistinct, like she was not really here at all.

That moment she saw it: on the bank of the river fluttered a photograph. Not daring to blink in case it disappeared, she stole through the snow to the edge of the river. Her back stiff from cold, she bent down and peered at the paper. There, lying on the ice was the picture of Mutti, her face unmarked by water or dirt. Sadie held her breath, and reached out for the photograph. She grasped it with both hands and studied the familiar face, the grey hair and friendly eyes. Lovingly, she cradled it to her chest, and smiled. She must place it safely in her wooden box, but just as she moved away from the bank, she saw a flicker as another piece of glossy paper caught a stray beam of sunlight.

It was just out on the ice of the frozen river, partly

submerged in snow. She slipped the first picture into her pocket and sat down on the edge of the bank. There was a drop of several feet, and she tried to ease herself down but slid faster than she intended, tearing her housecoat on a tree root as she fell. She picked herself up, and stood bruised and uncertain, trying to balance on the black ice. Forcing herself not to hurry, she glided on her patterned carpet slippers across the solid river to the second picture, and crouched down to peel it off the surface. This picture was of her father and she smiled between chattering teeth as she placed it carefully in her pocket, confident now that there were more to find.

Dark ivy clung to a gaunt elder overhanging the river, its deep green tendrils glimmered richly in the pale landscape. As she grabbed a strand to steady herself, she spied another photograph. She let go and skidded uncertainly further out, but this one was more difficult to reach and her slippers had soft leather soles that slid in every direction. She was dizzy from the bitter cold and the hard exercise, and saw the rooks surveying her with black eyes. Voices in her head urged caution, but unable to resist, she edged onto the centre of the river and, kneeling down, reached for a corner of the picture. It was too far. She inched closer and stretched out an arm. Her fingers were so cold that she could not command them properly, and the paper fluttered away once more. It was snowing now, and her path onto the river became obscured. The paper was lifted by a gust of wind and floated along the river towards the opposite bank. She cursed, '*Verdammt Scheiße!*'

The photograph lodged in a drift by a shivering willow. She took another few steps and came to a halt by the tree. Her cheeks were red raw from the wind, her lips tinged blue and her hair a tangled mass. Holding her breath, she reached up for the photograph wedged in the bank of snow. As her fingers brushed it, she felt herself being pulled downwards by invisible hands. They grasped at her, yanking her hair and clawing at her feet. The ice cracked open and Sadie fell slowly into darkness.

CHAPTER SEVENTEEN

JACK AND ELIZABETH had cleared away most of the rubble. The hole was patched haphazardly but at least it was no longer snowing inside the kitchen, and the floor was coated with a layer of grime that concerned neither of them. Elizabeth gave the stove a cursory wipe, put the ancient kettle on to boil, and when it began to sing, she poured out two steaming cups. Jack took his and sat hunched at the table. He was distracted, trying to do sums in his notebook, working out how much it would cost for a new roof and the minimum he needed to complete the golf course. He could afford no more mistakes, not a single one.

'Are there any biscuits?' said Elizabeth, interrupting his thoughts.

'In the larder.'

'I've looked. I can't find them.'

'Ask your mother.'

'I can't find her either.'

This was more surprising. Jack called, but there was no answer. It seemed strange that she had gone for a walk in this despicable weather, but she could be unpredictable.

'She's probably cleaning out the hens.'

Elizabeth went to the window and peered towards the barn.

'I can't see her, Daddy.'

Jack set down his pen. Where had his wife gone? The snow pounded against the windowpanes, and the trees creaked in the wind. This was not a morning to be anywhere except by a warm fire sipping hot tea. He abandoned his figures, opened the back door and saw a set of partially obscured tracks leading through the garden to the gate.

'I think she's gone outside.'

Jack saw that Sadie's stout walking shoes remained neatly on their Mackintosh square by the door. Her woollen coat and oilskins hung limply on the wooden peg. Jack had a nasty feeling in his belly. Sadie liked to make him cross, to worry at him like a blister, but she never tried to frighten him. She could catch a nasty chill going out in this arctic weather without proper layers. Jack shivered; he was not wearing his vest underneath his dressing gown and now that he had stopped schlepping sacks of straw and dirt he was getting cold once more. He pulled his overcoat over his pyjamas, put on some coarse woollen socks, his felt hat and three knitted scarves.

'Won't be long. I'd better check she's all right. Best put the kettle on again.'

He hoped he sounded casual; he didn't want Elizabeth to worry. She said nothing, but he felt her watching from the doorway as he ventured out into the blizzard. He could still discern Sadie's route across the land to the river, and as the feathery layers hid her tracks he followed the stream to the edge of his land. What madness or stupidity made her venture out in this?

Grimly, Jack realised that people had frozen to death on warmer days and with a fierce pang of guilt he remembered all the times that he'd wished she would leave him alone. He thought ruefully of the cakes she left out for him on the table, those little markers of concealed tenderness. He must find her to thank her for the baking. He loathed her cooking; she always forgot the things he did not like and was forever making him rabbit stews, but he knew that she revealed her love for him through her pastries. Years afterwards, he'd learnt that those strudels she brought him in prison used up her entire week's ration of butter. That's why she could only make them once a fortnight. The whole time he was away, Sadie and Elizabeth managed on a meagre half portion of butter, so that he could have his strudels. So that Sadie could show she loved him.

His face stung with cold; it bit into his cheeks and flakes settled on his chin turning his stubble hoary. He drew his coat tight around his shoulders and pulled his hat down low over his eyes. Where the devil had she gone? He reached the gate at the bottom of the field, clambered to the top rung and peered into the distance. The river was still; there was only the creaking of the ice and the eerie cry of the dark birds. Nothing moved. Jack could believe that he was the only creature on earth. Was this his fault? Did he drive her to this?

Unable to see any sign of her, he climbed back down and began to trudge the path along the riverbank. The jutting branches and fluttering bird shadows cast weird shapes upon the snow.

'I would like to sit in my house with my two women – my daughter and my wife.' His voice sounded thin in the big afternoon and he felt a little sick as he realised how much he wanted the company of his wife. He did not need to try and be English with her. She did not care. She had known him as the little Jew in Berlin and had loved him enough to marry him. He was suddenly light-headed and felt himself sinking into the snow. He cursed himself and his stupidity, yelling so loudly that his throat hurt, 'I am a fool!'

Fool, fool, fool!

His words echoed across the frozen river and he shuddered, drawing up his collar around his ears. There was a brisk flurry and he winced as the icy droplets hurt his eyes. He blinked hard and rubbed them. Damn this weather. He surged onwards through the gathering drifts, the bottom of his dressing gown hanging down beneath his greatcoat and dragging wetly along the path. He passed a rook perched on a bare bough of tree. The bird cocked its head on one side and stared back curiously, beak open in hope of food.

'Tell me if you have seen her,' he called in desperation.

It looked at him for a moment and then flew away. With an eager cry, he chased after it, buoyed by the wild hope that it would lead him to Sadie. He scrambled over the uneven ground as he raced to keep up.

'Wait my friend. Wait!'

The bird took no notice and vanished into the white void. Jack swallowed hard, and felt a painful lump in his throat. He must not give up. He must find her. He gritted his teeth, adjusted his knitted hat and stomped on.

The snow was coming thickly now and he could see only a few inches in front of him. He held out his arm and his hand disappeared. He knew, rather than saw, that the river was still beside him, and moving as quickly as he could, trudged on through the falling snow. His mind began to fill with sinister thoughts: what if he never found her? What if he found her and she was dead? Jack raised his eyes to the dark sky and through chattering teeth tried to bargain with the God he did not believe in.

'If you help me find her and she lives, I promise I will be a better husband. I will let her be a little sad. I promise I will be good to her. *I promise.*'

The trees groaned in the wind and a heavy fall of snow landed on his head, trickling wetly down his neck. He shuddered, swore and leant forward to shake it from his scarf. Losing his balance, he staggered and there was a sharp crack. Looking down, he saw Sadie's wooden box splintered beneath his foot. Fingers stiff and covered in painful chilblains, he gathered the shards and shouted into the storm.

'Sadie, it's me! Sadie.'

No one answered.

'I've come. Sadie, Sadie, I've come.'

Still no one answered.

He saw a snatch of pink fabric from her housecoat dangling

from a twig on the bank – she must be nearby. His heart pounding, he slid down onto the river and struggled across the ice, but the cascading snow formed a mantle all around him. He blinked away the flakes. Another flash of pink. Jack slithered urgently towards it.

She was lying on the ice, half buried by snow. With the fury of a wild bear, he cleared it from her body, and brushed her pale cheek with his hand.

'Sadie. Sadie. *Mein Spatz. Ich liebe dich.*'

Jack wrapped his arms around her and stroked her damp hair. She was so cold. There was only a faint tickle of breath on his cheek. Her eyes flickered, but they were filmy and unseeing. As he clutched her to him, he realised her housecoat was soaking wet, and the hem was starting to freeze.

'*Mein Gott, mein Gott,*' he muttered. '*Was soll ich nur machen?*'

It would take too long to fetch help; he needed to get her into the warm as quickly as possible. He took off his coat and laid it down on the ice. Then, he knelt down beside her, unpeeled her sodden clothes, undid his dressing gown and wrapped her in it as tightly as he could. Jack heaved her onto his fur-lined coat, untied his scarves and wrapped one around her head, another on her feet and slipped the third through the collar on the coat. Holding on to this scarf like a handle, dressed only in his red-striped pyjamas and heavy boots, he began to pull the makeshift sledge along the frozen river.

They reached the bottom of the field that led to the golf course and the dew pond. The snow had drifted and compacted to form a ramp. Panting, Jack used it to drag Sadie up the riverbank to the path, his pyjamas damp with sweat and steam rising from his back into the freezing air. His muscles burned, the air seared his lungs and throat and set his teeth on edge. He struggled to keep his footing as he carried Sadie through the field back home. At last they reached the garden and he dragged her the final few steps to the back door. Thumping on it with his fist, he called for Elizabeth.

'Help me . . . carry her.'

Elizabeth came running from the kitchen and threw open the door. She froze at the sight of her mother. Sadie's face was only a shade darker than the snow covering her. She was cocooned in white, like a giant chrysalis, her eyes shut.

'Elizabeth!'

Shaking herself out of her stupor, she helped her father carry her over the threshold. They laid her in the hallway, and Jack leant against the wall, struggling for breath. Sweat and snow trickled down his face and mingled with salty tears.

'In the sitting room . . . put her . . . is warmest in there.'

His voice filled the narrow hall and he could hear the sob stick in his throat as he spoke. Together they carried Sadie into the living room. With trembling fingers Elizabeth unbuttoned her from Jack's coat while he stoked the fire into a fearsome blaze.

'I'll stay with Mummy. You go into the village and send for a doctor.'

Jack shook his head, dazed with grief. 'I can't leave her. I won't.'

Elizabeth gave a small nod and was gone.

Jack stripped off his dripping pyjamas and climbed onto the sofa next to his wife, wrapped himself around her, rubbing her arms and legs to warm them. He was naked and cold but she felt colder still. She made him think of the tiny dead birds he had buried in the deep powder a few days before.

'Don't die, Sadie,' he whispered. 'I'm very sorry, please don't die.'

He rubbed his foot against her calf and kissed her cheek. There was a blanket covering them and he pulled it over their heads, so that they were encased in a crude tent.

'Don't leave me. Please, please.'

He reached his arms around her stomach and felt the soft yielding rolls. He clung to her, his teeth chattering, terrified that if he let go, she would die.

They lay together in front of the fire as the shadows grew long and danced in weird patterns on the stone walls. Jack did not release his grip but slowly fell asleep. He dreamt they were back in London. They were young, he still had his hair and Sadie's was chestnut brown. They were so poor, Elizabeth slept in a drawer in their bedroom, tucked in with the sweaters and tea towels. It was their anniversary but he had no money to buy his wife a present. In his dream, Jack climbed again the rickety cast-iron stairs to their fourth-floor flat and put the key in the lock. As he turned it, he heard Caruso crooning love songs on the gramophone from the place next door. He paused to listen, then pushed open the door to their apartment.

Sadie was standing stark naked on the table and when she saw him come in she began to dance. She swayed in time to the refrain lilting through the thin plaster wall. She was small and slender, her dark hair snaked down her back and she wore nothing but a pair of red high heels. 'Happy anniversary, darling,' she whispered and continued to dance. She turned her back and wiggled her round bottom. '*Mein lieber Schatz.* Do you like your present?'

As she spoke, she clicked her heels on the wood. She had lit the gas lamps and her skin glowed warmly in the dim light, her nipples dark pink. Seeing him stare she laughed and coyly pulled her long hair to cover her breasts. Jack stood, his back against the door, gazing at this girl-woman, silent with love.

He woke, embarrassed to discover that he had an erection. He was both aroused and sick with guilt; how could he have wanted this woman to disappear, to leave him alone when she had danced? She was still the girl in the red shoes. The fire had burned low, the embers orange.

'Jack?'

'My darling, you're awake.'

He pulled her tightly to him and began to cry. The tears trickled into his mouth and he licked them away.

'I am so tired,' murmured Sadie, her voice rasping and thin.

'Then you must sleep.'

He stroked her matted hair and tried to wrap his gaunt legs around her in case she was still cold.

'But first you must promise me. Never to do it again.'

'Do what?'

Jack closed his eyes and rubbed the soft down on her arms. He didn't like to say the word. It was a dirty, evil word.

'Leave us,' he whispered, 'promise me that you will never try to leave us ever again.'

'Oh,' murmured Sadie, 'so that is what I did.' She was warm at last, and it was so pleasant in Jack's bony arms. 'I promise.'

Jack kissed her on the mouth. His rough cheeks grazed her skin, and he touched the creases around her eyes with his fingertips.

The doctor diagnosed pneumonia and advised complete bed rest for a month. Sadie was forbidden from venturing outside until all the snow had melted. Jack told Elizabeth that it was an accident; her mother had neglected to put on her boots and slipped and fell on the ice. He nursed Sadie with forgotten tenderness; he brushed her grey hair and brought basins of hot water to warm her feet. He bought newspapers to try and interest her in the world once more, and sat beside her reading aloud. He only read yesterday's papers, because then she could be reassured that there was nothing so bad in them that the world would not continue tomorrow.

Yet, something had happened to Sadie on the ice. She remembered falling into darkness, floating under the frozen film and looking up at the heavens. She fell further, down through the middle of the earth and then another sky, until she emerged in a dark wood. A gnarled oak tree stood before her, giant fir-trees dwarfed her on every side, and she breathed in the scent of Bavarian pine. Lights twinkled inside a cabin and somewhere she could hear Papa singing. She walked through the cabin door, and Emil grinned up at her from his nest on the rug, before returning to pasting stamps in his album. Mutti patted the cushion beside her, saying, 'Come, you must dry yourself by the fire and have a little something to eat.' Sadie kicked off her wet shoes and padded across the floor.

Even lazing by the Dorset hearth, Sadie understood that she'd left a piece of herself in that other place. She knew none of this was possible, yet she felt different: same eyes, same nose, same round belly but something minute had shifted inside her and, to her surprise, she realised that she was glad Jack had found her. She liked sitting on the sofa, reclining on plumped cushions and toasting teacakes on the hot fire. She liked Jack combing the knots out of her hair, and listening to the click, click of Elizabeth's knitting needles in the afternoon.

The incident had triggered another revelation. When Sadie closed her eyes, she was overwhelmed by a passionate longing for turkey meatballs. Her mouth watered, and she could almost smell them frying on the stove. She remembered that Mutti had made them when she was small and they had been her favourite thing as a child. For twenty years nothing had been so bad that it could not be made better by turkey meatballs, then in the course of time she had forgotten them. One afternoon, when Jack briefly left Sadie alone with Elizabeth, she confided her yearning to her daughter, who took the task seriously.

Elizabeth listened as her mother explained how the taste

hit her tongue, until she too could hear her grandmother in the kitchen bashing spices with a rolling pin. She followed the instructions in the battered recipe book with its magical amalgamation of German and Yiddish, but the quantities were vague and imprecise. The book required her to cook with instinct, to imagine the flavour she wished to create and then use the book as a companion and guide. Her mother refused to eat the early attempts – if the recipe was wrong, Sadie would forget the taste once more.

Elizabeth was a small baby when they had fled Berlin and had no memory of her grandmother, but she began to know her through the book. The meatball method was in a chapter entitled 'food to soothe troubles' and slowly she learned to listen to her voice. She procured some turkey, ground it carefully, and then she heard a whisper, 'Mustard seed, mustard seed.' She pounded it with the old farmhouse pestle, added it to the sizzling meat and then presented it proudly to her mother, confident that this was perfection.

As Sadie ate, her face was radiant. 'This is a good thing,' she decided, comforted by the scents wafting from her kitchen. History could be carried forward in tastes and smells. Elizabeth was learning to cook from her grandmother; her children would know the tastes of the *shetetl* and the world *before*.

January was drawing to a close and it was Elizabeth's last evening before returning to Cambridge. The ground was wet and slick with mud, the grass brown and battered by the heavy snow. The icicles dangling from the rooftops dripped away into nothingness and sleepy badgers emerged to scavenge once more. As the snow retreated, shrinking first to the edges of the garden and fields, hiding under hedgerows, then disappearing altogether, Sadie rose from her bed. She took a long bath, washed her hair, dried it by the fire, put on a green stuff skirt, a cable knit sweater and went into her kitchen. Jack was not pleased.

'Go back to bed. You've been ill. Lie by the fire.'

'No. The doctor said I could get up when the snow was gone.'

She pointed out of the window. The evidence was irrefutable: drizzle dampened the ground, and the meltwater had turned the trickling stream into a torrent. There was something Sadie needed to cook before Elizabeth left for the station; the meatballs were an excellent start, but she wanted to teach her how to make a Baumtorte.

It was gathering dusk, the lights were lit and the stove burning when the two women lugged the tin bath inside to scrub it clean. They counted out the eggs, weighed the butter, flour and sugar and mixed them together. Tired from her illness, Sadie sank onto a kitchen stool, unfastened her stockings and washed her feet, then she climbed into the bath and began to tread the batter slowly between her toes, the mixture oozing creamily.

'Let me do that,' said Elizabeth, sitting down to take off her own shoes and socks.

Sadie shook her head. 'I must do this one. The next one is yours.'

Taking her time, she blended the ingredients, feeling them grow smooth and slippery beneath her skin. Elizabeth watched as she ladled the buttery mixture into great tins and toasted each layer under the grill. The cake grew tall, sprouting like a sapling, while dusk mellowed into nightfall. Soon it was dark outside, the sky was overcast with cloud and the soft rain continued to fall silently into the earth.

The church bells struck midnight and Jack came into the kitchen carrying his bottle of Scotch. The sweet scent of baking pervaded the house, and disturbed him –the fragrance of Baumtorte was always tinged with sorrow.

Sadie surveyed her cake-in-progress, chewing her lip. Once assembled, it would be as high as the one she had baked last summer, but this time it needed one extra layer. Tiers of cakes were spread out across the kitchen table. She spooned the final coating of batter into one of the tins and put it under the grill. She was no longer tired; she was hot and her arms felt sore from lifting and beating the eggs, but she felt a surge of energy as she lifted out the last tier and set it down on the table to cool.

Jack gulped whisky from a rose-patterned teacup and watched his wife curiously. Surreptitiously he poured a drop into the bowl set aside for the icing. Elizabeth giggled and said nothing but started to sift the icing sugar and stir in the lemon flavouring with a wooden spoon.

'No. No. I must do that. This is my Baumtorte,' Sadie protested.

'For goodness' sake. Let me make the icing,' said Elizabeth. Now that her mother was almost well, she was beginning to irritate her again.

Sadie conceded and allowed her to smooth it into a glossy paste. Then, together they piled the tiers on top of one another, using the icing to bind them, until finally the Baumtorte was ready.

'You should have the first piece,' said Elizabeth.

Sadie shook her head. 'I made it for you.'

Standing on a chair, Sadie cut her a slice, as thin as her little finger but several feet deep. As Elizabeth bit into it she felt a wave of sadness. She considered how lonely her mother must be, to bake cakes in order to remember. It was both strange and sad, and a fat tear trickled down her cheek.

Seeing her daughter cry, Sadie believed Elizabeth finally understood, and was comforted.

CHAPTER EIGHTEEN

JACK AND SADIE went to bed in winter, the big wind buffeting the walls of the cottage, and woke to discover spring in the garden. Pinpricks of snowdrops grew in icy clusters beneath the apple trees, their heads nodding in the breeze like a trembling all-day frost. The branches remained bare, the sky empty and cold, and yet there was the possibility of green things: everywhere there were tight curled leaf buds, the newly uncovered grass seemed lurid in its brightness and shoots poked the brown earth aside. Jack and Sadie inspected the garden arm in arm, pointing out the sprouting stems to one another, each patch of plants a surprise treasure hoard. As the snowdrops began to fade to brown, the primroses crept into view and shone like tiny suns growing from the earth.

After the primroses came clouds of daffodils, golden with bright orange trumpets. Sadie picked armfuls and brought them inside until every room was filled with vases of happy daffodils. The ones she liked best were white ones with pink rimmed hearts. In Berlin they had been banned from the parks, so in their first English spring they circled round and round Regent's Park, marvelling at all the flowers. Back then, she and Jack were still dazed and she was silent, unable to speak English. Not knowing it was forbidden, Sadie had picked one white daffodil, and it smelled of freedom. When Elizabeth was a child, Sadie bought bulbs for her to plant in the window boxes. The girl cut one open to look for the flower but it was empty and wet and white.

All England smelled of damp, fresh earth. As he went to his course each morning, Jack found himself walking with his mouth open taking great gulps of clean, moist air. He gathered the men on the field by the fifth hole; this was the one with the most splendid aspect, the land falling away beneath them and the tall grass glimmering in the morning light. They were not the only ones working – in the distance, on the edge of the village and only half concealed by a motley clump of trees, the bungalows were going up. Wilson's Housing Corporation had been true to their word and pre-fabricated buildings sprouted up across the cleared meadows. There was the far-off clatter of picks and clashing metal as scaffolding was hoisted. Jack sighed and thought of Old England, that mythical place before the Great War. Why did mankind want to ruin everything with his damned improvements? The English cottage was a thing of nature – it sprang up from the earth with walls made from local stone or mud and roof of slate or straw as if it had grown there. When abandoned, it sunk back into the ground like the corpse of a tree or a rabbit. He longed for the days when whole villages were pretty clumps of white cob houses and the visitor did not need to close his eyes when driving through the concreted developments that scarred the peripheries. When the course was finished he would plant more trees, white ash and elm, to shield his land from their ugliness. He stood on a mound, drew himself up to his full height and cleared his throat, since he wanted very much to be inspiring.

'Friends, we must press on, full puff ahead. I need nine holes finished before June. This will be the greatest golf course in the whole of England. We must work like hedge sparrows building their nests or the honeybee gathering nectar. We will triumph! And a bottle of Scotch to the man who moves the most molehills.'

He was determined that the course be finished on schedule;

it was a matter of necessity as he was nearly out of cash. He must be brave, like the champion Bobby Jones himself, hold fast and not lose his nerve. If he allowed even a second of wavering hesitation, he was finished. From first light he worked so furiously that the others marvelled at his energy.

He did not rest but laboured by the light of the bright spring moon, digging, digging. Night was another world; the trees, grass and houses might be the same – made from the same leaves, water or bricks – but they were transformed. Flowers closed their petals; the green grass turned purple and the wind changed key as it hissed through the rustling trees, whilst the trickling stream tore through the fields in a rush of noise. Night hid the unsightly bungalows, masking the concrete in darkness so that one could almost believe that the modern world had not yet impinged on the village.

Jack worked steadily, breaking up clods of soil with his spade, the edge glinting sharply like a square sword. There was power in his small frame and he laboured relentlessly – raking, cutting, smoothing. Dropping his tools in exhaustion, he halted shortly before dawn and traipsed back to the house where Sadie had left him breakfast on the table. There was a tall glass of milk, a fat slice of apple strudel and cold slices of lamb, the fat thick and white. He ate methodically, drinking the milk down in a single gulp then chewing the lamb, savouring the marbled lines of grease. He saved the strudel till last, licking the buttery pastry off his fingers and, half in a dream, picked out all the currants, lining them end on end around his plate. Leaning back in his chair, he gazed at the neat row and thought of Emil. Hearing the kitchen door creak, Jack looked round to see Sadie standing behind him, her eyes bright. She leant over and rested her chin on the top of his bald head.

'You remember too,' she said. 'I never knew.'

Before he climbed the stairs to bed, ready to sleep for a few hours next to the warm body of his wife, he retreated into his study to write to Bobby Jones. The sun was stealing over Bulbarrow Ridge, as he pulled out his sheet of paper and began.

> *Dear Mr Jones,*
> *I really hoped to hear from you before Christmas so either your sproncy American postal service is slower in coming than the Jew's messiah, or the aeroplane delivering my letters is tipping them out in the middle of the Atlantic.*

Jack decided not to acknowledge the third, most likely possibility, that Bobby Jones discarded his correspondence with no intention of ever responding at all.

> *I've been tardy in writing (though not so much as you, Mr Jones, if you will forgive this gentle reproof) as the Michaelmas season was eventful. My wife was ill but I am pleased to say that she is now much better. I am working very hard on the golf course. To tell you the truth, if it is not finished soon I am in the shit, as they say.*
> *I am holding a golfing tournament in honour of Her Majesty on the morning of the coronation and, on behalf of the Pursebury Ash Coronation Committee, I warmly and most cordially invite you to attend as our guest of honour.*
> *Your friend, humble servant, etc.*
> *Jack Rose*

He sealed up the envelope and placed it reverently on the stand in the hall, ready for Sadie to take to the post office. Worn out, his hands raw with blisters from shovelling, he went upstairs to bed.

March gave way to April and with it came the bluebells. Mr Betjeman described the bluebell as the quintessential English flower and the bluebell wood as a snippet of magic left behind as an oversight from the ancient world. Jack decided this was something that he ought to investigate, and so agreed to spend an afternoon with his wife in search of them. They drove to the top of Bulbarrow with the roof down for the first time that year, and Sadie, tilting her head right back, watched trails of cloud like wisps of smoke.

They had never seen anything like it: there were thousands upon thousands of bright blue flowers, as though the sky had fallen to earth beneath the trees. Sadie had thought she was too old for new things but the striking beauty of the place stirred her and she looked about greedily for the largest stretch of unbroken blue. They reached a patch of beech trees and spread beneath them was a cobalt cloud; the wood sloped gently down and the flowers covered the earth like a swirling waterfall, shaken by unseen currents. 'Here. Stop here,' she said excitedly.

She looked around her and stared; it was like being a little girl and seeing the sea for the first time. They picked their way through the trees but it was impossible not to crush the bluebells – the wood breathed with them – and Sadie wondered if her cheeks would turn blue with the scent. She picked one and tucked it behind her ear.

'You mustn't my darling,' Jack chided her. 'They're dying out.'

They laid a blanket beneath the trees, unpacked a box of vanilla biscuits and poured sweet Madeira wine into china teacups. Jack was nicely warm and lay back on the rug. He did not like to think of the fate of the bluebell, disappearing in the onslaught of progress. It was the fault of those wretched bungalows. This was a disappearing world and he was glad to be old – he would not live to see it all ruined. Shafts of sunlight fell to earth and illuminated clumps of the flowers. In the sunshine they were bright blue while in the depths of the shade they turned to deep indigo or shades of wine. He watched Sadie while she dozed, noticing the fine lines around her eyes and a mottled mark on her cheek, which he traced with his finger. He treasured these markings of age – they were like rings on a tree. He gave a wide yawn and, in the pleasant warmth of the wood, overcome by the scent of flowers and sweet wine, he succumbed to drowsiness and slept.

As they dozed, curled side by side on the picnic rug, the afternoon crept on. The sun disappeared behind a bank of cloud, the air grew cold and the damp woodland floor gave off the scent of leaf mould and ferns. The sky turned black, birds paused their singing and forest creatures sought shelter in the thicket. There was a terrific crash of thunder and, a moment later, a powerful flash of lightning illuminated the heavens. Jack sat up with a start and adjusted his spectacles, as another roll boomed out in the sky above and the storm shook the branches. Leaf curls raced along the ground, picked up by the gathering winds.

'Wake up. It's going to rain,' he said, shaking Sadie and scrambling to his feet.

Immediately the air vibrated as another bright crack of lightning danced through the sky. Sadie began to stuff the picnic things back in the basket, while Jack haphazardly folded the rug. Then the rain came: huge pellets of water hurled from the sky, battering the leaves and stinging their skin.

'Dance with me, Jack?'

'Are you a *messhuggenah hund*?' called Jack, already racing back to the car and slipping on rotting foliage.

'Are you a hen?' shouted Sadie after him.

Jack stopped in his tracks and turned around. 'You mean am I chicken-shit?'

'Hen-shit, chicken-shit, *alter kacker*, it's all the same to me. Dance with me old man,' she added with a smile.

Jack dropped the rug and, grabbing her round the middle, whirled her about, crushing bluebells, which released their scent, thick as smoke. He tried to move to the rhythm of the pounding rain on the leaves, while Sadie's hair stuck to her face like ivy strands, and Jack's spectacles streamed with water and misted with steam.

'You are a terrible dancer,' complained Sadie as he crashed her into an oak tree.

He leant forward and kissed her on the nose. 'And still you married me. Foolish old woman.'

The rain lasted for three solid days; they were marooned inside like Mr and Mrs Noah. Jack stared miserably out of the bedroom window – it having the best view of his course – and wondered how much harder he would have to work to make up the lost time. He thought of the wretched English understatement: 'April Showers' indeed – this was a biblical flood. Even Sadie baking 'wet weather treats' could not console him. He turned the bed into a model of Bulbarrow and, making the contours with eiderdowns and pillows, used knitting needles to mark the position of the holes.

Sadie came upstairs carrying a mug of hot tea to find him stretched out on the bed, peering over a large rumple and trying to visualise the eighth hole. It was still raining and the tin bath in the garden overflowed, while stagnant pools appeared on the lawn. The water meadows at the bottom of the hill had turned into lakes and the Stour was as wide as the Mekong. Sadie perched on the windowsill and stared out at the mist-covered golf course. A sigh came from Jack, who uncharacteristically ignored the biscuits she had placed on the saucer. She needed to cheer him up.

'Show me the course.'

'It's too wet. We'll drown.'

'Use the model.'

Jack looked at her in surprise; she had shown no interest in his plans before. Pleased, he took her by the hand and led her over to a patch of emerald baize.

'This is the first fairway. See. Down there is the dew pond.'

He pointed to an old hand mirror of Sadie's that twinkled away, nestled in the eiderdown. She gave him a smile of encouragement and he gestured to a knitted turquoise scarf that meandered along on the edge of the quilt.

'This is the stream. It will be marvellous.'

'What's that?' She pointed to a round purple stain by the knitting-needle flag on the third fairway.

Jack frowned, 'That, I think is a patch of strawberry jam.'

Sadie's face lit up. 'A strawberry patch. That would be nice. If you get peckish in the middle of a game, you could pick strawberries.'

Jack was uncertain whether this would be feasible in the middle of the fairway, but not wishing to quench her new-found enthusiasm pulled the cover a little and repositioned the flag so that the jam stain was at the edge of the rough.

'We could put it here, I suppose.'

He came to kneel beside her and cupped his hand round his ear, straining to hear an imaginary sound.

'Listen, can you hear the nightingales?'

A hairbrush forest and a white paper dove perched on a pillow and Sadie listened, for once captivated by Jack's fervour. Instead of the rose-patterned teacup she saw the small pond and the flowers that she must plant for him around its banks. She began to understand the challenge of playing out of the rough and, as she stroked the coarse horsehair blanket, she appreciated the sweep from the fifth hole. The coverlet fell away and she could see all the way down the bed-cloth valley into the Blackmore Vale, beyond the foot of the bed and out of the window.

While Jack continued to plot his model course, Sadie stitched him new flags. He gave her the old ones to copy but deciding that they were not properly made, she resolved on reworking them all. Jack tuned the wireless and they worked companionably, neither speaking, each absorbed in their task. Sadie sat on the windowsill where the light was good and meticulously double stitched the neat edges of the flags – she did not want them fraying or coming apart in the wind. She paused, the close work stinging her eyes, and watched the pounding rain battering the plants in the flowerbeds below; she hoped there would not be too much damage, at least not to her favourite rose. She looked beyond the garden to the golf course, gratified to understand the brilliance of Jack's scheme at last. It was much better to share it with him; if he was a madman then at least they were crazy together.

Yet, as she gazed at the field through the rain it looked as though the land was moving. Her eyes were tired – she rubbed them and blinked. No, it was still moving – the hillside was falling forwards and above the rain there was a rumble – the sound of earth moving.

'Jack, Jack!'

They looked in horror at the ground above the fifth hole. It was slipping away and sliding down the hill. The avalanche of earth gathered pace and there was a colossal roar as it crashed onto the fairway below. It juddered to a stop, leaving a brown river of devastation – trees were snapped in two from the force of the landslide and more were carried forth on the giant clump of earth.

Clad in oilskins, they rushed down to the field to survey the damage. In the gale, Sadie clung to an umbrella, which continually leapt away from her like a frightened bird. She tried to keep it over Jack, but he stomped away from her, indifferent to the pouring rain. Panting to keep up, she followed him onto the course, and as they marched across the third fairway, she admired the smooth grass that had sprung up verdant from the wet. The fifth hole was another story. It was always Jack's favourite, but now it lay smeared across the land below – an enormous pile of mud, rock and trees. Jack did not know what to do. Without a word he turned round and walked back to the house.

Sadie hurried after him. Water had found its way into her galoshes and they squelched and sucked as she followed. A trail of wet boots led from the back door into the study and she found Jack slumped in his chair, swigging whisky from the bottle.

'*Verflixt!* It's a catastrophe. I'll never finish on time. I'd need hundreds of pounds for repairs and there's no more money.'

He took another gulp and in his despair told his wife everything.

'I took a loan out against the business. I can't take out any more. I'll never be an Englishman. Never.'

He drained the bottle and gave a half hiccup, half sob. 'I may as well burn my list. Toss it into the fire and be done.'

He looked pitiful sitting in his wet things with water streaming down his cheeks. Sadie was not used to him like this; he was the one with the ideas, the one who took care of things. The optimist. 'What about the house?'

'What about it?'

'Is it mortgaged?'

Jack sat up. What was she suggesting?

'Yes. I took out a little one, to help with cash flow.'

'So you can take out another?'

Jack hesitated. 'I could. But I have nothing to pay it back with. And the bank will want the business loan repaid in a few months. It's a big risk, doll.'

Sadie tried to understand. She was unused to thinking about finances. 'If we don't take out another mortgage on this house then we cannot finish the golf course?'

'No.'

Sadie sat down on the stone floor and peeled off her wet stockings, setting them to dry on the hearth. She studied her toes, thinking hard before she began to speak. 'The course will be the greatest in England. There will be white doves and strawberry fields, streams filled with golden fish. It must be finished. You said so yourself.'

Jack stared at his wife in amazement. 'If the course does not make money and we cannot pay back the mortgage, we will lose the house. Do you understand that, darling?'

She met his blue eyes and nodded.

Later that evening, Jack found himself in his study and composed his weekly epistle to Bobby Jones.

Dear Mr Jones,

I can't help wondering if you get my letters. Or if you do, whether you even read them. While I would never presume to criticise (and this is intended with humble admiration) you really ought to reply to letters. It's very un-British not too. But after all, I suppose you're an American and so have to be excused.

Today, my wife surprised me. We've been married for a long time, Sadie and I, and we'd fallen into bad habits. I don't mean the leaving of socks on the bathroom floor and forgetting to close the chicken coop (though there is that too). I thought I'd lost her years ago, and then she came back to me.

I'm in a spot of bother over the golf course (boring finances and what have you). We sat together and worked out all the sums. Providing that the course is

*finished in time for the coronation and that we get fifty
members (at the price of one guinea each), we should
just get by. I'll have a golf course yet, Mr Jones!*

Your servant and fellow golfing enthusiast,
Jack Rose

*PS: You really should pay a visit to this corner of
Dorset – widen your horizons.*

The next morning the rain stopped, the men returned to work
and Jack showed them the damage. Basset shook his head
ruefully, 'A'ways knew there wis bad drainage in them fields.
A'ways knew.'

Jack's optimism had returned – every time there was a
disaster he met it and now even Sadie had faith in his vision;
he was five feet three inches of warrior-golfer. He was not
like those unfortunate fellows in the books by Mr Thomas
Hardy – he did not believe in fate; rather, one had to make
one's own good luck. His position on the hillock by the fifth
hole had been swept away, so he ushered the men to the point
just above the landslip. He balanced on a tree root and swept
his arms out wide, motioning to the landscape below. The
breeze toyed with his wisps of hair, picking them up so that
they floated around his head like a white halo. His battered
greatcoat – five sizes too big – hung around his ankles and his
eyes shone with inspired purpose. He looked rather like an
Old Testament prophet to the Dorset men, who gazed at him
curiously as the morning sun glowed in the east.

'Disaster has struck and still we stand firm! We shall not be
dissuaded from our purpose, we men of England!'

Curtis grumbled appreciatively and Basset, Ed and Mike
all spat on the ground, a sign of their approval. Jack rocked
precariously on his tree root.

'We must continue apace! Full speed ahead! No effort will

go unnoticed or unrewarded. I need plans. I need suggestions. I need inspired thought for how to mend and move forwards.'

He leapt onto a molehill before the gathered men and gazed at them expectantly. They stared back, unsettled by this demonstration of feeling and faith. Curtis was the first to speak.

'If you doesn't mind me sayin'. I think we ran into difficulties, cos we went against the land 'imself. We needs to follow 'im more. Smooth out this mess for sure, but less diggin' and movin' of earth.'

He pointed to the fields below and suggested alterations to the run of the course, taking advantage of the natural hazards of the land, so that only the greens were to be smoothed and levelled. Jack listened rapt. It was true – while he no longer wished to demolish the side of Bulbarrow as he had in the early days – he was still cutting into the land too much. He hated Wilson's Housing Corporation and their wretched concrete bungalows spoiling the meadows, but was he not as guilty? He had not listened properly to the dictates of his own fields.

In the distance the work continued on the new houses. They looked like teeth, rooted in muddy gums, decided Jack with a shudder. Curtis's plan seemed like a good one, but Jack realised it was flawed: if they stuck to it and worked ten hours a day, seven days a week, then the course would be finished by the end of August, but that was still too late. He watched the men, as small as mice from this distance, labouring mightily on the concrete houses. He needed them for his golf course. 'Basset, Curtis, Mike. We need to poach some Wilson men,' he said quietly.

Basset flicked a butterfly off his lapel. 'We needs more than that. I 'as got a plan.'

CHAPTER NINETEEN

A T MIDNIGHT, JACK met Curtis, Basset, Ed, and Mike at the bottom of the lane by the signpost known locally as Charing Cross. The night was smuggler's dark, useful for their purpose; all the lights in the village were out and the only sound was that of a badger snuffling around a dustbin, whose clattering made Jack jumpy. He felt distinctly nervous about what they were going to do and hadn't been able to eat any dinner. His stomach growled.

'What the bloomin' heck were that?'

'Sorry.'

'Right, 'ead count,' said Basset taking charge, 'There's five o' us here.'

'Well, 'ow many is there supposed t' be?'

There was a pause.

'I ent sure. Five wi' a bit o' luck.'

'Right.'

'Is everyone ready?'

There was a chorus of 'ayes' and the party headed down the hill into the blackness. They stole through the village until they reached the fork leading to Wilson's Housing Corp. The building site was half a mile down the road, situated on the outskirts of the parish. The men walked quickly, Jack panting to keep up with their swift strides. They stopped outside the entrance to the construction site. The large wooden gates were padlocked and a sign reading KEEP OUT was stapled to a post. Jack gave a worried huff, and thought for a moment that he could see words forming

– streaming forth from his mouth in vapours, *'Don't do it. Go Home . . . .'*

'Be 'ere in minute or two,' whispered Basset, exuding confidence.

Jack stamped his feet to keep warm and pulled his coat around him. He could only see Curtis by the twinkling of his eyes; one green eye gave him a conspiratorial wink. There was rustling in the bushes behind them and Jack jumped, his heart beating loudly in his ears.

'All ready,' hissed a voice.

A moment later, two figures appeared from the shadows and Jack could make out a slim man wearing a dented trilby hat and a stocky fellow sucking on a pipe, both men's faces illuminated by the glowing embers.

Basset took charge once more, 'Right you are. Mr Rose-in-Bloom this 'ere is Freddie Wainwright and Matt Baxter. They is workin' for Wilson's but would like very much to join us in our endeavours on the Pursebury Golf Course.'

Jack smiled cautiously in the darkness and silently shook hands. He reached into his pocket and retrieved a brown envelope.

'The bonus we discussed.'

'Thank ee.'

There was a jingle as Freddie produced a set of keys and proceeded to unfasten the padlock.

'Is there no security?' Jack wondered in a low voice, worrying about even being on an operation like this.

'Oh shouldn't think so,' answered Matt, with a casual toss of his white-blond hair, which shone in the gloom.

Jack thought that perhaps they ought to have checked this minor point first, and bit down on his lip – this couldn't be good for his heart. He was sure weak hearts ran in his family, or maybe it was Edgar Herzfeld's family – he knew they ran in somebody's. There was a click as Freddie eased off the padlock and swung the gates open. They squealed horribly and Jack shuddered. If there was anyone here at all, they must have heard that racket. But no one came. One by one they slipped into the still yard. It glittered with machinery: there was a small crane, cement mixers, towering poles of scaffolding and a small army of diggers. Half concealed in the shadows like a glowering beast of mythological power was the Mechanical Digger. It was the Dragon of St George, its bulk hidden in the darkness and its vast outstretched claw slumped against the wall.

'Is it sleeping?' Curtis hissed softly.

Freddie dangled the keys, 'Aye, till I use these.'

The others observed from a distance as the young man leapt up into the square box cab and turned on the engine. It stuttered, then gave a low roar and crept forward.

'Best move, he's not terribly good at reversin',' advised Matt.

The men stood flat against the fence and watched the creature crawl backwards on its metal legs. Jack was enthralled – he had not seen one so close before, and was at once horrified and amazed by its grotesque bulk. These were the things that did the work of thirty men. Jack felt a pang of conscience – this was a bit too much like stealing for his blood (list item thirty-three: the Englishman is scrupulously honest). Which was why, unbeknownst to the others, he had brought another envelope with a touch more cash. He scanned the yard for somewhere to stash it, spied a makeshift cabin and determined this to be the site office. While the digger entranced the others, he crept up the rickety steps and shoved his envelope underneath the door. Now he wasn't stealing, only renting.

'Mr Rose-in-Bloom!' hollered a voice.

Jack stood up quickly, banging his head on the door handle.

'Don't you want to ride in 'im?' Freddie called across the yard, apparently abandoning all attempts at secrecy.

Jack saw that all the others had crammed into the machine: Freddie and Matt sat on the seat, Basset, Ed and Mike hung out the windows and Curtis was perched on the roof, like a strangely shaped hat. Jack waved and hurried over. Basset reached down and pulled him up with a strong arm.

They had to shout to make themselves heard above the machine's racket. It could only creep along and Jack believed he could have gone faster if he were participating in a three-legged race. He was balanced precariously on the running-board at the side of the cab, and only Basset's restraining arm stopped him from tumbling onto the tarmac. Sweat trickled along his spine. He wondered that they had not been caught and fully expected at any moment the bells of a police car and for a Black Maria to pull up and cart him away. The others would be all right. He would be the one to go to prison – he was the Jew and the boss and would be blamed for corrupting these good English men. He considered whether it would be undignified to be sick.

'And we're 'ere,' said Basset, giving him a friendly pat on the arm.

Ed climbed down and swung open the gate leading to the bottom field, but the space was just too narrow and the digger tore one of the poles clean from the ground, leaving an unsightly scar along the metalwork. No one apart from Jack seemed in the slightest bit concerned. The beast was quieter in the field, its metal claws made less noise on the earth than the road. The yellow headlights cast a sickly hue upon the bulrushes and made a false moon shimmer on the pond.

Freddie was the only one who knew how to drive the beast, so Basset explained to him what needed to be done. Jack stared in awe as it dug a huge hole in the rough and deposited a tree, roots and all, into the chasm. The men gathered around the monster in the murk, clutching their hats and shaking their heads in respect.

'See how much stuff he can carry.'

'Aye. Aye. Fifty bloody horsepower,'

'*Fifty*. My God. My God. Never thought I'd see the day.'

'An' they do bigger ones, too.'

'Bigger'n him? Be bigger'n God.'

'Is it a pulley system?'

'Nah. A cable. Makes 'im a bit unwieldy, not so fast, like.'

'He really is some-att.'

'It's a nice mustard colour,' added Jack feeling left out.

Under Basset's direction, the machine manoeuvred the hillside back into place. The land was removed from the fairway and piled piece-by-piece upon the spot where the fifth hole used to be. Jack and Curtis sat on upturned buckets by the ponds and watched the machine work in its own pool of artificial light. While the others were entranced by the sheer power of the contraption, Jack was disconcerted. He was used to machines in his factory – great electric looms that wove the carpets and vats of industrial dye. He had imagined the countryside to be a rural idyll, free from the clamour of mechanisation. Unthinkingly, he took the flask Curtis proffered and took a hefty swig, 'Change, I suppose, has to come everywhere.'

Curtis stared through half-closed lids, his lined skin looking like chestnut bark in the gloom. 'Aye. He comes alrigh' whether we wants 'im or not. I remembers the days afore t' railways. Back in them days, every village had 'is songs an' each one were a bit differen' than 'is next door. Then, one day trains come, like bleedin' griffins, an' Dorsit isn't jist Dorsit no more, but a piece of big England. Them trains puffin' along tracks from Lon'on an' Bris'l brings all new stuff from the music halls. In one week – jist seven days an' seven nights – no one sings the ol' songs anymore. In fields at harvest time they doesn't sing "Ol Linden Lea" no more, but "Down the Lambeth Walk" and "Pretty Lil Polly Perkins o' Paddin'ton

233

Square". An' now no ones remembers them old 'uns 'cept me. An' my singin' voice is worse than a one-legged badger in a bear pit.'

Jack had no reply for the old man and only wondered how long it would be before this place hummed with traffic. The digger was growling up the hill once more with a ton of earth and stone clenched in its jaws.

'It'll still take time for the ground to heal,' murmured Jack.

'Aye, 'ee can move the earth but 'ee can't regrow that there grass,' said Curtis, with a slow shake of his head.

Jack glanced to the east and saw that there was the thought of dawn in the sky, and behind him a wren began to chirp. That was it. He scrambled to his feet, offering Curtis a soil-stained hand.

'Come on. It's time.'

Jack walked briskly up the rise to the others, with Curtis bleary-eyed, trying to keep pace. Feeling rather brave, Jack stood in the path of the machine and, waving both arms wildly, forced it to come to a stop.

'Eh, what you do that fur?' wondered Basset crossly.

Jack pointed at the sky. 'It's dawn. We must take it back.'

Basset studied the east sceptically. 'Got least an hour.'

'No.'

'Don't yer want some of them bunkers? 'Ee could dig you some in a minute. Bob's your uncle.'

'My uncle was Morris. And no bunkers. I don't want that thing tearing out chunks of earth. We must take it back right now.'

Jack was resolute; he stood very upright and looked Basset in the eye. The other man met his gaze and then shrugged.

'What ever yer wants.'

Basset whistled and signalled towards the road. In the cab, Freddie stuck up his thumb and the machine began its slow descent towards the lane.

Jack walked beside the digger as it crept along the road. The metal treads clattered horribly against the hard surface making him wince; he had studiously avoided trouble for more than fifty years and here he was actively inviting it – he could not be less invisible than he was at that moment, walking slowly next to a giant yellow mechanical digger.

It took him a moment to realise what was up. Dawn glowed rosy in the east and the air was full with the chattering of birds. A cockerel crowed in the distance and was immediately answered by another nearby. That was it. He could *hear* the birds: the digger had stopped and its vast engine had fallen silent. Up in the cab, Freddie fumbled frantically with the keys. Curtis tugged on Jack's coat, 'Don't look so worried, everythin'll be jis luvely.'

Jack swallowed hard as the window rolled down on the cab.

'Out o' juice,' announced Freddie.

'I'll get the spare can,' said Matt and climbed up to rummage around behind Freddie's seat. 'Ent 'ere.'

'Aw shit.'

'This is it. I'm going to prison,' said Jack and turned white.

Nimbly, Freddie climbed down and joined the others. They were at the bottom of the hill by Charing Cross. The nameless signpost creaked ominously. The hulking digger looked out of place, marooned in the middle of the road and blocking the narrow lane in both directions, its yellow sides brushing the hedge.

'Let's jis leave it here. Leave key's in 'im an' bugger off,' suggested Matt.

'Suppose some one nicks 'im?'

'Won't budge will 'ee. No juice.'

'Well that's settled then,' said Basset and marched up the lane.

The others muttered assent and began to follow, until Jack

was left alone beside the machine, 'Don't go. We can't leave it!'

'Come on,' called Basset. 'Nothin' yer can do. Wilson's'll be along in a bit.'

Jack stared at their departing backs as they sauntered up the hill, then with a final glance at the stationary digger, he trailed after them, as the red fingers of dawn streaked the morning sky.

The machine had done a splendid job clearing the debris from the fairway, but the green still needed to be levelled and reseeded and the tee rebuilt. The eighth and ninth holes had not been started and the seventh was not quite finished. All in all, there was a mountain of work still to do and Jack vetoed absolutely the illicit borrowing of any more machinery – they must continue by hand; a course of action made easier by Freddie and Matt bringing with them another dozen men from Wilson's Housing Corp. Sadie ordered rose bushes from Dorchester and planted them in clumps around the ponds and along the edges of the hazards. She threw seeds for wild flowers – scarlet poppies, cornflowers, love-in-the-mist, pink-rimmed daisies and cowslips – amongst the grasses in the rough. Jack faithfully recorded their progress in his weekly letter to Bobby Jones.

Dear Mr Jones,

Today was a strange sort of pagan festival that involved (as I find they usually do) drinking cider and shouting. We finished the seventh hole and toasted it (and poured a healthy drop into the hole – no doubt giving some poor earthworm a punchy breakfast). There was much laughter and even the womenfolk came along. My wife baked some excellent pear tarts and we ate them with the local clotted cream. It's

strange, I've eaten those tarts many times – they're
from an old Bavarian recipe – but they've never been so
delicious as with that little Dorset addition.
The damage (from a landslide this time, not the
woolly-pig) has been repaired and the course looks
simply marvellous. I wish you could see it. I'm crippled
with bank loans. Any more disasters and we're up
Stourcastle creek.

   I've placed an advertisement in The Times *– which*
I've taken the liberty of enclosing.

   Yours sincerely etc.
   Jack Rose

There was still the problem of the molehills. Knowing Jack
would not approve, Basset waited until he was safely out of
the way writing his letter, and then sent ferrets down the
holes to root out the moles. The sightless creatures emerged
terrified into the daylight, where Curtis and Basset crushed
their skulls with hammers. The trimmed green was soon
piled high with their minute, velvety corpses, which Curtis
quickly skinned, carefully preserving the pelts. Moleskin
gloves were much prized by fashionable ladies, and a few
elderly women in the village still knew how to make them.
Basset dug a grave at the bottom of the field and filled it
with the tiny bodies. Jack remained cheerfully oblivious to
their method, but was thrilled that his molehill problem had
mysteriously vanished.

On Wednesday morning Sadie ambled down to the village hall, carrying a fat chocolate sponge (laced with sugared cherry blossom) for the Coronation Committee. The sun beat down on the corrugated iron roof, and the ladies of the committee had abandoned the sweltering building for the village green. Sadie hovered unseen at the edge of the field, in the shade of a spreading chestnut. Coarse blankets were strewn haphazardly beneath the trees, and the other women sprawled in twos and threes, listening to Lavender Basset, who sat very upright on a wooden chair, rattling through the day's agenda. Beside her a mouse-like woman in a pale blue frock scribbled and blinked.

'Has anyone heard back from the electrical store in Dorchester?' asked Lavender.

A robust lady in a pair of olive slacks struggled to her feet and raised a hand. Lavender tipped her head imperiously, 'Yes, Mrs Hinton?'

'Tis as we feared, Mrs Basset. Bulbarrow Hill blocks all signals for the television. The BBC himself has been consulted. But there is nothin' to be done.'

There was a collective sigh, and mutterings of 'what a pity', until Lavender raised her hand again for silence. 'I know it seems unfair what with them French seein' it an' all. But we people o' Pursebury will not be defeated by pifflin' disappointments.'

'We will not,' agreed Mrs Hinton, settling back down on her rug.

'We need ideas, suggestions 'n solutions, ladies,' said Lavender.

'We can a'ways listen in on t' wireless,' said the mouse-lady beside her, in a meek voice.

'Whole village crowdin' round a wireless? It'll be a shambles.'

'Aye. No sense o' occasion.'

From the shade of the chestnut tree, Sadie listened to

238

the swell of noise. She thought back to the last great Royal celebration, the marriage of Princess Elizabeth to Prince Philip of Greece, five years before. Then, there had been no possibility of watching the event on the television set. Jack and Sadie had scrutinised every photograph in the newspapers, and Elizabeth's school held a pageant a few days later, with a girl in a white frock acting the princess and another, hair slicked back, playing the part of the prince. That gave Sadie an idea. She stepped out from the shadow of the tree and into the midst of the chattering women, her chocolate cake held aloft, and cleared her throat.

'Aye, pop the cake indoors, Mrs Rose-in-Bloom,' said Lavender, preoccupied with the crisis.

'I . . . em . . . I . . . have an idea,' said Sadie, standing her ground.

The women on the rugs stared at her in surprise. Sadie's cheeks pinked under the scrutiny. 'At eleven o'clock, when Her Majesty Queen Elizabeth the Second receives the crown from the Archbishop of Canterbury, we should be crowning our very own queen,' she paused, and smiled at the others. 'The Queen of Pursebury Ash.'

Lavender jumped up in excitement, knocking over the wooden chair. 'I like that idea Mrs Rose-in-Bloom!' She flung her arms out wide, eyes shining, 'We, of Her Majesty's Coronation Committee, Pursebury Ash Branch, refuse to be defeated or to permit this village to go without a proper coronation at the proper time.'

There were shouts of agreement from the assembled women.

'Excellent idea. Marvellous,' said Mrs Hinton, taking the chocolate cake from Sadie and trying to shake her hand at the same time.

'Now,' said Lavender, 'Over elevenses, me must discuss the matter of the Coronation Chicken.'

'Aye,' agreed the mouse-lady, with a stubborn scowl. 'If they're havin' it at Buckingham Palace, we are most certainly havin' it at Pursebury Village Hall.'

They spread a picnic out on the rug with Sadie's cake in pride of place. The sticky icing attracted a swarm of biting flies, which Lavender swotted with a roll of newspaper.

'No, not 'im,' said Mrs Hinton, snatching the paper. 'He's the one with the instructions. I saved him special.'

Mrs Hinton passed it to Sadie, 'Here you take a look, Mrs Rose-in-Bloom. You are a handsome cook and you knows all about foreign food.'

Sadie settled down on the rug, the wool scratching her bare legs, and studied the paper. It was a page carefully cut from *The Times*:

CORONATION CHICKEN (COLD) (FOR 6–8)

2 young roasting chickens; water and a little wine to cover; carrot; a bouquet garni; salt; 3–4 peppercorns; cream of curry sauce (recipe follows).

Poach the chickens, with carrot, bouquet, salt, and peppercorns, in water and a little wine, enough barely to cover, for about 40 minutes or until tender. Prepare the sauce given below. Mix the chicken and the sauce together, arrange on a dish.

'Ahh,' said Sadie, giving a little murmur of recognition, 'I heard Constance Spry herself on the wireless. She explained how to make this. I have poached chicken before. In Berlin. I can show you – if you like?'

Lavender blinked, forced a tight smile and then relaxed. This was the first time Mrs Rose-in-Bloom had casually mentioned her German past. But, Lavender supposed, it wasn't sordid like Mrs Hinton's younger sister whose 'past' had been a long-haired sailor from Kentucky. Mrs Rose-in-Bloom's past wasn't her fault, and perhaps it was better that she spoke of it from time to time.

CHAPTER TWENTY

ARLY ONE MORNING, after planting a flag in the restored fifth hole, Jack walked around his course chatting to Basset and Curtis. He held envelopes filled with wages; he liked to pay his men in person so that he could thank them for all their hard work. There was a palpable sense of antici-pation. He gathered his workforce around the flagpole and climbed on top of an upturned seed crate so that they could all see him. There were a full score of faces staring back up at him and he gazed at them, and then at his golf course. The land was so beautifully restored that in a few months no one would ever know it had slid down the hillside. The green fields shone in the morning sunshine, while white puffs of cloud drifted across the blue sky. A cuckoo called from where apple trees and cricket willows had been planted to screen the bungalows. The first of the year's dragonflies danced on the surface of the pond, causing Jack to feel a ripple of happiness.

'Thank you all for your hard work. Bobby Jones himself could not have laboured more mightily. There is only one more hole to be completed and then we will be triumphant!'

He took off his hat and waved it at the crowd, who bayed and whistled with enthusiasm. Then he noticed a balding man dressed in a grey flannel suit standing apart from the others, watching. Jack did not recognise him and, curiosity piqued, climbed down from his box. The others took this as the signal to go back to work, but the stranger in the suit did not move and instead addressed him in a confidential tone.

'Lovely spot you've got here.'

'Thank you,' said Jack smiling proudly. In his view this was the most beautiful spot in all of England and hence the whole of the world.

'Means I am very sorry to give you these.' The man opened his briefcase and handed Jack a tightly bound document.

'What is it?'

'Afraid it is a cease and desist notice.'

'A what?'

'Cease and desist. Means you must stop all work immediately or face a large fine and possible imprisonment.'

Jack sank down on the box, gripping the papers in his hand and scanned the first few lines. He'd always detested legal jargon – it was there to confound and intimidate, but it worked. Then it hit him: all this was his own fault. He always knew he shouldn't have stolen that mechanical digger, even if it had only been for a single night.

'It's Wilson's Housing Corporation out for revenge. I know it,' he declared miserably.

The man looked surprised. 'It's the council, sir. Nothing personal. You need to apply for planning permission for golf courses. Go through proper channels.'

This was news to Jack and fury began to bubble inside him. He hated bureaucrats – they were nasty, vague men who got in the way of good business in every nation in the world.

'It's a golf course, man! There are no buildings. Not even a stupid car park.'

The man gave a nasal groan. 'I understand. It does seem most unfair. But nowadays even golf courses need permission.'

Jack looked at all the men busily tending the fairway. 'Well? What am I to do?'

'Stop all work and apply for planning permission.'

'And how long will that take?'

'I can't tell you that, sir.'

Jack got to his feet and pointed furiously at the men working on the land.

'Look,' he said, trying not to shout, 'See them? I employ all of them. Am I supposed to send them all home? They thought they were to have another month's solid work. Have some pity, Mr . . . ?'

The grey man looked at him, and relented. 'Brown. Mr Brown. I can try to call an emergency meeting at the planning commission. Try to get this resolved quickly.'

'Please,' said Jack.

'But you must halt all work.'

That afternoon a telegram arrived from the carpet factory. As Jack read, a sick feeling churned in his belly.

DATE: 28 April 1953
Post Office Telegraphs
No fees to be paid unless stamped hereon.
TO: JACK ROSENBLUM, PURSEBURY ASH, DORSET
FROM: GEORGE FIELDING, LIVERPOOL ST,
LONDON

LOOM BROKEN STOP NEW MACHINE URGENT
STOP SEND FUNDS STOP REGARDS FIELDING
STOP

Jack stuffed the telegram into his pocket. There was no money to send – a new machine would cost five hundred pounds. All the money from remortgaging the house had been spent on the course. He would write to Fielding and tell the man to make more repairs. There was nothing else to be done.

Jack stood on the fifth tee and gazed down at the deserted golf course. After weeks of frantic labour the stillness was absolute and he shivered. He'd given the men two days off, promising they'd all be back to work and prayed that this would not turn out to be a lie. The countryside was as serene as ever – indifferent to his turmoil. A chaffinch flew from branch to branch and the wind hummed softly through the bulrushes.

'Smoke?' asked a voice.

Jack turned to see Curtis and Basset beside him proferring a packet of cigarettes. The three men sprawled companionably on the neat grass, exhaling thin flumes of smoke into the air, Curtis blowing rings, which hovered mistily above their heads for a moment before disintegrating.

'Wi' you look at that.'

Basset pointed across the hedge to a field full of sheep, where a black-faced ewe was lying on her side straining, and as Jack looked he saw that a wet membrane sack protruded from underneath her tail. She gave little cries and grunts, and he realised that he was looking at the nose of a black lamb trying to be born. The ewe gave a final groan and, with a rush of water and blood, the lamb slithered out onto the grass. The mother rested there for a moment, gave another push and a second form poured out of her and landed next to its sibling. The sheep panted, closed her eyes for several seconds, and then she was hauling herself to her feet. The umbilical cords snapped and she nudged her new babies, quietly chewing the membranes that covered their noses and mouths. The tiny creatures lay glistening on the grass until, after several minutes of their mother's busy licking, they gave a cough, then a splutter and finally began to wiggle their ears. Within five more minutes the lambs were wide awake and struggling to their feet, wobbling on their new limbs. Despite his despair, Jack gazed in wonder.

Curtis smiled and toasted him with his cider flask. 'I remembers my first lambin'. I were 'bout five or six. Sum time last century any hoo. Was on top o' Bulbarrow in the coldest March. There were still bloomin' snow. Not like them sissy winters we gits now. Lambs wisn't due for 'nother month. I wis mindin' them sheep and saw one of the ewes was makin' a rackit and I knows it was startin'. There was no barn or nothin' so out it came. Brand-new little chilver steamin' on the snow.' He slapped Jack on the arm. 'You alwas remember the first. You is a proper Dorsit man now. You sees it finish and then it starts again.'

That night Jack sprawled in bed with Sadie, their fingertips touching, watching a spider spinning a web between the low ceiling beams. The window was open and they listened to the rain falling softly on the creepers outside. A vase of pinks and violets infused the room with the scent of summer. There was the sound of scratching above their heads as mice scampered in the attic, and from the garden drifted the rustling of a fox and the purr of a nightjar.

'There is nothing we can do but wait,' resolved Sadie as she rearranged the bedclothes.

It was true. He had put all his faith in this country; councils were little governments and he must trust them to make the correct decision.

The letter popped through the letterbox two days later, as Jack was quietly pretending to eat his breakfast. Sadie watched as he tore it open with the silver knife, slowly read the contents and wordlessly handed it to her:

Dear Mr Rose,
   I am sorry to inform you that planning permission for the golf course at Pursebury Ash has been denied. A number of planning codes are in violation. Details of this decision may be obtained from the local planning officer Mr G. Brown.
Yours regretfully,
   Etc.

Sadie studied Jack's face. When he was working outside he appeared lean and strong, but now his skin was grey and he looked like an old man. He took off his glasses and cleaned them absent-mindedly on his shirt.

'Well, this is it. We're finished. *Fertig.*'

Sadie shook her head. This was not the Jack she knew. She watched as he slumped into his chair, rested his head on the kitchen table and shut his eyes.

'We'll sausage through,' she said.

'I am so tired. Too tired to fight anymore.'

Sadie poked him in the ribs. 'Get up.'

He shuffled round the table to avoid her but she simply poked him harder.

'Stop it.'

'Not until you sit up and decide what we are to do next.'

Jack raised his head and gazed evenly at Sadie. She was wearing her floral apron and curlers but her eyes were full of ferocious determination. 'How much of the loan money do we have left?'

'Not much. Less than two hundred pounds.'

Sadie frowned. 'I think there is only one thing you can do,' she said slowly.

Jack waited by the car at the top of Bulbarrow Hill, listening to a pair of magpies squabble. The evening was so warm that he was sweating in his jacket and his silk tie choked him. The leaves on the trees barely fluttered and in the patches of shade the first of the foxgloves were bursting into flower. A brown cow leant on a gate chewing the cud and stared at him nonchalantly. After what seemed an endless wait, he heard the distant whirr of a car engine and watched as a red Morris Minor chugged its way up the steep slope. In pursuit of his golf course Jack had taken many risks, even pushed the law a little, but the thought of what he was about to do made him frightened. He watched as the red car crept closer and closer and hoped Sadie was right.

The car drew up next to Jack's Jaguar and Mr Brown climbed out. He was not smiling. 'I would have much preferred to meet in my office. We could easily have discussed it there.'

Trembling and silently cursing his unsteady hand, Jack reached into his pocket and drew out a brown envelope. Inside was all the money they had left, every last penny.

'I want to give you this. I hope it might encourage you to . . . reconsider.'

Mr Brown recoiled from Jack in revulsion. He put his hands stiffly by his sides and took a step back towards his car. Slowly, he shook his head and his lips curled in contempt.

'Bloody Jews. You think you can buy us all. You disgust me.'

He hissed the words at Jack, his eyes narrow with hate. Jack stared in surprise. If it was not money they wanted, then why were they tormenting him? He'd believed Sadie was right and it was the same everywhere – they stopped Jews from doing business but when you paid your bribe, they let you go back to work.

'If you don't want my money why do you refuse me planning permission?' Jack asked, bewildered.

The other man got into his car, started the engine and began to drive off but then, clearly having a change of heart, wound down his window.

'You, sir, were in violation of at least seventeen planning codes under section A, subsection fifty-nine, paragraphs twenty-six to ninety-one. Seventeen violations!'

'But . . . I didn't know there were planning codes for golf courses.'

'A poor excuse. The gentleman building the other course made no excuses. Submitted a nice set of *professional* drawings.'

Jack only heard the first part of Mr Brown's outburst. 'What other course?' he asked, colour draining from his face.

'I can't tell you that! It's confidential. But it's for eighteen holes with a modern clubhouse.'

Jack rubbed his forehead and his throbbing temples, trying to digest this new information. There couldn't possibly be demand for two golf courses, and the other one had official approval, while his was outlawed. With a miserable sigh, he turned and slouched back to the top of Bulbarrow. He felt sick – he'd never criticised any government legislation before (list item number three) but at this moment, he knew that the council was monstrous.

He did not want to return home without good news. Sadie's suggestion had failed – backhanders were clearly more common in Mittel Europe than England, and now it was up to him to get them out of this fix. His heart hammered with adrenalin; he must find out who was building this new course – even though he was not sure what he would do then. He leant against the gate and, closing his eyes, listened to the soft hum of the flies flitting around the cattle. Absent-mindedly, he stroked the ears of a dappled cow, which began to lick him with its sandpaper tongue. How could he find out where this other *verdammt* course was? What he needed was someone on the inside. Hadn't Sir William Waegbert once been mayor. Jack recalled a splendid certificate embossed with the mayorial seal hanging in Piddle Hall. It was many years ago, but surely he still had the necessary influence to help.

A few minutes later Jack was hurtling down the hill in his green Jaguar as the sun glowed low in the sky, bathing the landscape in a warm haze. The clouds turned red then orange and the brown coats of the cattle shone scarlet. High above him a triangle of swifts flew home to their roosts, their cries filling the evening air. The sun finally slipped below the horizon and it suddenly grew cold, making him shiver and reach for the scarf on the seat beside him. A moment later, a deer streaked across his path forcing him to slam on the brakes. He waited whilst it found a gap in the hedge – its eyes huge and black with fear, legs shaking frantically – and then drove on.

Jack remembered the trip to Sir William's the previous year. Back then he was filled with trepidation, now he was travelling to see a friend. Jack was quite sure he would smooth out the altercation with the planning department – Sir William was an important man.

The lights came on in the houses and twinkled in the darkness, breaking up the gloom. Jack sighed – there had been money in carpets and he wished that he had paid a little more attention to his business, then he could have paid off his debts and the mortgage on the house. Now the factory needed a massive order, the sort that only ever came from governments – otherwise the bank loans would never be repaid. God only knew how he was supposed to pay for a replacement loom. As he gripped the steering wheel, Jack realised that he'd been happy. That Sadie had been happy. More than anything, he didn't want to go back to the city. He liked it here, and he wanted to live where there were deer and badgers and woolly-pigs.

Jack drove over the bridge across the river Piddle. It was called the Piddle here but became the river Puddle further downstream. It was said that the name was changed from Piddle to Puddle everywhere that Queen Victoria visited during her tour of Dorsetshire – the courtiers fearing that the word 'piddle' would make the Queen blush. Jack found this example of English prudery endearing – imagine being embarrassed by such a little word.

The stone eagles outside Piddle Hall glared down at him from their tall plinths, beaks frozen open in a silent shriek. He gave a tiny shudder and wound along the curving driveway where the avenue of looming oaks surveyed him with gaunt disapproval. A few minutes later, with a rumble of car tyres on gravel, he arrived at the hall and drove straight to the stables at the rear where he had been told to park the previous summer. The horses whinnied softly as he slammed the car door. His heart was beating fast. A little whisky and some good advice would help. There had been some changes since he was here last. What he presumed to be another stable had gone up, which even in the dark he could see was a handsome brick building.

He hurried to the main steps of the hall. Lights were on in the downstairs windows but the vast door was shut; the Waegberts were not expecting visitors. Jack yanked a huge, cast-iron handle that dangled down at the side of the entrance and a shrill bell pierced the night. Instantly, there erupted a chorus of barking, followed by voices, until finally he heard footsteps entering the hall. The door clicked and he saw with surprise that Sir William opened the door himself, a pack of spaniels wagging at his feet. Sir William looked equally amazed to find Jack on his front steps. There was a smear of something at the corner of the baronet's mouth, he still had his napkin tucked into his shirt and he stood there for a moment, paralysed, before his perfect manners took over.

'Come in, come in,' he said, ushering Jack inside.

'I am sorry to call like this,' said Jack apologetically, 'but disaster has struck and I need your help.'

Sir William stared for a moment. 'Oh dear. Gosh. We'll sit in the library and you must tell me everything.'

Jack followed him into the dimly lit panelled hall; it smelled musty and damp and, stifling a sneeze, he wondered that he hadn't noticed before. He was led along a winding passageway into a cavernous library with an elaborate chandelier suspended from the ceiling, though when Sir William clicked the light switch, it was a grimy lamp that illuminated the room.

'I'll be back in a moment. I must tell Lady Waegbert to continue without me.'

Left alone in the library, Jack surveyed the faded volumes decorating the shelves. They were all bound in the same worn crimson bindings and coated in a thin layer of dust, making him suspect that they had not been read in a long time. In the centre of the room stood an elegant wooden table with a rich patina that only needed a good polish with a touch of beeswax to have a glorious sheen once more. He wondered whether Sir William used this room very often – it had the smell of something packed away and forgotten.

A few minutes later Sir William returned with apologies and without his napkin. He gestured Jack to sit and they each took a carved upright chair and faced each other across the table. Sir William studied him, then with a tight frown got to his feet and went to a bookshelf. He pulled out several books, which turned out to be hollow carvings filled with a whisky decanter and glasses. His hand shook slightly as he poured two generous measures and slid one across the table to Jack. His face was pale and troubled, causing Jack to wonder if he had been unwell and, guiltily, if he should be here bothering him with his troubles.

Sir William toyed with his glass, downed its contents, then helped himself to another and, not appearing to be in a hurry for Jack to begin, started to trace patterns in the layer of dust on the table. Then, the baronet appeared to steel himself, crossed his arms in his lap and closed his eyes.

'Well, man, let's have it then.'

'You're sure? I don't want to be a bother.'

'You've come all this way. May as well let it out.'

Taking the invitation, Jack leant forward and in a low voice recounted his unhappy tale. Sir William let him speak without interrupting; his elegant face was impassive and Jack could not read his expression.

'I love the English. The most wonderful peoples,' Jack concluded, at the end of several minutes. The thick emotion in his voice emphasised his accent and he pronounced 'wonderful' with a soft hiss 'vf' at the beginning. 'I want this golf course so much. So very much,' he added, tears beginning to form in the corner of his eyes. 'Without it, I am ruined. I lose my house. *Everything.*'

Sir William said nothing. He settled back in his chair and studied the chandelier – the crystal shards were covered in filth and needed a thorough clean.

Jack waited in agony for him to speak and made one final plea for his assistance. 'Can you help me to discover who this rival is? Please.'

Sir William shifted on his narrow seat. He got up and began to pace the length of the room before moving to the stone mullioned window, where he stood gazing out into the darkness.

'It's me, Jack. It's my course.'

Jack did not hear him properly – could not understand his friend's words.

'Beg pardon?'

Sir William remained by the window with his back turned, so that Jack could only see the reflection of his face in the glass.

'I am building a golf course. Eighteen holes. Parking for a hundred automobiles. You must have seen the new clubhouse on your way in.'

Jack tried to speak and found he couldn't. He swallowed but his mouth had gone dry. He opened his lips to speak but again no sound came out. At last, he managed a whisper.

'We were friends.'

'Come. We were acquaintances,' said Sir William smoothly. 'I gave you membership to my golf course.'

'And you may have membership to mine. It will be the finest course and the most exclusive in the South-West.'

Jack reeled. He felt like the deer he had caught in his headlights and barely registered that Sir William was offering him membership to an exclusive English Golf Club. This was the last item on his list and the reason for moving to the countryside. Now he was being beseeched to join an elite club by a knight of the realm and he did not care. He spoke softly but his voice quivered with hate.

'I will never be a member of your club. I do not wish to be part of any society that includes you. You are *ein Landesverräter*.'

Sir William did not understand the word but he comprehended the tone, and it was true; he had used Jack and then betrayed him. He had found out that the Jew was not so stupid after all. After making enquiries, he discovered that there really was demand for a golf course out here in the sticks, and if someone was going to make money, Sir William was going to make damn sure it was he. These country piles took a fortune to run, and the Waegbert fortune was running low. Jack interrupted his thoughts with another furious tirade.

'I can never be English to you, can I? Did you want to teach the shitty little Jew-Kraut a lesson?'

The venom of the small man took Sir William aback. He disliked conflict of any kind – when he got the council to stop the building on Jack's land, they had promised him that they would not reveal who had lodged the objection. Sir William wondered how he had found out, certain that Jack had come determined to extort a confession – they were wily these Jews. 'How dare you address me like this? You're nothing but a vulgar counter-jumper. Go back to your tailor's shop.'

Jack blinked, opened his mouth and closed it again.

Aware of his guilt, Sir William became indignant and full of self-justification, 'You built a golf course on the side of a hill. It's preposterous. You can't have played a round in all your life. It would never have worked. I admit that, yes, you gave me an idea, but I am going about it in the proper way.

dream.'

Jack stared at Sir William in dismay. How could he have done this to him? He ached with the betrayal.

'I may not have played, but I studied Robert Hunter and Bobby Jones.'

Sir William gave a hard laugh of derision. 'You read Bobby Jones. I hired him.'

'I don't believe you.'

Sir William stalked to a desk in the corner and pulled out a piece of paper, which he tossed to Jack.

Dear Sir William,
    On behalf of Mr Jones I would like to accept the commission to design the proposed course at Piddle Hall. Mr Jones' fee is $1000 non-negotiable. Please forward all maps, land surveys and

Jack read no more. He felt a cracking in his chest and wondered if his heart could actually break. He stood up and walked out of the library, along the panelled corridor and out into the hall. Behind him Sir William called in a mocking voice, 'I am sure I can persuade the council to allow your course. It can be exclusive too. It can be the Jew course.'

Jack made no reply. He pushed open the front door and descended the stone steps into the cool, black night.

He was shaking so much that he struggled to steer the car and it weaved all over the road. He supposed he would have to sell it but strangely this thought did not upset him. Next he wondered how long it would take to sell the house. The pain in his chest returned and he hunched miserably over the steering wheel, too unhappy to cry.

When Jack reached home, he did not park in the garage or lovingly cover the Jag with the horse blanket but stalled it on the driveway and went straight inside. The house was quite still; Sadie must have given up waiting for him and gone to bed. He hoped that his late return might have prepared her for the worst. Only a few hours ago he had left in high spirits, full of optimism that a well-placed backhander would secure the necessary planning permissions and work could start again. He felt ill at the thought of telling her what had transpired. Guiltily, he remembered the last time he had sold her house, in London, over a year before. He wanted to pursue a dream and had been relentless in his ambition. Everything had been sacrificed for his golf course and finishing his list: the London life, the successful factory. They had given up their friends and Sadie had even abandoned her kosher kitchen for him. Shamefully he considered how poorly he had repaid her – he could not make it up to her, as he had nothing left. After nearly twenty years in England, he was once again as poor as he had been when they first arrived, only now he was old and without hope.

Jack wandered forlornly into his study to write one last letter, and for the final time he pulled out a piece of heavy white paper from the sturdy desk. He grabbed his whisky and drank straight from the bottle as he wrote.

Dear Mr Jones,
    My heart is broken. After all this time, after all
my letters, how could you agree to design Sir William
Waegbert's course? You did not even write to tell
me yourself. Sir William Waegbert has betrayed me.
But your betrayal is worse. I thought golfers were
honourable men. True gentlemen.
    I am finished but alas my golf course will never be
finished. I am empty. There is nothing left at all.

This is my last letter.
Jack Rose

With that, Jack sealed the envelope, put it out to be posted and wearily climbed the stairs to bed. Sadie was fast asleep, sprawled on top of the covers, her hair fanned out across the pillow and her mouth slightly open. Her breath made a curl of hair move up and down with each exhalation. Jack slotted his body in beside hers, slid an arm around her waist and laid his head on her pillow.

'I am so sorry,' he whispered.

CHAPTER TWENTY-ONE

WHEN THEY HEARD the awful news, the village suddenly remembered that Sir William was poor and had wasted his fortune on horses. They discovered that they had always suspected him; they guessed that the estate was bankrupt and Lady Waegbert gambled. With each telling the tales grew; Sir William turned into a vagabond who owed all the shopkeepers money and had letched over every daughter in the village. Lady Waegbert, it was said, was forced to pay her vast gaming debts in obscene favours, but none of this comforted Jack – he listened to half of it and believed less. It could not help him now. He had no pity left for Sir William – he needed it all for himself.

Jack lost his exuberance like a balloon the day after a birthday. He sagged and stooped so that Sadie felt she was watching him wither before her eyes. At first she baked him 'cakes to heal a broken heart' but either the recipe was faulty or he would not eat enough, not even when she decorated them with sugared violets. The course was silent; no one returned to complete the last fairway and the flags drooped in the stillness of the May afternoon. Inconsolable, Jack wished that the fields and hedgerows would acknowledge his despair. He wanted the flowers to shrivel on the bushes and the cherry blossom to fall to the ground in a pink snow shower, but to his disgust the starlings continued to sing, and the fish swam around the pond like slices of oranges amongst the weeds. He refused to see any of his friends and when Basset arrived to offer words of condolence he stole out to the course and would not be found.

Determined to reason with him, Sadie hunted him down to his favourite spot, hunched on a patch of grass by the fifth hole. In a single week, the fairway grass had sprouted thick and lush, and barely resembled anymore the neat crop of a golf course. Jack's trousers were dark with dew and he tore the petals off a daisy, all the while muttering incoherently under his breath. Sadie smoothed her skirt and sat down carefully beside him, wishing that she had remembered to bring a Mackintosh square, 'Why don't we stay in the village?'

Jack looked at her with mild surprise but said nothing.

'I mean, the house must be sold, but there might be enough left over to buy another place, a small cottage perhaps.' Sadie took his hand and rubbed the back of it with her rough, gardener's palm. 'We could be happy in a little whitewashed cottage. There are only two of us after all and I'm sure we could afford a box room so that Elizabeth could visit.'

Jack gave an unhappy cry, 'I can't do it, Sadie. I can't.' He could not bear to remain and watch new people desecrate his golf course, his dream of England. 'And really darling, what can we afford to buy? We've not even two hundred pounds.'

He tenderly removed a red money spider dangling from a curl of her grey hair. Undeterred, Sadie reached into her apron pocket and took out a copy of the *Blackmore Vale Gazette,* which she unfolded to reveal an advertisement in bold letters. 'See here. *Wilson's Housing Corporation is delighted to offer for sale charming bungalows with super meadow views. All mod cons. Deposit only one hundred pounds.* You see Jack, we can afford to stay.'

He tried to suppress a shudder and failed. With a bitter laugh, he took the paper from her and read the advertisement for himself.

'So, after all this time and effort, all we can manage is one of those concrete huts despoiling the water meadows. I can't do it. I can't. I'm sorry, dolly. I gambled and I lost.'

He did not need to say it. They both knew that the price of defeat was to leave, never to return.

Sadie did not raise the topic again and, since they must go, it was her task to organise the unhappy journey. She booked the removal company, began to pack up boxes and wrote to Elizabeth of the change in circumstance, but even then none of it seemed quite real. Slowly, they began to change the habits formed over the last year; they stopped sitting outside in the evening – in the city they could no longer stretch to the expense of a garden and so must wean themselves off fresh air.

'It will be good to be back in town,' said Sadie, trying her best to be cheerful, as they sat in the airless living room.

'Yes,' answered Jack. 'I'll go to the beigel shop each morning. No more stupid plans. No more lists.'

Sadie stifled a sigh and went back to packing boxes. She did not know what to do with Jack – his unhappiness was as relentless as his cheery optimism had been before and she longed for the old Jack to return. There was a knock at the front door that nearly made her drop the china bell she was holding. 'Can you get it? I'm busy.'

Jack scowled. 'I don't want to see anyone.'

With a huff, Sadie abandoned the packing box and went to the front door, where Curtis was standing on the porch.

'I 'as come t' see Mister Rose-in-Bloom.'

'Of course, come in,' said Sadie ignoring her husband's stipulation, rather hoping that the old man might be able to raise his spirits, but Curtis hesitated, pointing to his mud-caked feet.

'They is awful mucky.'

'Don't worry. We're leaving – let the new people clean it up.'

She ushered him into the living room but Jack had gone, leaving his half-finished whisky tumbler on the floor. She puffed up a cushion on an armchair and motioned Curtis to sit. 'May I get you a drink?'

'No thank ee.'

Curtis patted his pocket where he kept his hip flask of special cider. They sat there awkwardly, talking about the weather.

'Lovely and sunny.'

'Aye.'

'Though a trifle windy.'

'Aye.'

Curtis took a swig from his flask and offered it to her, but politely she declined.

'Let me find Jack.'

She went upstairs to the bedroom, to find Jack hiding in the corner.

'What are you doing?' she hissed, not wanting Curtis to overhear.

'I won't see any of them. I can't bear it.' He made no effort to keep his voice down.

Sadie frowned, folded her arms and shot him a look of fierce resolution. 'Mr Curtis is a guest and you are being rude. The English are always polite and welcome their guests.'

She added this last part in an effort to cajole him but Jack merely scowled at her and climbed into bed fully clothed, pulling the covers over his head.

'I'm not English and I'm not coming down.'

The following evening Sadie persuaded Jack to take a walk around the village, on the condition that it was late and the working folk were all in bed. The cherry blossom was nearly finished and it landed in her hair like brown confetti. Blue tits zoomed to and fro taking constant meals to their hungry chicks. The grass had sprouted and was the glossy green of early summer and she could hear the evening rattle of crickets in the fields. Out of habit they walked down to the parish notice board at Charing Cross but they were both too melancholy to talk. A smart poster painted blue, white and red was carefully pinned to the board and the second she saw it Sadie tried to turn back. But it was too late: Jack began to read.

Coronation of Her Majesty the Queen Elizabeth the Second,

Tuesday, 2nd June 1953. ~~Golf Match at~~
~~'The Queen Elizabeth Golf Club'. Tee off 6 am.~~

Celebrations Pursebury Ash Village Hall, 11 sharpish.

Latecomers not admitted.

Due to unforeseen circumstances the golf match is cancelled.

He stood bewildered, then rubbed his eyes, gave a loud cough and cleared his throat, 'Must be making hay nearby. Always bothers my eyes.'

Sadie looked at the forlorn figure and decided she could bear it no longer.

'I've had enough, Jack. The sooner we leave the better. I think we should simply pack up and go.'

'Yes. No goodbyes. We'll just disappear.'

On her way through the kitchen garden, Sadie noticed her sweet peas were beginning to form their first buds – in a week or two they would be flowering. A month ago Jack had cut hazel twigs and hammered them into the earth for her to twine the fragile stems of the seedling sweet peas around. She had ground up seashells and sprinkled them about the young plants to ward off slugs and snails but now they would flower once and go to seed.

Jack brought the car to the front door and loaded the cases. Sadie came scurrying out, locked the front door with the giant iron key and hid it in a flowerpot. As the car bounced along the uneven driveway Jack peered into the gloomy trees on either side and tried to resist taking a last look at the house. This part of his life was finished. He mustn't look back, he mustn't.

The car snaked along the narrow lanes as the moon caught the last of the cow parsley frothing in the hedgerows and the white wings of flitting moths. The night was thick with the scent of flowers; every garden seemed to have a lilac tree bursting into bloom and the air was heavy with sweet lavender. In his pocket, Jack had the brown envelope with all their remaining money: one hundred and twenty-nine pounds six shillings and ten pence. He had already decided how to spend it – they would take a room at the Ritz. The old, confident Jack would have spent all his money in the belief that more would come, and so he decided to feign optimism in the hope that it would return to him, along with his good luck.

They drove in silence as the car purred towards the main roads and the city. 'Do you want to stop for dinner?' Jack asked, puncturing the quiet, as they passed through a small town crouching amongst the hills.

'No. Let's just get there.'

Dorset smoothed into Wiltshire; then they were in Hampshire and the first of the Home Counties. The roads widened and they began to see other cars. Villages became towns, and then swelled into suburbs, until at last they were in London. The streets crawled with vehicles: taxis honked and red double-deckers cut in front of them. The sky disappeared behind the buildings and it was a starless dark. The city was a vast construction sight: blocks of flats sprouted like weird concrete plants and great cranes hung over the West End. They tried to drive up the Mall but it was already cordoned off for the coronation. Thousands of flags lined every street and hung from all the windows, and each display in the elegant windows of Harrods and Fortnum's celebrated the great event. They waited at lights on Piccadilly and then, at last, they reached the Ritz. A bellboy held open the car door and Jack handed his keys to a porter wearing a smart pillbox hat, who swiftly unloaded the car and then whisked it away to be parked out of sight.

Sadie wanted to be thrilled by the glamour and decadence of the hotel and managed a smile. 'Well, this is a treat, *Broitgeber.*'

Jack offered her an arm and, each acting a game of jollity for the benefit of the other, they went into the smart lobby of the hotel. The tiled floor shone with polish, a new and sumptuous red carpet accentuated the curve of the room and a magnificent vase of exotic lilies rested on a circular table. They weren't a native variety and must have been flown in especially at huge expense, decided Sadie. This opulence was not really to her taste – all she wanted was a comfortable bed. The clerk at reception, stiffly clad in tails, bowed his head as he saw Jack.

'Good to see you again, sir. It's been a while.'

'Too long. It's good to be back.'

'Clarence.'

The receptionist gestured to the bellboy, who ushered them into the lift and shut the cage, which with the stutter of machinery carried them to the fourth floor. He showed them into an elegant room, the ceilings high and the bed neatly turned down. The moment he left them alone, Sadie flopped onto the soft mattress and nestled into a pile of cushions, and watched as Jack went to the window and wrenched it open. Instantly, the sound of the city poured into the room, along with a dark ooze of smog. Sadie coughed. 'Close it, Jack.'

Jack shut the window with a bang. 'I wanted some fresh air.'

'Darling, this is London.'

He went to the drinks cupboard, 'Toast our return?'

'I don't mind.'

Sadie kicked off her high-heeled shoes; she hadn't worn heels for a year and they were pinching her toes.

'There's whisky, a twenty-five-year malt. Gin, vodka. The usual suspects. I can call down for a cocktail if you prefer.'

What she really wanted was a glass of milk and perhaps a boiled egg. She thought of her hens and of collecting the warm eggs and peeling off the downy feathers from the shells.

'I'll have a tonic water.'

He passed her a glass, which she didn't drink but held against her hot cheeks and forehead. She took in the creases around Jack's eyes, the shadow of grey stubble on his chin and the straggle of white hair. He removed his spectacles to clean them on his tie and she saw his eyes were red, laced with veins. He never used to be still – he was always moving, buzzing here and there with a scheme or a wild idea. Now, he sat with his whisky clasped on his lap, motionless as a heron watching goldfish in the pond.

This wasn't her Jack. Sadie wanted him spilling over at the edges with chaos and enthusiasm. She sensed with his abandoning the list that now England could never be home. They would live and die in exile.

She'd always done her best to ignore his list, but now she wondered. He'd almost succeeded in finishing it, and she had an inkling that if he had, they would have belonged to Pursebury Ash.

Sadie heaved herself up and went into the bathroom to get ready for bed. With a piece of cotton wool and a dab of cold cream she removed her coral lipstick and matching blush. 'My name is Sadie Rose,' she said into the mirror.

The new name still tasted strange on her tongue, and though it was a little inelegant, she would prefer to be Sadie Rose-in-Bloom – now that was a good name. If they had stayed in the village, she might have tried to persuade Jack that Rose-in-Bloom was the best choice for their passports. She supposed it didn't really matter anymore. During her life, she had many names and had lived in many places but Rosenblum belonged to another Sadie – the one who lived in Berlin all those years ago. They would never go back now – neither of them could understand the people who went back. *Before* did not exist anymore, however much one might wish it. That other world had gone and it was pointless to return and look for it.

She stared at her reflection until her vision began to cloud and her nose seemed to drift downwards towards her chin. This was not an English face, neither was it exciting or exotic – she saw a middle-aged woman fattening into old age, with a dusting of dark hairs on her top lip. She didn't belong anywhere: she wasn't English and she certainly wasn't German. *Jew.* It was such a small word and caused so much trouble. *Jewess.* That sounded more enticing, sexy even – but was not a word that fitted her, a plump woman born in the suburbs. She smoothed her blouse and tried to get the creases out of her skirt. It was tighter than it was a year ago – she needed to diet. Was it really only a year? In that time she had come to love the landscape and the seasons and the sky and the ducks and the stories.

Sadie realised that she was crying. She chided herself, '*Du blöde Kuh*. This won't do. Pull yourself together, silly old woman.'

She combed her hair, wincing as the brush caught on a burr. She untangled it, placing it on the corner by the sink. It was a tiny piece of the countryside and, somehow, she couldn't quite bear to throw it away.

CHAPTER TWENTY-TWO

J ACK COULD PUT it off no longer – it was time to call in at the carpet factory. He left Sadie after breakfast and drove to the East End. Even this corner of London was decorated with flags and coloured ribbons, although underneath the paraphernalia of celebration the bricks were dirty and soot stained, and there was the faint odour of rubbish decaying sweetly in the heat. The streets were teeming with stallholders selling beigels, buns, shoelaces, stinking fish, soap flakes and pickle jars, and Jack picked his way through the crowd to the narrow street leading to his factory. The gates were locked and he took a key from his pocket to let himself into the yard. He stood alone in the cobbled forecourt for a moment, listening to the low thrum of machinery.

The men working on the looms did not look up when he came onto the factory floor; they were far too busy threading and cutting to see him, and the bang of the door was lost in the clamouring din. Jack had forgotten quite how loud the great looms were – the crash and clatter of the machines vibrated through him and he felt the familiar pain at the back of his head begin to pulse. One loom was broken and silent, its metal guts spewed across the floor.

He walked to his old office, where his name still hung on a brass plaque, now coated in a layer of dust. Wiping it off with his sleeve, he went inside. There was a scurry of movement and Fielding scrambled to his feet, sending a pot of tea flying in his haste.

'Mr Rosenblum, sir. I am sorry. Wasn't expecting you . . . did you call?... I've just been here a minute. I'll leave now.'

Jack settled into the battered chair opposite the desk and motioned for the man to sit back down. The waste bin was overflowing, a dead plant rested on the windowsill and judging by the snapshot of Fielding's family on the desk, it was clear that he'd been here for some time. This was no longer Jack's office. Through the background whir and clack of the great looms there was a knock at the door and a young woman barged in without waiting for a response, clutching a folder. She stopped the instant she saw Jack.

'Please, come in,' he said beckoning her inside.

Hesitating, she handed the file to Mr Fielding and scurried out.

'I am sorry,' said Fielding, 'when you didn't come back, it was easier for me to work in here. It has a telephone.'

'It was the sensible thing to do.'

'Are you coming back?' asked Fielding, his voice betraying a note of desperation. 'Things have gone to the dogs without you.'

'I'm sure it's not so bad,' said Jack smoothly, taking the file.

He opened it and read the contents in silence. When he had finished, he closed the folder and leant back in his chair, wondering what to say. Fielding was right – it was bad, worse than bad. He took off his glasses, cleaned them as a matter of habit on his tie, put them back on and pushed them up his nose.

'I know this is my fault. I took money out of the business to start another concern. But these figures are dreadful. We're not even in profit.'

Fielding let out a tiny scream that sounded like a kettle giving off steam when it had boiled. 'It's God-awful! I wrote to you again and again and you never replied, Mr Rosenblum. I needed you to make decisions on things and you wouldn't. We need new machines like the other carpet factories. These looms are old and break down every other day. You never even responded to my telegram.'

Jack said nothing – it was all true. He was to blame and needed to make it right but he was too tired to hustle and scheme. Carpets just did not interest him like they used to.

He chose another two shades for next season's plush pile range: 'Rainy Day Grey forty-two' and 'Spring Green sixteen'. Neither looked anything like their descriptions, he thought dismissively. 'Spring Green sixteen' was a lurid colour – nothing like the soft, rippling shades that were found in the garden at Chantry Orchard. The grey of a rainy day on Bulbarrow was full of drama – there the black sky billowed with the swirling patterns of raindrops, while the wind sang in the telegraph wires. The colours on the dye chart looked flat and fake.

Jack tried to find his old self by doing all the things that used to give him pleasure: he went to the pictures to watch a daft cowboy flick and took Sadie to a play, the new Noël Coward. He didn't ask her how she found it, in case she wanted to discuss the finer points of the plot. As the greatest actors in England performed on Shaftesbury Avenue, he found himself wondering how tall the new trees had grown and whether they yet screened the bungalows from the vista at the fifth hole, and as he clapped during the curtain call, he realised that he had entirely neglected to watch the play.

They both struggled to readjust to London hours from Pursebury mean time, finding themselves yawning by nine o'clock and eating dinner unfashionably early. They walked arm in arm along the Mall, pretending to admire the flags and the gathering crowds. The trees were slender and had been gracefully pollarded, but Sadie didn't approve of the style.

'Look at them. Poor things, they're old and they've been all chopped about. They look like their limbs have been amputated. It's cruel.'

Jack prodded a trunk and a trace of city grime came off on

his finger. He realised that all the trees lining the avenue were coated with soot and thought sadly of the clean trees in his orchard. The day they had left he saw a toad there – it sat on a log, blinked its eyes and croaked. It wasn't a bad life that of a toad, he decided. No one would tell a toad that he was in debt and must leave his lily pad. Jack huffed – he urgently needed to contact the estate agent. Tomorrow. He would do it tomorrow.

Jack telephoned Edgar to tell him that they were moving back to town. Edgar had not been able to keep the surprise out of his voice and pushed for an explanation, but Jack could not bring himself to give one. They all met for lunch at Kensington Roof Gardens, a city garden growing on the sixth floor above a department store. Edgar and Freida were waiting for them at a table outside, in the section called the English Woodland Garden. There were a few sad-looking oak trees growing in eighteen inches of soil but there was a pleasant view across West London; Jack was able to see the pockmarked skyline stretching out towards the horizon and could make out the holes in the city – great gaps gouged out by the Nazi bombs.

The Herzfelds were baffled by their friends' return; while it had seemed rather quiet without Jack and his various schemes, they believed them to be happy in Dorset. Edgar had been looking forward to playing a round of golf on the new course come summer, and this sudden return struck him as odd. He did his best not to mention it.

'We thought we'd come here. The roof gardens have a good view and the woodland garden – well, it's not like your place . . .'

Sadie said nothing. This wasn't woodland; it was a gimmick – a garden one hundred feet above the ground was unnatural. She wondered if the trees were lonely, separated from those in the earth.

After lunch Jack and Sadie promenaded through Hyde Park, desperate for a proper expanse of green. Jack had not realised how claustrophobic he found the city; now he felt it tightening around his throat like a fist and he trampled the dusty grass in the park with relief. Wanting to prolong the afternoon, he suggested they go to a museum, but Sadie refused. Jack plunged his hands into his suit pocket, wondering what had happened to them since their return to London earlier in the week. It was almost as though the escape to the countryside had never happened; amongst the hedgerows and wooded streams they had found one another again, but here their lives started to diverge once more. Why wouldn't she come with him? Did she not like his company? After a few months of proper companionship, he did not want to revert to the old ways.

Jack went to the Natural History Museum alone. He hadn't been there since Elizabeth was a small girl – it was one of their Sunday afternoon treats before the days of the Lyon's Corner Café. He walked slowly up Exhibition Row, listening to the purr of the traffic. He had swapped his hazel switch for his London ivory-capped walking cane, but it was not as comfortable; the steel-tipped base clicked irritatingly against the street and he wondered how he had never noticed before.

He climbed the stone steps of the Victorian museum, admiring the handsome building and its relief carvings in the shape of extinct animals, birds and fish. He had never liked churches or synagogues but he loved this place: it was a grand cathedral to nature – the Notre-Dame of sea anemones and forest ferns. He paid his penny entrance fee and wandered into the great hall, which echoed with the clamour of children's chatter. It was strangely comforting, these young creatures being herded along by anxious mamas and papas, and he watched them for a few minutes, listening to their noise, before heading up the great staircase to the first floor.

The creatures in the glass display cases were all perfectly still, frozen in position for the next hundred years. Eagles hovered mid-flight, dangling from wire threads, and recorded bird song played through a crackling speaker. He gave a shiver at the taxidermy – animals should be barking and wriggling – but he found it weirdly fascinating. A fly hurled itself furiously against the inside of the glass, trapped. Its situation was hopeless; it had found a way in but would never get out, and would die there and be preserved at the bottom of the case, another tiny addition to the display.

There was an overpowering smell of camphor in this part of the museum and Jack stifled a sneeze. The specimens were old – most had been gathered during the Victorian rush for discovery of new things: machines, stars, fossils, species. The meerkats in the glass case in front of Jack were older than he was, although, he decided, they were probably not as old as Curtis. He wandered through a bat exhibit; they were tiny with razor-sharp teeth and floated against a sky of painted stars. One night last summer, he and Sadie had counted a hundred bats flying out of the roof to go hunting.

Pacing the exhibition halls, Jack realised he was in exile once more. Dorset was home. Without his ramshackle cottage and muddy fields he was rootless – he would never belong anywhere again. He stumbled upon a moth-eaten display and gave a bitter laugh. Wild boars. The largest was over two foot high and five feet long, with coarse black bristles covering his body and a pair of fearsome-looking tusks, cracked and yellowed with age. He remembered Curtis's description of the woolly-pig, '*a noble beast o' strength an' savagery*'. Jack crouched down and stared into eyes of orange glass. This was the closest he'd ever get to a real woolly-pig.

His nose made a smear on the window of the display case and the dead creature looked back at him mournfully, as though conscious of the indignity of its fate.

Sadie longed for grassy fields, so like a bee on a quest for the finest nectar, she went in search of the largest expanse of green in the city. She paced the well-worn paths through Hampstead Heath, inhaling the smell of mud and newly mown grass, which mingled with sooty fumes. Hobbling slightly, her feet sore in her tight, high-heeled shoes, she wished that she were barefoot in her garden. At least there were still ducks to feed. She remembered the time when she saw her mother feeding them poppy-seed cake in Hampstead Pond all those years before. Mutti might only have been a mirage, a memory flickering on the surface of the water, but at the time she had seemed so real.

It was a weekday afternoon and the park was busy with mothers and grandmothers playing with their little ones and feeding the birds. A young woman walked a swaying toddler to the water's edge, their summer dresses billowing in the wind. Two old ladies in pleated skirts and thick beige stockings sat gossiping in Yiddish and eating sweets from a newspaper twist, while another hitched up her dress and played hopscotch on a chalked board with a delighted child, who shrieked with joy as her grandmother jumped the squares.

Sadie screwed up her eyes, trying to picture her mother's face – tired smile, mole on her left cheek – then opened them and stared at the middle of the pond. Nothing. Although the little girl with her untidy plaits flying out behind her like streamers, reminded her of Elizabeth. The water stank of pond weed and stagnant water. A tufted duck perched on an old tyre poking up through the surface and stared at her quizzically.

'What do you want?'

It flapped its wings and opened its beak to display an empty mouth.

'Here you are then.'

She tossed the bird a corner of bread. A glossy mallard

swam over and tried to snatch it away, but the black duck objected with a loud quack and a fearsome hiss. In a minute there was a noisy chorus of squabbling birds. The sound echoed all around Sadie until, suddenly, she remembered. She was in Berlin and the Zoologischer Garten at crocus time. The flowers reached her knees, she was so small, and she shrieked as a duck snatched a crust from her outstretched hand.

'He's hungry, don't be frightened, my little one,' soothed Mutti. 'Watch!' Mutti laughed as she tossed a scrap up into the sky, watching as the birds swooped to catch them in open beaks.

Sadie threw another crust and a speckled duckling dived.

'See them fly, Sadie,' called Mutti, her shouts mingling with the call of the birds.

Now, standing in the London park all these years later, Sadie shut her eyes and listened: she could still hear Mutti's voice in the crying of the birds.

She walked away from the pond and onto the open heath. The green rolled down to the city, where buildings and concrete replaced the grass, but here the sky above was empty. It was one of the few places in London where she could see the expanse of sky – everywhere else it was hidden by roofs and she saw only slivers of blue peeping between the houses. She was overwhelmed with longing for the empty spaces and the fields of the Blackmore Vale – that was where her memories were hidden, like a mouse's nest in a cornfield. Walking along Bulbarrow Ridge she had remembered chasing Emil as a boy through the German countryside. They had been running through the long grass when he shouted at her to stop but she refused, thinking it a ruse for escape, and caught hold of his arm. He pointed to the heavens, where a buzzard hovered, its wings barely seeming to beat, before diving to earth. In her memory, the Dorset landscape replaced that of Bavaria and she chased Emil along the top of Bulbarrow. Only now, when they had returned to the city, did she finally understand. While she had lost their faces, in the open fields she had learned to remember them and somehow, they were waiting for her there.

Jack sat in the hotel bar thumbing through the *Financial Times*. He tried to interest himself in the headlines and failed, then noticed a copy of the *Daily Mail* on the table and started to flip through that instead. On page two, a news story caught his attention:

Blushes at Red Carpet Trip-Up
Officials organising the Coronation have been left red-faced after ordering insufficient carpet for the big day. More than a mile of carpet is needed but careless measurements by staff have left a shortage of hundreds of feet! So will the Queen break with tradition and be forced to walk up a Paisley swirl? A Palace spokesman declined to comment.

Jack felt a prickle of excitement as an idea began to emerge like a fox from its winter den. He seized the paper, and half an hour later arrived at the gates of Rosenblum's Carpet Factory. At a half-run, he tore along the corridor to his old office and flung open the door. Fielding was seated at the desk, eating a grey ham sandwich and speaking on the telephone but he lowered the receiver in surprise on seeing Jack, who stood backlit in the doorway, white hair shining like some kind of elderly, bespectacled genie. Jack thrust the newspaper at him and paced anxiously while Fielding read the piece.

'Well?' He demanded, when the other man had finished. 'Can we do it? Can the factory produce all that carpet in a week with one loom out of action?'

Fielding stared at him and then at the newspaper. 'It would be almost impossible.'

Jack banged the desk with a fist. 'But almost impossible is still possible.' He leant towards the younger man. 'This order is big enough to save us. Imagine in a week's time, Her Majesty walking up a red Rosenblum carpet.'

Carried away by Jack's enthusiasm, Fielding leapt from his chair, 'Do you think we'd get to have the Royal Warrant "*By Appointment to Her Majesty the Queen*" stamped on the side of the delivery pantechnicons?'

'I am sure we could.'

A flush of excitement suffused through the pallor on the manager's face, and Jack grinned.

'When this is over, I'm going to retire, Mr Fielding. I'm making you partner. I should have done it years ago, and then we wouldn't be in this mess. The decisions are up to you. I won't take any more money for loony plans. This is your office now.' Jack glanced down at the 'Tulip Surprise' colour swatch on the floor. 'And Mr Fielding, George, I'm sorry.'

Fielding stared at him for a moment in silence, and then nodded, 'Thank you.' He picked up the telephone receiver, 'Hullo, operator? Can you put me through to Buckingham Palace?'

Walking into the hotel, Jack knew he had done the right thing; his heart had gone out of the business and so it was right that he handed it on. He wasn't sure what he would do next, but he knew it wouldn't be carpets. The porter held open the door as Jack slipped inside. A second later, he dropped his hat in shock: there in the marbled lobby stood Jack Basset and Curtis.

For a moment Jack thought he was seeing things. Both men had dressed for the occasion: Curtis wore an ancient tweed suit and for once used smart braces to hold up his trousers, rather than his old spotted tie; Basset was in his Sunday suit with a neat neckerchief but still seemed out of place in the mirrored lobby. There were beads of sweat on his forehead and he rubbed his hands nervously. He shifted awkwardly from foot to foot and gazed about him, spying Jack with relief. Skidding on the polished floor in his hurry, Basset enfolded the smaller man in a large embrace, so that Jack was sandwiched against the wool of his suit jacket. A woman in a mink stole stared curiously at their little group.

Jack eased himself free and shook hands with Curtis, bewildered. He pointed to several stiff velvet armchairs.

'Shall we sit?'

Basset continued to lurk near a tall rubber plant, reluctant to join them, and Jack realised that he was self-conscious amongst the smart set.

'On second thoughts, let's go upstairs. Sadie will want to see you,' he said firmly, guiding them towards the lift.

Curtis started as the metal doors of the cage clanged shut. 'Aye. This is like them cattle cages at Stur market on a Monday. Feel like I is 'bout to be sold for 'alf a crown.'

When Sadie opened the door, her face went wide with surprise. It was nearly six and she was just beginning to wonder what had happened to her husband. She ushered them inside, busily straightening cushions, trying to tidy her hair and wishing she had cakes to offer. Having visitors and not being able to feed them was a travesty.

Basset undid his neck cloth and restrictive top button, and sank into one of the deep armchairs with a grateful sigh. Underneath his weather-beaten suntan he looked exhausted. 'Traffic was terrible. N'er see sa many cars in all my life. An 'ee wasn't no bloody use,' he muttered with a dirty look at Curtis.

'May I get you a drink?' Jack asked, always the host.

Curtis produced from his other pocket a large, familiar-looking flask. 'Brought 'ome brew.'

'Only thing 'ees good for. Stupid auld bugger,' complained Basset snatching the flask. He unscrewed the cap and after taking a swig passed it to Jack, who took it gratefully and helped himself to a deep draught.

'So,' said Jack, trying to sound casual. 'What has brought you to town?'

'I 'as al'ays wanted to see Tower o' London. My great-great-great-uncle Billy got 'is 'ead chopped off there an' I wanted to see. 'Bout time I sawed the world.'

Jack studied Curtis and saw a smile flicker at the corners of his mouth. Then, the old man's eyes narrowed. 'Yoos left without even a goodbye. I doesn't 'ave yer fancy ways, Mister Rose-in-Bloom, but where I is from, that's rude, that is. Enough to make you a ninnywally.'

'I'm sorry.'

'Right you are. 'Ave another.'

Curtis passed the bottle back to Jack who took a gulp.

'We came to give yer this.'

Basset fidgeted on the chair, pulling out an uncomfortable satin cushion, which he placed reverently on the floor. Then, he slid a hand into his breast pocket and proffered a telegram to Jack, who stared at it for a moment.

'Well, gowarn. Op'n it.'

'Yes, open it.'

Sadie, Curtis and Basset watched closely as Jack read the sender's name.

'It's from Bobby Jones.'

'Aye. Aye.'

Jack's hands began to tremble.

'Give it to me Jack,' said Sadie.

Unable to speak, he passed her the telegram and she unfolded it.

DATE: 15 May 1953
Post Office Telegraphs
No fees to be paid unless stamped hereon.
TO CHIEF EXECUTIVE DORSET COUNCIL
FROM BOBBY JONES AUGUSTA GEORGIA USA

NO LONGER SUPPORT SIR WILLIAM WAEGBERTS
GOLF COURSE STOP DID NOT REALISE MY
FRIEND JACK ROSENBLUMS GOLF COURSE
NEARBY STOP FULLY SUPPORT JACK ROSENBLUM
STOP WILL PLAY IN CORONATION MATCH AT
PURSEBURY ASH STOP

Jack took the paper from Sadie, read it and then read it again, all the while his head swimming. Basset decided that a little explanation was necessary.

'Clerk in council's office gave me this. Sold his dad some cows at good price last year like, an' 'ee thought it jist might interest me – yoos and me bein' friends like. Mr Jones sent this 'ere telegram to the council and another to Sir William. Auld Waegbert's shittin' a fury.'

Curtis could no longer keep quiet but jumped to his feet and began to prattle excitedly.

'Yer see, Jack, yer see? Din' I tell yer to keep an writin' to ol' Mister Jones? I said it were right thing to do an' look now! I bet it were the bit we told 'im 'bout the woolly-pig mischief what dun it, mind. That ud bring dew to a man's eye, right enuff.'

Jack swallowed hard, trying to take in this momentous news.

''Ee won't work no more for old Sir William Shitterton cos 'ee don't want to spoil yer chances at 'appiness an' success. Yoos alwa's said 'ee was a nice man, mind.'

'And he really wants to play in the coronation match? You're quite sure?' Sadie asked, incredulous.

'Aye. Says so right 'ere in black 'n' white.'

Jack could hardly believe that his letters had achieved such a profound effect. He had confided everything to Bobby Jones – in part because he had come to accept that Bobby would never, ever read them. But he had, and they'd inspired in the greatest, most illustrious golfer of all time a feeling of friendship towards him, Jack Morris Rose. It was a miracle. His head felt fuzzy and he needed another drink. He took the flask from Basset and drained it in a single swig. Was it possible? Could there be hope after all?

He stared at the others. 'So, I might get permission for the course? I can open?'

Basset looked a little ill at ease and stared at his grimy nails. 'Well. You'll jist 'ave to trust us a bit.'

Curtis fixed Jack with a steady gaze. 'Come 'ome,' he pleaded. 'Got ninth hole to finish. Can't let Mister Jones play on an 'alf-cooked course.'

Jack was struggling to absorb all of this new information and when he started to speak it was only to find he had forgotten his words.

'But what about the other course?' said Sadie.

Jack found his voice and wagged a finger. 'Yes, yes. Sir William will just hire another chap to design his perfect eighteen-holes.'

Basset's nose twitched and he stared at his feet before looking up and meeting Jack's eye.

'Well, it's a funny thing, but Sir William Whatnot seems to 'ave a terrible woolly-pig problem.'

CHAPTER TWENTY-THREE

S IR WILLIAM WAEGBERT was sitting quietly in the breakfast parlour and sipping a cup of tea with a nice slice of lemon when he noticed a deep, muddy furrow slashed across his manicured fairway. He rushed outside, shirt-tails flapping, and stared aghast at the desecration of his perfect green turf. There, on a scraping of muck, was a fat, round trotter print, bigger than that of any domestic pig. It was of such a size that it could only belong to a giant boar. Sir William had his gardeners rake over the damage and reseed the lawn but in the morning, as Sir William surveyed the garden from his bedroom window, he saw instantly that the woolly-pig had struck again.

Labourers arrived at Piddle Hall from all over the county to prepare the estate for the plans drawn up by the new golf-course designer. They dug and they raked and they preened and they pruned, but every morning, all across the grounds, they were met with fresh marks left by the furious rampaging of the woolly-pig. The course progressed like Penelope's web, advancing during the day, but unravelling every night.

Several miles away, Jack arrived home to discover that his course was complete. Basset and Curtis led the Roses through the garden gate and out into the field where, fluttering in the summer breeze, were nine chequered flags. Jack stood on the newly rolled ninth green and surveyed the finished scene with awe. It was done: his very own golf course. Basset and Curtis watched with interest as he turned white then pink, and briefly were concerned he was going to cry, but then Jack seized Curtis and kissed him solemnly, while the old man made popping sounds of surprise.

'You've done it. I despaired, I gave up but you didn't abandon me. This, this is friendship,' Jack concluded, gravely planting another kiss on the rough cheeks of the other man.

Sadie shook hands with each of them in turn, gratitude radiating from her eyes. Across the fields there was a thud and clatter as the last touches were put on the squat houses belonging to Wilson's Housing Corp, but nothing was going to spoil this moment for Jack. The sun burned through the clouds and the air was filled with the scent of flowers. The rose bushes Sadie had planted around the dew pond were budding open and formed clumps of crimson and cream against the green grass. Curtis produced his flask from his back pocket and held it up.

'A toast, to our very big success.'

Jack put out a hand. 'Yes. A toast to our success *and* to the Queen Elizabeth Golf Club. God save the Queen.'

Curtis grinned, took a swig and then passed the jar around the group. Each took a sip in turn, echoing the toast. Basset gave the flask to Sadie who, with scarcely a shudder, wetted her lips with the pungent liquid.

'God save the Queen,' she said, 'And all of you.' Unable to further articulate her thanks, she smiled and quietly retreated to her garden, leaving the men alone on the hillside.

'So how did you get permission?' Jack asked in wonder.

Curtis and Basset exchanged looks and chuckled. Then, Curtis flopped down on a bank of daisies, sticking his large leather boots out in front of him.

'This is an auld place. We doesn't care too much for these snivlin' rules. No busybody's tellin' me whats to do with my land, or nothin'.'

The ancient man spoke slowly, while Basset harrumphed his agreement.

'But I can get arrested. Go to prison,' said Jack, still worried, as he settled down between them.

Basset chuckled, 'Aye right. They takes you and they takes us all. They isn't goin' to do nothin'.'

From the top of the hill the church bell began to chime midday. As the deep note echoed around the valley, Basset got to his feet.

'Right you are then. That's my dinner bell, that is. Best get 'ome or Lavender will give us a right earful.'

With a friendly wave, he disappeared across the meadow, while the other two lay down sleepily upon the mossy banks.

'I is glad that 'ee 'as gone. Jack Basset is a nice enuff fellow but still a bit o' a noggerhead. No such thing as a woolly-pig, my arse.'

Jack laughed and wiped his forehead with his stained monogrammed handkerchief.

'Take a big breath, Jack, an' look at the gleam in the grass an' the sun in the sky.'

Jack filled his lungs with fresh air and looked again at the light shimmering along the grass. The wind rippled through it like waves on an emerald sea. He felt safe under this big blue sky. The village was at the edge of the world where the mundane rules did not apply. He remembered Curtis telling him months ago that this was part of the old world, an ancient place belonging to King Alfred or was it Albert? Jack resolved to be like one of the men of old and ignore the piffling rules of planning departments and councils. He disliked modernity and so he would be like the other men of the village and pretend it wasn't there. This was a corner of another place, with bluebells, willow herb, fat glossy ducks and mythical pigs.

'No one tells us what to do but Jack,' murmured Curtis softly.

'Oh?' said Jack in surprise with a sideways glance at his

friend, who was lying on his back, head propped on a molehill pillow.

'Not Jack Basset,' said Curtis. 'Jack-in-the-Green.'

'Jack-in-the-what?'

'Jack-in-the-Green. You know. The Green one. Robin of the Wood. 'Ee keeps everythin' in balance.'

He gestured to the concrete bungalows on the horizon. ''E'll flood out them houses, in time, turn 'em back to water meadow an' muck. Not these ten year perhaps, but 'Ee will.' He pointed with a stubby thumb at Bulbarrow Ridge. 'Aye. That's 'is back.'

Jack turned to gaze once more at the jagged outline of Bulbarrow against the horizon and realised that if he shut one eye and squinted it did resemble a giant man sleeping. The curls of cloud looked a little like smoke rings from the giant's pipe, which was in reality a lightning-struck tree. But, he wondered if this was the same as the tall tale of the woolly-pig. 'So, have you ever seen him, this Jack?'

Curtis chuckled. 'No one 'as seen Jack-in-the-Green. 'Ee's not like that – a thing or a man. 'Ee is the trees, an' the gleam in the grass an' the damp mornin' dew an' that feelin' you gits in an evenin' when the wind's in the ash leaves.'

Jack felt a strange sensation in his belly, and when he closed his eyes he imagined that he could hear the worms churning the earth beneath the grass. There was something familiar about Curtis's words, as though he was telling a story that Jack already knew.

'A barn owl's white wings under a full moon,' he said.

'Aye. An' in the stink of badger shit on a nice summer's night – that's a good 'un.' Curtis sat up and looked straight at his friend. 'That's 'ow we knew yoos was all right. You'd seen Jack.'

'I had? But no one sees Jack.'

'Aye. Not as such. But yoos dug this land all by yerself for what, thirty days and thirty nights. We all watches you from top o' Bulbarrow. That were Jack.'

He stared at Curtis in wonder.

''Ee's in the earth an' in our flesh. When a man can work tireless like, beyond what is normal for a little man, that's Jack-in-the-Green,' he explained with a twitching smile. 'Did yer not wonder 'ow a chap like yoos managed it?'

Jack marvelled – he had worked with incredible energy, barely tiring and with boundless enthusiasm but he had not considered where this vigour had come from.

'So Jack must have wanted this golf course then?'

'Aye,' Curtis pulled his hat over his eyes and from beneath the brim added, 'Fer now.'

Later that afternoon, Jack sat at the kitchen table working out the playing order and the pairs for the grand coronation match. Now everyone in the village wanted to play, so he was forced to decide the entrants by lottery – it was rather complicated and made his head ache. He did not like restricting the number of participants but he had only managed to secure half a dozen sets of clubs, and the game had to be finished in time for the coronation itself. He needed a smoke to help him think and went outside to sit on the front porch. The garden had changed in the week they had been away. Nothing waited even for a moment. The jasmine around the front door had burst into flower and some of the white blooms had already faded and withered brown. Jack admired the front door from the outside – an immense piece of handsome oak with solid iron studs. He breathed out a puff of smoke and gently ran his finger along one of the studs, but it pricked him and a drop of blood appeared under his nail.

'Bugger.'

He stood up and pressed down the heavy iron latch on the door, only to find it was stuck and that he had locked himself out. Usually, Sadie would let him in but she was at the village hall with Lavender and the Coronation Committee. Muttering, he sat back down on the doorstep; he would just have to wait for her to return. He stubbed out the cigarette and licked his finger. He had an idea: he could stop writing the blasted tournament timetable and go and have a drink with Curtis instead – there were important things to discuss. In all the time they'd been friends, he realised he'd never been to Curtis's home and was not even sure exactly where the old man lived, although he had mentioned his orchard several times. Jack also knew he kept sheep on Bulbarrow. On balance, the orchard was closer and so he decided to try there first.

He sauntered down the lane, admiring the colourful coronation posters, while women buzzed to and fro looking harassed. Curtis's orchard lay on the outskirts of the village, down a narrow dirt track, and it was quiet in this part of Pursebury. There were only one or two houses and those were in poor repair. It was marshy and dank in the wet, while in the summer it swarmed with gnats and fearsome Blandford flies. Once, a long time ago, this had been a pleasant part of the village with ten or more cottages and a stony lane leading to them, but then the river had changed its course and turned the road into a flowing stream. The cottages flooded and, in a few years, the wattle walls were washed away and the families forced to relocate up the hill. He gave a low chuckle – Jack-in-the-Green must have wanted it back.

He wondered how Curtis managed to remain. The river had been running its present course for sixty years, and hardly anyone remembered a time when this overgrown place was inhabited by anything other than sheep and wild deer. He opened the gate at the end of the track and went into the field at the bottom. It had been a damp spring and the sodden water meadows were filled with wild flowers – pale pink spotted-orchids, lemon balm and marsh marigolds. He tramped a path through the long grass towards a green shepherd's hut nestling in a far-off orchard that lay a good half-mile from even the dirt track. He was amazed that anyone lived in a place so isolated – the old man's nearest neighbours were a family of yellow wagtails nesting in the roots of an ancient sycamore tree that towered above the hedgerows.

Jack's feet were wet inside his leather shoes and, cursing, he realised that he should have changed into his galoshes. He pushed the wooden gate leading into the orchard and halted unthinkingly to gaze about him. There must have been a hundred trees and the grass around them was neatly trimmed, in contrast to the waving green of the surrounding meadows. The blossom on the branches had faded and early bees buzzed amongst the leaves. The shepherd's hut sat in the middle of the orchard, painted an olive colour that was starting to flake. It rested on four large iron wheels, red with rust, and a short ladder led to a small door in one end. A thin spiral of wood smoke rose from a narrow chimney on the side of the hut – Curtis must be at home. Jack paused on the top rung to admire the view of Bulbarrow. He could make out the medieval church perched on the hilltop and the thatched roofs of the village and, while it might be lonely, no one could deny that Curtis had picked a magical spot for his home. Rousing himself, Jack rapped on the door. There was no answer.

He knocked again, louder this time. Nothing. He wondered if Curtis was sleeping and if he ought to come back later. He edged round the side of the hut and tried to peer in the window but the curtains were tightly drawn, even though it was nearly six o'clock. He decided to try one last time and thumped on the door with his fist. The door creaked ajar. Gingerly, he pushed it open and crept into the cabin. It was warm and dark, and in the corner of the single room, he saw the red gleam of a wood-burning stove, throwing out a steady heat. There was almost no furniture – only a high-backed chair, a tattered fleece covering the wooden floor and a basket of logs. In a low cot Curtis lay fast asleep with his mouth open. Jack knew he should turn around and leave the old man, but there was something about the stillness of the sleeping figure that unnerved him.

'Curtis,' he called softly.

He gave the small form a gentle nudge. It made no response. Jack sat on the edge of the cot and lowered his ear to Curtis's mouth. No breath tickled him. He touched his neck and felt for a pulse. The old man's skin was cool.

Curtis Butterworth, the last of the old Dorset men, was dead. His life ended less than a mile from where it began, over a hundred years before.

Jack listened to the quiet of the afternoon. The smouldering logs in the old stove cast a warm glow around the cabin and a rosy flush upon Curtis's cheek, so that Jack could almost fancy he still lived. This strange old man was the greatest friend he had ever known, and yet he did not shed a tear. He felt numbness in his belly and slid to the floor of the hut. Curtis's stout boots were lined up next to the door and a bloodied brace of pheasant hung from a nail. He noticed something else. Pinned beneath the dead birds was an envelope with 'Meester Jack Rose-in-Blom' written upon it. He hauled himself to his feet and unfastened the letter, then, not knowing what he ought to do next, sat back down by the cot, and opened the envelope. Inside was a note, written on very thin parchment that looked suspiciously like toilet paper.

Deer Meester Ros In Blom

Yoos was the onlee one to trooly believe in dorsit woolly peg. Them others thinks it is only silly childers tail. Tis most unfortoonate. They is hignorant.

ONLY TROO DORSIT MEN CAN SEE IM, THAT WOOLY PEG. (an Dorsit men is the bist of all English men)

Not them piles of cow mook. They is noggerheads, ninny-wallies and effing turds.

Ate een deys after auwld midsommer Drink 5 pints cider _ per instructshons (resipee on back of this shit of paper) and look top bulbarrow. afore noon.

Yoos afectsionate frend,

Curtis

p.s Please take them pheasants. Tis a shame to waste em like.

Jack read the letter through three times. Curtis must have known he was dying. He had retreated into his hut like a wild animal that crawls into the hedgerow to die, and his last act was to pass on his recipe to Jack.

They buried Curtis with his last flask of special cider – everyone knew he could not face eternity without a good drink. Jack and Sadie had never been to a Christian burial before and they stood by the grave with the rest of the village, ready to throw a handful of dirt onto the coffin. Jack felt that there was a Curtis-shaped hole in the universe, an emptiness where once he had been. Curtis hadn't needed a list to be the best of all Englishmen.

After the service Basset erected a temporary headstone fashioned out of wood, on which he had painted the words that would be transferred to the gravestone for posterity:

'Curtis. Born Last Century. Died 28th May, 1953
aged somewhere between eighty-nine and
one hundred and thirteen-ish'.

In the now deserted churchyard, Jack held the wooden board as Basset wedged it into the soft earth.

'He were one of a kind. Unique like.'

Jack nodded, dumb with grief. He wished his friend could at least have lived to see the coronation and the start of the Elizabethan era – it was going to be a new world. Then, perhaps, Curtis belonged to the old one.

'Do you believe in the woolly-pig?'

Basset chuckled and then looked a trifle guilty. 'Don't go daft. I 'ad thought we was all clear 'bout that. Said I were sorry.'

'No, that's not what I meant, old friend. It was something Curtis said.'

'Aye. After ten pints o' cider, I'll warrant.'

Basset paused to stare into the horizon. 'I wish 'ee'd given 'is recipe to some 'un. It is awful sad that 'is cider dies with 'im.'

Jack reached into his pocket and felt the letter, but said nothing.

CHAPTER TWENTY-FOUR

'HERE,' SAID SADIE, handing a red-striped tea towel to Lavender, so that she could wipe the perspiration from her forehead. The kitchen at Chantry Orchard was transformed into an alchemist's den, with cauldrons of simmering water, trays of chopped herbs ready to be bound into muslin bags for 'bouquets garnis' and a mountain of feathers from the plucked chickens, now lying naked and headless in piles ready for the pot.

'Oooh. I think 'ee's done,' said Mrs Hinton, prodding a fat bird, poaching in a vat of water and Jack Basset's elderflower wine.

'Juices running clear?' said Sadie.

'Oh yes, chief-cook-lady,' replied Mrs Hinton with a toothy smile.

'Bring him out then,' commanded Sadie, handing her a fearsome carving fork and a large plate.

As one fowl was removed, Lavender plunged the next into the steaming basin, cursing as her spectacles misted up, 'Bugger it. I need bloomin' wipers on my specs like what Mr Rose-in-Bloom 'as on his smart motor car.'

'I'm right glad we is doin' 'im today. Imagine the kafuffle if we was to make 'im on Coronation Day?' said Mrs Hinton.

Sadie raised an eyebrow – she quite agreed. Fortunately the recipe was clear: the chicken must be made in advance and chilled. This was most considerate of Constance Spry, as otherwise Sadie suspected all the ladies of England would be expected to miss the festivities in order to cook for the men folk. On the great day, the entire country would eat the same luncheon, the nation transformed into a giant dining hall.

Mrs Hinton effortlessly jointed a chicken on a carving board, fat dribbling up to her elbows and greasing the folds of skin. With a polished blade, she diced it into neat bites and scraped the meat into a vast china serving-bowl. Lavender spooned in mounds of creamy mayonnaise, sprinkled on the curry powder and three entire jars of apricot jam.

'You got to check 'im, Mrs Rose-in-Bloom. You are the committee's head-chicken poacher,' said Lavender.

Dipping her finger into the mixture, Sadie took a long lick.

'Good. But needs something more.'

Mrs Hinton fetched the torn page of newspaper and recited the ingredients. 'Tomato paste, curry powder, jam, cream, mayonnaise, onions . . . No, we've not forgotten anything.'

But Sadie was an excellent cook and she knew when something was missing. She closed her eyes. 'Currants. It's wanting currants.' Emil's currants.

Lavender and Mrs Hinton watched curiously as she produced a box from the cavernous larder, and sprinkled in several handfuls. With a long-handled wooden spoon, she stirred the creamy-yellow mixture, and took another taste.

Her teeth tingled. 'Yes. It's right now.'

Lavender plunged in a teaspoon and sampled a mouthful. There was something else in the mixture, a nameless something that wasn't there before. She met Sadie's gaze. 'Yes,' said Lavender, 'Tis exactly right.'

Later that afternoon, Jack sat at the kitchen table and finished the playing order for the match, but he was distracted. Curtis had been with him from the very beginning, and Jack wished that he could have met Bobby Jones. They had spent hours discussing the genius of the great golfer and now, when by a stupendous miracle he was actually coming to play their course, Curtis would not be there to see it. With a heavy sigh, he took Curtis's letter from his pocket and read the crumpled note for the hundredth time. Was it possible? Basset thought it was nonsense and that Curtis was an old man who drank more special cider than was good for him and sometimes saw things. Only Curtis believed the woolly-pig was real, but then Jack remembered the grunting cry he had heard across the snow all those months ago. And that was why Curtis had left the recipe to him and him alone; the rest of the village were unbelievers.

'Well? Have you started making the cider?'

Jack looked up to find Sadie reading over his shoulder. 'I'm too busy. I'll get to it after the coronation.'

'You will do it right now, Jack Morris Rose-in-Bloom,' she declared, her hands lodged firmly on her hips.

Jack was surprised at her vehemence. 'Why? You don't think it's real?'

Sadie shook her head. 'It doesn't matter. This is how he wanted you to remember him. You must honour the wishes of the dead, and this is how he wants you to say *Kaddish*.'

'But what about the golf game?'

'What about it?'

'It's the same day. I'll have to drink all that cider, then play in a golf match with Bobby Jones, watch the coronation and then climb up the hill – while I'm blind drunk.'

Sadie raised an eyebrow. 'I am sure you'll manage.'

Jack realised his wife was right – this was the way to remember his friend. He read through the recipe. There were half a dozen other ingredients that needed to be added to a regular batch of cider, although Jack hadn't heard of most of them. He didn't want to ask for advice as to do so might raise suspicions. There were some odd items: Enchanter's nightshade, mangleworzle, wolfbaine, water from Chantry Orchard spring collected at dawn. With Sadie's help he managed to track most of them down, adding each as he found it to the vat of cider left in the stable from the autumn. It hissed and emitted noxious fumes that smelled a little like Curtis.

The next day was the first of June and the eve of the coronation. On the wall in Jack's study were chalked the pairs for the tournament. Bobby Jones was due to arrive at half past six the next morning and would play in a three-ball with Jack and Sadie. The calendar was pockmarked with crosses and there was only one blank square remaining. Jack put a red line through this last date, and remembered how he and Curtis used to count the days together. There was nothing more that Jack could do for his friend, except fulfil his last instructions, scrawled on the piece of toilet paper.

The cider was nearly ready but there was still one missing ingredient – the wings of a jitterbug. Jack ignored his usual armchair, choosing instead the low stool favoured by Curtis. He closed his eyes and remembered his first conversations with the old man. They had climbed Hambledon Hill, where Curtis gave him his first taste of special cider and told him about King Albert and the Wessex knights. There had been hundreds of jitterbugs in the sky that night.

He fired up the car and drove to Hambledon, parking in the lay-by and walking along the tree-lined path to the gate at the foot of the hill. It was much darker than last time, and he shivered as he recollected stories of the head-hunters. He let himself through the gate to the grassland and scrambled to the top of the hill, stumbling over thistles and loose stones. Eventually, he sat under the starless sky on the coarse grass at the summit, wheezing for breath. In daylight he could see five counties and on a clear day as far as the Isle of Wight, but now at a quarter to midnight all the lights in the villages were out, and he could only guess the direction of Pursebury. He wished he had left his headlights on. Just then, he saw a flicker and suddenly, there were the first jitterbugs swaying before his eyes – tiny green stars shimmering amongst the grass stems. He took out a flask containing the half-brewed cider. With one more ingredient it would be special cider: his first batch. A glow-worm inched up a grass strand, drawn to the sweet smell of the alcohol, and crawled on the side of the flask, its light casting a glamour.

'My apologies,' said Jack and pushed it down the neck of the flask.

He peered into the liquid. For a second the contents seemed to glow green in the darkness.

Back home, he was far too jittery to sleep. Not sure whether it was nerves, excitement or the cider, he decided to walk out to his course and double check that everything was in order. There would be no time in the morning – they would be teeing off almost as soon as it was light. He traipsed through the shadows to the silent fairway where he could only make out the white flags. The stream sluiced over pebbles and a far-off fox shrieked at the shrouded moon. Jack unfastened the cider top and took a dubious nip – it burned and tickled all the way to his toes. It was still out here on the greens, but in a few hours it would be teeming with people – the entire village was coming to watch and cheer.

At the prospect of all those spectators, Jack pondered whether he ought to practise his swing – he had cleaned and polished his irons and they lay sparkling in the hallway but, as yet, he still had not swung a club. He had waited so long that now it seemed right to hold off until his first try was under the direction of the great, the one and only, Bobby Jones. Jack took another swig and picked up a stray switch of hazel that had blown onto the fairway. Carefully, he placed his hands around the wood, spreading his fingers along the shaft as he tried to perfect the Vardon grip. He widened his feet, leant forward, flexed his knees and swung. The makeshift club swished through the air with ease. Jack smiled – he would be fine. How difficult could it really be?

He marched through the darkness to the fifth tee. This was his favourite spot in all the world – he used to sit here with Curtis and enjoy a good silence. He wondered what time it was, but had no way of knowing, having given his wristwatch to Curtis all those months ago. Now, the watch was buried with him, and Jack imagined that he could hear it ticking from deep beneath the ground.

Jack shook Sadie awake at five the next morning.

'Wake up. Get up. You need to be ready.'

Thick with sleep, she opened her eyes to see Jack sitting on the edge of bed proffering a cup of tea. She took it from him and noticed a stray leaf sticking to his head and a wild glint in his eye.

'Did you sleep at all?'

'I sleep tomorrow. Today is the great day. Get up.'

He nudged her gently in the ribs.

'Come on. Come.'

Sadie gave a tiny groan and rolled out of bed.

While she dressed, Jack sat on the sill and gazed from the window towards the lane. Rows of blue, red and white bunting were tied to the trees; Union Jacks dangled from the eaves of all the houses and the whole village gave the appearance of having been scrubbed – cottages had been whitewashed, windows cleaned with vinegar, and sills given a lick of paint.

Elizabeth was waiting for her parents in the kitchen.

Sadie smothered her daughter in kisses. 'What a wonderful surprise – I thought you were watching the coronation in Cambridge.'

'Yes. But then, I thought I'd rather be here.'

Jack beamed. 'You do know we have no television signal?'

'Daddy, you don't have a television.'

'True. True. It is a little late to add you to the playing order.'

Elizabeth shrugged, 'I'd prefer to watch anyway.'

'Good, good.'

Jack rubbed his hands together in eager anticipation. Elizabeth's unexpected arrival was a sign – this was going to be a splendid day. She'd managed to hitch a lift all the way from Cambridge to Stourcastle and what were the chances of that? Discovering his daughter raiding the larder this morning had made Jack very happy. He took his first sip of cider – five pints was a lot to get through, and a little nip might help his game. Soon, Basset arrived armed with the morning newspaper. He had declined the offer to play, preferring to caddy instead, and placed it on the table. The family crowded round to study the pictures of the Abbey set up for the coronation.

'Carpet looks good,' said Jack, 'but so it should. Highest quality wool. Well, five hundred yards of it are anyway.'

Jack watched as the sun came up over the chicken shed. He was worried; it was nearly half past six, the tournament was due to start, and there was no Bobby Jones. He took another draught from his flask.

Basset cleared his throat and pointed at the kitchen clock. 'Thinks we'd best go. Can't let the first match start late, now can we?'

Effortlessly, the large man picked up both Jack and Sadie's clubs and walked down to the golf course. The little group heard the sound of the crowd before they could see them – the air vibrated with cheering voices and whooping shouts. The edges of the course were thronging with people, hundreds of them by the trees. Jack saw twinkling on the top of Bulbarrow and realised a moment later that it was the reflection of binoculars from hundreds more people, who had all flocked to watch from the hill.

'Good God,' he whispered. 'Everyone in Dorset's here.'

'Aye. An' there's a bus from Wiltshire,' added Basset.

Jack's stomach gurgled – now that the moment was here, he was more than a little anxious and, to crown it all, Bobby Jones was late. He felt Sadie slip her hand into his. Just then, there was an enormous rumble overhead and the sky seemed to shake, forcing the women to cling desperately to their hats. The trees shuddered and the cries of the crowd were drowned out, as a small, very noisy biplane swooped down. It circled lower and lower, searching for a place to land and then, engine spluttering, touched down on the flat top of the hill. The crowd stared as it sped along the ridge before stuttering to a halt. A moment later, a figure climbed out over the wing, pausing to pull out a bag of golf clubs, and then bounded down the hill. As the engine lapsed into silence, the crowd roared with excitement.

Jack, Sadie and the other golfers waited expectantly on the first tee, all watching as the figure drew closer until, finally, he reached them. He was immaculately clad in brown tweeds and polished golf shoes, his skin lightly tanned from the pleasant American sunshine.

'Bobby Jones,' announced the man, warmly clasping Jack's hand.

'Jack Rose-in-Bloom. We're so pleased you could make it.'

Bobby Jones continued to grip his hand firmly. 'Wouldn't have missed it for the world, Jack. I've kept every single one of your letters. I savoured them all year long. Gee, at first, I couldn't believe you were for real.'

Bobby opened his jacket just wide enough to display the letters carefully stashed in the inside pocket, and Jack puffed with pride like a robin with the fattest worm on the garden wall.

'Shall we?' Bobby Jones enquired politely, in his soft Augustan drawl.

As he gazed at the expectant faces in the crowd, Jack

wavered. He turned to Bobby Jones. 'Would you do the honour of playing the first shot and opening the match?'

'Why sure.'

Jack stood next to Sadie, keeping a respectful distance, as the great man walked to the first tee. A hush fell over the crowd. Bobby produced a wooden tee from his pocket, pushed it into the ground and then, with a motion of exactness, placed upon it a white ball. He stretched his arms above his head and swivelled his hips to loosen them. With unhurried calm, he selected his driver and, at last, assumed his famed stance. He was totally at ease, body balanced and poised; then he raised his club and, with the smoothest of movements, brought it down in a steady sweep. There was a satisfying click as the ball flew into the distance. Jack gazed in awe as it flew straight down the fairway and landed with a gentle thud at the edge of the green and rolled neatly to the base of the flagstick. The crowd clapped its raucous appreciation.

Now it was Jack's turn. He took another swig of cider to steady his nerves. His knees shook as Basset handed him his driver, and he walked up to the tee. He closed his eyes and visualised Bobby Jones's swing – so natural it flowed like water. Jack stood with legs shoulder width apart and flexed his arms. This was the moment. He sensed everyone watching him as he placed the tee carefully in the earth and popped the small white ball on top. He settled over the ball, brought the club up high, and swung down with a powerful swoosh and then . . .

Nothing.

Jack glanced down to see the white ball staring back up at him, still perched on the tee.

The crowed bellowed its approval. No one had ever seen a game of golf before and they were certain Jack's technique was masterful. 'Why doncha take another swing,' said Bobby Jones kindly.

Jack managed his second shot with slightly more dignity than the first: the ball rolled twenty yards down the hill before coming to rest in the rough, causing him to wonder, if perhaps, it might have been better to practise.

Now it was Sadie's turn. Jack had worked very hard to convince her to play; he bought her a beautiful set of lady's clubs and at first only the knowledge that they would be wasted otherwise, had persuaded her. But now, to her surprise, she was rather looking forward to it. She had never held a club before and had not even practised her grip on saucepan handles. Still, she reasoned, she couldn't be much worse than Jack. She studied Bobby Jones very closely and, after slipping her tee into the ground, tried to mimic his stance. It felt surprisingly comfortable and she was quite relaxed as she filtered out the din of the crowd. She raised her club, and then brought it down in a seamless arc. There was a crack, and she watched in utter astonishment as the ball sailed through the air and landed in the middle of the fairway.

'Sweet Jesus,' said Bobby Jones in amazement. 'Your wife has a perfect swing. She's a natural.'

Jack turned scarlet with pride.

Sadie won the women's match by twelve strokes and Bobby Jones the men's by a hundred and three. Jack was not the worst golfer in the competition and actually made it into the top three simply by not losing his ball. Twenty-seven balls were lost completely and two players forced to withdraw as no more replacements could be found, but no one seemed to mind and the crowd hooted encouragement at every stroke. When the match ended there was a small celebration on the final fairway. The crowd whooped as Jack awarded the women's medal to his wife and the first ever Queen Elizabeth Golf trophy to Bobby Jones. Bobby held it aloft and posed cheerfully for photographs before climbing back into his

plane and taking off into the hazy sky. The crowd continued
to cheer until the small biplane disappeared over the horizon.

After it had gone, Basset cleared his throat and raised
himself to his full height for the final announcement.

'I wish to ask Mr Jack Rose-in-Bloom, with the full
authority of the Coronation Committee, if he would do us the
honour of crowning the Pursebury Queen at the coronation
today in the village hall at eleven o'clock.'

Jack was dumbstruck – he took off his glasses and cleaned
them again on his tie. He tried to speak but there was a strange
feeling in his throat.

A short while later he sat down in the garden, enjoying
the pleasant sunshine on his bald head. He was deeply
touched at being asked to crown the village queen, but also
a little concerned – considering the amount of cider he was
supposed to imbibe. According to Curtis's instructions, he
needed to scramble to the top of Bulbarrow before midday.
The coronation was due to start at eleven, but in his limited
experience Jack knew that village events rarely ran to time –
he was also dubious about being able to make the steep climb
after five pints of the brew. He concluded it was best not to
think about it.

He took another gulp; it burned his throat and made him
choke – this was the proper stuff all right. He drifted off to
sleep and dreamt of Curtis. The old man was alive again and
they sat on the grass above the fifth tee, sharing the flask.
They watched the big clouds buffeting across the sky and the
swifts soaring amongst the beech trees. Jack handed him the
cider and Curtis took a long drink.

'Ah. Now that's there is proper stuff,' he said, giving a great
yawn.

'I followed your instructions.'

'I know yer did. But tisn't many chaps what can make it.

Takes a special summat.' Curtis chuckled. 'Yoos is a proper Dorsit man now. A real good Englishman. An' yoos knows what that means.'

'Dad.'

Elizabeth roused him from his deep doze. 'Dad.'

Jack opened his eyes and was instantly filled with sadness – his friend was dead once more.

'It's half ten. You need to go down to the village hall.'

'All right. All right.'

Jack took Elizabeth's arm, admiring her new outfit; she was wearing a navy frock that flared above the knee, and her newly short dark hair was glossy beneath a matching blue hair-band. Furtively, he took another gulp of the strange smelling liquid. He had lost count now of how much he had drunk but supposed that this was a good sign. Gratefully, he leant against his daughter and together they made their way down the lane.

Jack had a seat set up outside the village hall; it was the same wooden one as everyone else, but his had a cardboard cut-out of a bishop's mitre behind and a shepherd's crook. Behind the audience rows, twenty long tables covered with white cloths and strewn with red roses had been laid out on the village green, ready for the luncheon. Banners blew in the wind and children waved flags. Jack took another stealthy swig from the flask and squinted into the sun – he could just make out the clock tower on the church from here. It was ten forty-five – they were still on time. The Pursebury Queen's throne rested in the centre of the green on a raised platform that was bedecked with a canopy of flowers and, Jack had to admit, it all looked rather wonderful. He took another drink. Elizabeth blew him a kiss and he beamed back; she was easily the prettiest girl in the crowd. Sadie came and sat beside him, and he cast an approving eye over her; she was wearing a crimson dress and looked very fetching. Then, the Pursebury

Players struck up the national anthem and the village rose to its feet. Sadie gave Jack a peck on the cheek. 'Look, the parade is starting.'

She got up and went to the edge of the green for a better view, leaving Jack alone. He had been far too preoccupied with his golf tournament to listen to any other details. He only knew that it was all supposed to finish before twelve and that the woolly-pig would appear on the top of Bulbarrow at midday sharp. It was most strange; the more of the special cider he drank, the more certain he felt that the creature would come.

Jack sweltered in his regal robes. The music was soothing rather than rousing, and he fought against sleep. Once again, he glanced at the church clock. Eleven. Running late now. Never mind, he could walk fast. He got to his feet and swayed as Elizabeth caught his arm.

'Are you all right?'

Jack passed her the jar. 'Have a sip of that.'

Elizabeth choked. 'Daddy, what is it?'

'Secret.' He pressed a finger to his lips. 'I'll tell you when I'm dead.'

She looked a little worried as her father collapsed into his chair and began to toy with the bishop's mitre. Basset ambled past and winked at him. 'A' right, Jack – ready?'

Jack tried his best to look official but Basset gave him a second glance – something wasn't right. He sat down in the empty seat next to him and sniffed.

'You got special cider.'

Jack handed him the flask and Basset took a loud slug of booze.

'I am confiscating this. You needs to be sober.'

Jack hiccupped happily. 'I'm fine. Just fine and dandelion.'

'Aye. I'll jist sit here. We is runnin' late.'

Jack sighed and tried to focus on the church clock – everything was getting a little fuzzy. Eleven thirty. He still might make it. The national anthem started again and the ladies-in-waiting took their places at the foot of the throne, while the children gathered on the grass. The adults all waited expectantly in neat rows; there was a scent of carbolic soap and clean skin.

'Basset, do you want to crown the Queen?'

'What does you mean?'

Jack stared at the village clock. Eleven forty-five. If he left now – said he had a headache, a gangrenous leg or something – and ran to the top of Bulbarrow, then he might just make the woolly-pig. Two children began to sprinkle confetti petals on the grass up the central aisle, where the village Queen was to walk, and Jack got to his feet – it was almost his moment.

'You could crown the Queen.'

Basset's face fell. 'You is jist nervous Jack. You'll be grand.'

There was a hush as the Queen descended from her horse-drawn carriage. She was a tall, buxom girl but she understood the magnificence of the occasion and walked with a stately pride. All the faces on the green turned to watch her – they were filled with such hope and expectation, and Jack realised that he couldn't disappoint them. He would have to miss the woolly-pig. He hoped Curtis would understand, and muttered under his breath, 'I can't let them all down, my friend. It wouldn't be British.'

He grabbed Basset and lurched dangerously.

'Jack Basset. Walk with me.'

'I'd be honoured.'

Slowly, arm in arm, the two old men followed the Pursebury Queen up the aisle. All heads turned to watch them as they passed; the small, purple-robed bishop and the round, suited farmer. Sadie thought she would burst with pride as her husband proceeded past her seat. He moved so carefully, aware of the importance of the day to the village and to avoid toppling over from the cider.

304

Basset stopped at the end of the aisle. The Queen was already seated on her throne and Jack climbed the steps to kneel before her. She tapped him on the shoulder with her sceptre and he stood. Doing his best to remain steady, he turned to the crowd. He couldn't see any of their faces and colours began to pool together – there was a sea of white dresses, another of swaying grass and the sky was throbbing blue. Flying above them all was a squadron of jitterbugs. They cast their weird green light over the village and flitted in looping patterns amongst the trees. On the horizon Jack could see Bulbarrow Ridge, and the jagged hawthorn branches uneven against the smooth skyline. Was the woolly-pig there waiting for him?

A child knelt at his feet, holding a cushion on which lay a golden crown. Jack bent down and raised it up to the crowd. He took a step towards the Queen and she lowered her head to receive the diadem. It glinted in the sun, blinding him for a moment. He paused, crown held aloft, and turned once more to Bulbarrow. And there on the top he saw it: a giant boar with great carved tusks as white as bleached bone, its coat thick and matted like a sheep's fleece, its snout long and upturned like a pig's. It was a creature of majesty and magnificence, and it seemed to Jack that it saw him and met his gaze with its shining green eyes. As the clock struck midday, Jack placed the crown on the head of the Pursebury Queen. Then, the hour bell finished chiming and the woolly-pig was gone.

POSTSCRIPT

ELIZABETH SHADED HER eyes with a hand, searching the sun-soaked garden for her father. She spied him sprawled on a deckchair under the shade of a cherry tree. He was fast asleep, the sound of his snores harmonising with the hum of the bees, his walking stick propped beside him. She watched as blossom rained down on his bald head like confetti.

The flowerbeds were overgrown with ragged-robin, clouds of pale blue forget-me-nots and ground elder; bindweed choked the roses and ivy grappled with the clematis. Slugs had eaten away the red snapdragons, leaving silvery trails along the low stone wall. The grass was long; it had not been cut for several weeks and had begun to go to seed under the creaking plum tree, but Elizabeth said nothing about the general state of neglect because Jack was insistent – Sadie had liked the weeds, so this was a garden where everything was allowed to grow. The only sign of interference was the small space cleared around her mother's beloved rose bush. There was a single peach-coloured bud that smelled faintly of cinnamon, but the bush was turning black and half of its leaves were dead.

Jack stretched luxuriantly and gave a great yawn. 'It's hard work being old. Very tiring.'

Elizabeth laughed. 'I know.'

'Poppycock. You're not even fifty.'

'I'm fifty-three.'

'Exactly. You've barely started. I only got going at fifty-three.'

He got to his feet, leant on his stick and adjusted his skewed hat. 'Shall we?'

They strolled through the garden and into the field where the meadow grass was a lush, May green and speckled with wild flowers – scarlet herb robert, celandine and ox-eye daisies. A stream meandered through the middle, trickling over pebbles and tiny pieces of broken crockery to fill the large dew pond at the bottom. Fat buttercup lilies trembled on the surface while lazy dragonflies flitted amongst the reeds.

Jack produced a flask from his jacket pocket, took a gulp, and then gave a loud hiccup.

'You shouldn't drink that stuff, Dad. Can't be good for you.'

'Nonsense. This is what's kept me alive so long. I'm completely pickled – like a herring.' His shoulders sagged. 'If only I could have got your mother to drink more of it.'

Elizabeth stroked the white hairs on his arm and watched as he knocked back another mouthful of cider. His eyes watered – she was not sure if it was the alcohol or the memory. With a shake of his head, he resumed the climb, and Elizabeth clambered up the slope behind him. He moved with the measured gait of an old man but he still had a brightness in his step, a little half jump, and while Elizabeth was perspiring, his cheeks were barely pink.

They came to a stop beside a neat grave, marked with a tattered flag. Jack dropped his stick and sat on the grassy mound. Elizabeth's breath was still coming in heaves and gasps.

'God I'm unfit. Give me that,' she said snatching his leather flask. As she gulped down the fiery liquid, she felt her heart slow and her panting ease. She slumped beside her father and stared out across the fields. The land sloped smoothly to the bottom of the valley, where the river Stour dawdled amongst the trees. The only blight on the landscape was an ugly clump of concrete houses that were partly obscured by a copse of cricket willows. Several of the houses had fallen into the river when it flooded the year before. Jack fumbled in his pocket and handed her a package.

'A present.'

Elizabeth took it from him and peeled off the brown paper. Inside was a leather-bound volume, inscribed in a slanting, old-fashioned hand. It was Sadie's recipe book – all the women in her family had learned to cook from its pages. She felt a tightness in her chest. Closing her eyes, she sniffed the spine and remembered the first time she had used it, cooking meatballs for her mother. For a second, she imagined that it would smell like a glorious concoction of all the recipes inside: chicken soup with *kreplach*, vanilla crescents, beef *cholent* and honey, but it only reeked of dust and damp age.

Elizabeth wiped her hands on her jeans before leafing through the fragile pages. 'My German is just good enough . . . oh.'

A faded blue pamphlet was sandwiched between the pages of the Baumtorte recipe, like an extra layer in the cake. It slid onto her lap. 'This is your list, Daddy.'

Jack peered at it over the top of his spectacles. 'So it is. Good bookmark.'

He studied his daughter. She was starting to look more and more like her mother. He guessed that was the fate of all women. A woodpecker hammered at the bark of a gnarled oak and a pied wagtail trilled his flute-like tune. Jack smiled. This was his last summer. He couldn't explain how he knew, but he did. He sensed it, like the swallows knew dusk was coming, or the black-nosed badgers sought their winter hideouts deep underground, sensing the coming snow. These were his last yellow meadow vetchlings, and he'd never again pluck splinters from his backside after accidentally sitting on prickly sowthistle.

'Tomorrow, bake a Baumtorte,' he said, turning to his daughter.

She smiled at him, 'All right.'

And bake one more layer. A layer for me. But he didn't say this aloud, not wanting to upset her. She'd find out soon enough. Besides, there was nothing to be sad about. This was the way of things. Jack was the last of them – they had all left for the churchyard at the top of the hill and weekenders from the city had taken over their homes. Even Basset had gone last spring, aged ninety-odd.

Sadie's grave was apart from the rest, nestled into the hillside and marked by a flagpole instead of a headstone. Jack knew that even after fifty years in England, his Sadie would not want to be buried in a churchyard. He sat for a moment in silence.

'This was the fifth hole. My favourite. Look at that sweep,' he said.

'It was a wonderful course, Dad.'

'No, it was the greatest course in all England,' he said, correcting her. He pointed to a slight rise at the edge of the trees, where the land was flattest. 'That was the fourth hole. Not so lovely as the fifth but a fine hole nonetheless. Your mother always made a birdie on the fourth.'

He chuckled at the memory, while Elizabeth stared at the shining fields, trying to remember them as they had been – a series of fairways, smooth greens and waving chequered flags. The greens had long since reverted to wild meadow grass; the holes had closed over and sunk, while the hedgerows crept from the rough and onto the fairways. Now, the land was a mixture of tangled grass, unkempt hedges and scrub – the gorse grown thick and fierce, the friendly yellow flowers belying the vicious spikes, and brambles spread amongst the trees, while blackthorn tore across the tees. Yet, underneath all of this lingered the remains of the golf course, slumbering like Sleeping Beauty, hidden by the knot of bushes, grasses and branches. A long time ago, Bobby Jones had played here.

'What happened, Dad? Why did you let it go to ruin?'

Jack rubbed his nose. 'Well, we were open for quite a while. And then demand seemed to slip away and, of course, we got old. But we had a good time of it. Your mother was quite a golfer.'

He paused and gazed out at the fields below with a gleam in his eye.

'But the real reason is that Jack wanted it back.'

'Jack?'

'Jack-in-the-Green,' he said. 'He's a woolly-pig, a will-o-the-wisp or the red sun sinking behind Bulbarrow Hill on a summer's night. Everyone should know Jack. And if ever you tell the *bubbeh-myseh* about the crazy old man who built a golf course on the side of a hill, you must remember Jack-in-the-Green.'

With that, he turned away and started his journey back down the slope, leaving Elizabeth alone on the hillside. She noticed a hulking oak at the edge of the rough with peculiar knobbles and calluses that looked weirdly like bone sticking through the bark. Then she saw that it was not bone, but dozens of golf balls embedded in the trunk, and that the bark, in time, had grown over the balls and absorbed them into the great rings of the tree. It was one of the strangest things she had ever seen.

The sunlight filtered through the leaves, casting green patterns on her skin. The roots were thicker than sapling trunks, and plunged deep, deep into the earth. In her mind, Elizabeth saw that they formed an inverse shadow tree under the ground, even broader than the great branches above her head. The roots reached down beneath the soil, stretching under the Stour and below the sea. She pictured them surfacing on a forest floor in Bavaria, where an ancient oak tree creaked in the hot summer wind. She inhaled the sudden scent of pinecones and peat, and remembered her mother telling her bedtime stories about a cabin in a dark wood and a boy named Emil.

A green acorn dropped onto the faded blue pamphlet in her hands. She looked down at the peeling cover – *Helpful Information and Friendly Guidance for every Refugee* and, opening it, started to read her father's list. Each item was annotated with Jack's scrawl. Several extra pages had been inserted, all covered with his writing. There were more than a hundred points, detailing every aspect of daily life – '*an Englishman is scrupulously honest . . . an Englishman always says thank you . . . an Englishman apologises even when something is not his fault . . .*'

She turned to the final item, reading it aloud, 'Item one hundred and fifty-one – This last item supersedes all previous list items. If you see a Dorset woolly-pig you are a true Dorset man. And as any noggerhead or ninnywally knows, the Dorset man is the best of all Englishmen.'

Elizabeth closed the leaflet, slipped it back inside the recipe book and hurried to catch up with the old man walking steadily down the hill.

Acknowledgements

The first thank you is to the people of Ibberton in Dorset. Many decades ago, they welcomed my grandparents, Paul and Margot, to the village and after years of living in exile helped them find home. My parents, Carol and Clive, have provided endless emotional support and horticultural advice, as well as home-made biscuits and damson jam. I am most grateful to Katharina Schlott and Sharon for sharing their remarkable knowledge of vintage German curses, and to all my family and friends, especially Joanna, Michael, Katy and Rachel. Maureen Solomons generously allowed me to use her parents' names for Jack and Sadie. Thanks also to Elinor Burns, and my supervisor and mentor Janet Todd. I am deeply grateful to my agent Stan for his friendship and advice. Thanks also to Jocasta Hamilton, Reagan Arthur and everyone at Sceptre for being such a delight to work with.

Lastly, thanks to David – without him, I would never have written a book at all.